Stealing Time

Book 1 in the Stealing Time Series

by KJ Waters

Other works by KJ Waters:

Shattering Time, Book 2 in the Stealing Time series is available now at most fine booksellers.

Blow – A Short Story is available online as an ebook.

You can read the first two chapters of Shattering Time, the continuation of Stealing Time, on my website at www.kjwaters.com. Subscribe to my newsletter on the website to receive the first five chapters of Shattering Time free and stay up to date on all my upcoming releases!

Stealing Time
A Blondie Books Novel

Published by Blondie Books
Copyright 2014 by KJ Waters
Updated May 9, 2017
Cover art by Blondie's Custom Book Covers and Jody Smyers Photography.
ISBN 978-0-9862508-6-6 ASIN B00PJMWD65

Created in the United States of America
   www.kjwaters.com
   www.blondiebooks.com
   www.jodysmyersphotography.com

This book is dedicated to

my beautiful sister-in-law and my best friend who both are fighting the

good fight against the Big C.

Prologue

Friday, August 13, 2004, Punta Gorda, Florida

It was three o'clock in the afternoon but day had turned to night. The hurricane's grayish-black fingers descended—reaching, clawing, and greedily devouring the land.

The plan hatched in Scott's mind had been helped along by a little too much vodka. If he took a video of the hurricane and sold it to a news station he could make his Florida gig last a little longer. Scott had graduated from college in June and managed to spend most of the summer hanging out at the beach, waiting tables, and clubbing every night.

His mom's biting comment from their morning phone conversation still replayed in his head, "Scott, all your friends are starting jobs and you're down there partying like a loser on spring break!" She didn't understand. With work to look forward to the rest of his life, why not have a bitchin' summer first?

With luck, he could catch the eye of the storm by setting up in the apartment pool house to record the second half of the hurricane. It was a once-in-a-lifetime chance. Charley was making a direct hit at nearby Captiva Island with 140-mile-an-hour winds. Here, only a half an hour from Captiva, the winds were whipping around pretty bad, but couldn't possibly be anywhere close to 140, could they?

Power and cell service had been out for the last few hours but luckily his iPod still worked. He switched between the news and jammin' out to the Black Eyed Peas' "Let's Get It Started."

A loud crash rattled the front window and caused him to spill vodka on his pants. "Damn it!" He stood up and yanked open the blinds. His neighbor's white plastic lawn chair clung to the window at an odd angle. It was crazy—he had seen the guy sitting in it only a few hours ago.

The chair fell off and tumbled away. The rain still came down in torrents but the trees flailed around less than before, didn't they? Maybe the eye was approaching!

1

He flipped the iPod to radio to catch the latest weather report. "The eye of the storm is approaching southeastern Punta Gorda. The outer eyewall of the storm has the most severe winds so be prepared for more intensity as the center of Charley approaches. The eye may only last a few minutes so don't be ..." Scott pulled the earphones off and dropped the iPod on his chair.

"Woooo hoooo!" he yelled, trying to psych himself up. It was now or never. He crossed the tiny living room, snatched his video camera from the kitchen counter, and shoved it in a Ziploc bag and into his cargo shorts pocket.

He grabbed his Detroit Lions windbreaker off the edge of the couch, put it on, and walked outside. The jacket soaked through in seconds but the hood protected his eyes from the driving rain.

Surprisingly, the wind was relatively calm outside the door— maybe the eye was here! Scott continued along the ground floor toward the side of the building closest to the pool.

As he turned the corner, the wind caught him full on, almost throwing him to the ground. Adrenaline coursed through his body and made his legs shake. *Why was it windy again? It was supposed to be the eye of the storm.* Fear began to worm its way past the booze and made his stomach clench.

He looked toward the parking lot where the rain blew at an impossible angle. He swore that it went upward at times. The stronger gusts made the palm trees bend nearly to the ground as if a giant gorilla shook them. Buffeted by the wind he inched his way toward the pool. A section of metal roof as long as his apartment flew across the road and smashed into a car. The battering wind held it in place. Scott jumped at the noise that echoed in his mind like his mom's shrill voice. Fear weighed him down. He looked back toward his apartment. *Don't wuss out!*

The fence separating the parking lot from the pool kept him steady as he pulled himself along. A huge palm frond smacked him in the face and blew away. He touched his forehead and his fingers came away bloody. "Shit, back off Charley!" The storm threw the first punch, but it was just a scratch.

A loud crack sounded overhead. Scott covered his head in reflex and let go of the fence. The wind threw him to the ground and shoved his face in the mud. "Aaaaaagghhhh!" he screamed. A palm tree smashed down inches from his legs where it crushed the fence he had been holding.

Heart racing, he looked back at the apartment building again. His brain screamed—*STOP, GO BACK!* His heart said—*You're almost there!* Rolling over, he crawled toward the pool house in a fight against the wind that wanted to fling him into oblivion. He grabbed a light post to pull himself upright.

All he needed was a few more feet to the overhang and through the door to the safety of the pool house. A red blur from the parking lot caught his eye. Scott turned in time to watch it slam into his chest. Pain punctured the vodka haze as the metal pierced his flesh. He tried to put a name to the red horror that trapped him, pinning his body against the pool house. Scott worked it out in his mind just before everything went blank, "Fucking stop sign!"

Chapter 1 – Stormy Weather

August 13, 2004, 4:30 p.m., Orlando, Florida

When Ronnie Andrews sat down on the red velvet couch, a cloud of particles let loose and floated in the sunlight like fairy dust. Her real name was Veronica, but she hated it with a passion and had changed it to the shorter version in high school to get away from the formal, stuffy sound. Now, the only time she heard it was when her mom was upset with her.

"Seriously Steph, how can a hurricane hit here *today* on my birthday?" Ronnie said to her best friend Stephanie McKay. She was one of the reasons Ronnie had moved 1,200 miles away from her mom in Virginia Beach. "I've only been in Florida for three days!"

"Listen," Steph said turning up the volume on the TV. "They're telling us where it's going to hit."

"Hurricane Charley is completely devastating Punta Gorda on the southern Gulf Coast of Florida as we speak. Here is the current trajectory of the storm." The suit-clad Terry James pointed at a map of Florida. Was he wearing a toupee? His hair didn't look quite right. "Charley is projected to hug the coast moving north and entering Tampa Bay. Governor Jeb Bush has issued mandatory evacuations for low-lying areas surrounding Tampa. If you're in an unstable structure such as a mobile home or manufactured house you need to evacuate now."

"Hey weather dude, tell us if it's coming to Orlando!" Steph shook her fist at the TV.

The power and danger of Charley intoxicated Ronnie who was both excited and terrified by the storm. Part of her wanted it to be a raging nightmare, just for the dramatic effect. The other part of her wanted to go back home and hide under her childhood bed.

"Steph, that reminds me. Jeffrey has to be at the lab all night to monitor the storm and he canceled on me." Jeffrey Brennan, Ronnie's boyfriend, was the other reason she had moved to Orlando. They had been dating for the past year and a half. Last March Jeffrey moved to Florida for his job in a weather lab or an applied physics lab, or something like that. Her mind usually shut off when he began talking about it so she wasn't completely certain what he did.

"Jeffrey canceled on your birthday?" Steph made that familiar Scottish 'auch' of the Glaswegian variety. "Remind me again why I'm supposed to like him?"

"Steph, c'mon, I've moved down to be near you both. Can't you make an effort to be nice to him? You're the only two people I know here," Ronnie said crossing her arms.

"I'm sorry, love, I just wish you'd find someone who isn't so ..." Steph smiled at Ronnie. "You know."

"What, smart and handsome?" Ronnie said. It really bothered her that Steph and Jeffrey didn't get along.

"No, I was thinking you should find someone who isn't such a *tadger*." Steph's Scottish slang still took Ronnie by surprise, even though they had been friends for nearly seven years.

Steph sat down and put her arm around Ronnie's shoulders. "Listen, why don't you pack an overnight bag and we'll go to my house." Ronnie's cat Fluffy jumped on the couch wanting some love, too. Steph petted her long white fur. "It probably won't even hit here. Just some rain and a lot of *stramash* over nothing."

"You remember what happened to me during Hurricane Isabel? I don't wanna to go through that again!" Ronnie said. That storm had hit her hometown of Virginia Beach last September and power had been out for ten days with temperatures over ninety every day.

"Yes, I do. I was glad to be down here," Steph said while giving Ronnie's shoulder a squeeze.

The phone's ring made Ronnie jump. She looked at the caller ID. "It's Jeffrey." Steph made a face and turned away to focus on the cat.

Ronnie stood up and walked a few steps into the kitchen to get a little privacy. "Hello."

"Hey baby, Happy Birthday!" Jeffrey said. "I'm sorry I had to cancel our dinner plans for tonight."

"It's okay, I understand," Ronnie said, not fully understanding but not wanting to sound hurt.

"Can you come here and spend the night?"

"You mean the lab? A few hours ago you said it was against company policy," she said.

"Things have changed. I really need you here."

"Oh, so now you *need* me there, huh? That's an interesting way to put it," she said. "Steph invited me to her house." Ronnie peeked around the corner and stuck her tongue out at Steph who rolled her eyes.

"But Ron, I have a special birthday dinner for you," Jeffrey said. They were supposed to go to Del Frisco's, a fancy steak and seafood restaurant for her birthday. Now it would probably be sub sandwiches or something equally uneventful. Not that it really mattered. "And I have a special present for you, too."

The heat rose in her cheeks. "I thought I wasn't allowed to be there." She covered the mouthpiece and whispered to Steph, "He wants me to go to his lab."

"He does? The wee bastard," Steph said not looking up from Fluffy.

"Ronnie, you coming or not?" he interrupted.

"If you're going to shower me with food and expensive gifts, I might consider it. But what about Steph?" She glanced back at her friend who looked away scowling.

"Come on, the lab is a lot safer than Steph's. It's underground with its own generator, and I have all the supplies we need." Typical of Jeffrey to miss the point about Steph's feelings.

"Hang on a sec." She covered the receiver. "Are you okay with me going to Jeffrey's lab instead of your place?"

"I wish he'd make up his mind. He's on, he's off. Bloody hell," Steph said.

Jeffrey always seemed to know how to get his way. "Yeah, I guess," Ronnie said.

"So you're definitely coming over? You're coming here now?" he said.

"Yes, I just said I was coming. Why are you so worked up?" Usually, he was cool, calm, and collected.

"I just need to know. I have a few things to prepare for you, babe."

"I still don't understand why you have to be at work today. Most companies are closed for the storm." She was a little mad at him. He had hardly spoken to her since she set foot in Florida.

"Look, I've got one shot at testing the equipment with a storm this size and intensity. There is no reason you can't be here testing out *my* equipment."

She laughed. "Oh, you're dirty!"

Steph set Fluffy down on the couch, stood up, and turned her back on Ronnie as she gathered her purse and the birthday gift she had brought for her.

"But babe, you've gotta leave now. I'm looking at the radar and the outer bands of the storm are really close," Jeffrey said.

"Are you sure? We just watched the news. It sounds more like it is heading north of here."

"Charley is wobbling right now so it's hard to say exactly what it will do. Listen, babe, I'll make it worth your while."

Worried about Steph now Ronnie said, "I gotta go. Tell me how to get there."

He gave her directions and they exchanged "I love you's."

"So," Steph said walking toward the door with her purse over her shoulder. "You're going to the gobshite's mysterious lab, are you then?"

Ronnie never completely understood her dislike of Jeffrey. "Steph, I'm sorry. Are you going to be okay?"

"I'll be fine. Been through hunners of storms. Just don't get yourself into a palaver over that man of yours." She hugged Ronnie. "You'll get your birthday pressie from me tomorrow. And for God's sake take the K-Y this time. You don't want your fanny sore." They had always laughed about that word, especially when anyone talked about their fanny pack. In Scotland, it meant something different.

"You're horrible!" Ronnie smacked Steph's arm and laughed. "But you do have a point."

"Love, I gotta get on the roads before the skies open up and drown me." Steph opened the door.

Ronnie hugged her friend. "I'll call you in the morning to be sure you're safe."

"You be careful." She gave Ronnie one of those hard looks that made her feel like she had better listen.

"Ta-ta." Steph walked quickly to her car. Her dark gray pencil skirt and crisp white sleeveless blouse flattered her hourglass figure. Ronnie wished they were parting on better terms.

The wind picked up and blew Ronnie's long blonde hair in her face. She waved at her friend, but Steph ignored the gesture and drove away. She was mad. Ronnie would have to make it up to her tomorrow.

The sky was spectacular—a third of it was clear blue and sunny. A dark boiling cloud took up the remainder like a science-fiction movie with poorly done special effects. Every shade of gray swirled and raged looking like she could reach out and touch it. The edge of the cloud, one of the outer bands of the hurricane, appeared razor-sharp as it cut its way through the sky.

A combination of panic and excitement buzzed around her head. Hurricane Charley was at her doorstep—she better get out of here. Ronnie went back to the apartment and found the small bag she had just unpacked that morning and filled it with a change of clothes and her toiletries. Fluffy looked at her with beautiful blue eyes framed by silky fur. What she needed was to be comforted rather than left alone in a strange new place. They had only been there a few days and Fluffy didn't take well to change. Would Jeffrey let her bring Fluffy? Probably not. He didn't really like cats.

For a second Ronnie considered waiting out the storm with her precious kitty, but the thought of Jeffrey's teasing words and tan chest convinced her otherwise. She quickly set up a safe place for Fluffy to ride out the storm, "Bye, sweetie, I'll be back tomorrow. You be good." Fluffy stared at her with her giant sad eyes. She shut the door and tried not to think of what a bad owner she was.

Ronnie climbed in her 1996 Thunderbird, set her overnight bag on the passenger seat, and pulled out the directions she had scribbled on a scrap of paper. West on I-4—that was the one road she could find since the exit was right outside of her apartment. She backed up and nearly ran over a man, who flailed his arms angrily at her before trying to open the car door. In a panic, she leaned on the horn. This had the desired effect of startling him so he would let go. She jammed it in reverse and then peeled out of the apartment complex. When she looked in her rearview mirror she saw the man running after her.

"Well, that was weird!" Ronnie said trying to calm down. Bad enough a huge storm was about to hit, but to have a crazy man attacking her car only made things worse. She turned on the radio for a distraction as well as an update of the storm. The weather report provided a snapshot of Armageddon so she turned it off while she fought to steer through the increasing winds.

On I-4 she drove toward Jeffrey's lab and tried to shake the feeling of impending doom. A few large splats on the windshield startled her, followed by a gust of wind that shoved her car out of the lane. Ronnie overcompensated the turn and hydroplaned on the slick highway. "Crap!" She jerked the wheel in the other direction while the car fishtailed down I-4, barely missing a white Toyota and the guardrail. The driver honked at her and gave her the finger. Her heart nearly beat out of her chest.

Panic returned in full force. Would she make it there without crashing? Did the lab have a covered garage to protect her car from the storm? How would Fluffy deal with the stress of the move and now the hurricane? Who was the weird guy and did he live in the same complex as her? The questions assaulted her and she was fully worked up by the time she pulled off the highway at Jeffrey's exit and called his cell.

He led her through a few turns to a huge building. A wave of excitement washed over her when she saw him—all six feet of his fit, lean body. His dark curly blonde hair plastered against his face from the rain and wind. It had been a month since they had been together and she felt giddy thinking of what they would do later.

She rolled down her window. "Hi honey, I'm here," Ronnie said.

"Hi, Babe." Jeffrey leaned in to kiss her, his face wet from the rain. He smelled great. "I'm so glad you made it. It's getting bad out here already."

"I know. I almost got blown off the road," she said.

"Blown, eh? That gives me an idea for later."

"Jeffrey! You are such a perv!"

"Here scoot over, I want to drive."

Ronnie climbed over the center console to the passenger seat and Jeffrey took the driver's seat. He reached a security gate and inserted an ID card in the box. He parked the car in the covered employee lot and took her in the back entrance using the card to open the basement door.

"I've paid off LT at the guard desk to turn off the camera just while I sneak you in." He took her bag and hoisted it over his shoulder before grabbing her hand.

They walked quickly through several corridors and reached a metal door. Jeffrey used the keypad and his security key once again. The room was about the size of her apartment living room and full of computers, monitors, and cabinets. There were no windows and there was only one door in the back of the room. Out of place in the back corner, squished between the desk and the wall, sat an inflatable mattress with sheets, pillows, and a blanket. A TV on top of the desk had weather coverage on.

Terry James, the local weatherman, nearly frothed at the mouth with excitement. "We have a new trajectory. This is very important for those who have just evacuated from the Tampa Bay area." His face was serious, but the mystery of toupee or not toupee as Steph said, was distracting. Jeffrey set her bag down near the bed as they both listened intently.

"The mandatory evacuations from low-lying areas for the Tampa Bay area are no longer in effect. The new trajectory is here." Terry pointed to a cone-shaped path in red and orange covering a huge swath with Orlando in the center.

"If you are in coastal or low-lying areas anywhere in the path of this storm you need to get to a shelter immediately. This is a dangerous storm, in fact, it is one of the strongest to hit southwest Florida since 1960 when Hurricane Donna devastated the area."

Jeffrey took her hand and kissed it. "Babe."

"Shhhhhh!" Ronnie said. Excitement and dread bubbled up in her chest.

Terry continued, "Hurricane Charley has sustained winds of 145 and gusts up to 175 miles per hour. This makes Charley a Category 4 storm. We are expecting it to weaken over land but by the time it makes it to Central Florida it will still be a Category 1 or 2 hurricane with sustained winds from seventy to 120 miles per hour."

Jeffrey stood behind Ronnie and pulled her close, his arms around her waist while they watched. "A Category 2 storm would result in damage to roofs and poorly constructed buildings. We can expect trees to be down with extensive and perhaps total power outages. There is a potential for loss of potable water as well so fill containers with clean water to last three days." Terry went on to detail the areas that would likely be flooded and what kind of damage to expect. Ronnie drank it in, feeling the pull of the storm, the seduction of its power.

Jeffrey turned her around. "Do you know what this means, babe?" He hugged her and picked her up off her feet. "With a direct hit, I can try out my equipment and see how it handles hurricane-force winds!" He set her down and kissed her. He pulled away and muted the TV. "Babe, this is really big! I've only used lab-simulated hurricane-force winds. The original path of the storm was supposed to miss us." He walked a few steps to his desk. "With a direct hit, I'm going to get funded as long as the equipment holds up." He picked up a bottle of champagne and opened it.

"I'm glad you're excited. It scares me, Jeffrey." Ronnie jumped at the sound of the cork popping. "Dom Pérignon! Jeffrey, you've really gone all out!" Although it did seem like he was celebrating the storm as much as her birthday.

He handed her a plastic glass, filled another for himself, and lifted it, "A toast to the birthday girl." Ronnie touched her glass to his. *Plink.* They laughed at the pitiful noise the plastic made. She took a big sip and the cool bubbly liquid slid down her throat, adding to the electricity running through her veins. "You go wash up and we'll eat. I have a special dinner for us." He nodded to the door at the back of the room.

Ronnie opened the door and found a small sterile bathroom with a brass drain in the middle of the floor. It smelled like paint and bleach. She closed the door behind her.

   ***

Jeffrey opened the desk drawer and pulled out a small medicine bottle and twisted the top off. He walked to the food that sat on the edge of the desk in take-out containers. Opening the Styrofoam lid, he took a plastic fork and gently lifted the crusty top of the twice-baked potato and emptied the contents of the bottle into the steamy pocket. He could hear the toilet flush. With his finger he mixed it around and gently put the potato back together. With his fingernail he marked an *X* on the top of the Styrofoam and closed the tab on the container.

   ***

Ronnie washed her hands and dried them with the paper towels and opened the door.

"Here sit down." He held out the chair. On the table sat carry-out containers from Del Frisco's Steakhouse, the same place he was going to take her to before the storm interfered. He opened the box in front of her to reveal a feast of lobster tails, veggies, and a twice-baked potato.

"Oh man," she said, "my absolute favorite. Thanks, babe."

He leaned down to kiss her. "Yes, nothing but the best for Miss Andrews. Jeeves, get the lady more champagne." Pretending to be a waiter, he poured her another glass, napkin draped over his arm.

This quelled some of her fears about moving so far from home. The awkwardness between them since he left Virginia started to evaporate. She could feel the knot in her stomach unravel a little. The champagne was helping, too.

They enjoyed the feast and talked about the storm and the new job she would be starting on Monday. Ronnie watched his hands and his mouth as he talked and ate and couldn't help but imagine them on her. After dinner, Jeffrey handed Ronnie a small box wrapped in gold foil paper.

"What wonderful wrapping, did you do it?" she asked.

"What, are you kidding? Of course not. It would look like crap if I had. Open it." He looked like the Cheshire Cat with a huge smile and mischief in his eyes.

She slowly unwrapped the box and opened it. It was *the* watch—a rose gold antique watch she found in London in June with Steph on her post-graduation trip. She had just finished her master's degree in business and wanted to tag along for Steph's biannual trip to Glasgow, Scotland where her family lived. They had taken a long weekend and visited London. In a quaint antique shop they found this watch. She couldn't afford it but Steph had taken a picture of her wearing it.

"It is beautiful!" Tears stung her eyes while she moved to sit on his lap so she could hug and kiss him.

"Where did you find it?" she asked. "I can't believe it."

"I didn't. I stole your picture and had a replica made. It's not exactly like the one you saw since all I had was the 2-D picture."

"They did a great job, Jeffrey. It looks exactly like it." She put it on her wrist and he helped fasten the safety clasp. "Definite brownie points, Jeff. When did you steal the picture?"

He smiled triumphantly. "I took it when you were in the shower the last time I was up in Virginia Beach. You didn't notice it was missing, did you?"

"No, you sneak!" She kissed him again.

"I had the idea when you came back from your trip. I tried to get the one you saw in London but it sold before I could buy it. This one is better though—waterproof to eighty feet, extra clasp to make sure it doesn't ever come off, and brand spanking new."

"I wouldn't want to swim or go spelunking with it on." The rectangular face was made out of the rose gold as well. It was a beautiful piece.

"Oh, you can swim with it. It is not going to come off. I'd like you to wear it all the time, maybe not spelunking in a muddy cave, but all the time." He kissed her softly again. "Think of it as part of me protecting you from the world. It's especially made to give you good luck!"

"Aw, that's so sweet. I'll wear it all the time."

Neither of them were ready for an engagement. This watch was about the closest thing she could think of to a commitment. It must have cost a lot just in gold alone not to mention the price for someone to replicate it.

"Hang on, I have to check something." He walked over to his computer and typed for a few minutes. She watched TV but they were just going over the trajectory again. She wondered how Steph was doing and remembered Fluffy. She felt a bit sick to her stomach. Was she freaking out? And what was Steph going to do during the storm?

Chapter 2 - Struck by Lightning

"Ronnie!" Jeffrey said.

"What?" Ronnie closed the door and turned to see his profile as he typed on the computer.

"You've only been here three days and you've already attracted a major hurricane. I've been here for five months and nada! How'd you do it?" He turned toward her and smiled.

"Ha ha! Rather bad luck I'd say." Ronnie remembered the dread she felt earlier. "Jeffrey, what if something happens to my house? We postponed the closing because of this stupid storm."

Jeffrey had talked her into buying a house instead of renting. Steph suspected that it was a twofold plan—first to keep her from moving in with him, and second to keep her in the area if her new job didn't work out. Ronnie had some insurance money from her father's passing five years before. Until now it had been too hard to spend it. But buying a house was a great opportunity to use her inheritance for a down payment and to also make some repairs on the house—a way to invest in her future, as Jeffrey put it.

"Ron, maybe that's a good thing. If there is damage then you don't have to sign the papers."

"I never thought of that. But what about the owners?" she asked.

"They've got insurance and tons of equity on it. Aren't they the original owners?"

"Yes, they bought it new in 1952," she said.

"They could fix it and sell it later. Don't be stupid because you feel bad for the old geezers. The market is hot and they'll have no trouble selling." He turned back to the computer to type for another minute before finishing with dramatic staccato strikes at the keys, then stood up.

"I know. You're right."

"Come here and let me distract you." He walked over to her with a smile playing on his lips.

"How are you gonna do that?" Nothing could distract her from the storm and the sense of impending doom.

Jeffrey wrapped his arms around her, his mouth pressing into hers, tongues mingling. He worked his way down her neck nibbling and licking, sending chills through her. He grabbed her legs and picked her up before setting her gently down on the desk.

"Well, that might distract me a little," she said breathlessly.

"I missed you, babe." He sucked on her upper lip and darted his tongue in her mouth. He then stepped backward and unzipped her shorts.

"Oh looky here! You brought out the fancy panties for my enjoyment." He slid his hand inside her shorts to feel the silky smoothness. She stood up so he could remove her shorts and looked down because she had forgotten what she put on—lacy pink see-through silk—his favorite because it barely hid her contours.

He pulled the shorts off and tossed them on the floor. "Let's see if we're matchy-matchy today." He pulled off her shirt. "Oh, yes the full set!" He put his mouth on the pink silk bra and bit through a little. "Are you thinking about the storm right now?" The thrill of the storm had gotten her aroused, but his lips were taking it to another level.

"What storm?" She shoved his head back where it had been.

He deftly worked the clasp in the back so he could remove her bra and toss it on the floor. He took a step back and looked at her sitting only in sheer panties.

"What?" His staring embarrassed her and she resisted the urge to cross her arms. They usually kept the lights low and the bright florescent lights of the office seemed too revealing.

"You're just so perfect. God, I could eat you up." He made good on that a short time later with her still on the desk. She quickly reached climax with images of Charley's gray and black swirls in her mind as Jeffrey's mouth pressed into her flesh and caused a flood of pleasure.

They moved to the blow-up mattress where he removed his shirt and shorts. Her hands reached for his chest and her lips touched his warm skin. They devoured each other, lust taking over logic, passion and need pushing them to a fast and furious climax, much like the storm raging outside.

An alarm at 9:30 startled both of them.

"Everything okay?" she asked while shifting to climb off of him. Smacking her butt with one hand, he guided her nipple into his mouth with the other. Then he pushed her hips and she rolled off of him.

"Yep, just a warning. The storm is at its peak." He grabbed his shorts and pulled them on, then walked across the room to his computer. Ronnie lay down on the makeshift bed and covered herself with the sheets to enjoy the cool cotton against her naked body.

Jeffrey turned up the TV. Ronnie could hear the storm coverage but couldn't see it. A reporter was on the phone talking about buildings damaged and trees uprooted. A few homes were damaged by fallen trees and streets were flooded. Power was out to the entire viewing area, but Jeffrey's lab had electricity, thanks to the generators. She thought about Steph and hoped she was all right. Was her house damaged? What about the apartment and Fluffy?

A strange feeling bubbled in her stomach. Ronnie got up and slipped on Jeffrey's T-shirt and found her underwear in a pile of clothes near the desk. The feeling worsened. Was she going to be sick? Jeffrey was busy at his computer and she quietly made her way to the small bathroom and closed the door behind her. Was it something she had eaten?

The cold water felt good as she splashed it on her face. Ronnie looked at her reflection in the mirror. No outward signs of being ill. Too much champagne? She took a deep breath in an attempt to quell the rising nausea. The room spun and she sat down on the toilet, head in her hands. Sweat broke out on her face and she knelt down to lift the toilet seat. "Oh crap!"

A sudden change in air pressure overwhelmed her, making her drop on all fours. Her ears popped and she swallowed trying to clear them. Was the storm intensifying?

An agonizing bright light seared into her eyes and she squeezed them shut in an attempt to block it out, without success.

The building must have been struck by lightning! *Struck by lightning. Struck by lightning.* She could hear her father's voice reading *The Hobbit* to her as a young girl. A pang of sadness added to the confusion.

A low vibration shook the bathroom tiles. A dark mist sucked away all light. Ronnie was flattened to the floor by some unseen force and couldn't fight it. Strange smells assaulted her—horse manure, almonds, and wet soil. She pressed the side of her face against the cool cement floor in an attempt to stop the dizzy spin of the room.

What the hell was happening? A chill ran up her spine. Nothing about this was right. Fear choked out any rational thoughts. She tried to call out to Jeffrey but her body was paralyzed, her voice disconnected. It was a living breathing nightmare.

A gut-wrenching tearing ripped apart her soul. She tried to scream. Ronnie floated up to the ceiling to see a lifeless shape on the bathroom floor below, surprised to see anything in the dark. Holy crap, that was her own long blonde hair spilled across the concrete floor. She reached out to touch her arm but was jerked a million miles an hour upward into the darkness.

Shadows engulfed her. A sensation of motion disturbed her equilibrium. She was hurtling up into the ebony sky and away from her body splayed in Jeffrey's lab. Her arms reached for something to hold onto, to make it stop, but came up empty.

Was she dying? There was supposed to be a calming bright light to head toward. Instead, there was only emptiness, a buzzing that lulled her to an empty dark place similar to the twilight just before falling asleep—alert, yet fuzzy and drifting into oblivion. It sped up, she could feel the wind on her face, her hair whipped behind her, but now she was falling like a rocket returning to Earth, pulling her down, stretching her toward destruction.

Suddenly the back of her head struck the ground. Stars floated in a pool of blackness and pain overwhelmed any thoughts. Finally, her mind began to clear and it occurred to her if she were face down on the floor how did she hit the back of her head? Under her hands, she could feel something soft and gritty but everything was pitch black.

Panic returned. What was happening … and what the hell was that smell?

Chapter 3 - A Chance of Showers

August 13, 2004, 8:30 p.m., Altamonte Springs, Florida.

Steph glanced at the clock and was surprised that it was already 8:30. She had left Ronnie's around 5:00—where had the time gone? The worst of Hurricane Charley would be here soon and she was just finishing up her preparations. The masking tape made a loud noise as she pulled off a long strip and covered her picture window from the bottom left to the top right and repeated the process on the opposite side.

Something in the yard caught her attention. Hamish! Her precious kitty had worked himself into a tizzy with the storm approaching and darted out the door the second she opened it. Her stomach had been in knots ever since, imagining him outside during the storm.

She tried to get the cat's attention by tapping on the glass. He looked over at the window but kept creeping through the bushes with his ears flattened against his head. Steph ran to the door and pulled it open. "Hamish, come here wee kitty-boy," she said trying not to sound panicked despite how she felt. He crept toward her, crouched low to the ground. "That's a good lad." He was definitely freaked out. Swinging the door open, she said, "C'mon Hamey-wamey."

He scurried into the house and immediately disappeared into her closet, his favorite hiding place. "Whew! At least he's back inside." The stupid cat had completely stressed her already frayed nerves. With the storm coming and Ronnie ditching her for the gobshite, it had been a miserable few hours. Steph really didn't want to be alone. Hopefully, Nick would arrive soon. She had called him from the car on her way home from Ronnie's hoping he would not mind camping out with her for the duration of the hurricane. At the moment he was at his mom's helping her prepare for the storm.

Nick was her best friend, after Ronnie of course. Truth be told, he was drop- dead gorgeous and a really good man. Tall with light hair and broad shoulders and a footballer's body, he was always at the gym and had begged her for months to join him. They had been friends since she moved to Florida but never dated. Always out of sync—one was always in a relationship when the other was free.

"Water!" Steph said almost forgetting the most important storm preparation. She went back to the kitchen to finish filling her pots and pans as a backup in case the city water pumps went out during the storm. Digging under the cabinet she pulled out every pot and lid she owned. She started with the biggest one and set it under the faucet. While it filled, she took the ice cube tray, cracked it into a Tupperware container, and refilled it. Nick said that the ice could be used to keep the fridge cold after the power went out if she had enough.

He was full of great advice. Being a Florida native he had been through enough storms that this all came naturally to him. She opened several water bottles, dumped an inch of water out of them and put them in the freezer, also Nick's suggestion. Scotland had big storms but not like this.

Her doorbell chimed. "Oh good, he's here!" She made her way across the kitchen, through the living room to the front door. Nick stood on her doorstep soaked to the bone.

"Hi, sweetie!" He moved in for a big hug but she pushed him away.

"Nooo, you're all wet!" She leaned over and gave him a peck on the lips. "Get in here before you let that awful Charley into my house!" A huge gust of wind blew rain inside the foyer. Nick walked in and stood there dripping.

"Ah, you sure I can't get a hug, Stephie?" He wagged his eyebrows at her.

"Stay right there! Don't move!" Steph ran just past the kitchen to the linen closet in her bedroom and pulled out a towel. She sighed to let out some of the stresses of the day. He was here and everything would be okay. She returned to the foyer and handed Nick the towel. "Take off yer massive track shoes, while yer at it."

He dried off his light brown hair making it stand on end and toweled off his muscular arms and legs. "So did you take care of the water like I suggested?"

"Oh, damn it!" She ran back to the sink, switched the water off, and lifted the big pot onto the counter. Through the kitchen window, camphor and crepe myrtle trees flailed about helpless to the wind. "Nick, I've left a few huge potted plants outside in the back garden."

He walked into the kitchen and looked out the window. "That's a damn shame. They'll probably get damaged."

"I was hoping you'd …" she said, smiling winningly at him.

"Hoping I'd go out in the middle of the storm and fetch 'em? Ooh, no you don't!" he said.

"But Nick, they're my precious babies!" Her garden was everything, having spent endless hours designing, digging, planting, watering, and doting.

"They were too big for me. I moved all the smaller ones inside already. Should have moved them before the …"

"Nope, you're not gonna work your Scottish womanly charms on me."

"Please, that big pot was from my mum." She pointed at the largest one with a rosemary plant in it.

"Aw, Stephie, you had to mention your mum," Nick said. Her mom was diagnosed with breast cancer a year ago and Nick had been there for Steph during her emotional breakdown, made even more difficult since her mom was in Glasgow.

He looked outside and back at her. "Wumman, yer trubb-bull with a capital T!" He made a sad attempt at a Scottish accent.

"Oh, yer gonna be a love and do it for me?"

"Just that one pot, Steph!" He held up one finger.

Fifteen minutes later Nick had moved ten pots into the already full garage. It looked like a small jungle with her Jeep Liberty barely visible through the forest of potted plants. She handed him another towel.

"Interested in a shower?" She swiped a finger across his dirt-covered arm.

"Only if you join me."

"Haha, noooo, I don't think that's gonna work!" Her face felt hot and her stomach did a flip. "What about your floozy, what was her name?"

"Tiffany and I didn't know she was sleeping with the entire staff at the gym." He reached out and hugged her making a point of wiping as much dirt on her face and arms as possible. "Aw, but you're so dirty. I think you'll need to clean up, Stephie."

"NICK!" She pulled away. "Stop that!" She smacked his arm and wiped the dirt from her face on his shirt. He scooped her up and carried her to the bathroom. She laughed and kicked her legs trying, but not trying, to get free. He delicately set her down in front of the shower.

"Let me help you with that shirt. It looks like it's become a burden to you." Nick said with a smile crinkling the skin near his eyes.

Steph pushed him away. "Wait, first tell me what this is?"

He stopped in the middle of taking off his shirt and looked at her. "It's my buff chest Steph, really? Do I have to explain everything to you?" he laughed.

"I mean us getting naked. Where is this going?"

"I'm pretty sure we're *going* to take a shower." He pulled down his shorts to reveal wet boxers and a very obvious level of excitement.

"Oh." Steph tried to look away, but he was so defined. His chest was clear, no hair at all, showing each individual ab and his chest was perfectly shaped. A bit too muscular for her taste but, oh my God, he was built.

"Trying to distract me with that, eh?" She nodded toward his crotch.

"No, just a consequence of you in wet clothes. Can I help you with that soggy shirt madam?" He laughed while reaching out to take the hem but waited for her to say it was okay. Steph wanted to join him but it was just strange to think of Nick in this way. She had never seen him naked before.

"I get it. So this is just a shower, nothing else?" Steph said pulling off her shirt.

"Yeah, sure. Just a shower with a friend. No biggie. If something happens, it happens. But no pressure, if you're not comfortable with it I can use the other bathroom." He bent down to pick up his clothes.

"No, no. I'm okay with this, I think." She looked down to take it all in but held her arms across her chest. She was reluctant to take the next step.

"Good," he said.

Steph reached to turn on the shower and he pulled the bra strap down off her shoulder. She turned her back toward him and pulled it back up.

He stepped in the shower and she could see his boxers on the floor. Steph had the strong urge to run into the other room but not without peeking at him first. She poked her head around the shower curtain and he smiled, reaching out for her hand. She didn't want to, but he pulled her into the hot water.

"Are you going to take those off?" he laughed.

Her shorts, bra, and knickers were still on. They were soaking wet now. "Yes. No. Auch!"

He laughed and unbuttoned her shorts. "Here, I'll help you." He unzipped and peeled them down. She stepped out of her shorts and looked down at his face surprised to see the lust in his eyes. How could he want her? She was so pale. Plus he knew way too much about her past relationships.

They heard a loud crashing noise and a howling. "Oh my God, that's Hamish!" Steph jumped out of the shower, re-clasped her bra, and grabbed a towel. She ran to the back of the house and looked out of the window. Nick was right behind her putting on his wet shorts.

Steph's heart pounded in her chest. The trees whipped around and debris covered the windows. She opened the kitchen door. "Hamish! Hamish, come here kitty." Water sprayed inside the house while the wind howled through the tall trees.

"How do you know that was Hamish?" Nick asked.

"I know his cry. He must have gotten out when we moved the plants."

"I'll go check." Nick grabbed his shoes and walked toward the back door.

Steph put the rest of her clothes on and looked around for her shoes.

"Do you have a flashlight?" he asked.

"Yes, on top of the fridge," Steph said. "I'll be right there!" She watched him walk out of the back door into the stormy darkness. What the hell were they doing going out in this storm?

Chapter 4 –The Hands of Time

Ronnie heard strange noises all around. Oddly enough it reminded her of Girl Scout camp with the smell of horses, the clink of metal, and the creaking of leather. What would horses be doing in Jeffrey's lab? She tried to sit up but her body refused to respond.

"Jeffrey! Help me!" Ronnie thought but nothing came out. Pure unadulterated fear overwhelmed her. Using all the strength she could muster Ronnie forced her body to respond, rolling onto her side. Where was Jeffrey? Was he hurt?

Everything was cloaked in darkness, but gradually a fuzzy yellow light appeared around the edges of her vision.

A man's voice off in the distance said something unintelligible. Was Jeffrey coming to help her? "Regina, Regina!" An unfamiliar voice called out. "Oh, Regina. Are you badly hurt?"

Ronnie tried to answer but her mouth would not form the words. The desire was there but the connection to her brain seemed severed. Who the hell was Regina? The security guard must be confusing her with someone else.

"Regina, why are you on the road?" the man said as he touched her head, her arms, and then he picked her up and carried her. There must be a nasty bump on the back of her head because it screamed out in pain with every step he took. Maybe it was someone from another lab? How could he see where he was going in this blackness?

A small voice said, "I fink she's been run over by a carriage. I seen her run out of that big house, sir."

"Thank you, lad," the man said.

"I seen 'er meself. She was running and looking behind her. That's when it 'appened," the boy said, sounding like *Oliver Twist.*

Where had this kid come from? He shouldn't be in the lab during a hurricane. And why was he speaking in an English accent?

"Lad. Fetch Doctor Wiggams at once. Send him to the Ingram Estate," the man said, also speaking in an English accent.

"Yes, sir."

"My dearest Regina. Please speak to me!"

Ronnie tried again to say something but she couldn't force any words out. Without warning, he set her down roughly on something solid, making her brain scream in pain.

"Driver. Return us at once," The man said while inanely patting her hand. Whatever they were sitting on lurched forward nearly pitching her on her face but he caught her. "Regina, fear not, I will care for you."

A steady jostling made Ronnie's head nearly split in half. Stars danced recklessly around her blurry yellow vision. She put her head between her knees to keep from fainting and tried to place the familiar noises. Focusing on the individual sounds, Ronnie could swear she heard chains clinking and the steady beat of horse's hooves. Desperate to confirm the bizarre sounds, she tried to make her eyes work, but only saw yellow shadows. There was a distinct odor of horseflesh and leather, but these things were not in Jeffrey's lab. They couldn't be. Panic filled Ronnie's chest, adding to the pounding in her head. What the hell was going on? She must be in the bathroom in Jeffrey's lab—this must be a dream, a very weird and painful dream.

After an eternity the movement stopped. "Johnson, Fetch my butler, Robert, for me at once," the man said.

A few minutes later a deeper male voice said, "Mr. Ingram."

"If you please, assist me with my sister. I must deliver her to her bedchamber without delay." She heard footsteps on hard wood. "Please." He huffed and almost dropped her but quickly recovered. The pattern of movement changed as if he were carrying her upstairs. She redoubled her grip around his neck.

"The antechamber door," he said, thoroughly out of breath.

A door creaked open and she was set down gently on something soft. The room smelled of smoke and melted wax.

"Regina," he patted her hand again. "Are you injured? Why were you not in the company of Lord Barton where I had left you?"

She wanted to ask why he was calling her Regina. Instead, a garbled mumble came from her lips. Something was touching her foot and Ronnie realized she could see a shadowy outline of a man messing with her shoes. Closing her eyes again she tried to think. There were no shoes on her feet a few minutes ago. Ronnie pulled her foot away from him and touched it. Her hand shook as she felt the hard leather. Her fingers came away dirty. She wiped them on her leg and felt soft fabric. A few minutes ago she had nothing on her legs. Her pulse pounded in her head, reminding her of the recurring fever dream she had as a kid where King Kong was chasing her down. She was definitely not in Jeffrey's lab anymore.

24

"Regina Elizabeth Ingram!" The man grabbed her foot again, pulling off the shoe and let it drop to the ground. Unlacing the other shoe he removed it. She closed her eyes again hoping to clear her head. How could she be here? And more importantly where the hell was here?

Her vision was returning in small increments but everything seemed too yellow and fuzzy. The man paced back and forth, tapping his fingers on his thigh. He was in his mid-twenties and was wearing the strangest clothes. They looked like they were torn from the pages of a history book—a ridiculously long black velvet coat with a gray tunic and gilded lace down the front. Underneath he wore a white frilly shirt with lacy sleeves and a matching cravat around his neck. He was slim with long, wavy brown hair.

The room was strange as well. It reminded her of the old houses of the famous authors and dignitaries she and Steph had toured in London. Except that this room didn't have shabby faded wallpaper. Everything looked new and expensive. It was baffling. How did she get here? How would she get back?

"Regina. I beg of you. You must forgive my intolerable behavior." He walked over to her and knelt down at her feet taking both of her hands. "The citizens of London are rioting in the streets all for the parliament's New Style. In a fortnight it will begin and we lose eleven days of our lives. Never would I have believed that I would be a witness to such madness." He kissed her hands and she looked at the top of his head.

What was he talking about? London? That would explain his accent—he was English. Ronnie was afraid to say anything. Better to just let him talk and maybe she could figure out what was happening.

He continued, "There are only fourteen days in the month of September. How will I ever get full rents from all of the tenants? Sister, I beg your forgiveness for my outburst. I am required to pay full wages for the month but with only a fortnight of work going out. It is a great strain on my bankroll."

How could there be only fourteen days in September?

"You must understand our family fortune is at stake if you do not marry Lord Barton."

"Who?" Ronnie said, not able to keep quiet.

The man's hand grazed her cheek. "Sister, I do not know why you are pretending not to understand me, but I beseech you to stop playing this unpleasant game."

"Game!" This time her voice came out in a croak. "Why do you think I am playing a game? I just want to know where I am!"

"Regina! I have to insist that you stop this charade." He pronounced it shar-rard. "The doctor will arrive in this chamber promptly and you must obey my commands." He shook her shoulders a little, making her wince in pain.

"Commands? Get off me!" She lifted her arms to brush his hands off her shoulders and tried to stand up to get away.

He pushed her back down. "You will do as I bid, Sister." He slapped her hard on the face. "I will not allow an insolent girl in my household."

Ronnie's head reeled with the blow. She closed her eyes, pressing her hand to the heat on her cheek where she had been slapped. Tears rolled down her cheeks without any warning. This was not a dream—she wouldn't feel a slap like that in a dream.

A knock on the door interrupted them. The man opened the door to let in a woman dressed in a full-length black dress. She held a large tray and nodded her head before speaking, "Mr. Ingram, sir. Miss Regina, ma'am." She bustled past them and set the tray down on an old-fashioned desk in the corner of the room.

The woman looked strange as well. She had a very rigid posture. Her bustline was way too high to be natural and her shoulders seemed to be pulled back at an unusual angle. Without thinking, Ronnie touched her stomach and felt the stiffness of something under the light green silk dress that she somehow was wearing. The tight clothes made her feel claustrophobic. Glancing down at the dress she saw something that horrified her more than the strange clothes. The hand was very pale, small and … NOT HERS!

Before she could stop herself an "Oh my God!" escaped. The man and woman turned to stare at her. Looking from one face to the other, she wanted to scream. Could she be in someone else's body? *Don't freak, don't freak!*

Chapter 5 – Doctor Who

"Regina, are you not well?" the man kneeling by her side asked.

"I … it's just …" the back of Ronnie's head pulsed with each beat of her heart and made it impossible to think.

The door opened and a woman peeked in. She wore a loose floor-length black dress that attempted to cover an advanced pregnancy.

The man said, "Catherine, you should be in your lying-in chamber." He walked over to her and took her hand. "Doctor Wiggams was adamant."

"Husband, I found it unbearable to be stuck in my chamber knowing poor Regina was dreadfully injured," Catherine said.

"I will allow you a few minutes to check up on our dear sister but then you must rest." He kissed her hand again and she smiled at him.

"I am so alone in that chamber since my companion is no longer there to sit with me."

"Catherine, you know we cannot keep such extravagant help anymore." Jack's expression grew angrier. "Our finances are not able to support such luxuries. I will allow you but a few minutes to check up on our dear sister but then you must rest." He kissed her hand again and she smiled at him.

Catherine turned and sat down next to Ronnie on the couch and took her hand. "Regina, dear. What has happened to you?" Soft brown eyes showed kindness and concern.

"I have no idea. I must have bumped my head. Why are you calling me Regina?"

She let go of Ronnie's hand as if it was on fire and sprang up from the couch, standing a few feet away, "Your name is Regina Ingram. Do you not know your God-given name? Have you any knowledge of what has happened to her, Jack?" Catherine asked, but kept looking at Ronnie, her brows knitted with worry.

"I escorted her to visit with Lord Barton to discuss their betrothal. They were talking and I left to take care of some business with the bank. When I returned I found her lying in the street. A coach and team of horses had run her down." He shook his head.

"Where was Lord Barton when the coach collided with Regina?" Catherine asked.

It was becoming difficult to focus on what they were saying. Was it possible that she was in Regina's body? Or was this a strange hoax with actors putting on a show? Nothing explained the strange hand. She held it in front of her face and wiggled it. The hand moved as if it were her own.

Ronnie's attention was brought back to the conversation when Jack's voice rose in anger. "You will not take that tone with me! I did not take the time to find out. Instead, I brought our dear sister home and called for the doctor."

Tears welled up in Catherine's eyes and she turned away from him.

The maid came over and interjected, "Mr. Ingram, sir. I was just thinking that perhaps Miss Regina might want to be moved to her bedchamber? The doctor will arrive shortly."

This seemed to distract Jack from further reprimanding his wife. "Yes, yes. Let us move her into the bedchamber. Please, Margaret, retrieve the tea service and tidy up this room for the arrival of Doctor Wiggams."

Catherine avoided Jack's eyes and handed Margaret a key. Margaret passed her a sympathetic look and gave a small courtesy. "Thank you."

Jack offered his arm and Ronnie used it to get off the couch. The room spun and she almost blacked out. He took a step forward, but she stopped him.

"Give me a sec," she said and put her head lower to make the stars stop dancing around.

"Indeed, what is it that I am to give to you?" Jack asked, confusion in his voice. "Would you perchance prefer me to carry you?"

"No, I don't think so. Just go slowly." He supported Ronnie and she felt a bit sturdier as they made their way through a doorway into a smaller room while Catherine watched intently.

Jack led her to a small bed with a maroon coverlet surrounded by curtains that could be drawn to keep out drafts. A fire burned in the fireplace making the air smell of wood smoke.

Ronnie sat on the edge of the bed to catch her breath. It must have been stuffed with hay or something very stiff. She settled herself into the soft down pillows and Jack pulled the coverlet over her legs. This room was full of old-fashioned furniture and beautiful maroon, pink, and white silk wallpaper that looked like it has just been put up.

Her mind was racing a million miles an hour. Where had Jeffrey and the lab gone? Was she really in another body? She had to find a mirror to confirm, maybe her hands were just a little weird here, she told herself. But they were not her hands, these were smaller and her own fingers were longer.

"Doctor Wiggams is here," Catherine said from the doorway. A short round man with oily gray hair shuffled into the room. He wore an old-fashioned tunic, white shirt, and ill-fitting black pants with hose. He dramatically set down a large leather case on a table near the door.

He shook Jack's hand and said, "Mr. Ingram, your servant sir." He bowed to Catherine, "Mrs. Ingram."

Doctor Wiggams gave Ronnie a sour look and said, "Miss Ingram, what has befallen you?"

Ronnie had no idea what she should say to the man. The truth would be her first choice, and boy did she ever want to tell them that, but given the serious demeanor of the three people staring at her, she decided against it. She stuck to a very brief version of the truth. "I dunno." Her voice sounded very small, and very *not* British.

"Why does she sound like *that*?" Catherine said, pursing her lips and furrowing her brow at Ronnie.

Jack took a step toward the bed, "I came upon Regina lying in the road just outside of the courtyard of Farthington Manor. I believe that she was struck by a carriage."

"Miss Regina, pray inform us of everything that you remember from this incident," Doctor Wiggams said.

Ronnie drew a complete blank. These people acted as if they knew her and surely would know how she was supposed to sound. She decided to imitate Catherine's smooth English tones and said, "I woke up in the road, not being able to see." It was simple, direct, and the truth. It would have to do.

Doctor Wiggams continued, "Miss Regina, what is it that you remember just prior to the accident?"

"Nothing," she said, hoping they could be done with the questions.

Margaret's return with a tray of tea took everyone's attention away from Ronnie for a second. She sat up more on the bed and tried to figure out what the hell was going on. How could she be here with all these old-fashioned characters? Margaret handed the key back to Catherine, who slipped it into a pocket in her dress.

Catherine made a strange noise and Margaret caught her as she collapsed. Jack rushed to her side and Jack and the doctor moved Catherine to a nearby chair. She was not responding.

The doctor rushed to his black case and pulled out a small vial and opened it. He put it under Catherine's nose. She woke up with a start and sat back against the chair.

"You must give me leave to examine your wife," the doctor said, looking toward Catherine. "She should not have been removed from her lying-in room," he scolded Jack.

"Yes, Wiggams, of course, you are quite right." Jack helped the doctor stand Catherine up.

Catherine pointed a shaky finger at Ronnie, "It is this girl here that has made me ill with her queer words, her dangerous touch."

Jack looked at her in surprise. "You speak nonsense, my dear. Let us get you to your bedchamber to rest."

"What did I do?" Ronnie said and immediately regretted it when everyone in the room looked at her.

"Do you see husband, the odd turn of phrase. Where is our sister, where is Regina?"

Ronnie felt her face heat up and looked from Margaret to the Doctor. They looked as surprised as Jack did but she recognized the terror in Catherine's eyes.

"Come now, you shall need your rest," Jack said as he turned to Catherine to guide her out of the room with Doctor Wiggams on her other side.

Ronnie sat back and let her head sink into the soft pillow while she tried to wrap her mind around the situation. Catherine had noticed something was different about her. What would be the repercussions of her pointing it out?

Ronnie was startled when a voice said, "Miss Ingram, would you care for some tea?" She had forgotten that Margaret was still in the room.

Ronnie nodded. Margaret picked up a china teapot from the silver tray and poured it into an elegant cup, added a little milk from a jug, placed it on a saucer and handed it to Ronnie, who sat up and tried to keep the strange hands from shaking.

She sipped from the white china cup trying only to focus on the warmth and flavor. But her mind would not rest. She sorted through all the worries that were stacked up waiting to be addressed. How could she be here, wherever here was? How would she get out of this place and back to Jeffrey's lab? And what would Jack do with Catherine's suspicions?

Chapter 6 - This Time

"If you want to see about Mrs. Ingram please go ahead," Ronnie said to Margaret, sensing that she wanted to check on Catherine.

"Oh, bless you, Miss Regina. Are you sure you will be all right while I'm gone?" Margaret said.

"I will close my eyes and rest," Ronnie said eager for a minute alone.

Margaret curtsied and left the room. Ronnie could hear her footsteps down the hall. After listening for a minute to see if anyone else might show up, she pulled the blanket off her legs and sat on the edge of the bed. The room spun and those dreaded stars were back flitting around her eyes like gnats. She waved them away and lay back down while they made a reluctant retreat. There had to be a mirror in here somewhere. She looked around and found nothing,

Now would be the perfect time to escape. It sure would be helpful to be able to stand up without blacking out. *Deep breath, let it out.* This was the mantra her mom had taught her to calm down. There had to be a way get out of here. A loud grumble from her stomach interrupted her thoughts. The smell of food on the tray made her mouth water. Weird too because she had been so full after her birthday feast of lobster tails and twice-baked potatoes with Jeffrey in Florida. How could she be this hungry already? If she really were in another body that would explain it.

Ronnie put her head between her knees with her legs dangling over the side of the bed and took several deep breaths. She put her head up and the lack of stars floating around was a surprise.

Venturing one foot on the ground then the other Ronnie stood up, holding onto the bed. A mere ten steps separated her from the food. It wouldn't be smart to leave on an empty stomach, now would it? Just a quick dash and grab. Her stomach rumbled again, urging her on. "Hush." She patted it, hoping she would be able to keep the food down.

This could be her only chance to get out of here, away from Jack's heavy hand and Catherine's suspicious eyes. She tentatively took five steps on unsteady feet—and five more. She grabbed a plate and took a piece of cake to place on it, nearly flinging it onto the floor on the way back to the bed.

She sat on the bed and took a heavenly bite. It was fresh and moist with a hint of warmth from the oven. She laid back on the bed and chewed. With the task of food retrieval off her mind, she began to take in her situation.

Her cheek still felt hot where Jack had slapped her. Up until the slap, she may have convinced herself it was merely a dream. But dreams didn't deliver a cold hard smack in the face. No one had ever hit her in her life. Mom and Dad hadn't believed in spanking. There was the occasional scuffle with her brother, Dave, but he never hit her.

She had to get out of here. But where would she go? How did she even end up here? It made no sense at all. Another tear escaped. Damn tears! She wiped at them as if that would make it stop. Ronnie had to find her way back. The alternative of staying here with Jack as a cruel captor was not an option. Where the hell was here? She looked around the room for anything that would give her a clue.

On the table next to the bed was a yellowed piece of paper. Ronnie picked it up. The light was so low in the room she reached over to turn on a lamp. To her surprise there was none. She looked at the ceiling for an overhead light and again nothing. Over on a small table near the window sat a candle.

She tilted the piece of paper toward the light from the fire to see it better. It felt rough in her hands as she unfolded it. In peculiar letters that made every *s* look like an *f*, it read "Feptember, 1752. *The Ladies Journal of Fashion.*" As in the year 1752? She read it again. *1752.* Under the title in small letters, it read *London.* Could it be a relic or something reproduced?

Ronnie felt queasy and lay back on the bed. Did she go back in time? It was way too elaborate to be a hoax. And for God's sake, she wasn't even in her own body. That was not something that could be faked. She closed her eyes and tried to make the room stop spinning.

She pictured Jeffrey in profile sitting at his computer. How would he handle this situation? He never seemed to be out of control of anything—his life, his job, or his emotions. In minutes he would have a methodical approach and a plan of action. Footsteps sounded nearby. Ronnie opened her eyes to see Margaret entering the room.

"Miss Ingram," Margaret curtsied.

Ronnie sat up. "Hello, Margaret. Do you know what this is?" She held up the paper still clutched in her hand.

"Course I know what it is. It's your ladies' journal, ain't it, ma'am," Margaret said.

"How old is it?" Ronnie asked.

"Bless you, ma'am, wasn't it only delivered last week? Surely you remember, Miss Regina? Goodness, this is your favorite journal. Always reading you are, ma'am, when time allows," she said.

"So this is the current issue? The newest journal?" Ronnie asked.

"Sure and certain it is, oh yes ma'am." Margaret leaned over and looked at it again. "September 1752, I think it says, but my reading ain't too clever. 'Tis the latest from the printers, I'm right sure."

Seventeen freaking fifty-two. How was that possible? The clothes were appropriate. The furnishings and wallpaper fit. She scoured her brain for anything she knew about 1752.

Holding the journal she lay back down on the bed, her mind blown. What had happened to the real Regina? *Will I be stuck living Regina's life?*

The more immediate problem was about to walk through that door. What if Jack hurt her again? Fear shot through her, making her pulse thump in the injury on the back of her head. Could she walk right out of here? She still wore the light green dress—the shoes were in the other room. It would help if she were steadier on her feet. Noticing the cake on her plate she took another bite, chewing over her options.

Chapter 7 - Timely Discoveries

"Miss Regina," Margaret interrupted Ronnie's thoughts. "Are you feeling a mite brighter now that you've had a bit of a rest?"

"A bit better now," Ronnie said, keeping up the fake English accent.

"If I may be so bold, ma'am reckon I know what you need. Some of Mrs. Baird's cake. Ain't nuthin' better." Margaret walked over to the tray of food and filled a plate, poured a cup of tea and brought it to Ronnie.

"Oh, thank you, Margaret." Ronnie devoured the second piece of cake. The tea was almost hot enough and did a lot to restore her.

Ronnie ate and thankfully Margaret quietly tidied the room while she continued her ruminations. Did she switch places with Regina like *Freaky Friday*? Would another hurricane bring her back? That was rather unlikely to happen in London. She eyed Margaret. Was this woman really from 1752? By all outward appearances, it would seem so.

As she took the next bite a glint of metal caught her eye. She lifted the white lace of her sleeve and saw rose gold. It was the watch—the one Jeffrey had given her! If she were in Regina's body how was the watch on her wrist?

Was Regina already wearing it when she ... what would you call it ... arrived? Looking down at the strange hand she moved the lacy sleeve aside to look at it again hoping Margaret didn't notice. It was new like the one Jeffrey gave her and didn't have the smooth edges of the antique she had seen in London. But it wouldn't be an antique in this time period. Is that what connected her with Regina?

The shopkeeper said it was from the early nineteenth century, so that didn't fit. Could she have brought the watch with her? An image of her body lying lifeless on the floor of the lab bathroom hit her. Is that where her body was?

If she could see the back of the watch she would know. Jeffrey's watch looked completely different with the modern backing and waterproofing. Ronnie didn't want to draw any attention to herself with Margaret nearby so she continued eating the cake.

The antique she had found was in London and here she was in London. Is that why she was here? She laid back down, head spinning with implications of time travel and being in 1752.

"Miss Ingram, are you feeling a bit out of sorts, you're looking as pale as a death. Shall I run and fetch the doctor?" Margaret headed toward the door.

"No!" Ronnie was dreading seeing the doctor. "I'm just a bit tired."

"Well, I never! Bless me if they're not on their way here as we speak." Margaret went out of the room. Ronnie touched the watch and turned her wrist over. The clasp was complicated. Before she could figure it out she heard footsteps coming into the room. Pulling the sleeve over the watch she looked up. On first sight of Jack's tidy figure, Ronnie inhaled sharply.

Margaret followed Jack into the room wringing her hands. "Mrs. Ingram, sir? Is she unwell?"

"Catherine is resting comfortably," Jack said. He headed toward Ronnie.

The doctor opened the black case he had left on the table. He took out a sheet of thick paper and rolled it into a tube.

"Miss Regina. Forgive me, but 'tis vital that I should listen to your innards and make a thorough examination of the rest of you." His hot foul breath wafted toward her. She turned her head away and breathed through her mouth.

Jack moved to the other side of the bed to give the doctor room and to block her escape. "Regina. You will lay quietly while Dr. Wiggams attends to his duties with you."

What does it look like I'm doing? Ronnie thought, but kept her expression neutral, not wanting to see the wrath of Jack again.

The doctor brought the rolled-up paper close to Ronnie's chest. *What the heck was this quack going to do, give her a paper cut?* He put one end against her chest and the other end to his ear in a makeshift stethoscope.

"Would you be so kind as to make yourself cough, Miss Ingram if you please?" he asked. She coughed. "And now say, 'menmenmcnmenmem.'"

Ronnie felt ridiculous but she did as the doctor said, eyeing Jack. He gave her a dark look.

Dr. Wiggams unrolled the paper and put it back in the case. "Mr. Ingram you have described an injury to her head. Will you show me where this damage appears to manifest itself?" He didn't even look at her as he spoke.

Jack grabbed her head and twisted her face toward the pillow to expose the lump on the back of her head. Ronnie tried to pull away from his grip but he held her down, not letting her move an inch while the doctor felt the lump and all around the injured area.

"Ouch!" Ronnie yelled. "Stop it. That hurts!" She tried to grab Jack's arm but he shoved her harder into the pillow.

"Pray be still, Regina!" he said calmly but in a low tone. A don't-push-your-luck tone.

Jack let go and she gave him an angry look. "That was not necessary. I would have let him look!"

Jack pointed a slender finger at her face. "Madam, you *will not* speak to me in that tone." It was the same thing he had said to Catherine in the same hateful way. Ronnie looked away not wanting to further incite his anger.

The doctor dug around in the case again and brought out a white ceramic elongated bowl with a cut out of its middle. He placed a towel on the bed next to Ronnie and sat the strange-looking bowl next to her. She looked at Jack and Margaret, hoping for some clue as to what he was doing. Their expressions didn't change.

"Please tell me what happened to you, Miss Ingram. You must start from just before the accident that has befallen you," Doctor Wiggams said.

"I don't remember anything," she said in her best fake English accent. "The only thing I remember is when he," she pointed at Jack, "picked me up and carried me in here."

The doctor said, "Mr. Ingram, may I ask your permission to bleed Miss Ingram? I consider it of the utmost importance to return her humors to balance."

"Bleed me?" Ronnie said. So the doctor had a dry sense of humor. Maybe he wasn't so bad after all.

"Most certainly Doctor Wiggams, indeed you have my permission," Jack said.

Ronnie looked from one man to the other hoping to spot the twinkle of the eye or a smirk giving away the joke. She looked at the strange bowl next to her.

"Oh no, you're not!" She scooted to the far side of the bed away from the doctor trying to make a break for the door. "Oh no!"

Jack blocked her escape and gave her a look of pure evil.

"Madam, pray forgive me, but I cannot cure you of your malady if you do not allow me to do so," Doctor Wiggams said. Before she could get up from the bed Jack grabbed her arms and pushed her back against the pillow.

"Regina, what devilry has got into you? I insist that you will obey me at once!" Jack grabbed her upper arms and held her firmly on the bed. "I have had enough of this wicked behavior. You will be punished if you do not make yourself still."

Ronnie had no doubt that he would hurt her, in fact, he already was doing so. His face, so close to hers, flushed red with anger.

On the table near the bed, the doctor was arranging his rusty blood-stained instruments. He approached and cleared his throat. Jack let go of her arms and took a step back.

"You're not going to use those on me are you?" Ronnie asked.

"Madam, I will use what is appropriate in my professional opinion. Pray permit me to help you, Miss Ingram." The doctor pushed up her sleeve, uncovering the watch.

"What in God's name is this?" Jack said touching the watch face.

Ronnie jerked her arm away. "It's a watch!" Ronnie covered it protectively with her hand because she knew the watch might be her only way to get back home.

"Regina! I demand to know from whom did you get this bracelet!" Jack yelled.

Heat rose in her cheeks. Regina must not have had it for very long, if at all if Jack didn't know about it. In a violent grab, he jerked her out of the bed, making her stand in front of him.

"From where did this pretty trinket come, Regina?" he said.

Afraid he might hit her again she answered him without thinking, "Jeffrey gave it to me." And immediately regretted it.

"Geoffrey? Who, pray is Geoffrey?" Jack asked, his face taking the hue of the coverlet.

Ronnie scrambled for an answer and came up empty.

"I am at a loss to understand you, Regina, indeed I am! You have the sheer impudence to tell me that a man whom I do not know is giving you gifts without my consent?" He tried to grab her arm again but Ronnie took a step backward and bumped into a table. He took advantage of the distraction and raised his hand to slap her across the face again.

"Jack!" A man's voice interrupted his motion.

Margaret pushed the man, trying to get him out of the room. "Mr. Stohl, sir, I cannot allow you to enter Miss Regina's bedchamber."

"Mathias, the good of you to stop by cousin," Jack said. He stepped away from Ronnie and lowered his hands.

"Please help me," Ronnie said, thankful for the interruption. "He has already hit me once."

Margaret stepped away from Mathias, looking nervous. "Miss Ingram, are you sure it is acceptable for Mr. Stohl to be in here?"

"Yes, yes, please let him in," Ronnie said not sure who he was, but maybe he could keep Jack from hitting her again.

The man walked toward them. "Robert informed me upon my return zat Fräulein Regina has been in an accident," he said with a slight accent. German maybe?

"Good to have your assistance," Jack welcomed him. "Indeed I am at my wits' end with my wayward sister. Doctor Wiggams, this is Catherine's cousin, Mathias Stohl from Prussia. He is staying with us for a few months as he establishes his business connections."

While the men said their hellos, Ronnie sighed in relief at Mathias's arrival. For the moment he had defused Jack's anger. He was a good foot taller than Ronnie, or rather Regina, with broad shoulders. He wore a black suit and white silk stockings that outlined his meaty calves. The man was stunning with big dark eyes and full lips.

"Since you are here, perhaps you would be good enough to assist me with my sister," Jack said.

"I am your servant, dear cousin." Mathias gave her a serious look. "Fräulein Regina, please be so good as to forgive my intrusion. I heard the commotion and was worried about you."

"How very kind of you, Mathias," Ronnie said, keeping up the fake English accent.

There was something very unusual about Mathias. Ronnie couldn't quite put her finger on it but it was almost as if he were hypnotizing her. Could it be his good looks? Surely not, he was very attractive but Ronnie was twenty-seven years old and not the sucker she used to be for a pretty face. Correction, twenty-eight years old. Today was her birthday. The dinner with Jeffrey seemed like an eternity ago.

"Mathias, we were just discussing Regina's treatment. Doctor Wiggams believes my sister is in need of a bloodletting. Perhaps you can step in and help her see sense," Jack said. "She has always been somewhat taken with you."

The doctor snorted and glanced at the two men.

Mathias ignored the doctor and returned Ronnie's gaze with a winning smile. A jolt of electricity coursed through her veins. He was in his mid-twenties and blessed with an overload of charisma. She smiled back, not wanting to trust him, but he had already wormed his way in with the bold move to stop Jack from hitting her. Would he protect her again?

"Mr. Ingram, Mr. Ingram, if you please, sir! I have other patients who are in need of my services. I must bleed Miss Ingram so I can be on my way," the doctor said.

"Regina, you must do as you are told and sit on the bed and let Mathias remove the bracelet so the doctor can do his work," Jack said. His tone was civil and a whole lot nicer than it had been before Mathias arrived.

Jack came up close to Mathias and whispered something. Ronnie strained to hear him, but couldn't make out the words. She sat down hard on the bed. There was no way she was giving up the watch. It was the only connection to her world.

"If you please, Fräulein Regina. Pray allow me to assist you *mit* your bracelet." Mathias pulled up a chair and sat in front of her. He was being very careful with her, sitting back in the chair giving her space. "May I see zis curious bracelet?"

Ronnie looked at Jack and put her hand over the watch protectively. "No!"

He smiled at her. "Come, come my dear girl. Your brother desires for you to remove zee bracelet. If you do not do so the pretty zing will be soiled from the bloodletting."

She shook her head.

"Jack will have the bracelet come what may. Would you allow me to remove it? Or do you want to do so?" he said while glancing back at Jack.

"I don't see why anyone needs to remove it. It's not Jack's. It is mine." She felt like a small child defending her toys.

"Enough!" Jack bellowed. "Remove the wretched thing from her arm, Mathias. If I take it off her, by God it will not involve any discussion."

"Jack, calm yourself. There is no need to raise your voice. She will comply. Will you not, Fräulein Regina?"

"Can't the doctor use the other arm?" she asked, hoping there was some way to keep the watch on. It was a link to her life, and maybe her only way back. There had to be a way to keep it.

She turned her wrist over and tried to undo the clasp herself, hoping that she would be able to keep the watch if she could shove it down her bodice or something. With her thumbnail, she pulled on the clasp and it opened, but the safety lock was fastened and she struggled with it for a minute. Mathias patiently sat and watched her. Glancing up at him after a minute, she found him smiling at her yet he stayed still in the chair.

Finally, Jack said, "Mathias, take the accursed thing off her now. The doctor has other patients to attend."

Mathias waited for her to make the first move. Jack took a step toward her. She held her arm out to Mathias.

"Are you sure, Fräulein Regina?" Mathias said.

"It is better than the alternative. Please give it to me when you take it off," she said.

Mathias reached out, pulling her arm to rest on his oversized knee. His pants were pulled taught across his leg and showed the bulge of his thigh muscles. Big hands worked deftly at the delicate clasp and he had it off in seconds. Before she could reach for it Jack snatched it from Mathias and put it in his pocket.

"Give that to me!" Ronnie said standing up and brushing past Mathias.

Mathias grabbed her shoulders from behind and said, "Fräulein Regina, be so good as to let Herr Viggams finish his treatment. Please, Fräulein, it is in your own best interest." He turned her around to the bed before pushing her gently down. He seemed enormously tall from her sitting position.

"Regina Elizabeth Ingram, I command you to allow Dr. Wiggams to complete his medical ministrations." Jack shook his finger in her face while trying to be calm.

Mathias put himself between Jack and Ronnie. "I have utter confidence that Fräulein Regina will be an obedient patient. Vill you not? Fräulein Regina," he said in a softer tone, and then whispered, "Please sit still, for if you resist, I believe zat Jack vill not be so gentle with you."

She met his steely look, wanting to listen to him, but the stakes were very high for her as well. The watch was still in Jack's pocket, only a few steps away. She took a deep breath, hardening her expression.

He mouthed please again and she melted. He was right, she wasn't going to get out of this with Jack fuming a few feet away. At least Mathias was there to intervene. He seemed to have a calming effect on Jack.

Ronnie eyed Jack. How was she going to get the watch back? He gave her an angry look and she turned her attention to Mathias who smiled at her and patted her hand.

"Do let Viggams assist you *mit* your humors," Mathias said.

She wanted to jump up and grab the watch out of Jack's pocket, but that would get her nowhere. Instead, she tried to tamp down the anger and let these men get their way, for now.

Chapter 8 - No Connection

Jeffrey poured some coffee and added one Splenda. He usually didn't get tired, his work was so stimulating. It must have been the sex making him sleepy. A quick flash of Ronnie's naked body and her orgasm face reminded him that it had been worth it.

He rubbed his eyes and stretched. A few more minutes and he would start the sequence to bring Ronnie back. From the experiment on the cats, he had discovered that for some reason time advanced differently when they went back. It wasn't predictable either—sometimes it would be a few minutes on his end and hours where the cats landed. Other times it would be days, even though the experiment clock read the standard half an hour. For Ronnie, he had set the timer for fifteen minutes, not completely sure how a human subject would tolerate the process. It was always best to err on the side of safety.

That toupee guy was on the news again, Terry something, and was waving his arms excitedly. He unmuted the volume.

"Charley has delivered a one-two punch to Winter Park. A water main break is flooding downtown adding to the damage that is already evident by the downed trees. Significant damage to inland areas is to be expected. Let's go to Bill Cheska in the field. Tom, what are you witnessing in Winter Park?"

"The wind is really whipping trees and debris around." Bill had on a blue-hooded jacket that was completely soaked and he could barely keep his eyes open for the wind. "You can see behind me the canopy of the gas station is gone, blown off in a huge gust of wind. Branches are everywhere littering the ground and just down that street," he pointed to his left, "is the flooding from the water main break." The wind buffeted his body.

"Damn, that's bad," Jeffrey said. His condo was in Winter Park. He would probably not have water for a while, or at the least would have to boil it. He muted the TV and looked at the computer. He started the coding for Ronnie's return. It would take a few minutes to get the process started.

"Hold on Tom, this just in, a wind gust of 110 miles per hour was recorded at Orlando International Airport. This is the strongest gust I've ever seen in Orlando. I will have to check the records, but folks we may have just made history, again. Already in the last twenty-four hours, we had two tropical cyclones striking the same state when Bonnie made landfall in northwestern Florida," Terry said.

"Is that right, Terry? What a summer we're having. First Alex last month, Bonnie, and now we have Tropical Storm Danielle just upgraded from a Tropical Depression 4," Tom said.

An error popped up on the screen: *No connection to subject.*

"What?" Jeffrey's fingers shook as he retyped the command. There must be a mistake. The same message appeared. "No!" She must have taken off the watch! What about the backup? Would it be enough? This had not happened before with any of the cats. They had *always* returned. Always. But cats couldn't take off their fucking collars with the tracking device. People could take off their watches. Why the hell would she take it off? Even if she had been killed, the sequence would return her body and keep the connection—but only if the watch was on her damn wrist.

He clicked on the power grid icon. Good—it had full power. Ronnie had to be brought back soon before the power dissipated as the storm moved away. In Virginia Beach, he had successfully designed and tested the power capture device. The system could collect and store the power of the storm, but it wasn't capable of harnessing all that was needed to pull her back, yet. For now, it had to be done during the peak of the storm to boost the stored power.

"What the hell is happening, Ronnie? Put the goddamned watch back on!" His fingers were missing keys. Maybe it was an error in the code. He retyped it very slowly, double-checking everything before hitting enter. The same error message came up again. "FUUCCK!"

Jeffrey pushed his chair away from the desk and stared at the screen in disbelief. "God damn mother fucker!" He picked up a water bottle and threw it across the room but felt stupid when it bounced off the blow-up mattress. Ronnie's clothes were strewn across the floor. Would he be able to get her back? Fear hit him hard and made his stomach clench. He walked around the room thinking and tapping his finger against his leg. Of course, he needed the access code for the backup! Would it be enough? He had never had to use it before but that is exactly why he created it—in case the subject lost the connection.

A scene of destruction on the TV showed a huge live oak tree as it smashed through several cars and landed across the highway. He muted it. Jeffrey pulled out the notebook where he had written all the instructions. Flipping through the tidy handwritten pages he found the diagram with the coding he needed. Jeffrey sat down hard in his chair and began typing. Every line double-checked before he hit enter.

The computer mockingly replied: *No connection to subject.* He typed it all again and checked it. *No connection to subject.* There was the outside possibility that she threw up the capsules he put in the potatoes. If she only had a small portion of them in her system, the backup would not work.

"You bitch. C'mon." He typed it in again, he made a few changes to the code. *Connection with subject.* He sat back staring at the screen.

"Connected! Yes!" He continued the coding with adrenaline buzzing through his body, making his hands shake again.

Halfway through the sequence, an error message appeared again: *Lost connection to subject.* "C'mon." He slammed his hand on the desk. "God dammit. Ronnie!" He could see her face smiling at him. She was happy, having fun. Maybe she wanted more time there? "Damn it, Ronnie. It's time to come back!"

Knock, knock. Someone was at the door to the lab. Who could that be? He walked across the room and opened it to find Hanna Volpe, the scientist responsible for the wobble that changed Charley's trajectory. She worked in the lab next door.

"What's going on over here? Sounds like you're murdering someone." Her brown eyes sparkled.

It was ironic how true that might be. "Oh, just having trouble with the codes. You know, frustrating." He looked back at the computer. "I gotta get back to it." He willed her to leave but she took a step into the room.

"Oh, look, you've left your bra on the floor. Good taste, Jeffrey." She smiled at him. "Victoria's Secret."

An image of Hannah's large pale breasts assaulted his mind. "Hannah, I've got to get back to this." He sat down at the computer with hopes she would take the hint.

"Just heard you yelling and wanted to check on you. Are you happy with my storm steering skills?" She sat on the edge of his desk and smiled.

"Of course, you're brilliant! I still want to know how you do it." Jeffrey said not wanting to be rude. She had done a lot for him today by navigating the storm over the lab.

"Trade secret Jeffrey. You can pay me the rest tomorrow. I can see you're busy cussing down the walls right now. I want to know what's going on here. Surely you don't need a hurricane to get laid. You could have had this for free." She pulled her lab coat away from her perfect hourglass figure. "A half mil is a lot of money, Jeffrey. I hope you've spent it wisely!"

"I did. But remember, I've bought your silence too so keep it under wraps," Jeffrey said. It had been worth every penny, but only if Ronnie came back alive. If not Hannah would become a huge liability.

"I will remember," she said and smiled sweetly.

"I had my doubts about your skills, Hannah. You must be stoked that you've cracked the code for manipulating the weather. Disney is going to be pissed if they find out though, not to mention the Kennedy Space Center."

"Ha, yes, I know Jeffrey. Also, a good reason for us to keep this all under the radar for now. My research will be published at some point but I'll use another storm for that write-up. It looks like I'll have other opportunities this summer."

"That is music to my ears!" he said turning back to the keyboard. "Have a good night."

"I'll let you get back to work. I'll catch you later, Jeffrey. Be good now," she said and walked out of his lab.

He refused to look at her wide hips and firm ass as she added an extra wiggle just for him. Oh, what the hell, he watched her open the door and his eyes languished on her ass and then her calves. They were not the sleek muscle of Ronnie's but were nice enough to imagine around his ears.

He looked back at the screen. This project was on its way down the crapper if he didn't do something now. If he didn't get Ronnie back in the next hour she would be lost. Focus, focus. He gulped the rest of his coffee, gone cold now, and created a work-around.

Chapter 9 - Scarificators

"Fräulein Regina. It vill be over before you know it," Mathias said in a light German accent as he picked up her hand, touched her palm lightly and looked into her eyes. "*Bitte*, be so good as to lie back, let me give you something else to think about vile the doctor tends to you."

There were worse things to get lost in than his golden-brown eyes. Ronnie lay back on the bed and watched Mathias who stood over her and arranged her left arm in the long bowl that seemed to be made for her with a cutout at the top to let her upper arm sit comfortably, as the rest of her arm lay inside the bowl. Her wrist dangled out of the bottom cutout.

"All you are required to do is to lay still. Zere is but a mere pinch and zen zee rest is a simple matter." Mathias lightly pinched the inside of her elbow in demonstration, and then picked up her hand and smiled at her.

She wanted to appease him but remembered the filthy instruments the doctor had removed from his case.

Dr. Wiggams looked at Mathias and said, "Excuse me, sir, you cannot stay there, you are in my way." The charms apparently did not extend to the doctor.

"Pardon me, Viggams, I shall remove myself from your endeavors." She couldn't take her eyes off of Mathias as he walked to the other side of the bed. He rewarded her with another smile.

"Have you seen one of these apparatuses?" Doctor Wiggams held out a small brass cube with a tiny handle at the top. Jack took it and looked at it from every angle and handed it back.

"No, Doctor, I confess I have never seen such a thing before in my life. What is it, Wiggams?" Jack said.

The doctor made a show of holding the item up for all in the room to see as if he were on stage. "I found this gem at St. Bartholomew's Hospital last month. I procured my own copy of the fine instrument just this week. Isn't it beautiful?"

Ronnie and Steph had visited the small hospital museum at St. Bartholomew's in June. It stuck out in her mind for two reasons. One it had some connection to Sherlock Holmes, maybe a few scenes from a show or something? It also sported the only statue of Henry VIII in London out in front of the hospital.

"Yes, it is a stunning piece. What is the purpose of this odd cube?" Jack asked.

Wiggams looked smug now that he was back in control of the floor. "That, sir, is a scarificator." As if that explained everything.

Mathias caught her eye and blew up his cheeks, making his eyes wide. She looked away, not wanting to be on his team yet. Was he calling the doctor a puffed-up windbag? He stroked her palm again with his thumb making her turn to jelly.

"Allow me to demonstrate." Wiggams returned to Ronnie's side and placed the scarificator on the inside of her elbow. It felt cold against her skin. No doubt it was some stupid hoax he had been suckered into spending his money on. Mathias cocked his head to the side with a skeptical look on his face.

"Mr. Ingram, pray come this way so that you may have a better view." Jack obliged and stood next to the bed so he could peer at her arm. Margaret came in close too.

Wiggams allowed a dramatic pause and then touched the small lever at the top of the device. She heard a click and felt a sharp pain where it touched. "Ouch." She jerked her arm away but he was ready and held it while his other hand steadied the bowl under her elbow. Ronnie looked at her arm, well, Regina's arm, and was shocked to see blood pouring out of the one-inch gash the small device had made.

"Bravo!" Jack yelled! Margaret clapped her hands.

Mathias shot the doctor a dark look and held her hand tight. "Fräulein Regina, vas it tolerable?"

"Yes, it just startled me," Ronnie said.

"That, Miss Ingram, is the beauty of the device," Wiggams said. "The patient is unaware of the seven blades that hide beneath the beautiful brass exterior. This allows them to relax and enjoy the experience." He held up the underside of the contraption to show everyone the small slits where the blades hid. A single drop of blood landed on the maroon coverlet disappearing into the fabric. Wiggams placed the scarificator back in its leather case.

"Fräulein Regina, please do tell me honestly. Did you enjoy zee experience?" Mathias said in a quiet but dramatic tone showing big brown eyes.

Ronnie shook her head, "Not so enjoyable." She tried to look mad, but Mathias was starting to break through the wall she had put up.

"Ye Gods, it is a remarkably useful tool for a surgeon to have on his person!" Jack said with enthusiasm.

"How long are you going to let me bleed?" she said a bit too loud but wanted the doctor to hear her over the fuss he had created with the torture device.

He turned around to face her and for once actually looked at her. "Have no worries, Miss Ingram. I am here to be sure you are well cared for."

That was not so reassuring. Mathias squeezed her hand and said, "Just close your eyes and try to think of something pleasant."

Ronnie laughed at that. Oh sure, relax knowing that one of the only possible connections to her own time, the watch, had just been taken away. Relax knowing that Jack and his giant friend were there to make sure she obeyed.

"I need that bracelet back," she said to Mathias, quietly while the doctor and Jack talked each trying to impress the other with the latest news. Jack didn't seem to recognize it as a watch and she wondered if they had been invented yet.

"Jack insisted zat I hand it to him. I am sorry." Mathias said. "I can ask him about it later if you vish me to." He glanced back at Jack and his face became serious.

"I have to have it. It is really, really important." In fact, her life might depend on it.

"May I ask vere did you obtain the bracelet, Fräulein Regina?" he asked.

How to answer that question? My boyfriend from the future? Yeah right. That would go over well. She bit her lip. "A friend gave it to me. It is really important that I wear it at all times."

The smile left his lips and he looked a lot older. He turned away and ran his free hand through his hair. He returned his brown gaze on her. "Vye do you need to vear it at all times?"

Crap, he had to ask that. "I'm not really sure, but I think something bad might happen to me if I don't." No that didn't sound like a freaking nut job. "I don't know how to explain it."

They sat in silence, as he ran his thumb over her palm, sending waves of excitement through her belly. The smile left his eyes and he looked down at the coverlet.

With his gaze elsewhere Ronnie found it nearly impossible to keep her eyes off of him and she studied his face. Long black eyelashes framed his eyes and he had full lips and a strong jaw. His hair was short and a bit wavy where it was slightly longer on top, and his five o'clock shadow was visible. He glanced at her and she looked away embarrassed to be caught staring at him like a wide-eyed lovesick teen.

After a while, her eyes grew heavy. She looked at her arm and the blood was flowing freely, filling the bowl a few inches deep. Maybe a few pints? "Doctor, are you nearly done with the bloodletting?"

Wiggams glanced at her and said, "Be patient Miss Ingram. It will only be a few more minutes."

Wiggams and Jack continued talking on about banks, rents, and riots. "Close your eyes, Fräulein Regina," Mathias said in a soothing voice. He squeezed her hand. "I vill vatch over you vile you rest."

"Okay." Ronnie had to force the words out. Mathias continued to stroke her palm and she could feel his eyes on her but it was too much to stay awake. She drifted off to sleep.

***

Ronnie awoke with a start and for a second had no idea where she was. A small white cloth covered her arm and the doctor said, "Press on this for me please, Miss Ingram." At least the cloth looked clean.

Mathias no longer held her hand. He sat in the chair next to her reading a book.

"Mr. Ingram, I will call on you tomorrow and check on your sister and wife. You will need to keep both ladies comfortable until I return." Wiggams gathered his instruments and put them in his black case.

"Of course, I will keep them both in the comfort of my embrace," Jack said.

Mathias stood and bowed. "Good day, Wiggams."

The doctor nodded to Mathias and he and Jack left the room and Ronnie could hear their voices echo down the hallway. She closed her eyes again. A deep tiredness spread from her chest to her bones. The image of her pooled blood in the bowl yanked her out of the stupor and she looked at her arm. The white cloth rested there but the bowl was gone. What did they do with the blood?

She heard footsteps and was stirred back to a tired but awake state. Jack's angry voice startled her. "Would you prefer your punishment now or after you tell me about the bracelet?" He pulled the watch from his pocket and dangled it in front of her.

Chapter 10 - Storm Damage

Steph grabbed a towel to wrap around Hamish when they found him. Cats could be real bastards when they were injured. "Where are my bloody shoes?" She wandered around in a panic until she realized they were near the kitchen door. She remembered Nick's naked body and cursed the kitty again. She sent up a prayer to St. Gertrude, the patron saint of cats.

The cry had come from the side yard. Steph made her way to the back door. "Nick, Nick!" She called while holding the screen door open. "Where are you?" It was hard to hear her own voice with the roar of the wind. An undistinguishable noise came from the side yard. It had to be him. Hesitating in the doorway, Steph had a mini panic attack. *Why the hell am I going out in the middle of a hurricane?* She held the towel over her head for protection and ran toward his voice.

"I hope I don't regret this!" Steph splashed her way through the pond that now occupied her lawn. A glow from the living room gave her just enough light to see the path through her rose garden toward the side yard.

"Steph! Over here!" Nick yelled.

A clump of leaves blew into her face! "Ahhhh!" She flung them aside.

He ran toward her, flashlight beam flailing around as he did. "Are you okay?"

"Yes, did you find Hamish?" she asked as she struggled to hear him over the storm.

"I don't know. Come here!" he yelled right next to her ear. The wind was deafening with the taller treetops swaying at unreasonable angles. She pulled the towel down to block the blinding rain from her eyes.

Nick led her to the white-fenced area near her neighbor's yard. Steph could see a huge live oak branch on the ground with an orange tail that stuck out beneath. She ran over to the horrific sight. "Oh my God, Hamish!" Moving around to the other side she could see the kitty's huge golden eyes. A low noise escaped from his panting mouth. Nick grabbed the far end of the branch and tried to move it.

"I'll lean on it and you pull him out!" he yelled over the storm.

Steph pulled off the towel, smearing her hair across her eyes. A sound like a freight train roared above her and a gust of wind nearly knocked her over followed by a spray of small branches and leaves. A loud crack sounded above and all the lights in the house went out. Heart in her throat, Steph stood up and ran to the side of the house pressing hard against the white cinderblock under the eaves. A huge dark shape fell seemingly in slow motion landing a few feet away shaking the ground beneath her feet. Sparks shot out and she covered her face.

A tree or telephone pole landed right where Hamish and Nick had been. "No!" She yelled. Through her trembling legs, she could feel other trees falling—some close and others in the distance. It must have been a huge gust of wind to bring so many trees down at once.

"Nick!" She did not want to move for fear of the blue-white sparks and snakes of electricity that were all around her. An orange blur ran across the yard and hid in the bushes. "Hamish!" At least he was free and alive.

Her hands tingled and her hair stood on end. A faint sweet smell of ozone wafted around but dissipated quickly with the rain and wind. The sparks faded and it was pitch black all around except for Nick's flashlight beam splayed across the grass. She had to help him. Would she step on a live wire and be electrocuted trying to get to him?

Steph tentatively stepped away from the sparks and made her way toward the flashlight. The Wind whipped around and made a horrifying howling in the trees. The storm sounded more ravenous than when they had first come outside. It was hard to make her way across the yard but she wasn't sure if it was because of the wind or that she couldn't see a damn thing. She shuffled her feet so she wouldn't trip and made her way toward the flashlight terrified of what she might find. "Nick, Nick!"

The flashlight beam moved. Was the wind blowing it or was Nick moving? Her foot snagged on a fallen branch and she landed hard on her hands and knees. "Nick!" She could hardly hear her own voice, the noise above her drowned everything out. The storm was getting stronger and more trees would be down. This was not a place they should linger.

She stood up again and wiped her hands on her shorts before moving toward the flashlight, still shuffling her feet like an old lady. Another roar sounded in the trees and the wind knocked her backward to the ground where she landed on her butt. Once back on her knees, she crawled to the flashlight beam. A shower of leaves rained down on her back followed by a deafening crash in the neighbor's yard. One of her trees had fallen on their house and a horrible bang vibrated through her body.

"Nick!" she screamed in a complete panic while crawling toward the flashlight.

"Steph!" Nick said. "Steph, where are you!" He shined the flashlight directly in her eyes and she winced in pain.

A wave of relief flushed over her and she sobbed, "Oh my God, are you okay?"

"I am! My arm isn't! I was trapped. But I'm free now." He pulled her to her feet and they walked slowly to the house with the flashlight guiding them over strewn branches.

Her beloved begonia bed had been destroyed by a fallen branch, but she didn't give it much thought with her mind on her friend and the pitiful cat. Nick pulled on the storm door handle but the wind held it shut. Finally, the gust let up for a fraction of a second so he could pull it with his right hand and then wedge in a foot to leverage it open. They made it inside the house and the storm door slammed behind them.

"Steph, are you all right?" Nick said shining the flashlight on her from head to toe. "You're bleeding." He took her hand and she could see her palms were scraped. She had a pretty good gash on her shin as well.

"What about you? Are you okay?" Steph said, taking the flashlight from him. He had a muddy scrape along his cheek. She worked her way over his body and stopped at his hand. "Oh my God, Nick!"

"Shit! That's hideous!" Nick grabbed his hand and held it protectively against his body. "Steph!" He looked at her with huge dark eyes.

"Nick, stay calm. Let me see it again." His pinky finger was not where it should be.

"Don't fucking touch it!" he said.

"I won't, just let me see what we're dealing with here." He held it out for her to see. "Oh God." Her knees buckled and she nearly fainted. It took everything she had to not run away screaming. "Oh, Nick, I am so sorry." His pinky finger was bent at a ninety-degree angle from the second knuckle and a bone stuck out of it. Blood trickled down his hand to mix with the mud.

Steph moved the flashlight unable to look at it any more. "Oh, my God, I am going to boak." She ran across the house to her bathroom, barely making it. Steph stood dripping over the toilet, muddy water pooling at her feet. The flashlight rested in the puddle and she picked it up and flushed the toilet.

"Steph!" Nick yelled. "I'm standing here in the fucking dark, come back!"

"Damn it!" She had the only flashlight! "Oh no, Nick. I'm such an eedget." Steph retraced her steps back to him.

He stood there dripping wet and holding his hand, face twisted in agony. "We need to clean that. Come here." She took his arm and then led him to the sink. "I'm so sorry. I've never been very good with blood. Does it hurt?"

"That's the weird part. I didn't even know my finger was hurt until I saw it. My arm is killing me though. Bet it'll start hurting when I wash it," he said.

"Auch," Steph made a Scottish noise and looked away. Her stomach lurched and she was afraid she would be sick again.

"It's gotta be cleaned, look at all that dirt in there. How are you going to do it?" Steph asked.

"I don't know. Can you get some other lights going, Steph, so I don't have to stand in the dark when you run off again?"

"I'm so sorry, Nick." She rummaged around for the matches and lit a few candles she had left out in case the power went out. "I have a lantern too, somewhere. Oh and here's a flashlight for you." She reached on top of the fridge and handed him a smaller flashlight. He stuffed it in his pocket. Nick picked up the liquid soap and squirted some on his injured hand and started washing it. "Do you think they'll be able to fix it?"

"I hope so. Did you bring a change of clothes?" she asked but knew the answer. He had come at the last minute from his mother's house and arrived soaking wet. There was no power to wash or dry anything.

"No," he said, working the soap toward the broken finger.

A low rumbling noise made them stop. They looked outside at the pitch blackness and back at each other. Blue flashes lit up the sky to offer a snapshot of the trees leaning sideways and dancing in unison.

More blue flashes sliced the sky. She wasn't sure if it could be lightning or transformers blowing. Either way it was unnerving.

Through the floor, she could feel the thudding of trees crashing to the ground or on houses, every few minutes another one. Steph could only imagine whose life had just been destroyed by each one.

"Surely they can fix it, Nick." She risked another horrifying glance at his finger.

"Should I pop it back in place?" He turned around to look at her.

"Ooooh, God," she leaned against the bunker. "Oh please let me leave the room if you're gonna do that."

"I was going to ask you to do it for me."

A wave nausea passed over her.

"What? After that last display I'd never ask you to do that. I'm just messing with you Steph—trying to lighten the mood." He forced a smile. With the candles casting shadows on his face it made him look like a villain in a B movie.

"Lighten the mood! Nick." She wanted to smack his arm, but he was carefully working his way toward the hideous finger and she didn't want to bump him.

A huge crash shook the house. Steph jumped back in surprise.

Nick yelled, "Holy shit!" He turned around. "What the hell was that?"

Steph grabbed the flashlight off the countertop and rushed to the garage. Wet hot air greeted her when she opened the garage door. The flashlight reflected off the floor and she shined it toward the ceiling.

"Oh no! Nick, a branch came through the roof!" A few pots lay cracked and spilling dirt on the floor. She set the flashlight down on a shelf and dragged the other pots to the side in case the roof collapsed. Luckily the branch had missed her Jeep Liberty.

"Steph!" Nick stuck his head in from the kitchen. "I think we should get to your safe spot."

A safe spot was an interior room with no windows in case of a tornado. A safer place would be a basement but Florida didn't have many basements due to the high water table.

"Oh God, Nick." She put the potted plant down and wiped her hands on her butt. Handprints remained. "I've got a few things ready for us in my closet."

"Show me. I want to be sure it's the safest place," he said.

"Did you get your hand cleaned up? I don't think we should leave it for long." She avoided looking it. "We should cover it so you don't bump it or ..."

Another huge gust of wind roared overhead sounding louder in the garage than it had in the house.

Nick rinsed the soap off his hand and grabbed a few paper towels, wadding them up over the damaged finger. "C'mon Steph! Charley is intensifying, we need to get to a safer place!"

He grabbed another flashlight and she took a few lit candles. They made their way through the kitchen, then the living room, on their way toward her bedroom. The windows rattled and they ran the last few steps into Steph's bedroom.

Chapter 11 – Stolen Time

"That is mine. You have no right to take that from me!" Ronnie said, reaching for the watch.

Jack shook his finger at her. "On the contrary, I have every right to know who is giving you gifts, Regina. Most especially now, on the eve of your betrothal. You will tell me about the bracelet and give me complete details."

It occurred to Ronnie that if she didn't remember what happened before the accident, how could she explain the watch?

"Regina! I demand that you answer me at once!" Jack yelled, making her jump.

"I … it …" Her brain was not working with the loss of blood. "He gave it to me," she said, realizing too late she didn't say who.

"I demand to know who gave it to you," Jack bellowed.

Mathias stepped closer—he was curious as well.

"I got the watch from Jeffrey."

"Geoffrey? Does this fine gentleman have a surname Regina? Indeed I am hoping he is as rich as a prince and will make a better match than the lord I have chosen for you." Jack's voice carried a sharp edge—a scary I-will-hurt-you edge.

Jeffrey was rich, at least in comparison to anyone she had ever dated. Although a graduate from MIT and a brilliant scientist, his wealth came from his father's dot-com business. "I don't know his last name." Damn, she was talking without much of a filter. Her brain was definitely fuzzy from the bloodletting. What was Jeffrey's last name? Then she remembered—Brennan. But she did not share that information with the two men staring at her.

"God's blood! You accepted a gift from a man and you do not know his surname? At what time and place did he give this to you?" He held the watch up, examining it more closely. "By heavens, I do believe that this is a well-made piece of solid gold."

"I knew his last name. I just can't remember it now." Ronnie tried not to say another word since it was just digging a bigger hole for herself but, against her will, the words just came out. "He gave it to me on my birthday."

"That cannot be true, for I was with you nearly every minute on your birthday. Regina, I do believe that you are playing a game with me. Did you steal the bracelet?" Jack said.

Maybe this was her way out. Surely stealing wouldn't be as bad as a strange man giving Regina, a young single eighteenth-century woman, expensive gifts. If only her brain wasn't complete mush. What answer would be more likely to get the watch back?

"Yes. I stole it," she said before she could stop herself.

"Great heavens, Regina! Have you become a thief as well as a liar? Did you steal it from Lord Barton? Is that why you were running away when you were struck by the carriage?" He paused in the tirade and looked at her, his mouth a slit.

Not sure which question to answer and really what could she say? She settled for, "I don't know." Ronnie was not sure how to make the questioning stop.

"For goodness' sake Regina, you are about to marry the man! There is no reason for you to take his possessions, like a common footpad!"

Ronnie sat quietly as Jack rattled off questions and suppositions. It was all going too fast for her soggy brain. She took a deep breath. Her gaze landed on Mathias and he looked away. No more charming smiles from him.

"Mathias, I need you to restrain Miss Regina while I teach her a lesson." Jack moved toward Ronnie.

All the color drained from Mathias's face. He looked at her wide-eyed and then stared at his feet. "Jack. You cannot ask zat of me. I vill not oblige you in zis matter!"

In a panic, Ronnie tried to climb across the bed to get away from Jack. He caught her in mid-escape by grabbing the back of her neck and shoving her face down on the bed. "Take her arms," he said to Mathias. Jack landed on top of her, knocking the air out of her lungs.

"Jack, you cannot do zis to your sister! She is a lady and an Ingram!"

Ronnie screamed out. "No, don't!" She kicked her legs behind her to try to connect with Jack but he was on top of her already.

Jack fumbled for a minute with her clothes. "If you will not help me teach her a lesson then by God, you will need to show yourself the door."

"No!" Ronnie yelled. "Please don't!"

"Jack," Mathias said pulling on Jack's arm. "You cannot do zis to her. She is a respectable young lady."

Jack pulled away from his grip. "Mathias, I cannot believe you are arguing this point. She would not obey me. I cannot allow her to be untruthful, or to steal things from others without a care in the world. If you will not assist me then pray leave us forthwith. This is not your affair."

"Mathias, don't leave! Help ..." Ronnie said, but before she could finish, Jack hit her backside.

For a split second Ronnie's eyes locked with Mathias's. The pain she saw reflected in his expression was haunting. He really cared about Regina.

"Please don't!" she begged Jack again. "No!" Ronnie tried to struggle against Jack's grip but intense pain interrupted. *Smack! Smack!*

Jack muttered angry curses under his breath. Tears fell down her face and soaked into the maroon coverlet. Cold air caressed her legs and the assault continued.

"Jack, no, no, I cannot vatch you do zis to her," Mathias said.

A weight was lifted off of her. Ronnie gasped for air, unaware that she had been holding her breath. All she felt was overwhelming relief at being able to fill her lungs again. She looked back at Mathias who restrained Jack.

"Unhand me!" Jack said. "This is not your affair, Cousin."

"Do not let your anger interfere *mit* logic. You have delivered your punishment," Mathias pointed at her. "You can see you have made your mark upon her flesh and corrected her foolish vays. She will be a better sister for it, of that I am certain."

"I warn you, Mathias, you are not to interfere in my affairs. She is my ward, my responsibility, I will instruct her as I must!" Jack said, his face beet red.

"It is done. She has learned a lesson on how far to try your patience, have you not, Fräulein Regina?" Mathias said.

Ronnie scooted off the bed and let the dress fall to cover her legs. "Yes, Jack, I will not disobey you again." It seemed to be the only way to appease the seething Jack.

"Do not let her leave this room!" Jack said to Mathias and stormed out.

Chapter 12-George Washington's Blood

Ronnie lay down on the bed and hid her face. The bed moved as Mathias sat and touched her shoulder. "Fräulein Regina, I apologize for Jack's behavior. I have never seen him mistreat you before."

She ignored him and let out all the pain and confusion, unable to keep her emotions in check. No one had ever hit her, not even once as a kid. The bed moved again as Mathias stood. He returned quickly and handed her a napkin.

Ronnie wiped her face and took a deep breath. "Thank you, Mathias!"

"I allowed him to strike you, it vas *schrecklich* ..." He spoke rapidly in another language. Jack had said he was from Prussia—that was what, Germany now? He stopped speaking, probably realizing he had switched to his native tongue.

"No, you made him stop. That took a lot of courage. Who knows what he would have done if you'd not intervened. I can't thank you enough, Mathias." She wiped a few last tears and took a deep breath.

He walked over to the window while running his fingers through his hair. "Fräulein Regina, I ..." He stopped and turned around. "I have failed you. I vas there and stood by ... I should have done more." He turned his back to her, but she could see the emotion on his face before he did.

"You did help me," she said. "He would have done a lot worse if you hadn't stopped him." Ronnie had felt the anger in Jack's beating. She could hear the noises he made and it scared her. Who knows how far he would have taken it without Mathias's intervention.

"*Ja*, it took every ounce of my control to not damage him," he said while looking toward the door.

"That would have been something." There was hope then that maybe he could help her get the watch and get away from Jack. "Mathias, I have to ask you something."

"Yes, Fräulein Regina?"

She stood up and took a few steps toward him but stopped short. Black spots swirled around her head like fall leaves in a hurricane. Mathias wrapped his arms around her in an awkward hug to keep her from falling. In the split second before she fainted, a déjà vu flashed but it was gone before she could grab it.

He set her gently down on the bed and stood above her with a worried look. "Shall I call for zee surgeon, Fräulein Regina?"

"No! I'm just dizzy because that idiot bled me and that other idiot beat me."

Mathias walked to the water basin, wet a cloth, and brought it to her. "The bleeding vas to benefit you, Fräulein Regina. Every doctor uses zat technique to bring your humors back to balance."

She took the cloth and wiped her face. "Mathias that is a bunch of hooey." He looked puzzled, he probably didn't know what hooey was. "It doesn't do anything but make you lose blood. People who are sick or hurt need that blood to recover. Look at George Washington! He had a throat infection and they took five pints of blood from him. Do you know how that ended?"

He squinted his eyes. "Who is zis George Vashington? Fräulein Regina, I don't know what you are …"

"America's first president, George Washington, died of dehydration and loss of blood!" she interrupted him.

He looked at her blankly. "America? I have heard of zee colony. But, forgive me, Fräulein Ingram, I have not heard of George Vashington. *Bitte*, tell me who he is."

She thought he was joking but he was completely serious. Oh my God. If that journal was right it was 1752. Would he have heard of Washington yet? She had been to Mount Vernon many times and tried to recall the dates from the museum.

"Holy crap!" Ronnie clamped her hand over her mouth. She hadn't meant to say that out loud. In 1752 Washington inherited Mount Vernon from his half-brother. He was … she thought for a minute … born in 1732. So George Washington would be twenty years old. Someone in London surely would not have heard of him yet.

"Fräulein, are you not vell?" he said. "If you please, let me call for zee doctor."

"No Mathias please listen, the colonies will revolt in 1776, and they will form their own country. It will be called the United States of America. George Washington will be the first president." Ronnie said, and realized by the look on his face that he thought she had lost her mind.

"Fräulein Regina, have you not learned a single zing from your tutor? The colonies have already revolted during zat skirmish three years ago. The colonies are under English control."

Ronnie took that in. Was he talking about an early attempt by the colonies to free itself from England or was *this* history different? She had read some time-travel stories where there were significant differences in history. She needed to know what the date was. But would he think she was completely crazy for asking? Not much to lose, it seemed he already thought she was nuts.

"Fräulein Regina!" Mathias stepped closer to her. "I am certain I need to get Viggams in here at once."

"No! I'm okay, really."

"Okay?" He looked puzzled. She really needed to stop using modern words, he was becoming suspicious.

"Mathias, please don't make me see that horrible man ever again," she said grabbing his arm.

"Zen please help me understand who George Vashington is and vye is he dead? Vat does he have to do *mit* bloodletting?"

"It doesn't matter, Mathias." She touched his arm and he looked into her eyes, obviously still confused. "Tell me about this revolt, Mathias. What did they call it?"

"I have lost all faith in your tutor. The revolt vas only a few years ago and you do not even know vat it vas called. It was a three-year war with the Atlantic Colonies. Zey made an attempt to force the English out and create zee United French Colonies."

"The United French Colonies. That's absurd. The French were kicked out of the colonies after the French and Indian War, Mathias."

"I must speak with your brother, *Ach mein Gott*," he raised both hands as if to push the idea away. "I do believe that your ignorant tutor has been inventing history to teach you utter and complete nonsense."

Ronnie's head was spinning. She had been a straight-A student and never had she heard of the United French Colonies. She would have learned that, certainly. Could this be a wormhole, where she went back in time to a different set of circumstances with a different history?

"Mathias, what year is it?"

His brows furrowed, "Vye voud you have need of zis information?"

"What is the date, Mathias?" She was losing patience. "Please tell me the day, month, and year."

"Zee Year of our Lord, 1752. August zee second."

"It is 1752! So the journal was right! Oh my God!" Ronnie examined his face to find the humor, the lie, the teasing. His face was an open book. Nauseous now. "I'm going to be sick!"

Mathias reached under the bed and handed her a chamber pot. He took a few steps backward to give her some room.

Ronnie stood up and turned around, throwing up into the foul-smelling decorative clay pot. He handed her a fresh cloth from the tray of food in the corner. Her head continued to spin and she couldn't make it stop. She sat back on the bed and could feel the pain in her thighs and tried to make sense of what he had just told her.

She looked into the disgusting pot and back at him. He took it from her and walked out of the room, returning empty handed. So it really was freaking 1752. A hundred more questions occurred to her but she couldn't make her brain form anything intelligible to ask him.

"Fräulein, I am most confused by your questions. *Bitte,* tell me you are not in need of zee surgeon."

"Don't bring the doctor in, he is useless." Ronnie took a deep breath and let it out slowly, trying to calm down. "Are you sure it's the second?"

"Yes, I am certain of zee date. I do not understand zee importance."

She left on the thirteenth and now it was the second? Same month and two hundred and fifty-two years later. What the freakin' hell?

He stood there awkwardly. "Do you vant some vater?" He pointed to the pitcher that sat on a wooden cabinet with a marble top.

"Yes, please," she said, still numb. How could she be in this time period, this skewed history? What could have brought her here? The only clue was the watch and it was no longer in her possession.

"Vye did you need to know the year, Fräulein Regina?" he asked, pouring water into a cup. He said it so gently, so kindly, she wanted to tell him.

"Mathias, it's so confusing. I don't remember anything before the accident," she said. "Can you tell me anything about my life before today?" Maybe he could tell her something that would help her figure this out.

He handed her the cup and she took a sip. The water was cool and tasted of metal. She felt light-headed again and lay back on the bed rolling to her side. He took the cup from her and set it by the pitcher on the dresser.

"Vat precisely voud you like to know?" Mathias asked.

"Anything. My childhood, whatever you know about me, how do I fit into Jack's family?"

"Vell, Fräulein Regina, indeed I am at a loss. Zis is really most difficult. I do not know vere to start."

"Mathias," she reached out to touch his hand. "Pretend you are telling someone else about me as if I knew nothing of this girl." She pointed to herself.

"How extraordinary." He took a deep breath and exhaled. "I vill try." He stood up and walked the length of the room and turned around to look at her. "You are zee sister of Jack Ingram. He is heir to zee Ingram family fortune zat is sadly somewhat diminished in recent years." He paused and she nodded to encourage him to continue. "Jack has not managed your family's finances as your father vas able to do so successfully. It is not his fault, for he vas not expected to take over zee family business, being the younger son. He was preparing himself for an apprenticeship elsewhere."

He sat down on the bed next to her and glanced at her occasionally as he spoke. "Your older brother, Samuel, died of zee pox, as did your *Mutter und Vater* this two years past." He looked again and waited. "Do you not remember?"

"No. I don't remember anything. It is as if I were born somewhere else." Boy was that the truth.

Mathias's eyes widened. "You do not remember ven zey were laid to rest?"

"No, I don't," she said. "Were you here when they passed away?"

"I vas in Prussia *mit* my family. Maria married an Irishman and has made her life here in London. It is only now that I have come here to be near her and to strike out on my own account." His hand combed through his hair. "My *Vater* recently …" he pressed his lips together and stood up walking toward the window. "He is *im Himmel*."

"Who is Maria?" she asked. "What is *im Himmel*?"

He turned around. "Your cousin Maria, my sister. You do not remember her?"

"I'm sorry, I don't." She spread her skirt to cover her ankles.

"*Vater*, oh I apologize, I lapsed into German. *My father*," he sighed making an attempt to articulate the *th*, "I vill try it zee English vay so you can understand me. My father is in Heaven. I lost him last year and it prompted me to move to be near my sister."

"Oh, I am very sorry for your loss."

"*Danke. Bitte*, shall we continue your questions?"

"Yes, if you don't mind. Do you know why I was meeting Lord Barton?" she asked.

He walked back toward her. "Lord Barton." He looked at the ceiling and back down at her. "You were meeting to discuss your betrothal."

"When was Regina …?" she stopped, realizing her error. He looked surprised. "When am I supposed to marry him?"

"A fortnight hence. Lord Barton is aware of your family's finances and is asking for a larger dowry for your hand in marriage. Jack is furious. He has been enticing Lord Barton's attentions by encouraging you to visit him." His brows furrowed and he looked angry. Or maybe disgusted. She couldn't tell.

"Vat is more, Lord Barton is nearly twice your age and is easily as round as he is tall." He looked at her again, trying to read her face.

"He is! Oh!" She looked away. Yuck, this poor girl had to marry a fat older man to help her family's financial situation.

"Do you not remember him?"

"No I don't," she said. "How old am I?"

His eyes widened again. "*Gnädig mich*, Fräulein Regina, are you saying zat you really do not know your age?"

She shook her head. "No, I don't."

"We celebrated your seventeenth year in July."

So Regina was merely a bargaining chip for advancing her family. Crazy world where a seventeen-year-old girl was forced to marry a man over forty. Ronnie wondered how Regina felt about this. Hopefully, she liked this man. Visions of a hideously fat man forcing himself upon an innocent girl clouded her mind. It was probably standard practice for marriages in this time period.

If I can't get back to Florida will I have to marry Lord Barton? The thought struck her like a ton of bricks. Oh, God. That would be horrible. It was bad enough she would be stuck here, but to be forced to marry some awful creepy stranger and bear his children in eighteenth-century England! She put her hands on her head and tried to block out the rest of the thoughts that were pooling in her mind like the blood in the bowl. Her stomach lurched and she touched it in hopes it would calm down.

"Mathias?"

"Ja, Fräulein Regina."

66

"I need to get out of here. I can't let Jack hit me again. I can't marry Lord Barton. I can't." The tears falling down her face surprised her. She wiped them away, embarrassed at the intensity of her emotions.

He sat on the bed and put his arm around her shoulders. "Do not fret. It vill turn out all right. I have heard it said zat every woman is terrified before her nuptials."

The kindness and concern in his eyes melted her. "Thank you, Mathias. I'm serious though. This cannot be my life. I can't do it. I'm not meant to be here. This place, this time. I'm ..." She stopped not ready to tell him more. He was Jack's cousin and, although he was being kind to her now, it likely would not extend past a polite conversation, despite any feelings he may have for Regina.

He handed her the napkin she had used before so she could wipe her eyes and nose. "I can't be here. But look, I am here. It makes no sense," she said waving her arm around. "And I need the bracelet back. It is really, really important, Mathias."

"Zee bracelet?" He stood up. "*Bitte,* forgive me, but I do not understand zee importance of zee bracelet. You have said earlier zat something bad vill befall you should you remove it from your wrist. What in *Gott's* name would make you believe such a thing?"

She could feel the heat rise in her cheeks. "I just do. I need it for protection."

A small woman with graying hair and a black dress walked in the room. She was carrying a tray of food and set it in the corner. She bowed to Ronnie and then turned to pick up the tray that Margaret had left. "Miss Ingram," she bowed in her direction and left the room. A woman standing just outside the door motioned for Mathias.

"Excuse me for a moment." Mathias left the room. Ronnie could hear them talking but couldn't make out what they were saying. Mathias came back in. "I have some pressing business to attend to Fräulein. Vill you please excuse me?"

"Wait, you're leaving?" she asked.

"Mrs. Stenack vill be just outside zee door of your bedchamber tonight to keep a vatch on you. Should you need anything, you simply have to knock on the door and she vill help you," Mathias said.

"Okay." She looked out into the antechamber but couldn't see Mrs. Stenack. "Will I see you tomorrow?" She bit her lip.

"Zat I am afraid I cannot say. I have a number of appointments throughout the morrow. If I am able to I vill call on you before noon." He gave her a tentative smile.

"I hope to see you then."

"Good evening, Fräulein Regina." He bowed and walked out of the room.

Damn, damn, damn! She was just beginning to figure this out. And Mathias was softening up to her. Why did he have to leave now? She had to get out of this place. The room was on the second story, it might be possible to climb down, but if she fell it wouldn't be pretty. A whiff of the food from the tray made her stomach growl. The cake hadn't done much to slake her hunger.

She lifted the metal cover and a wonderful steamy smell wafted in her face—beef stew with potatoes and carrots, and what must be Mrs. Baird's bread. There was a pot of tea and what looked like a bread pudding. She pulled up a chair and stuck her spoon in the stew, suddenly ravenous, thoughts swirling around in a confusing muddle of United French colonial wars and fat old men. There was no way she could stay here in this time period. Would there even be a United States on this path of history? It was such an awful thought. Maybe it was a dream, a difficult, horrible dream … with beatings thrown in. How could she return to Florida, the normal Florida she had left with a hurricane swirling overhead and a normal USA intact?

When the bowl was halfway empty, an overwhelming tiredness started in her chest and spread to her arms. Her eyes grew heavy and her brain slowed. The room wobbled a bit. She stood up and the floor refused to stay still as she made her way to the bed. *"Crème de la crème a la Edgar,"* she said as she laid her head down, thinking of her niece's favorite movie. Her eyes were closed before she could think another thought.

Chapter 13 - Catherine's Intuition

"Catherine, did you rest well this night?" Jack said, sitting on the edge of his wife's bed.

"I must confess, my rest was much interrupted. Husband, I must speak with you about the matter which has disturbed me so."

"It is not my son that has kept you up this night?" Jack said before taking his wife's hand.

"Dear me, no. It is Regina and her queer behavior last night that has been troubling my slumbers so much," she said, pulling her hands out of his.

"Regina? What is this you speak of? Forsooth, has my sister disturbed you in your bed during the night? Great heavens, I had a woman at her beck and call outside of her chamber, and her door was locked!"

"No, husband, she did not come to my bedchamber. Remember my fainting spell last night? It is Regina who has caused me this troubling affliction. God help me, but I fear that she is ..." Catherine wiped away a tear and looked at him.

"Come, come Catherine. Tell me, how is Regina disturbing you so much as to interrupt your sleep?"

"Do you not recall her queer voice? The strange words she used. The unusual behavior and her ridiculous claim to not know who she was?" Catherine clutched a piece of linen and dabbed her eyes.

"Indeed, it has troubled me greatly too. She behaved in a monstrous way when Wiggams was doing his utmost to help her. The child was so willful and outright rebellious I confess that I was forced to punish her defiance. Furthermore, she had this fastened around her wrist." Jack pulled out the golden bracelet.

Catherine gasped. "Her talisman! Do you think it is a sign of the devil, husband? Truly, you must lock that in your desk forthwith. It should not be seen in this room again."

"A talisman? No dear Catherine, the gaudy thing is nothing of that nature. Regina firstly said that a man gave it to her, and then changed her story to tell me that she stole it from Lord Barton."

"Her lips mutter evil. Mark my words, the child does not speak God's truth, these are wicked words!" Catherine looked away from the bracelet. "Go, take that accursed thing away now. For I am certain the man who gave it to her is not a man at all. He is the devil."

"The devil you say? Great heavens woman what workings of your mind lead you to this absurd conclusion?" Jack asked. It angered him that she was turning a simple injury and the girl's subsequent confusion into such an accusation.

"You have spoken of it yourself. She was defiant. Has our dear Regina ever been defiant on past occasions? Please, I beg of you, you must remove that object from my sight." She pointed to the bracelet, her hands shaking.

"As you wish my dear Catherine. I will return promptly," Jack said. He left Catherine in tears and looked at the gold bracelet. It had a very unusual centerpiece. He unlocked the door to his private chamber, hid the object in his desk, and locked that as well. On his return to her room, he had a difficult time putting together the picture his wife painted of his dear sweet sister. However, Catherine was correct about one thing. Regina had been most difficult last evening.

Returning to his wife's bedside, Jack continued, "Catherine, I am deeply sorry that all of these strange happenings have upset you so much."

"Jack, I fear that her mind—indeed her very soul perhaps—has been overtaken by the forces of evil, maybe the devil himself. She is spitting out falsehoods, she has forgotten how to behave, and worst of all ..." She dabbed at her eyes again, "she has attacked our son. I felt it when she was so close to me in the room. I touched her hand and the heat from it burned me. A few minutes later I collapsed upon the floor. My dear husband, I fear for my son's life with your sister in this house."

"Our son! You are saying that the devil has taken possession of Regina and is trying to harm our unborn son? Catherine!" Jack stood up and clenched his fists. "Damme! She is my sister. You have always wanted to have her removed from our lives. This is merely another of your devious schemes to be rid of her!"

"That it is not. You saw me struck down, falling to the floor." Catherine looked away, trying to compose herself. "Would you not agree, that it is clear she does not act like herself? Gracious, she does not even know her own name! She speaks strangely. It is as if she is someone else. I believe she is possessed by evil humors Jack. And I cannot allow her to harm the baby." She put her hands on her swollen belly.

"My inclination is to allow Lord Barton to take her off our hands. By heavens, the betrothal agreement is in place. Barton wants her, I know he does. In his eyes, I can see the earthly desires he feels for her. We just need to get him to agree to our terms and she will be gone from here for good."

"Husband, it will be too late if she attacks the baby. What if he is damaged by the evil emanating from her person? What might happen if she were to come into my chamber during the nighttime?" she twisted the lace.

"I will put a woman outside her door this night as well, to be sure she remains in her chambers. She will be watched and you will be safe, my dear. Our son's safety is of the utmost importance to me," Jack patted her arm.

A knock at the door interrupted them. Jack crossed the room and opened it.

"Sir, Robert has informed me that Lord Barton is here to call upon Miss Regina," a young female servant said. "If you please, I was told to say that it is most unusual for his lordship to arrive unannounced."

"Tell Robert to make him comfortable. I will have Regina ready for him as soon as I can," Jack said to her.

"Very well sir," the woman said.

"Catherine, here, at last, is good news. Barton has come to call upon Regina. We will hasten along the process and have him sign the betrothal papers today. If Regina is out of our home she will no longer be the troublesome burden to us that she has become. Barton will be responsible for correcting her wicked ways."

"Pray convince Lord Barton at any cost to take her off our hands, I beseech you husband. And until such time as she leaves this house, I beg you to keep her from this room. I used to spend such happy hours listening to her reading to me, but for the sake of my unborn child I cannot abide her anywhere near me."

"Never fear Catherine, your safety is all I am concerned with. My sweetness, I will be cunning with him. I will not give up our monetary advantages to the match, however. Please rest well this day and recover from your frightful experiences." He kissed her hand and walked out of the room.

He made his way down the stairs and in his mind worked out the ways to strike out and have Lord Barton sign the papers that very day. What a victory this would be. He would fasten his hold on the lord while removing his wayward sister from the household.

Chapter 14 - Morning Negotiations

A bright light bore deep into Ronnie's skull, intensifying the headache that had begun some time ago.

"Ronnie, we finally found you," a deep, and thankfully, American voice said. A handsome black man bent down to help her off the floor, his bright white teeth smiling at her.

"Yes, I'm Ronnie."

The man wore a navy-blue jumpsuit with a tag on his shirt that said Bart Lordy. That name seemed familiar.

"Bart Lordy." It felt funny on her tongue as she said it aloud.

"At your service, ma'am." His eyes glowed from the flashlight. Bart put his arm around her to help her walk, although she was steady on her feet. Why she needed help was not exactly clear. He used the flashlight to guide them through a dark hallway. "We can catch up with Jack around the corner."

"Wait, you're taking me to Jack? No, please don't." She pulled out of his arms, turned and began running the opposite way. It was too dark to see anything and she bumped into a wall.

"Ma'am, please," he said from a few feet away while shining a light on her. "Everything will be all right. We just need to have you answer a few questions and then you can go back to your brother."

"He's not my brother. You can't make me go back there. You can't!" The man took her elbow and turned her back around.

"But he said you were lost. He was trying to find you." He scratched his head and looked down the hallway.

"No, please help me get away from him. He is …" Ronnie heard a loud noise.

Ronnie opened her eyes to bright sunshine pouring into the room. Reflexively she shut them against the pain. It was way too bright. The curtains weren't the right color. One eye opened again tentatively. They were supposed to be white. No wait, that was in her Virginia Beach house. This must be the apartment in Florida. Her mouth felt like it had been packed with cotton at the dentist's it was so dry. She pictured the bedroom in Florida. Where were the blinds? She sat up abruptly to get a better look, now panicking, with the dream still vivid in her mind. Sharp pain felt simultaneously in her head and butt brought her fully awake. "Ouch!"

Everything came back at once, sparked by the maroon color, and flooded her mind with horrible images of the day before. She really had to pee. "Damn maroon curtains!"

She grabbed her head, "Ooh, crap it hurts." The dream was fading and she reached out for it, wanting the kind rescue worker to be standing before her. However disturbing the dream was, it had at least taken place in America in modern times.

A small knock on the door caught her attention. A young woman with a lace cap peeked in and said. "Mornin' miss."

Without a thought, Ronnie shot past her and through the antechamber and opened the door to the hallway. She smacked directly into a very large person.

"Out for a morning stroll, Fräulein Regina?" Mathias said smiling down at her.

"Mathias. What are you doing here?"

"Ah," he turned away embarrassed. "Cousin, zis is not seemly. You vill need to cover your person if you are to leave your bedchamber." He smiled, face turning red.

The servant came out into the hallway and nodded, "Miss." She handed Ronnie a dressing gown. Ronnie looked down, realizing she was in a thin white linen shift, the garment women wore under their dresses in this time.

"Oh, thanks." Ronnie put her arms through the sleeves and pulled it tight around her waist. God, how embarrassing! She had fallen asleep in her dress last night, someone must have come in and undressed her. Why didn't she remember that? They must have drugged her. The thought left her feeling very vulnerable. What else had they done to her while she was out?

"It is a fine morning. May I enquire vere you are rushing off to so early?" he said and then nodded toward the door. He wore fresh clothes and his face showed no sign of the five o'clock shadow from the day before.

"Oh, that." She glanced at the door and looked at his substantial frame. "I have to go to the bathroom."

"Zee bathroom? Vere on earth is such a place? Is zis another of your strange vords?" he asked a smile playing at his lips.

"I have to pee." She had to go so bad she didn't even care how embarrassing it was. He looked at her blankly. What did they call it in 1752? "Mathias, I have to—make water."

"Oh," he cleared his throat and turned a shade redder. "Is your chamber pot not zere?"

"Miss, miss," he called out to the maid. "Vye is her chamber pot not in its proper place?"

The maid looked horrified. She walked to the bed and looked underneath and then held the pot up. "Begging your pardon, miss, but it is here, where it always is. Mr. Stohl, sir, please, I have done nothing wrong!"

The look on his face said it all. He thought Ronnie had lost her mind. "Do you need Viggams, Regina? Talking of a room of baths, forgetting the chamber pot. I do believe you are not vell."

"No, no I am fine." Now she was a shade redder. Oh my God, of course, there was no indoor plumbing. "Just a bit groggy," Ronnie said.

Margaret bustled into the room carrying a tray of food. "Good morning Miss Ingram. How are you feeling? Mr. Stohl, good morning to you, sir."

"I'm better. Thank you, Margaret. What is for breakfast?" Ronnie said.

"Miss, it's your favorite. Poached eggs and toast." She set the tray down. "Now, miss, I understand you are receiving a visitor quite soon, so we had best get you dressed."

"What visitor?" Ronnie didn't like the sound of that. It was probably the horrible doctor.

"Dear me, Mr. Ingram didn't say. He only asked that I should help to make you respectable for company." She opened the wardrobe and looked at the choices. "Blue silk?"

"I bid you good day ladies, I vill check on you later, fräulein." Mathias bowed and shut the door.

Ronnie's bladder screamed out for relief. "Margaret, please excuse me for a moment," Ronnie said. There was no way she could go with an audience.

"Miss," Margaret curtsied and left the room.

"Wait, what do you use for toilet paper around here?" She looked in the pot. It was empty but still reeked.

"I do not understand, Miss Ingram," Margaret answered through the door.

"Never mind. Give me a minute." Ronnie pulled up the thin linen shift that was like a long-sleeved nightgown, coming down past her knees. She wore nothing underneath and looked over Regina's legs and nether regions. It was quite unnerving to see Regina's bits, as Steph liked to call it. Most of the time since arriving here she didn't think of herself being in a different body. It was too upsetting. Now she felt like she was invading Regina's privacy.

Ronnie squatted over the chamber pot and hoped it wouldn't tip over and spill on the floor. God did she ever miss modern plumbing. She looked around for something to wipe with and saw a napkin on the tray. She used it, the not sure where to put it and decided to hide it under the bed. Did they really not use toilet paper here?

She opened the door and Margaret pushed past her into the room. "Miss Ingram, we must make all haste to get you dressed." She held up something that looked like a corset. Margaret fussed and primped over Ronnie and finally, she was dressed in a clean shift and thick socks Margaret called stockings that were fastened in place with a garter just below her knee, and a few pleated skirts she called petticoats. She put the corset on Ronnie and pulled the laces in back.

"Now for your pockets, miss," Margaret said putting two oblong white pockets of fabric around her waist so they laid along her hips.

Ronnie watched all of this without saying anything since Regina would have been used to the dressing routine. Margaret pulled out of the wardrobe a strange basket-like contraption with straps.

"What is that?" Ronnie asked.

"Miss. Your panniers are the most important aspect of your dress. It shows your status." Margaret fastened the odd basket around Ronnie's waist. She picked up the blue silk gown from the bed and placed it over her head, and arranged it down over the pannier. Her hips were enormous in this strange outfit, but it explained the shape she had seen on Margaret. She must be wearing a much smaller version.

There was a light knock at the door. Margaret opened it to find Jack in a long black tunic and coat similar to his outfit yesterday. "Sister, are you ready for our meeting?" There were no signs of the vicious mood from last night.

"My meeting? Who am I meeting with?" Ronnie asked.

"Dear sister, Lord Barton has called upon you. He is waiting in the parlor, dreadfully vexed about your accident," Jack said smiling.

"Margaret, is she nearly ready? We want her as desirable as possible," Jack said.

76

"Why do I need to be desirable?" Ronnie had a sinking feeling.

"Regina, we have talked and talked of this. We no longer have much dowry to offer Lord Barton for your hand. It is your duty as a good sister," he chucked her under the chin, "to encourage him to see things our way. We need him to desire you more than a deer desires a mate."

Margaret snickered.

"What?" Ronnie said.

"Regina, dear sister, it is merely business. If he is desirous of you, if he covets you, we will be more successful in bending him to our will. He has to be foaming at the mouth with desire for your ministrations so he will agree to forgo a traditional dowry. However I trust that you will not allow him to actually deflower you else we will have no means to force his hand." He smiled a winning smile as if this was what brothers and sisters usually discussed.

He sensed her uneasiness and walked over and took her hand. "Regina, he is a very wealthy man. He will take care of us in the manner that I have been unable to do since Mother and Father departed this life. As long as we can get past this absurd shift-in-time tomfoolery, we will be saved by the brilliant match I have made for you."

"What shift in time?" Ronnie said. Maybe this was her way back to Florida!

"Regina, we really do not have time for this. You know of the shift that is due to happen in a few weeks. We have all spoke of nothing else since the king announced it," Jack said.

"What shift in time? Jack, you have to tell me!" She grabbed his sleeve.

"Enough of this unwomanly behavior Regina!" he said in a show of anger buried just below the surface.

Margaret placed a towel around her shoulders and brushed her long hair, then twisted it in small coils as Jack continued.

"Regina, I will not tolerate any more of this queer and ungodly behavior. This is your chance to assist our family." He squeezed her shoulder hard, looking into her face. "You will capture Barton's imagination. Use your womanly charms! Give our lusty Lord Barton something to desire."

"Oh dear," Ronnie said, wanting to run out of the room. Instead, she sat quietly trying to dampen the scream working its way out. She shifted in her seat as Margaret pinned her hair up in small coils.

"Regina, I pray you, your most sincere effort is required to secure this betrothal faster than a fly on a close-stool, or you will very much regret it," he said, giving her a hard look and releasing his grip. "He is a lord, a member of England's aristocracy, and will be the saving grace of our family. You will do as I bid."

"Will you be there while I'm, um … entertaining Lord Barton?" she could feel her heart beating faster. God this day was going to suck. And she was getting no closer to finding a way back to her own time.

"Most certainly I will be there at first. However I am going to stay with you but a few minutes before taking my leave, so as to allow you to complete the task," he said.

"Jack, how am I supposed to do this?" Ronnie said. This farce of her playing Regina was going too far.

"My dear sister, you will entice him with your treasures of buxom beauty. You will beguile him with the prospect of pleasurable wicked dalliances, you will entrance him with those fine soul-searching eyes. Dear sister you will *do it*! You will make him desire you!"

"I will do my best," Ronnie said cringing at his words.

"Margaret, complete your administrations so we can meet Lord Barton without delay. Send for me when she is prepared." He turned on his heel and left the room.

Ronnie sat still as Margaret finished her hair and affixed a small hat to her head with pins.

"Miss, please stand."

Ronnie stood and Margaret pulled the corset tighter and smoothed the fabric of the dress over her midriff and hips. She presented shoes for Ronnie to put on her feet.

"Margaret, how will I charm him? I don't know how to do this."

"Miss Ingram," Margaret said. "If you'll forgive the familiarity, in my experience, men are all the same. All you need only to do is to make him feel attractive and smart. You have to actually do things, skittish little tricks as makes him feel frisky. Why, a swift turn of the hip, a flash of your ankle." Margaret demonstrated, lifting her skirt to show her boots.

Ronnie wondered if modern men even looked at ankles anymore. "I would like to brush my teeth, what do I have for that?" she asked.

"Miss, brush your teeth?" Margaret laughed. "I never heard of such a thing! We may have a horsehair brush tucked away in your washstand." Margaret walked over to a small cabinet under the pitcher of water and bowl for washing. "Why bless my soul, I have found it. Dragon's blood is here 'n all somewhere."

She poured some water into the bowl and set the soap in her hand. "Miss."

Ronnie looked over the horsehair brush. It was larger than a modern toothbrush and made from a piece of bone. The bristles were black at the base, whether with dirt or mold, Ronnie wasn't sure, but it didn't matter. There was no way she was putting that in her mouth. She picked up the bottle of dragon's blood and pulled the cork. It was a dark red and smelled spicy like cinnamon mixed with another rancid odor. "Dragon's blood? What is this stuff, Margaret?"

"Tooth powder, miss."

Ronnie decided to skip the dragon's blood and disgusting toothbrush. Instead, she dipped the corner of the cloth in the water and scrubbed her teeth. They were still fuzzy afterward but not nearly as gross as when she woke up. She washed her face and patted it with the cloth.

"Tell me what I am to expect. I'm really nervous about this meeting with Lord Barton."

"I haven't the foggiest idea miss. Betrothal negotiations is what them's called, but they ain't nothing I'm schooled in." Margaret fussed and primped over Ronnie as she talked. "In my family, the right and proper thing they done for me was to have me teeth pulled for my husband."

"What?" Ronnie turned around, upsetting the tin of powder she held in her hand. "Oh, sorry."

Margaret gave her a funny look and bent over to wipe up the powder that had spilled. "No need to apologize, miss, that's what I'm here for. As for my teeth, my old mum had it done. Makes sense, don't it? After all, it saves all the expense of the blacksmith pulling the beggars out one by one, as they rot."

"So you have no teeth?" Ronnie couldn't help but ask. It was a rude question and this was confirmed by the look on Margaret's face but she said nothing about it. The thought of her teeth being pulled was too horrific. A young girl with perfectly good teeth to go through all that pain. "How do you eat Margaret?"

"I have my dentures of course." She opened her mouth to show uneven, brown and horrid smelling dentures.

"Oh I see," Ronnie said, nearly gagging at the site of rotten bits in her mouth. Oh, my God, this was a barbaric time. How could hideous dentures be better than natural teeth?

Jack knocked on the door and walked in to interrupt her horrible thoughts of kissing someone with dentures, not to mention the act of eating with those godforsaken things.

"My dear, you look exquisite," Jack said to her. "Margaret, you have outdone yourself."

"Thank you, sir," Margaret said.

Jack led her down the stairs and walked in front holding her hand as she tried to walk in the kitten heels and wide dress that took up nearly the entire stairway. She was hardly able to breathe for the corset pulling all her ribs together and shoving her breasts as high as possible. It was ridiculous and devoid of any sex appeal whatsoever. What if Lord Barton had smelly dentures? She had never been good at faking her feelings. Would he see the distaste on her face? Maybe he would not be looking at her face. Would he be fooled by her twenty-first-century self, packaged as an eighteenth-century girl?

"Regina," Jack said as they made their way down the steps. "You are my puppet. Is my meaning as clear as crystal?"

"Yes, I will do as instructed," she said, hoping she would be able to.

Ronnie took a deep breath. Maybe Lord Barton would know about the time-shift and how she could get back to Florida. "You mentioned the time-shift earlier. Can you tell me what that is so that I can be well-versed if Lord Barton brings it up?" Ronnie asked.

"I will discuss that with you later. Your task right now is getting the betrothal agreed upon. Do what Lord Barton wants of you. Play the doxy, but do not act the doxy, got it?" he said.

"Sir, Lord Barton is in the parlor awaiting your arrival," An elderly gentleman, one of Jack's servants, said as they walked into the hallway at the bottom of the stairs.

They made their way along a corridor filled with paintings of old men in really old-fashioned clothes. She was glad of the long dress and long sleeves, as the air was chilly downstairs. She made note of the front door as they passed it, hoping to make use of it at some point for a hasty exit.

Jack opened a door at the end of a hallway and they both stepped into a beautiful room full of morning sunlight. A flutter of nerves made her short of breath. How was she going to pull this off? What horrible things would this man want from her to sign the betrothal papers, and would she be stuck here to marry him?

Chapter 15 - Bare Flesh

"My dear!" Lord Barton stood up and smoothed his suit. He was heavy with pale shiny skin and a brown wig. Uneven yellow teeth showed a broad grin. At least there were no dentures to contend with. He was just a little bit taller than she was and to say he was unattractive was being kind. No wonder he was considering marrying her. She would be quite a catch. But the poor Ingram gene pool would take a nosedive if they had any kids.

"Miss Ingram. Indeed it is a great pleasure to see you again." Lord Barton walked over to her and kissed her hand. He looked a lot older than the forty years Mathias had mentioned. Ronnie searched for a redeeming physical quality and found none. His eyes were brown and hooded. He was dressed in a long gray jacket with lacy sleeves poking out and a lacy cravat at his neck. Ronnie forced a smile and let him kiss her hand. His face was powdered and so was his brown wig that contrasted with his gray eyebrows.

He turned his gaze to Jack. "And Mr. Ingram. How very pleasant to see you again."

"I wish you a very good morning, Lord Barton, and I welcome you to my home."

"Oh but I have you to thank for bringing this delightful creature to me," Lord Barton gushed. "I was desolate when I heard the news you were hurt. My dear, are you now recovered from your accident?"

"Yes, I feel a bit better." He put his hand on her waist and guided her to a small couch.

"My pet, pray sit there and talk to me about your injury and recovery," Lord Barton said.

Ronnie tried to sit down but the ridiculously wide dress would not allow. She made several attempts and finally sat gracelessly in the center of the small couch, the majority of the space taken up with the huge panniers on either side.

The men exchanged looks both perplexed at her attempts, but finally, Lord Barton sat down next to her and tried not to sit on the dress.

His gaze fixed steadily on her chest. "I hope you have called the surgeon to assess the poor child. Is she feeling well enough to put up with visitors?"

"Why, yes," Jack answered, smiling. "Dr. Wiggams was here just after the accident. He balanced her humors and told her to rest. It was most restorative. You will be gentle with her I hope, sir."

Ronnie found it a bit infuriating how they discussed her as if she weren't present.

"I will be as gentle as a hummingbird." Barton picked up her hand and began stroking it. His fat lips grazed her palm. It was all she could do to not scream and jerk her hand away. He sensed something and let go.

"It is indeed my greatest pleasure to be here with you, Miss Ingram. Pray tell why you left me in such uncommon haste at our last meeting?" he said, drawing each word out slowly as if she were a child.

"I don't remember, Lord Barton." She smiled at him, trying to keep from gritting her teeth.

"Because, my dear, indeed, I do believe that we were beginning to make some progress on the negotiations," he said as he scooted closer.

"Maybe we should take a walk?" Ronnie said, eyeing the garden out the window.

"A walk. That would be very pleasant," Jack said. "I will leave you two together, as unfortunately, I must make haste to attend a prior engagement. Will you excuse me?"

"Certainly." Barton leered at Ronnie, licking his lips as he eyed her chest again. "Miss Ingram and I will be more than happy to take our perambulations alone, I am sure."

Oh God. She gave Jack an exaggerated look of desperation.

"My lord, pray be gentle with her," Jack said and turned to her. "Regina, I trust you to be a good obedient sister and to take care of Lord Barton if he should require anything." His eyebrows lifted in question.

"Yes, I will take care of him." She looked wide-eyed at Jack with a frantic oh-my-God smile.

He ignored it and turned on his heel to walk out of the room.

"How about that walk?" Ronnie turned her attention back to Lord Barton.

"Oh my dear, forgive me, but I am not dressed for an outing in the garden. And you my sweet plum, your clothes are not suitable either. Gracious me, just look at you. My little beauty you are ravishing. You quite take my breath away."

She smiled. "Thank you so much."

He scooted his fat bottom closer to her on the couch, closing in on her.

Remembering Jack's threats, Ronnie stayed put despite her strong urge to scoot away. "What were we doing yesterday? I've not remembered much since my accident."

"Yesterday, I was expressing my deep feelings for you. Of how my heart had capitulated to the beauty of your nubile young ..." He looked at her chest again and touched her arm, running his pudgy fingers along her sleeve.

"Oh?" Ronnie said again, forcing herself to not cringe at his touch.

"I was merely discussing wifely virtues and husbandly desires. Do you not remember my dear?" he asked, smile fading.

"No, I don't remember anything. I ran from here and got hit by a carriage. Please tell me why I ran away. I have to know."

"Got hit by a carriage! What a quaint turn of phrase you have my dear, I never realized before. Do please accept my most humble apologies, Miss Ingram. My behavior was unseemly. Most unusual for me, I do assure you, and I believe I may have upset you yesterday. I hope you may find it in your heart to forgive my unmannerly display of verve." His face changed from lustful eagerness to a more serious look and his hand dropped to his lap.

"Please tell me why I was so upset. I really don't remember." She was curious now.

"We discussed what I wish for you to do so that I may sign the papers." He looked away, pulling a lacy handkerchief from his sleeve and wiped his face.

"Yes, please tell me what it was."

"I will do so if you will agree to stay with me and not jump up and run down the road. It really was most embarrassing to explain to my household. Perhaps you have had a chance to think on it. My hope was that when I came to call today you would be accustomed to the idea," he said.

"Please tell me what it was," she said as he picked up her hand.

"It was my earnest desire for you to ..." he paused, playing with her fingers, "for you to sit on me."

"Sit on you?" she asked. "On your lap?" That wasn't so bad.

"Ahem, no, no. Not exactly," he dabbed his forehead with the lace. "Gracious me, dear, dear. So you do not remember then?"

"No. The accident made me forget." So it was worse than sitting on his lap then. "Please tell me the rest."

"Well my dear," his eyes lit up, "I wanted you to perch your pretty little behind on my face and then smother me." He looked away, his face having changed from pasty white to a pale blush, starting at his neck and rising upward despite the powder.

"Smother you?" That would certainly be one way out of the marriage. "Like to suffocate you?"

"Goodness no! Oh no, no. I want your sweet ripe young flesh upon my face, preventing me from breathing but only for a short time. I will hold my breath and you will allow me to breathe when I request it. Nothing more."

She stood and took a step backward. "What?"

"Yes, oh please, I beg you, it would mean the world to me! Damme, I would sign the papers, without a dowry, no further contracts at all," he said, standing up and taking a step toward her.

Ronnie turned away from him, feeling sick. He wanted her to smother him with her butt? No wonder Regina ran away. What a freaking perverted gross man!

"I don't understand," she turned toward him. "Why would you want me to do that?" Ronnie could feel panic rising, making her voice higher. "Is this something I would do once we are married?"

"Why? It is something I have always desired. Truly I think it would be very exciting indeed," he said, the blush was in full force now. He tried to smile but it came across as a more of a squint. "I would want you to do it again, yes, of course, as often as you would allow. Mind, you would have to remove your petticoats and shift though. I want your lovely bare flesh on my face, filling my senses."

"My flesh ..." The words died in her throat. "You are serious?"

"Never more so, never more so. Miss Ingram, this is the small favor I ask of you, to indulge me in my little peccadillo. In return, I should demand no dowry, indeed I would quite put it aside. It really is not so much to ask. Is it now?" he said, wiping his face again.

"I don't know. Is there anything else you would want instead?" she asked and then regretted it. What other horrible things had this man already fantasized? Seemed as this was his free pass to fly his freak flag.

"Oh my word yes, but you already said no to those things yesterday," he said twisting the handkerchief in his hand. "I had all kinds of fine games for us to play. Until you ran out of the room when I suggested this act."

"I did?" she asked.

"Miss Ingram, I am so ecstatically happy to see you again. I was afraid I would scare you off, you see. But since you are here in front of me now, you must have given it some thought. After all, I suspect if you gave yourself up for our joyous flesh-on-flesh union, it could be something you might enjoy yourself, do you not think so? Does your heartbeat not race and skip at the thought of such sensual frolics?" Lord Barton said.

"Um." Ronnie sat down hard on a chair away from Lord Barton and felt the bruises from her spanking yesterday. "I really don't know what to say."

She looked at him closely, trying to match this perversion with the man who otherwise looked somewhat dignified. He smiled, exposing his yellow uneven teeth, making her stomach do a flip. She could see a bit of food stuck between two of his top teeth.

"As I was saying when you left me yesterday," his eyes affixed to her breasts, "I will not interfere with your person in any way while you sit on my face. I will not probe you. My joy would be simply to wallow in the excitement of feeling your bare flesh upon my face until I cry out for want of air! Oh, my goodness Miss Ingram, what fun, what exquisite excitement. Perhaps for you too?"

Ronnie shifted in her chair when he spoke of probing. Images of his horrible mouth on her made her stomach turn.

"Perhaps we might arrange a discreet half an hour with you smothering me with your sweet little behind, but letting me breathe when you so desire it?" He wiped his face again, his breathing getting faster, eyes alight with excitement. "And afterward I will sign anything you want. We can then marry soon." He opened his mouth and began panting.

That was exactly what Jack had requested, to get Lord Barton panting. Now what?

"Even if I wanted to I wouldn't be able to do it now. My brother spanked me last night. It would be too painful today." At least there was an upside to what Jack had done. Maybe it would get her out of it without making a bad situation worse.

"Oh, my dear, that is a terrible shame … spanking, you say. My dear … oh, my … a terrible, terrible shame." The smile on his face did not show worry, rather his eyes lit up at the prospect of her being spanked. "But why would he punish you, my dear? You had been run over by a carriage for goodness' sake."

"I didn't want the doctor to bleed me," she said, hoping to stick to the truth as much as possible.

"Oh dear. I am very sorry to hear that. However, I have another idea then my sweet one." He glanced down her bodice.

Ronnie didn't like the sound of that. He was so creepy, leering at her. She stood up and backed away "Oh you do?"

He stood up and moved closer so he could slide the shoulder of her gown down, revealing more cleavage and her corset. "You could remove those stays and let me ..." He stared at her exposed flesh.

Ronnie shuddered. Oh God this was awful. The man wasn't going to let her just make promises, he wanted the goods delivered today. She stepped away from him with her skin crawling. She knew his eyes were on her.

"Forgive me my sweetness, I do believe I am moving a little too fast for you. Just as I did yesterday," he said, sitting down again. "Why not sit beside me and we will talk of common things for a while. Perhaps I am a mite too eager for us to resume our negotiations." He patted the seat next to him.

"Yes, that would be good. I need to get comfortable first." She smiled, glad for the reprieve from his advances. Ronnie sat down and rearranged the pannier to sit a bit lower. These things were a damn nuisance.

"It so happens I have a close friend who is having a time-shift party on the second." He moved closer to her and played with her fingers again. "What say you accompany me? You could have your brother chaperone if you would like."

"A time-shift party? That brings up a question. What is the time-shift? Jack mentioned that yesterday, and again just before we came in here." Maybe this was her way home.

"Your brother has spoken of it to you just now? What has he said about it? What has he said about me?" He sat on the edge of the seat so as to turn toward her, his knees touching her thigh.

"Only that he wanted to get past it and work out the details of the betrothal with you," Maybe the party was around a time travel device or something?

"I see. Does he have something up his sleeve, Miss Regina? Can I call you that?" he asked.

"Yes."

"Aha! So he does have something planned in connection with the time-shift?" His smile faded.

"No, I didn't say that. I meant yes you can call me Miss Regina. Can you explain the time-shift to me?"

"Why?" He sat back against the couch and pulled out his handkerchief again and patted his face delicately. "Did he ask you to try to obtain information from me about the time-shift?"

"No, he didn't. I'm asking because I don't know what it means. It might be important to me." She didn't like the change in his tone.

"Forgive me, madam," he stood up and looked down at her. "I want to know what Mr. Ingram has told you about the time-shift and the New Style. The event is only a few weeks hence, and I'm suspicious about you Ingrams. What have you got planned for September the third?" His tone was angry.

This wasn't going well. Maybe Jack did have something planned for Lord Barton? Ronnie sat back against the couch with her face feeling flushed. "I really don't know a thing, Lord Barton. Sit back down next to me, we were just getting cozy."

He paced across the room and walked back, his face twisted in an ugly snarl. "Frankly, madam, I am truly disgusted by the pair of you. You are trying to take advantage of me. I thought that we had more than just a business arrangement between us, but I can now see that you are playing fast and loose with me!"

"No, that's not fair. I misspoke. I really don't know anything about Jack's business. I can't even remember our last conversation, only yesterday. I don't know anything about a plot against you," Ronnie said, panic rising.

He glared at her. His ears now several shades darker than his already beet-red face.

She stood up. "I'm very sorry that I have angered you, Lord Barton. I was merely answering that you can call me Miss Regina. I wasn't telling you that Jack was up to anything. Do you think he would trust anything to me, a mere girl? Surely you know I am not privy to any of his business dealings."

"My dear girl, how in God's name can I trust you now? You reject my friendly advances—heavens, you even recoil at my touch! What could a scheming little girl like you offer me but a cold bed and financial ruin?" He clenched his fists like an angry child.

How had this conversation shifted to anger and doubt so quickly? Ronnie could feel Jack's seething wrath and she resisted the urge to protect her rear end in response to her imaginings.

Chapter 16 – Am I Kind?

"I …" Ronnie could almost feel Jack's anger renewed with this impending failure. "Lord Barton that is a very unkind assessment of me. You started our conversation with the idea of me sitting on your face. You need to give me a chance to ease into the situation. I'm young and not used to such talk."

"But the truth is, you are revolted by me, are you not, Miss Ingram?" He pursed his lips and looked like a full-fledged sourpuss. "Madam, your eyes betray you."

"I am not revolted by you, I am just not used to any attention from men," she lied. "You are very forward and it has taken me by surprise. Please forgive me if I've insulted you."

"My dear it is only right and proper that you should have attention from men. Are you not aware that you are very beautiful? Your face, your womanly assets, your elegance?" he looked from her lips to her chest, and to her waist. "Why I would not expect for you be attracted to an old man like me. But it is of no consequence."

"Lord Barton, I am sure I can grow to love you. You seem very nice. I believe you would take very good care of me and that's all a woman can really ask for in life."

His face softened a bit. "Really? Do you think you could grow to love me?"

"Yes, I do. You seem very kind. Are you?" Ronnie said, hoping he would start talking about himself and relax a bit.

"Am I kind? Gracious me, what an extraordinary question." He sat down, his weight shaking the chair. "I assure you I can be, however, I will not be so kind if you betray me."

"Then it is in my best interest to be loyal to you and take care of you. You will see, I will make a very good wife." She would make someone a good wife but not in the eighteenth century and *not* with this man. Jeffrey might get the chance if she could get back to Florida.

"Miss Ingram, I fancy that you are trying to charm me, and I am not going to fall into the trap that your brother has set. After having talked to you for an appreciable time now, it is apparent to me that you have been schooled as to what to say to me." He stood up, straightening his waistcoat. "Unfortunately, your schemes have come to naught, because you are not wise enough to keep your pretty little mouth closed about the time-shift and your brother's plans."

"Seriously? You insult my intelligence?" She bit her tongue, wanting to say he was a revolting perverted old man and she would not be caught dead sitting on his fleshy old face. Instead, she tried to calm down, "Again, I am very sorry I made you so mad and have the hope that we can further our talks another day."

"Made me mad?" he looked confused. "Why should you assume you have driven me to insanity? I am not the candidate for the madhouse, madam, I can assure you of that. And now I think our meeting is finished, Miss Ingram. I must find Mr. Ingram." He bowed clumsily looking like a very different man than the one she had met a half an hour earlier.

Ronnie stood up and watched Lord Barton walk out of the room. "Good day, Lord Barton."

He nodded his head toward her, "Good day, Miss Ingram," and turned on his heel.

She followed him to the door and shut it behind him. "Oh crap! That was a disaster." Panic washed over her. Jack would be furious! What would he do to her now? She wiped her hands on her blue velvet dress, the corset jabbed into her ribs and she adjusted it. He would hit her again and probably worse.

It then occurred to her, she was alone for the first time since arriving here. Renewed hope bubbled in her chest. She looked around the room for a door she could slip out into the garden but found none. She pressed her ear to the door to the hallway. Where would she go? She had nothing with her, no money, or any semblance of a plan. Maybe she should just get out and let the details be sorted as the day progressed.

Ronnie opened the door quietly and stepped into the hallway, not sure which way to go. The front door was to her left but that might be too busy. She turned to her right and followed along the corridor hoping to find a back door. She passed several closed doors and found the kitchen. It was busy with several people busy preparing the next meal. She paused and Margaret caught sight of her. Damn!

"Why Miss Regina," Margaret called out. "The tea has already been delivered to Lord Barton, has it not?"

"Yes, yes …" Caught by surprise Ronnie didn't know what to say. "He left me, Margaret."

"He is no longer here? Lord help us, Mr. Ingram is going to be vexed if he has left before he can say a proper farewell," Margaret said wiping her hands on her apron and walking past her. "Oh, dear me, Miss Regina, this is not what we was expecting." Margaret began twisting her apron. "I must find Robert and see if his lordship has departed."

A few minutes later Robert confirmed that Lord Barton had left in a huff. With Margaret and Robert talking near the front door Ronnie quietly walked away and searched for another way out of the house. Surely there would be an exit in the kitchen? She made her way toward the back of the house and found Mathias walking down the hallway toward her.

"Fräulein Regina, how very nice to see you again. How vas your meeting *mit* Lord Barton?" he asked, a smile lighting up his face.

"Hello, Mathias. Let's say it was not an overwhelming success." Ronnie was happy to see his smiling face but disappointed that her escape was interrupted.

His smile faded. "Zee meeting *mit* Lord Barton did not go as planned? Let us speak of zis in private. Perhaps I may be of assistance *mit* your brother. Does Jack know of zee failure?"

All she wanted was to leave this horrible place and get back to Florida, but again her attempts were thwarted. He stood there, waiting for a response. "No, he left the two of us alone and it fell apart shortly after." Ronnie could not look Mathias in the eyes. He might see how Lord Barton had changed her.

"Fräulein, this is deeply upsetting. I varrant that your brother vill not take zis news vell. Allow me to accompany you outside, so zat we can discuss zee matter further." He took her arm and led her to the front door and they walked out into the grounds.

As they followed a pathway around a grassy knoll, Ronnie played over in her mind what to say to him. Could she explain the disgusting acts Lord Barton had proposed? A knot formed in her stomach. Mathias would be furious. It was really unfair for Regina, or her for that matter, to marry such a twisted old man and to most likely bear his children and possibly die in the process. She would make sure that wouldn't happen. Even if it meant being homeless in London.

Finally, Mathias said, "*Gut*, vee are away from zee prying ears of zee servants. *Bitte*, tell me vat has taken place here this afternoon ven you conversed *mit* Lord Barton. It is clear zat he has upset you." He motioned for her to sit next to him on a garden bench. "Make yourself comfortable here and vee vill try to make sense of vat has occurred."

Ronnie sat, feeling the pain from the tender flesh where Jack had spanked her yesterday and shoved the pannier down from her ears. The same flesh that Lord Barton had wanted her to … ugh! How could she tell Mathias? She busied her hands by playing with her skirt, not wanting to dive into troubled waters.

"*Bitte,* fräulein. I assure you, you may put your trust in me. I vill only be able to help you if I understand vat took place." He sat down next to her and took her hands.

She didn't want to repeat what the horrible little Barton had said, but Mathias was right, there might be something he could do to help. "That man." Ronnie started, but not in the way she wanted to. "He is revolting on so many levels. Why should I have to marry him?" She didn't have to try hard to sound like a disgruntled seventeen-year-old.

"Forgive me asking, zis but is Lord Barton who has angered you? He is revolting? Please tell me vye zis is so." He squeezed her hand. "Tell me vat he has done to upset you so."

"Mathias, he …" She looked away not able to say it to him. This wasn't going as she wanted but at this point, there really was no turning back. "He asked me to do rude things before he would sign the betrothal papers. Really *awful* things."

"Pray tell vat things has he spoken of to you?" Anger echoed in his voice.

"Not normal things." She took a deep breath. "Do you know if Jack was planning something to do with the time-shift?"

"Fräulein Regina, do not change zee subject. *Bitte*, I beg of you, I vill need to know vat he has said to you if I am to defend you. He vill be as angry as a tethered bull when he finds out that Lord Barton left on such uncertain terms."

Ronnie took a deep breath and turned her head away. "Jack is going to hit me again, isn't he?" She fought back tears but lost the battle.

"I vill not allow zat behavior from my cousin. He should not be abusing zee women of his household. I have seen how he treats Catherine and it makes my blood boil. For heaven's sake, she is *mit* child and should be left alone to rest." He picked up her hands, "Fräulein, you must tell me everything and I vill do my best to smooth things over with Jack. He vill not retaliate, for vee vill stand together."

Ronnie studied his face, still debating, still stalling. "Mathias, I don't know if I can say these things to you."

"You must," he said.

She shuffled her feet, nearly losing her shoe. That would be awkward since she couldn't see her feet with the stupid huge dress in the way. "He asked me to sit on his face." She pulled her hands away from him and looked away.

"I do not understand. Did he ask you to sit on his face? What ludicrous madness is this?"

"He asked me to remove my petticoats and sit my bare flesh upon his face."

Mathias stood up with his fists clenched by his sides, looking like he was ready to kill someone. "Did he indeed? *Ich schwöre bei Gott, allmächtiger!* He has deeply insulted you, sweet Regina. I should like to string him up by his ..." he glanced down at her. "I am most sorry for zis outburst, but it is more zen I can stand."

"When I said no to that using the excuse of Jack hitting me last night he asked me to remove my stays and ..."

Mathias's face reddened and his lips disappeared in a thin line of anger. He paced down the pathway. "How did he conclude zis disgusting conversation? Tell me of his next suggestions after his depraved and foul insults to such a lady."

"He saw that made me very uncomfortable and changed the subject by inviting me to join him for a time-shift party. I was curious to know what the time-shift was so I asked him. He got really mad. Wanted to know what Jack was planning behind his back."

"Mad?" Mathias asked.

"I mean angry, furious."

"Go on, *bitte*."

"He accused us both of plotting against him with the time-shift and the New Style," Ronnie said, studying Mathias's face.

"Plotting against him? Indeed! Vat plot can zis be, Regina? I have heard a few rumblings about a scheme surrounding zee time-shift but not from your brother."

"I have no idea." She played with her fingers in her lap and could feel his eyes on her. "Did you think over what we talked about last night? You could help me get away from here, from Jack and Lord Barton." She didn't know how much time they would have before Jack returned and wanted to get to the point with Mathias.

"Yes, I did. But I fear zat I cannot . . ." He combed his hand through his dark hair and looked down at his feet.

"I understand. I really do." She took his hand. "You can come with me if you want." He was the only person who could help her. But would he tell Jack of her plans?

"Fräulein," he looked away. "Vords fail me, I am at a loss to know vat to do. Vat voud vee do? Vere voud vee go?" he said more softly, more tenderly.

"Miss Ingram!" A male voice yelled out.

Ronnie panicked. "Mathias please, let's leave now. We can go somewhere else!"

The gate opened and a servant bowed, "Miss Ingram, your presence is requested at once. Please follow me."

Ronnie stood up and turned to follow the man. Mathias took her arm. "Be so good as to place your trust in me, Fräulein Regina. I vill talk *mit* your brother. You may rely on me to be on your side."

They both followed the servant back to the house. Ronnie was certain she was making the wrong choice. She should be running away, not going back to Jack's grip. Jack would be furious at Mathias's intrusion in the Ingram's affairs again, and she would get the brunt of Jack's anger. She would never get away from this place and would never find a way back to Florida. Ronnie paused at the lintel and Mathias put his hand on her shoulder.

"I am here for you. Let us go forth and face Jack together."

Ronnie's stomach clenched. This was going to be horrible.

They entered the building and walked along a hallway to the front of the house. The servant knocked on a door and Jack asked them to come in.

"Regina, where have you been?" Jack stood at a heavy wooden desk. This must be his library, for there were leather bound books on shelves. "Hello Cousin, I was not expecting you to be party to this conversation."

"Regina has asked me to accompany her," Mathias said. Did he stand just a little taller when he spoke?

"Well, perhaps you can help us find an explanation for the news I have received. I have just been informed that Lord Barton has called off the betrothal," Jack said.

"He has?" Ronnie said bracing herself for the onslaught. She looked at Mathias for support. He nodded. She was very glad that he was there. Maybe Jack would control himself.

"I …" Jack stopped and glanced up at Mathias. "He …" Jack's face was nearly purple with rage as he walked over and stood in front of her. "Understand this, Sister. This may mean financial ruin for us! Damme, why in God's name would you destroy us in this way? To bring destruction to Catherine and my son." He grabbed her arms and shook her, "What have you done to our family? How could you be so headstrong and selfish? To bring disaster down on all of us?"

Mathias took a step closer. "Jack, please, listen to her. Let her tell you vat has happened. Cousin I'm sure you vill find it in your heart to forgive Fräulein Regina, once you are fully aware of the situation."

"What right have you to provide your opinion on such matters, Mathias?" Jack said turning his anger to Mathias.

"Sir, violence is no vay to solve a problem such as zis. Be gentle and understanding *mit* your sister, pray listen to vat she has to say! Striking zee poor girl vill not make *ein bisschen* of difference to zee situation." Mathias looked down at Jack calmly but didn't back down.

Jack let go of Ronnie and walked to the window. She rubbed her arms where he had grabbed her. *Please don't send Mathias away!*

After an uncomfortable ten minutes of listening to the two men discuss the issue, Jack sat down at the desk with his head in his hands.

Mathias gave her a sympathetic look and motioned for her to sit down. She eyed the chair and knew her pannier would not allow her to sit. She shook her head.

After a few minutes, Jack said, "You are both coming with me."

Ronnie looked at Mathias and back at Jack. "Where are we going?"

Jack grabbed her arm and marched her out of the room, down the hallway, and out the back door. Ronnie looked backward at Mathias, but he shrugged his shoulders.

Chapter 17 - Batteries

Nick looked in the walk-in closet and said, "This will do." They shut the door and she looked up at the ceiling in hopes it would hold up to the storm. The comforter from Steph's bed and a few pillows already sat in a pile from her earlier preparations. Food and water waited in a large Tupperware container in the corner of the closet as Nick had instructed.

He dragged her shoe rack with his good hand toward the closet door and pitched it out into the bedroom.

"Hey, why'd you do that?" Steph asked.

"Look at me Steph, I'm six-foot." He sat down hard and leaned against the wall. "I think we'll be in here for the duration. Do you have the weather radio?"

"Shoot. No. It's in the kitchen. I'll get it," Steph said.

"Don't you have a clock radio that uses batteries near your bed? Just grab that." He looked pale and uncomfortable. He dug around in the plastic bin in the corner and inspected it. "Food, water … did you put batteries in here?"

"Batteries!" She remembered they were in the drawer by her bed and had meant to put them in the bin but hadn't gotten around to it. She got up and opened the door, hesitating to go out where a tree could fall any minute. A huge branch was smashed up against the window which thankfully appeared to be intact.

She took a few steps and grabbed the clock radio, jerking the plug out from the wall. Reaching into the drawer, she rummaged around, feeling the ground shake under her. It was another tree down and closer this time. "Dammit, where are they?" Steph realized she had taken the batteries to the kitchen. "Ooch!" The clock radio took double-A batteries, she would have to steal them from something else. She looked around the room until another powerful gust of wind roared outside. "The remote!" Once she found it she yanked the batteries out and made her way back to the closet. He was going to cuss her out for missing one of his most important storm preparations.

"Nick, I left the batteries in the kitchen, I think. I'm pretty sure I bought them." Steph handed him the radio and the batteries. "I found these in the remote."

"Okay." He took the backing off the radio and inserted the batteries.

"Okay? You're not gonna rail me for forgetting?" He must be feeling poorly if he wasn't even going to lecture her.

"Got the fight knocked out of me Steph." He nodded his head toward his finger, "I'm not going to be good for a lecture for a while yet."

Nick had shoved a row of clothes away from where he sat so he would have some headroom. She grabbed a handful of dresses on hangers and dumped them on the bed.

Nick looked pale and shiny. "Are you okay?" He really looked like death warmed over.

"I feel kinda gross, Steph." His voice sounded shaky.

"Water. You need some water." She cracked the top open on a bottled water and handed it to him. "Lay down. I've got some ibuprofen here, too." The bottle was near the top of the heap, added as an afterthought.

"No, I think my collarbone is broken. I'm gonna sit right here and not move." He sat stiffly and gripped his wrist.

"No, Nick! Why do you think that?"

"It hurts like hell, Steph," he said. "I don't want to be a wimp or anything but I'm feeling really shitty."

She could see the pain in his eyes. "Let me see. Show me where it hurts."

"Here." He said touching his clavicle. "I tried to get out of the way of the transformer when it fell but it caught me on my back and shoved me to the ground."

"Oh, Nick, I'm so sorry." She looked at the bone running along his upper chest but couldn't see anything but mud.

"It took me a minute to worm my way out from under the damn thing. I had to use both arms to get up." He wiped a drop of sweat off his forehead. "Didn't you hear me yell?"

"No, the storm was too loud. I thought you were dead, Nick. It's my fault for asking you here."

"Don't be silly, Steph. It's the damn cat's fault for ruining a perfectly good shower." His smile nearly covered the pain in his eyes.

Steph laughed, remembering how he looked in the shower. "Oh, God, Nick. That's right." Was that fate's way of intervening? Maybe she shouldn't start anything with him. They had been such good friends, she would hate to lose that closeness they shared if it didn't work out romantically. He was probably her best friend here in Florida. The possibility of moving things along with him was very tempting though. His body was so hard. She shook her head trying to get that image out of her mind. The Nick in front of her needed help, the Nick from the shower would have to stay in her imagination for later examination.

"Do you want to change clothes?" she asked. "You're soaking wet and filthy."

"I don't want to move a muscle. The thought of pulling the shirt over my arm isn't so appealing." His face pinched in pain.

"I'm gonna get into something dry." Steph couldn't stand the wet clothes plastered against her skin. She opened the closet door to run to the bathroom and peeled off her clothes as she went. She hung them on the towel rack and dried off while walking back to her dresser naked hoping Nick wouldn't come out and see her.

She pulled a loose T-shirt and shorts out of her dresser. The humidity was creeping in since the power was off. It wasn't too hot yet but there was no hope of power coming back on that night. When she opened the closet door she found Nick cradling his arm.

"Is it getting worse?" she asked. It was really hard to see him in so much pain.

"Yeah, a bit. Did you see Hamish before the transformer fell down?"

"Yeah," she brushed her soggy blonde hair out of her eyes. "I could see his tail. He ran off just after the transformer fell. Poor wee man, he's still out there."

"I hope he's okay." He sounded tired. "Wait, they're giving us an update on the storm." He turned up the volume on the radio.

"This is Mixx FM radio, Tom the Treeman here," the DJ said.

"Hi Tom, it's Debbie from Altamonte Springs. We lost power about an hour ago and I've got a tree on my car out front and another one that just landed in my living room." Her voice sounded like a pack or more a day.

"I'm sorry to hear that. Is everyone okay?" Tom said.

"Yes, we're all hiding in the bathroom. Just me, my husband, and the dogs. What should we do with the tree? I mean it's right in my living room, landed on the couch. Thank God no one was sitting there when it fell."

"I'm so glad you're okay. You should stay in the bathroom until the storm is over. It's a small storm, as hurricanes go, but sustained winds have just been reported at ninety mph at Orlando International Airport. You don't want to be anywhere but in an interior room away from all windows and doors."

"We are. The tree went right through the house. I mean, bam, straight through the roof and landed on the floor. I think our house is going to be ruined. The water is just pouring in, running down the walls, and soaking into the rug," Debbie said.

"As long as no one is hurt count your blessings. You can always find a new house. Stay put for now and keep listening. This is Tom the Treeman on Mixx FM radio brought to you by Nathan's Tree Trimming. Get your trees trimmed before hurricane season to protect your property. A bit late for that, right Nathan? Be smart and stay safe. Call in and tell us what is going on in your neighborhood. (727) 235-6330. Now an update from Accuweather TV-12."

Nick finished his water and chucked it at the plastic bin of supplies.

"This is Terry James from Accuweather TV-12. The National Weather Service has issued a tornado watch for the following counties." He read a list of the entire area. They listened intently until Orange County was announced.

Steph wanted to ask him about his arm but thought better of it. "So how much longer do you think the storm is going to last?"

"Shhhh!"

"We have an unofficial gust at Charlotte Regional Medical Center of 172 miles per hour along the coast," Terry said.

"I've never even heard of wind speeds that high, ever!" A feeling of dread crept over her. What if Nick started to crash or needed medical attention. There was no way an ambulance would come in the middle of this storm.

"Hurricane Charley is a very compact storm. At landfall it was about twenty-five miles wide, so unless you are in the path of the storm you will not be impacted by the strongest winds of the eyewall. If you are in the path of Charley, be ready for a Category 1 or 2 storm-force winds. It is beginning to lose some steam but remember it made landfall as a Category 4 storm with winds in excess of 145 miles per hour. Even if the wind speeds drop by fifty miles an hour that still means Charley is a Category 2 hurricane," Terry said.

Nick wiped his forehead. "Damn, that is terrible."

The man on the radio continued, "Even if the storm weakens considerably, we are looking at potential wind gusts of one hundred and fifteen miles an hour in and around Orlando."

A deafening boom made both of them flinch. Steph jumped up and opened the door to the closet and ran over to the window. A white glow came from a few streets over. "Nick, come here!"

Chapter 18 - Deer in the Headlights

Jack grabbed Ronnie's elbow and marched her out of the room. Mathias followed and tried to smile but it came across as a look of pain. They crossed the house, exited a back door, and walked across the cobblestone courtyard toward the stables. Jack gave instructions to a stable lad while Ronnie and Mathias stood uneasily in the courtyard waiting. The wind shifted directions and she could smell horse manure. It reminded her of the moment she arrived here in this time. The sky was gray and a faint odor of something weird caught her attention. It smelled like pollution, but these were cleaner times, weren't they?

Ronnie shuffled her feet and waited for Mathias to say something. After a few minutes of uncomfortable silence, she asked, "Where is he taking us?"

"I do not know. Verever it is I varrant it vill not be a pleasant afternoon," Mathias said while running a hand through his dark hair.

"Is he taking us to Lord Barton's?" Her stomach clenched. She could not bear to see that horrible little man again.

Mathias shook his head. "Fräulein, I fear zat Jack has stopped acting as if he vas a rational man. Zis is a vim, verever vee are going it has not been planned. I am just pleased zat I am by your side." He smiled weakly at her.

"Me too, Mathias." Why Jack had included Mathias on the little journey was not clear, but knowing he was with her helped calm her nerves a little.

Mathias and Ronnie made small talk both too nervous to say much. Ronnie's mind was spinning at the possibilities of where they were going. About ten minutes later Jack approached and then motioned them to enter a small carriage pulled by two bay horses. The driver took her hand, helping her up the two steps into the coach. He opened a small door and she squeezed the ridiculous pannier'd hips through the door sideways, then tried to adjust to the small space and sit down. The seats were light brown shiny leather with brass studs along the bottom edge. It reminded her of something out of the reruns of *Bonanza* she had watched as a kid with her massive crush on Little Joe.

Mathias climbed in, ducking his large frame to fit in the small door and sat down opposite of her with their knees tangling. She moved over to one side to give him more room. Jack climbed in and sat next to Mathias since Ronnie and the dress took up the entire seat on her side. Jack looked stunned—like a deer in the headlights. It was much better than his angry look, but it scared her nearly as much.

Mathias turned toward Jack. "Jack, *bitte*, you really must listen to your sister's account of vat took place ven Lord Barton called today,"

"Cousin, this is not of any import," Jack waved his hand dismissively. "In but a few paltry hours Regina has destroyed my months, if not *years*, of effort in making this marriage a reality. I have no further patience with either of you. I have only one question, to which I shall soon find an answer."

"You have but one question? Vat, pray tell, is zis vitally important question, Jack?" Mathias shook his head. "Vill you ask vat has happened to Regina? Or are you desirous to know vat vile indignities and insults she has had to endure because of your match?"

"I most certainly will not! Now the subject is closed. I do not care to discuss it further," Jack said, turning to face out the window.

"Where are you taking us?" Ronnie asked.

Jack grunted. His face was red and his mouth was a line of anger. She decided to let him have the last word for now. After half an hour the driver stopped the carriage at a private home just outside of the city. The driver stepped down from the carriage and walked up the pathway to the small shabby cottage. He knocked on the door and waited. Ronnie's heart raced. She tried to catch Mathias's eye, but he would not look at her. The door opened and a heavyset man in black robes and a white collar stood there looking puzzled. They were too far from the door to hear the conversation but the driver gestured toward the carriage and the man stepped outside and motioned for them to come in.

Ronnie's legs were shaking as she made her way down the path toward the house, still sore from the spanking but more than that, her nerves were getting the better of her. Jack gripped her upper arm and Mathias walked behind her.

"Greetings, good Father," Jack said to the man, letting go of Ronnie's arm to offer his hand.

"Good day to you sir," the man answered. "I am Father Blenheim. Please come in, if you will, Mr. Ingram."

They entered the small stone cottage. The floor was made of compacted soil and it was sparsely furnished, a big contrast to the Ingram Estate.

"I am Jack Ingram and let me introduce my sister, Miss Regina Ingram," Jack said. He waved toward Mathias. "And this gentleman is my cousin, Mathias Stohl."

Father Blenheim smiled and shook Jack's hand, then Mathias's, and nodded to her. "How can I be of service to you, Mr. Ingram?"

"Father Blenheim, I am here today to ask if you will examine my sister. I fear that she may be possessed by evil spirits."

"What?" Ronnie caught Mathias's eye and saw the deer-in-the-headlights look Jack had in the carriage as if Jack had handed it to him.

"I would be happy to provide such a service, sir. I would just ask, can you afford the fee, Mr. Ingram?" Father Blenheim said.

They spent a few minutes negotiating the cost and Ronnie watched Mathias. He finally looked at her and mouthed, "Be careful." What did that mean? Careful of what?

With negotiations complete, Father Blenheim lit a candle and held it close to her face. "Child, do you know why you are here?" The man's double chin shook as he spoke and she could smell his foul breath. Greasy salt and pepper hair was visible under his black velvet hat.

"No," she said.

"I will examine you to find out if you are indeed possessed by the devil," he said.

Ronnie could feel the heat rise in her cheeks. She put her hands to her face and looked at Mathias. He looked away, shaking his head. "The devil?" she said not at all liking this turn of events.

Jack lowered his eyes and said, "Catherine is frightened of you, Regina. She can see that you are not the same girl we knew yesterday."

"Jack, the accident has made me lose my memory, that is all," Ronnie's throat tightened, making her voice sound shrill.

"No child! You are *not* the docile lamb I have known my whole life. Inside …" He pointed at her chest. "You are obstinate, difficult, and unruly. And I confess that it scares me, Regina. I have to know if the devil has taken possession of your mortal soul. I need to protect my son, indeed all my family, from such threats."

Ronnie now took the deer-in-the-headlights mask from Mathias. What would they do if they thought the devil was inside of her?

"Jack, come now, zis is going too far," Mathias said. "I fear I must object to this examination."

"It is no matter, Mathias. She is my sister and I will decide what must be done," Jack said. "I wanted you to bear witness as you have been in her company of late and so you will need to take care."

"I have no vorries about Fräulein Regina's mental state. I believe zis is cruel and wholly unreasonable to put her through such an examination, Jack!"

"Gentlemen, Miss Ingram," Father Blenheim interrupted, "if you please, good sirs, in situations such as this it is imperative that we make all haste to fight the demons you fear may be present. We must begin at once. Let us pray." Father Blenheim looked at Mathias, who walked toward the three of them and stood between her and Jack. "The Lord's Prayer." He held Ronnie's gaze for a second and then looked at Jack.

Ronnie knew the Lord's Prayer. She said it every night each summer when she would stay with her grandparents. The men bowed their heads and began reciting.

They all delivered the prayer in unison. She looked down at her fist, her thumbs were digging into her fingers and she tried to relax. "Our Father *who art* in Heaven."

The men said, "Our Father *in which* art in Heaven."

Father Blenheim stopped and looked at her. "Miss Ingram, do you know this prayer?"

"I do," she said, intimidated by the three men staring at her.

Father Blenheim continued and they all recited along with him. Ronnie could feel a trickle of sweat running down her back as she continued, "Hallowed be Thy Name. Thy Kingdom come, Thy will be done *on* Earth as it is in Heaven."

The men said, "Hallowed be Thy name. Thy Kingdom come, Thy will be done, *in* Earth as it is in Heaven."

Mathias's eyes were huge and she looked away, not liking what she saw there—fear. She said, "Give us this day our daily bread; and forgive us our trespasses as we forgive those *who* trespass against us."

The men said in unison, "Give us this day our daily bread. And forgive us our trespasses, as we forgive *them that* trespass against us."

Close to tears now, Ronnie hoped there were no more differences between the modern and Anglican versions. She was nearly out of breath, her heart was beating so fast.

They continued, "And lead us not into temptation, but deliver us from evil." Father Blenheim looked at her as he said the word evil.

They all said in unison, "For Thine is the Kingdom, and the power, and the glory, for ever and ever. Amen."

Ronnie took a deep breath and looked at Jack, trying to gauge how bad of a mess she was in. There were only a few minor differences but it had seemed monumental to them. Jack would not look at her.

"Miss Ingram, I will need you to remove your gown," the priest said to her while taking a step closer.

Ronnie stepped backward with her hands up. "My gown? Why do I have to take off my gown?" Mathias looked away, with his hand jamming through his hair.

"Let me help you, Regina, dear sister," Jack said reaching for the massive skirts of the gown.

"No!" She pulled away from him. "Tell me why I need to remove my gown," she said, her voice sounding higher and angrier than she had intended.

"Because I said you must, that is why," Jack told her. "Do you see how it is, Father? Last week she would have obeyed me. There would have been no discussions, no questions."

"Father," Ronnie said, "please tell me."

"Miss Ingram," Father Blenheim said, "My child, you will please make yourself still. My experience in these spiritual matters tells me that I have to look upon your skin for the marks of the devil. That is all I will do."

Mathias took a few steps toward them, fists clenched. "Sir, zis is preposterous."

"Mathias, he will merely look upon her skin. It will do her no harm." Jack said, taking a step toward Ronnie.

"I don't have any marks of the devil on me. That is ridiculous!" she said, feeling completely out of control. If Mathias had looked relaxed she would not have this feeling of impending doom. How could she make this stop?

Jack reached for her dress again and Ronnie yelled, "No! I'll do it!" She loosened the laces and pulled the gown over her head, getting it caught momentarily on her shoulders, and Mathias helped her pull

106

it over her head. He took the dress and put it on the back of a chair. She shivered in the cool air of the cottage as it pulled the warmth from her body. Standing stick straight in front of the three men in her petticoats, corset, and ridiculous pannier, she tried to keep her teeth from chattering.

The movement of Mathias wiping at his face caught her eye. Oh God, he was crying. This was really bad.

"Miss Ingram, if you please, would you lift your right arm and pull back your shift?" Father Blenheim held the candle toward her. His hand was shaking a bit, making the melted wax jiggle.

She pulled the light linen material up to her shoulder to reveal her entire arm. The priest held the candle up to her skin and looked closely. It reminded her of a skin cancer check. He pulled out a small piece of parchment and made a mark on it—a figure he drew, indicating the mole she had on her wrist. She looked at Regina's arm. It was slender and quite pale, a contrast to her own tanned arm.

Her mind raced. Marks of the devil? She had heard this phrase before but couldn't remember the context. Ronnie took a few deep breaths to try to calm down.

"Please uncover your left arm." He held the candle close to her and she saw it shake even more. The man's fleshy face was near hers but he would not meet her gaze. She pulled the sleeve up to her shoulder and watched as a small drop of hot wax fell onto her arm.

"Damn it!" she yelled as the wax burned her skin and immediately regretted the words. The three men looked at her, mouths agape. The priest made a strange hand signal with pinky and forefinger raised while holding the ring and middle fingers down with his thumb.

She grabbed the wax that was already hardening and peeled it off. It left a red mark the size of a quarter. "Sorry," she said, looking at Mathias.

Father Blenheim stood up and made the sign of the cross and mumbled a prayer that Ronnie could not understand. He pulled out the parchment and wrote for a minute. Ronnie wiped her sweaty hands on her shift and tried to catch Mathias's eye. He would not look at her.

"I need to complete the examination," the priest said. He was not addressing her any more, but probably talking to the devil he thought was inside.

"Gentleman, if you please, you will want to avert your gaze," he said, turning his head, making the rolls of fat on his neck bunch. Father

Blenheim stood behind her. She could feel his hot breath on the nape of her neck. He moved the shift to uncover her back.

"Mr. Ingram, I will need you to see this," Father Blenheim said.

"What is it, Father?" Jack said, walking closer. The priest held the candle toward her shoulder blade.

"Oh," Jack said.

Father Blenheim stepped away from Ronnie and made the sign of the devil again. "I need to examine the rest of your body." He didn't make eye contact. "Lift your petticoats," he said motioning her to turn around.

Deep breath, let it out. The priest pulled up a chair and sat down, making his huge stomach shake with the impact. His face was expressionless. Ronnie's legs shook. How much further would this go?

She pulled the white linen up, revealing her stockings and garters. Father Blenheim pushed the stockings down. The candle lit up her skin and Father Blenheim struggled past his fat belly to bend down to get a closer look.

"Now turn around," he said, "and pull your skirts higher if you please."

She turned around to face him and lifted her skirts as far as modesty would allow. Ronnie glanced down at Regina's legs to see if there were any offending marks, but all she saw was pale white skin.

"Father, have you nearly finished?" Mathias was facing the wall.

"Higher," the priest said, a little too loud this time. "Can we remove her pannier, sir?" Father Blenheim said to Jack.

Mathias said, "*Nein*, Father, zat you may not remove."

She pulled the fabric up and pressed it between her legs, exposing her upper thighs, but not allowing him to see more nakedness. If she pulled it any higher he would see everything since she had no underwear on. Heat rose in her cheeks again. This bastard was getting off looking at her.

"Miss, I will need to see more. You must move your hands so I can finish my exam," Father Blenheim said, almost breathless.

"No, I will not!" Ronnie let the petticoats fall covering herself, feeling completely violated by the pervy old man.

Mathias walked to her side. "Zat should not be necessary. You have surely seen enough, Father."

"I will decide what is enough," Jack said. "Mathias, I brought you here to show you what kind of spawn of the devil poor Regina has become. She is not the sweet Christian child you used to know. Have regard for how she treats me! Have regard for how she is defiant even to the good Father."

"Jack, she is a lady of gentle birth, from a highborn family. Zere is no reason to uncover her innocence in zis shameful vay, in front of gentlemen," Mathias said while taking another step closer to her.

"By all that's holy, do you not see that this is the very thing that I am trying to show you, Mathias! There is someone else lurking inside of our sweet innocent Regina. Indeed, Catherine noticed it that first moment she saw her after the accident. The queer words she uses that we know not where they come from. That is why she fainted and had to be taken to her room."

"She fainted because you were horrible to her, Jack," Ronnie said, not able to hold back. "You insulted her and knocked her down with your harsh words."

"How dare you!" Jack grabbed her right arm and jerked her toward him, lifting his other hand to hit her. Her free hand went up to protect her face.

"*Nein!*" Mathias yelled.

When the blow never came she looked up to see Mathias and Jack struggling.

"You vill not abuse Fräulein Regina again!" Mathias said, holding Jack's wrists, keeping him from striking out at him.

"Unhand me!" Jack struggled feebly against Mathias.

Father Blenheim clutched his parchment and quill and stepped away from the fray. "Mr. Ingram, please desist from wrestling in my house. I cannot have you breaking my few humble possessions."

"I cannot stand by and let you hurt her again!" Mathias said as Jack's face reddened. "I vas not highborn, my beginnings vere indeed humble, but I vas taught that it is a sin to abuse vomen." Mathias let go of Jack and stepped back with his hands raised in front of him. Jack lunged forward and threw a punch at Mathias's head. Mathias blocked it and said, "You do not vant to strike me, Cousin."

"God's blood, I will strike you for interfering in my affairs!" Jack threw another punch and Mathias deftly dodged it.

Ronnie jumped out of the way of the two men fighting for control, her heart beating madly.

"I vill not stand by and let you hurt her again. Nor will I let a priest gaze upon her virgin flesh." Mathias lunged forward and took Jack by surprise. He stumbled backward. "Fräulein Regina is a lady and deserves to be treated as such."

Jack shoved Mathias and made him stumble backward, but he caught himself, stopping short of the fireplace.

Father Blenheim grabbed his mug from the table and stepped away. "Mr. Ingram! I must insist that you must stop this abominable behavior in my home."

Everyone ignored Father Blenheim. Ronnie stood shivering and eyed her gown that had been thrown over the chair. If she had it on she would have already run out the door.

"Mathias, good cousin, do you not see what she has become? The devils that possess her have allowed her to put you under her spell. She is a conniving enemy who is set to make you throw your life away! And what will you have as a result?" Jack said.

"Satisfaction!" Mathias caught Jack squarely on the jaw with a right hook.

Jack's head swung around and he stumbled backward. He stood dazed for a few seconds. "Cousin, you have struck me! How dare you!" He put his fists up in a fighting stance.

"Cousin, are you too blind to see zat she is not an enemy? She is a lovely young lady who does not deserve to be abused." Mathias swung a fist at Jack's head but missed. Jack returned a blow and hit Mathias in the stomach.

Mathias paused momentarily absorbing the blow, then exploded upward, hitting Jack in the jaw with an uppercut. Jack crumpled to the floor like a rag doll, landing inelegantly with arms akimbo. Mathias stood over Jack with eyes wide and hands ready to fight.

"Holy crap!" Ronnie yelled.

"Mr. Ingram!" Father Blenheim cried out and knelt down at his side. "Mr. Ingram wake up."

Chapter 19 - Questions

"Fräulein Regina," Mathias said. "Put your gown on, vee are leaving!"

Ronnie pulled the gown over her head. She reached behind and made an attempt at tightening the laces.

Mathias pulled at the laces and spun her around. "Fräulein Regina, come *mit* me!"

"What about my payment!" Father Blenheim shouted after them. "Who is going to pay for my services?"

"Settle it with him," Ronnie said pointing at Jack. "He's staying here for a while." Mathias grabbed her hand and they ran out the front door toward the waiting carriage.

"Sir," the driver said, stunned at their sudden appearance.

Mathias climbed up onto the driver's bench, grabbed the man by the lapels, and deposited him gently on the street. "We will be borrowing Mr. Ingram's coach for a few hours."

"I do not think so Mr. Stohl. I … I …" The driver said adjusting his lapels.

Mathias helped Ronnie into the cabin part of the carriage. "Make yourself comfortable, fräulein."

She sat back against the seat inside the covered carriage, adjusting the pannier, and stared in disbelief as the driver tried to climb back on the carriage.

Mathias pulled him off and said, "Sorry my friend, I recommend you find your employer inside zee cottage." He climbed up on the driver's bench and flicked the reins to urge the horses forward. Ronnie slid back against the seat, stunned at the turn of events. She glanced behind hoping Jack wasn't chasing them but the road was empty. Even the driver was gone.

After a few minutes of seeing nothing but empty road behind them, Ronnie began to relax. Mathias had been incredible, knocking Jack out, but where were they heading? How would she figure out how to get back home?

The noise of the carriage prevented her from asking any of the hundred or so questions that came to mind. What would Jack do? Would she need another hurricane to get back to Florida? She sat silently watching the eighteenth-century London landscape pass by as her mind circled around the unknowns like a vulture above a carcass. Coaches, men on horseback, people in old-fashioned clothes passed in a blur, her mind too much in turmoil to take it all in.

Tears welled up and Ronnie frantically wiped at them. It was such a relief to be free of Jack and the prison the Ingram Estate had become. The fear of being stuck there clung to her but its grip had lessened with Mathias's actions to get her free. It had all happened so fast. Had Mathias thought this through or was this a whim like Jack taking her to Father Blenheim's? How had she jumped through time and across an ocean to London? How the hell was she supposed to get back? The watch seemed like the only link to her past and that was no longer in her possession. Damn Jack had screwed that up. She wasn't even in her own body for Christ's sake. None of it made any sense.

The carriage slowed down and stopped alongside a row of shops. Mathias climbed down from the driver's bench and opened the door. He gave her a grim expression as he took her hand and she made her way down the few steps to the packed dirt street.

"Fräulein Regina. I am utterly sorry for putting you through zat. I …"

"Mathias," she took his hand and squeezed. "You were amazing. Thank you so much for defending me."

He returned the squeeze and released her hand. "Fräulein Regina, I vill need to carefully consider all zat has happened—everything has been so sudden. Zere is an inn just along the road. Vee vill take supper and talk of vat can be done." His eyes wouldn't meet hers.

Ronnie and Mathias walked in an awkward silence down to the end of the row of buildings to a small coaching inn, a building with timber beams on the outside and a tall steeply sloping roof. It was dark inside, but the atmosphere was perfect for staying hidden from anyone looking for her. The aroma that filled the room was a mixture of stale beer and hot bread, the former reminding her of her old haunts in college. They walked toward the back, passing a few men near the long counter area, and chose a corner table away from everyone. A man approached the table and Mathias ordered for them both.

Ronnie had so many things to ask Mathias but she was suddenly too shy to say much of anything. Everything had just changed for both of them, her situation improving dramatically, but his now appreciably worse. It was hard for her to face him, knowing she asked for this, but hadn't really thought through what it would mean for him.

"Fräulein Regina, I have to most humbly beg your forgiveness," Mathias said.

"Why? Mathias, you've done so much for me. I should be apologizing for putting you in this situation." She couldn't help but smile at him, she was feeling a mixture of giddiness about being alone with him, and nervousness about how to proceed. How would she tell him the truth? Would they figure out a way to get her back home or would she be on the run with him in this strange world?

"Fräulein Regina. You do say the most unusual things," Mathias said smiling at her.

Ronnie felt her face go hot, the accusations from Jack about her odd behavior still fresh in her mind. "I'm sorry."

"Don't misunderstand me, *bitte*! I do not mean zat in an insulting vay. I mean you do not speak like other women I have met. The vords you use. The strange accent. Indeed you are different in a very special way." He leaned in toward her.

"Thank you, Mathias. I don't know how to pay you back for everything you've done for me." She wanted to touch him, to take his hand, but she didn't. Instead, she tried to diminish the everlasting smile pasted on her face.

"Fräulein," he smiled and a deep blush started at his neck. "I have no desire for your thanks. As *Gott* is my vitness I have only done vat I felt in my heart vas right. My fervent hope is zat my actions have not increased the danger you are in."

She smiled at him warmed by the tenderness in his words. "I'm just glad to be away from Jack. I think that was the biggest danger—staying near him."

"Regina," he said softly, reaching out to take her hand. "I swear I vill protect you from your brother. I do not have much to offer, except my vord as a gentleman zat I vill make sure he never lays a hand on you again."

She was surprised at the rough solidness of his hand. Very different than Jeffrey's manicured hands. "You were amazing back there, defending me and then …" The tenderness in his expression melted her. "Punching Jack. Did you see how he crumpled to the floor?" Ronnie said.

A small smile lit his eyes. "It vas not my intention to put him on zee ground. I had no idea he vas as delicate as fine chinaware."

She laughed. "You were brilliant. And Father Blenheim desperate for his payment as we left. What a horrible greedy man!"

Mathias laughed, his dark eyes sparkling in the low light of the inn, reminding her of the night she met him. Doctor Wiggams had been so rude and he had laughed it off with all the confidence in the world. The waiter returned and placed two steaming plates and two pints of something brown and foamy in front of them.

"I hope you like fish pie," he said, carving into it with a knife and shoveling a huge bite into his mouth.

Ronnie wasn't sure what fish pie was but it didn't really matter. It was food and she was starving. She cut into it letting out a swirl of steam and took a bite. Oranges, fish, and a few mystery items mingled on her tongue. Raisins? It was really tasty with a thick lard crust. "Thank you, Mathias. It's really good."

They settled into the meal, both quiet for a few minutes. She watched Mathias as he ate and wondered where he would take her. An image of his big arms wrapped around her protectively gave her a thrill, followed by a twinge of guilt about Jeffrey. Those thoughts were shoved aside, as she didn't want to ruin the moment.

"Jack will be furious when he wakes up. What will he do, Mathias?" Ronnie imagined the fury Jack would feel when he realized they were gone.

"I do not know what Jack will do." He looked up at the ceiling and sighed dramatically. "I could not bear another minute of zee priest leering at your nakedness. Zee vay he behaved vas not zee vay a man of God should ..." He slammed his hand down on the table and looked away, his lips disappearing into his angry expression.

Ronnie jumped, surprised at the noise and his vehemence.

"I could not allow it to continue. And Jack threatening to strike you. He has never been a violent man toward you before yesterday." He took a long draft of the drink.

"Mathias, I have to ask you something,"

He stopped in mid-gulp looking at her over the mug. "Hmmm?"

"What was that about the devil's marks back there at Father Blenheim's?"

He set his mug on the table and sighed, leaning back against the dark wooden chair. "Father Blenheim is a vitch finder, and a mangy one at zat."

"A witch finder?" she did not like the sound of that.

"They provide evidence to convict people of vitchcraft. Unfortunately, it is most common to convict the innocent." He pressed his lips together in a frown. "And judging by zee man's wretched dwelling, not a particularly successful one. Jack must have been desperate to seek out zee services of such a man."

"Oh my—" She stopped short of saying God. "Mathias, they can't convict me of being a witch, there are laws against that. Is he going to put fraud charges on me?"

He rubbed the stubble along his jaw and leaned back against the chair. "Regina, I do not know vat law you are speaking of, but a few months ago a voman was convicted of vitchcraft."

"She was? Here in London?" she leaned back in the chair biting her lip,

"Yes, she was hung down zee road at Tyburn. Zere vas such a spectacle made, as you can imagine. Zee crowds vere horrendous," he said, pain showing in his eyes.

Another difference in history, just like the United French uprising. This one affecting her more personally, though. Ronnie and Steph had visited Crieff, Scotland where in her time the last witch was convicted in 1715. There had been a law passed in 1735, if she remembered correctly, preventing trials for witchcraft in Great Britain.

If Jack was gathering evidence to convict her as a witch she was in a lot of danger. What the hell had she gotten into? There had to be a way back to Florida before this got too far along.

Chapter 20 - Seeing the Seer

Mathias took a long draft of his ale again and set it down. He leaned forward, closer to Ronnie. "Jack has started the vitchcraft proceedings by collecting evidence today at Father Blenheim's cottage." Mathias combed his hand through his hair. "I do not know how committed he is, but I suspect since vee have left his company on difficult terms he may be a bit more serious about taking further steps now. I sincerely hope I have not made things vorse for you."

"What could Jack do with Father Blenheim's evidence?" she asked, then picked up the mug in front of her. It was cold and left a trail of bitter hoppy flavor on her tongue.

He leaned forward looking directly into her eyes. "Vith the right evidence he could take you to court for a vitch trial and if you vere convicted ..." He crossed his arms, leaning back again.

"Witch trial?" She sat back in the chair and looked down at her food no longer hungry. Flashes of the Salem witch trials superimposed on the fish pie. "What is the punishment for being convicted as a witch?"

"If one is convicted zee sentence is hanging or burning," he said while covering his mouth, pain showing in his eyes. "Believe me, I could not sit idly back and vatch Jack build a case against you."

"Tell me why the priest was doing all of that. What was with the drawings and the pointing?" She could feel her cheeks getting hot with the memory of the man examining her bare flesh.

His hand ran through his hair again. "Zey vere looking for marks of zee devil."

"Marks of the devil? That's what the Father said, but what does that mean?"

"Spots, moles, rashes. I confess as I understand it, for all I know zey could find anything and call it a devil's mark." He took another bite of the fish pie and wiped his mouth with a napkin, holding it there for a second.

"Why would they do that? I don't get it."

"The reasoning of zee Church is a devil's mark is any mark on your body vere zey claim zee devil suckles you and makes you his slave. Its presence means zat you are a witch."

She blanched. "That is disgusting! Who comes up with this crap?"

116

"Regina, you use the strangest phraseology. Of course, it is not my belief zat you are a vitch, and I am not persuaded zat even Jack believes it. However, vitch finders can be very persuasive *mit* a jury, though vat vee think is of little import. If Jack decides, for vatever reason, to pursue zis, he has a mountain of evidence against you." He took another sip of the ale and put the mug down violently, spilling a little. He dabbed at it with the napkin.

"Mathias, what evidence does he have?" Her stomach clenched.

"The mistakes you made when reciting zee Lord's Prayer."

"I was nervous with everyone staring at me." She bit her lip. It was so much worse than she thought.

"Vat is more, he found vitch's marks on your person." He looked away, shifting in his seat. "I am sorry to say it Regina, but zee Church attests zat a vitch is supposed to be unable to say zee Lord's Prayer without making a mistake." His eyes were a shade darker and his mouth was set in a grim expression.

"Is this all it takes to be proven a witch?" she shook her head.

"Regina, trust me. I vill not allow Jack to take you to court." He leaned toward her.

"Where are we going now? We can't go back to Jack's."

"I am taking you to a seer," he said, lifting his pewter mug. He took another drink and it left a small mustache of foam that he wiped with the back of his hand.

"A seer?" Ronnie looked down at the fish pie, her stomach turned.

"A fortune-teller, a soothsayer some call it. I fancy zat we need a broader view of the situation," he said, meeting her eyes and then looking away.

"Okay," she said, shrinking back in her chair.

"Again zis strange vord. Sometimes I find you hard to understand."

"I mean, yes, I think that might help." She had never put much faith in such things as fortune-tellers. Were they better or worse in this time period? "What is she going to tell us?" Her stomach did a flip. How would she ask if there was a way back to 2004?

"I am not entirely certain," he smiled. "Perhaps she can use her special powers to divine the reason vye you do not remember anything zat happened before zee accident."

"Is this seer nearby?" She pushed the innards of the pie around with her fork and identified some more items.

"Indeed, she is, the lady is not too far. We vill have to go in zee carriage. I do not think your shoes are suitable for a long valk."

She wiggled her feet, forgetting what she had on, and remembered the kitten heels that were supposed to excite that horrible Lord Barton. They finished the meal and Mathias walked her back out to the coach.

"Mathias, can I sit next to you up there?" She pointed at the driver's bench area.

"I suppose but you are a lady, you should be protected inside zee carriage," he said.

"I don't care. I want to be near you. We need to talk about the seer. I'm a bit nervous about what to ask."

He took her hand and helped her up the driver's bench, sat down next to her and released the break. "If it begins to rain I vill insist you get inside zee coach, Regina." He looked up at the ominous clouds.

Ronnie felt a spark of excitement at the storm approaching. After all, she came here during a hurricane. The seer and the storm could be her way back! The coach jerked as it moved forward with the horses straining against the weight of the carriage. She relaxed a bit and marveled at the cobblestone-lined streets and small shops with bland signs above the doors. It was absolutely beautiful.

"Do not be nervous about Madam Zangari. She is zee best in London. My sister has consulted her for years," he said looking at her.

A woman was walking with huge panniers under her dress, reminding her of a French cartoon she had seen years ago where all the women were drawn in a way that exaggerated their giant rear ends and bosoms with tiny waists. It seemed about as ridiculous as being thought a witch.

"I urge you to be very forthcoming when speaking to her. If you hold back if you are misleading, she will know and may refuse to help us," he said.

"Oh, that's not intimidating. Nope." She pictured the evil queen from *Snow White*—dark hair, shadowy lined face, poison apple offered by a withered hand.

Mathias laughed. "Please do not fret. I vill make sure it all goes vell for us."

Us? That made her feel better. He wasn't just taking her to a seer. It was about them. She looked at his strong profile. Everything about this man said strength, goodness, and gentleness. She had no idea why she felt so strongly about this but it felt like she had already tested him on these qualities. Had she ever felt this way about Jeffrey? They were close but it was more of a physical closeness than an emotional one. She could trust Mathias with her life she was sure of it. Would she trust Jeffrey with her life?

"I'm hopeful Madam Zangari vill be able to provide some answers. Maybe for my questions as vell." He glanced at her, and back at the road.

"What questions do you have for her, Mathias?" She bit her lip. This had to go well. She needed his help to find a way back home.

"I vant to know vat has happened to you zat you do not know who is Regina." He smiled and held her gaze for just a hair longer than necessary. Then he picked up her hand and kissed it.

A spark ignited in her chest with a wave of excitement. She looked away not wanting him to see how much he had affected her.

"Tell me vat is zee last thing you remember before zee accident?"

"Nothing." But it was a lie. She remembered Jeffrey's hands on her, the bathroom just before she -- what had she done? Gone through a wormhole back in time?

"You do not remember anything before zee accident?" He watched her carefully.

"I don't remember anything from visiting Lord Barton." That much was true. "The first thing I remember is when Jack picked me up and carried me into his carriage. I don't remember anything before that." Anything from this time period that is.

He shifted position so his leg was touching hers. She let it stay there. It felt solid and warm against her, somehow reassuring. They sat in silence for the last few minutes of the ride. Mathias parked the carriage in an alleyway and helped her down. This was it, Ronnie would have to come up with some way to ask Madam Zangari how to get back to Florida. Nerves got the best of her and her mind scrambled for some way to word the request.

Mathias promised a young boy who lived in a nearby house some money when he returned if the boy would keep an eye on the carriage.

He turned to Ronnie, "Vee need to find shelter before the rain starts."

She looked up at the sky. The clouds bubbled and boiled above looking a lot like Hurricane Charley had before Ronnie left her apartment. He took her hand and helped her over a large mud puddle and didn't let go as they continued to walk.

"My sister last saw Madam Zangari just before her daughter was born," Mathias tucked her arm under his. It was chilly out and she enjoyed the warmth of his body.

"Your sister? What did she ask Madam Zangari?"

"She wanted to know if zee baby voud be a son. She was hoping to please her husband *mit* zee news, if it vas so."

Mathias looked down at her as they made their way into an alleyway. *Boom!* A loud crack of thunder made them both jump. A stray cat startled and ran, hopping nimbly over a stone wall and Ronnie looked at the sky. Was this good timing or what? A storm hitting at the very minute she would meet the seer?

Mathias knocked softly on the door to the cottage three times and waited. Ronnie's stomach was in knots. Would this woman be able to help her get back to Florida? The door opened and a middle-aged woman dressed in every possible shade of brown looked at them with haunting black eyes. She looked from Mathias to Ronnie and back while squinting suspiciously.

"Good day madam. I am Mathias Stohl, brother of Maria McConnelly. I vish to have a reading, if you please," he said.

The woman took a step backward and let them in. She stepped into the alley to look both ways before shutting and locking the door behind her.

"Your name is Mathias?" Madam Zangari said with a strange accent.

"Zat is correct, Madam, yes I am Mathias Stohl. I have been here on other occasions *mit* my sister, Maria."

Ronnie watched them exchange facts in short bursts. Mathias towered over the tiny fortune-teller. She seemed to be feeling out the situation. After about ten minutes of discussing Mathias's family ties and connections she finally looked at Ronnie.

"Why are you here with this man?" Madam Zangari's voice was low and raspy, and she sounded angry.

"Uh," she said feeling stupid. "I … I, uh, came here for advice on my situation." Ronnie's hands were sweaty and she wiped them on her skirts.

The woman turned around abruptly and disappeared into another room. Ronnie stared at her in disbelief.

Mathias shrugged his shoulders and smiled weakly. "She is remarkably talented as a fortune-teller, but do not expect drawing-room manners and politeness." Mathias took her elbow and led her into the adjoining room.

The room was musty and dark and in the center sat a table covered in a light tablecloth with a small candle on it. A cupboard holding a few white plates without any other decorations or personal touches was along the wall, near a door. The fire in the fireplace warmed the room and added eerie shadows all around. The door burst open, making Ronnie jump and Madam Zangari appeared holding a tray with a teapot, white teacups, and a small white container. How would she ask about returning to her own time? She still hadn't figured out how to phrase such a question.

Madam Zangari nodded toward the table and told them to sit as she set the tray on a long dark cabinet against the wall. Mathias held a chair out for Ronnie and then pulled up a chair next to her. He squeezed her hand and smiled.

A flutter of brown and two teacups appeared in front of them. A flick of her hand and impatient eyes commanded them to drink. Mathias nodded, picked up his cup, and slurped loudly. Ronnie copied Mathias and sipped the hot liquid. The tea was unsweetened with a strong rich flavor but was almost too hot to drink.

She kept taking small sips. This was not a relaxing cup of tea—it was part of the consultation. A flash of lightning echoed around the room, creating eerie shadows, followed by a loud crack of thunder. Would the storm take her back to Florida?

A strange feeling crept into Ronnie's mind. She could feel Madam Zangari's dark eyes on her and looked up to confirm it. Ronnie suspected this was the way she came up with her words of wisdom, studying clothing, mannerisms, and body language. Hopefully, this would not be a dead end. There had to be a way back home. She glanced at Mathias, who paused briefly in his sipping to give her a reassuring smile. If he trusted Madam Zangari, she must have some merit.

Ronnie's mind raced, running through how she could phrase her questions to this strange woman. It was hard to come up with much. The abrupt comments so far from her didn't leave room for a lot of confidence. The thunder rumbled outside, now sounding farther away. She looked at Mathias and he nodded to her and gulped the remainder of his tea. He set his cup on the table. Ronnie gulped the last bit of tea and put her cup next to Mathias's.

"You will pick up the cup and swirl it three times," she said to Ronnie, who promptly obeyed and set the cup back down. Madam Zangari took the handle and turned it so it pointed at Ronnie. "You are older than you seem." This was true. She was twenty-eight and Regina was eleven years younger. "You are out of place, not comfortable where you are." All true, but that would be true of nearly everyone who came in. Madam Zangari shifted her gaze to Mathias. Ronnie sat back in her chair. Well, that was certainly worth the long trek.

Mathias picked up his cup and swirled it three times and set it down with the handle facing toward his hand. Skinny fingers reached for Mathias's cup. Madam Zangari studied it and without looking up she said, "Her name is Ronnie."

Ronnie gasped and her hand clamped over her mouth. Not once had she said her real name in this time period. There was no way this woman could have guessed that. A chill crawled up her spine and the hairs on the back of her neck rose.

Chapter 21 – Fear and Loathing

Mathias turned in his chair his eyes wide. "Is zis true? Is your name Ronnie?" He grabbed her hand pulling it toward him as if to pull the answer out of her.

Ronnie squeezed his hand and said, "Yes, that is true."

His eyes grew wider still. "But your name is Regina."

"You can tell that from my cup?" Ronnie said to Madam Zangari, her mouth suddenly dry.

"No," Madam Zangari answered, "for me to help the both of you I need her to open up to me, it is vital that she speak honestly. She needs to know I do not play you false."

Ronnie said, "Well, you have my full attention now."

Madam Zangari gave a brief smile. She looked into Mathias's cup at the leftover tea leaves. To Ronnie, it just looked like a clump of wet tea leaves scattered around the inside of the cup.

"See here?" She pointed to the right of the handle. "This is the near future. This is the past." She moved her skinny finger to point to the left. "Your past is peaceful. Your future is full of turmoil and pain."

"Vat else can you tell me, madam?" He combed a nervous hand through his hair.

"You are risking everything you hold dear to you by helping this woman." She looked at Ronnie and squinted her eyes when she said *this woman*. "It might be too late to save yourself, but you are doing the right thing."

Heat rose in Ronnie's cheeks. Oh, God. If she was right something bad was going to happen to Mathias because of his kindness. A sharp pain shot through her head and faded as quickly as it had begun. Rubbing her temples she studied the woman, who seemed to be cast in a deeper shadow than before. Mathias sat back in his chair, a big hand running through his hair again.

"Are you needing anything else then?" Madam Zangari asked. Of course, she had hooked them with what she had told them so far.

"Vee vant to know, *bitte*, vat are vee to do now?" Mathias asked.

Madam Zangari sat back in her chair while crossing her arms across her ample chest. Mathias pulled out a few coins and set them on the table. "What is it that you would like me to use?" she asked. "Cards, palm, something else?"

Mathias looked older now in the dim light, a five o'clock shadow beginning to show, and dark circles under his eyes. "Vat do you think?" he asked Ronnie. "Voud you allow her to read your palm?"

Ronnie nodded and offered her right palm face-up on the table. The blue-green veins on the old woman's hands stood out almost grotesquely in the shadowy room. Another rumble of thunder growled in the distance. The storm continued moving farther away. Was her opportunity slipping away with the clouds?

Madam Zangari gently picked up Ronnie's hand and stroked her palm, looking into Ronnie's eyes and then let go of her hand abruptly. "No!" She pushed the money back at Mathias and stood up and took a few steps away from the table. "I cannot do a palm reading for you."

Mathias stood up fists clenched. "Please, you have to help us!"

Madam Zangari looked at Ronnie and back to Mathias, shaking her head.

"Vee need your help. Please, I beg you," Mathias said.

Ronnie was stunned. If this woman couldn't help them what the hell were they going to do? She could feel the pulse beat on the back of her head where she had landed on it yesterday.

"Please Madam Zangari, we are desperate. You have to help us!" Ronnie's voice got louder and higher as she spoke.

Madam Zangari crossed her arms and looked toward the door. Another loud crack of thunder echoed, making several items in the room vibrate. Her eyes grew larger making her look a lot like Snow White's stepmother.

Mathias reached into his pocket and pulled out a handful of coins. "I implore you, Madam Zangari. Just one more reading. Please help us."

"Why can't you do the palm reading?" Ronnie asked.

Madam Zangari turned a dark gaze on her and spat out, "You have a black spot on your soul."

Mathias sat down hard on his chair. "Vat?"

Ronnie reached out and took his hand, squeezing it. "What does that mean?" Ronnie asked.

"A long, long time ago, something happened," Madam Zangari said.

"Vee have to know vat happened." He looked at Ronnie and her heart nearly stopped when he let go of her hand. What if he wouldn't help her?

Ronnie heard a very small noise from within the adjacent room behind Madam Zangari but she was too intent on the conversation to give it much thought.

"Miss, you are not who you appear to be," Madam Zangari went on. "Someone, a man, is using you for his own advancement. Bad things will continue to happen to you while you are under his spell. Beware of gifts from this person."

"Jack!" Mathias said.

"You are in the gravest danger," Madam Zangari said to Ronnie. "In time you will be set free, but the seeds of your destruction have already been planted."

"The seeds of my destruction?" Ronnie's lip trembled. Would she ever see her mom again?

Mathias stood up and walked the length of the small room and back. "Great heavens madam, what are we to do now?"

"Is there something else you can do for us?" Ronnie asked, desperately hoping she would say yes. She had to know how to get back home.

"Sit down!" Madam Zangari spat, slamming her palm on the table. She glared at them. "There is but one thing I can do. Whether it will work is beyond my powers to know."

"I will do anything," Mathias said and sat back down in his chair but couldn't keep his hands still. They were in his hair, then tapping on the table. The woman tapped her finger on the table too. Mathias reached in his pocket and put more coins in front of her. It was like a payphone. To keep talking you added more money.

Madam Zangari left the room with a swish of brown and returned a minute later with a large white bowl partially filled with water. She set this gently in front of Ronnie, the water rocking back and forth, threatening to spill on the table. She positioned the candle so that Ronnie could see her own reflection in the wide shallow bowl. It was strange to see Regina's face and not her own, blinking back at her. She had a small mouth and big eyes, giving her a doe-like appearance. Loose brown hair framed her face.

"I believe you have a question to which you need an answer." Madam Zangari had returned to her seat across from her.

Ronnie's heart skipped a beat. How would she phrase that question? They would both think she was crazy.

"You must gaze into the bowl and ask the question in your mind. Repeat it and let everything else fade away from you—this room, your friend, and your troubles. Repeat the question but once more and then you must fall into the reflection." The woman must have lit incense or something that gave off a pleasant spicy odor.

Ronnie took a deep breath and let it out, creating ripples on the surface of the water. At least she didn't have to say it out loud. She waited until the water settled and she could see the strange young face reflecting back at her. *How do I get home?* She pictured Jeffery's lab, her apartment, and Steph's smiling face. She repeated the question, making her feel a bit like Dorothy from the *Wizard of Oz.* After a few minutes, she lost herself in the reflection. *How do I get back home?*

Starting from the center of the bowl, overtaking the doe-eyed face, an image of a flame appeared. Was it just a reflection of the candle? It grew larger and made her cough and gasp for air. Her throat squeezed closed and she felt as if she were being strangled.

A mass of yelling people, dirty-faced and angry, dressed in old-fashioned clothes, were in front of her. A terrible feeling of despair, loneliness, and horror overwhelmed her. She took a deep breath, hoping to get air into her lungs but her throat was closed. Ronnie clawed at her throat. Gasping and terror rising, she couldn't breathe and the angry voices were louder. Forcing her eyes away from the bowl, she saw Mathias staring back at her, his mouth open in surprise. Icy dread spread through her bones. She felt like crying, but the feeling was beginning to fade.

"Regina, tell me vat did you see?" Mathias asked.

Ronnie tried to clear her head of the image and form words to describe the vision. Before she could, she saw a man walk through the door behind Madam Zangari. It was Jeffrey! The dread switched to excitement. He had come for her and could get her back home! "What are you doing here?" she said, standing and smiling. Mathias and Madam Zangari turned toward the door.

Mathias stood up and started toward the man, fists clenched and a furious look on his face. Ronnie was baffled. How did Mathias know Jeffrey? Why would he be mad at him? She looked at the man again and realized it was not Jeffrey.

Chapter 22 - A Blast

Nick cradled his arm as he got up to walk to the window. His shoulder positioned out of place. "Where the hell is that coming from?" He stood next to Steph and looked out onto the glowing light in the midst of Hurricane Charley.

"You heard that noise right?" Steph's heart was beating fast, making her short of breath. Who lived on that street? She racked her brain trying to come up with a face, a family that was over there. "Oh my God, I wonder which house is burning." If the fire spread to her house they would have to leave in the middle of the storm. Where would they go?

"Steph, the wind is blowing this direction. I hope the rain puts it out." The worry was written on his face.

"Do you think anyone died? Oh, this is really bad." She wiped a tear away. What if the blaze came this way and Hamish was too injured to get away from the fire? She wondered what that stupid precious kitty was thinking out in the middle of the storm.

"I sure hope not. Come on. Let's get away from the window," he said. "The storm is really picking up now. We're likely to have more trees down and who knows ..." He squeezed her shoulder, "Maybe a tornado."

Steph's stomach was in knots. "The rain will put the fire out, right?" Steph followed Nick back into the closet and closed the door behind her. Would this tiny closet be enough to protect them from a tornado?

"Steph," he looked at her, pain evident in his expression. "That was an explosion."

"It was? Are you sure?" In all of the horrible scenarios of the storm's wrath, Steph never dreamed of an explosion. Her stress ratcheted up a few more notches.

"The one thing that I can't get out of my mind is what caused it." He winced as he lifted his arm and let it fall back down again.

"What do you think caused it?" Steph asked.

He looked away. "I'm not sure. But the first thing I thought of was natural gas."

"Oh, no. Nick?" She covered her mouth. That kind of fire would not go out with the rain. That was the kind of fire that burned down whole neighborhoods.

"Yeah, a big *oh no*. A fire that won't go out until they turn off the gas." He opened another water bottle and sucked it down, the plastic crackling as it emptied.

"And the wind is blowing this way?" Steph stood up and opened the closet door. The room was lighter than before and the glowing had taken up more of the night sky. "Nick, it's getting closer!"

Her doorbell rang and she could hear pounding on the door.

"Who the hell is that?" Nick said.

"Come with me, I don't want to answer it alone," Steph's heart was beating madly and she was short of breath.

Nick reluctantly got up and followed her out to the front door. She stopped in front of it and waited for him to open it. She looked out of her front window but couldn't see anything in the pitch blackness of the storm.

"Who is it?" he yelled with his face pressed to the door.

"Stephie, it's Mimi, please let us in!" Mimi lived behind her house in the direction of the fire.

Steph opened the door and stared into the drenched faces of Mimi and her granddaughter, Felicia. "What are you doing out in this?" They looked like drowned rats with their hair plastered to their heads.

"Steph, our phones weren't working and the house behind us is on fire. It's heading this way!" The granddaughter was in her mid-twenties and held a terrified Chihuahua in her arms.

Steph introduced Nick and they exchanged uncomfortable hellos all around. Nick pulled his phone out of his pocket and tried to get a signal. It had been soaked a few times now so it wasn't even turning on.

"The flames came right up to our fence and we watched it light on fire. I grabbed Sugar," Mimi nodded at the dog, "and Felicia and I got out of there fast. Can you try your phone? We have to call the fire department." She mussed the fur on the dog's face, wiping water off her head.

"Oh, I'll get it." Steph got up to find her cell phone. She had not tried to use it yet. It was in her purse that she had left in her closet and dialed 911. There was no signal. She picked up the landline and got no dial tone.

128

Steph walked back. "No signal on either phone. Ladies come with me to my spacious closet." They all went into the master bedroom and looked out the window. "What's it like out there?" Steph asked Felicia.

"Trees down everywhere. It was hard to walk the wind is blowing so badly." Her voice shook and her lower lip quivered when she talked.

"The fire is getting closer. Look I can see the glow through the windows in your neighbor's house," Nick said. "What's our plan of action if it gets close?"

Everyone looked at Steph. "Well, I don't know. I guess we're going to a neighbor's house. We're certainly not going very far in this storm!" Steph felt a giddy panic pressing upward from her stomach.

A loud roaring drowned out their voices and they all smashed into the walk-in closet. They stood and looked uneasily at the ceiling. Steph put the lid on the box of supplies and asked Mimi to sit there. Felicia sat with the dog on her lap in the corner. Nick stood near the door looking massively uncomfortable. He was lying down just a while ago feeling nauseous.

"Well this is cozy," Nick said rubbing the stubble on his chin. He opened the door and peeked out at the neighbor's house. "Steph, we have a problem."

She stepped gingerly over Mimi's legs toward Nick.

"The neighbor's house is on fire." He opened the door a bit wider so she could see. Sure enough, the wind blew smoke and sparks off the neighbor's house toward Steph's. The entire sky was lit up, an eerie orange glow flickered in the dark night.

"We've gotta do something, what if those people are burning up in there?" Nick said.

Steph felt weak in the knees and leaned against the doorjamb. "What can we do, Nick? You're not going to pull anyone out with your arm like that."

"Steph, I've got another arm and maybe they just don't know where to go." He looked back out at the fire and put his hand on the window.

"And maybe they're not even there? Maybe they've left town or were on vacation or something." She had been frantically getting the house ready for the storm. "I just can't remember if they were here or not." She had seen the kids in the pool occasionally, but not really spoken to the parents. "Mimi, were your neighbor's home today?"

"Yes, I think so. I was so busy bringing in all the pool toys and furniture I wasn't really paying attention," Mimi said. "Yes, I waved to little Melody when she was swimming." She pushed the wet gray hair out of her eyes.

"I've gotta do something. Steph. I'm not just going to stand here and let them burn up." Nick turned away from her.

"What the hell are you going to do?" Steph grabbed his good arm. "You can't go out there Nick, you just can't."

Mimi looked at them from the closet door. "It's too bad out there. We almost got brained by a huge branch coming down. Barely missed us." She shook her head, her bronze-colored eyes huge and watery. "Nick, please. You have to stay here."

Steph knew that look. He was determined. "I'll just slip out your back door and …" He stepped further away from Steph.

"Oh no ye don't Nick. I'm not gonna have you go off and get hurt worse. You're here because I asked you here, you're my responsibility," Steph said while holding firmly to the good arm.

"I'm my own responsibility, Steph." He pulled his arm away. "You're not the boss of me." They had been saying that to each other since the first week they met as a joke. This time it rang true and the irony was not lost on her.

He walked over to the front door with Steph close on his heels. He pulled the flashlight out of his pants and shined the light around.

"Nick, really? You're gonna risk your life for some people you don't even know?" He was infuriating. How could he go out in the storm after it had already broken two of his bones, maybe more?

"Steph, it's not about me. If I can help them I have to do it. They have kids. How can you just wait here and hope for the best?" He walked to the kitchen and she followed him.

"Nick!" She wasn't going to lose him. She already thought he had died once today. "I can't let you."

"Um, Steph, I think it's more like you can't stop me." He grabbed a dish towel, and wrapped it around the one already on his gory finger and held it in place with the rest his hand.

"Then I'm going with you," Steph said her hands clenched at her sides. "I can carry a kid if I need to and make damn sure you don't do anything too stupid."

He stopped and looked at her. "No. I don't want you to come." He went to the door and slipped on his track shoes, not bothering to unlace them. "Steph, you stay here and look after Mimi and Felicia. Keep an eye on the fence. If it catches fire you'll not have very long to get out of the house. That wind is blowing the fire quickly and it's fueled by gas."

He put his hand on the door handle. She leaned against the door blocking his way. "I'm coming and you're gonna have to deal with it."

Nick held her by her shoulders. "You are going to stay here, Steph." He stopped and held his arm, face twisting in agony.

"Nick, seriously, look at you. Your arm is a mess, don't do this!" She was nearly crying. She couldn't stand by and watch him go back out in the storm. It had already damaged him enough.

He walked briskly to the window, cupping his good hand to see out the window. "Shit! Shit!"

"What!" Steph said.

"I can see a flashlight beam in the house. I'm going over there. You stay here in case I need you to pull me out."

"Oh my God, are you sure?" Steph said looking out the window.

"Yes!" He slipped out of the door and was engulfed by the rain and wind.

Steph cupped her hands on the kitchen window. She couldn't make out his form at all. "Goddammit, Nick!" Steph ran back to the bedroom and looked out her window. The entire sky was orange now and she could see a blurry image of her yard and the neighbor's house. The room smelled of smoke.

Steph went to the closet. "Nick went to the neighbor's house to help them escape the fire."

"No!" Mimi stood up and went to the window. "I can see him. Look there he is!"

Steph looked out her bedroom window. "He's going in the house!" Steph cupped her hands to block out the glare of the lantern and the glow it cast around the room.

Nick disappeared inside the house. Steph looked at her watch. God she wished he had stayed here. They all stood there looking out the window waiting, hoping he would return unharmed.

Chapter 23 - Queen Anne's Revenge

A strange buzzing noise echoed in Jack's mind. His face hurt. He sat up surprised to find himself on a dirt floor.

A man helped him up. "Mr. Ingram, thank goodness, you have awakened. Here let me help you to a seat."

"What has happened? Where am I?" Jack said, brushing the dirt off his suit.

"It is with my sincerest apologies that I must inform you that your sister and cousin left here a matter of minutes ago. I did all in my power to detain them," the man said.

"Regina and Mathias are not here?" It was coming back to him now. Mathias had gone mad and struck him. Hatred echoed in his head and he pressed at his temples to make the ringing stop.

"Sir, they have taken your carriage and horses as well. Your driver is here and he was just informing me of the loss," the heavyset man said. Jack recognized him now, it was Father Blenheim. Jack looked around the room and saw his driver.

"Mr. Ingram, I resisted the attack for all I was worth but Mr. Stohl removed me from the carriage. I attempted to recover my position but he overpowered me and rode off," the driver said.

Jack stood up, a bit unsteady on his feet but he was determined to see for himself. He pushed open the door to the cottage and looked for the carriage. "God's teeth! I cannot fathom what has gotten into Mathias." He stomped his foot and slammed the door.

"Mr. Ingram, I have sent my lad after them on horseback. I trust he will return with all haste with news of their whereabouts," Father Blenheim said.

Jack sat down in the chair and put his head in his hands. "Father, I need you to complete the paperwork for this evidence and please put everything in writing if I am to proceed." It was more important now than ever to pursue this. Regina had taken this too far, as had Mathias.

Father Blenheim smiled. "I will have papers ready for you in the next hour if you care to wait. However, there is the trifling matter of my payment before I can proceed."

Jack paid the priest the sum requested and sat back, waiting for him to complete the work. His driver stood outside, waiting for the lad to return.

A half hour later the back door burst open and a boy came in, shouting in excitement, "I have found them, Father!" The driver followed behind him.

Jack stood up. "Father, I will more than make it worthwhile for you if you can see your way to allowing my driver and I to take the lad and your horse to find them? Could we borrow another horse to achieve this goal?"

"Aye, sir that will indeed be acceptable." Father Blenheim turned to the boy, "Lad, will the horse be able to take you and Mr. Ingram to the location you describe?"

"Aye, Father, I do believe he has strength enough to ride there," the boy assured him.

The rain came down in torrents running down the street. They had found the coach along the road and Jack sent Father Blenheim's boy back with the borrowed horse. Jack leaned against the building under the eaves trying not to shiver uncontrollably and spoke to a lad who had been paid by Mathias to watch the carriage. He was soaked through his clothes from riding in the rain.

"Lad, if you please, where are they now?" Jack shook the boy by the shoulders.

"Sir, I beg of you, I did not know it was your carriage. They went into the old gypsy's cottage, that one with the red door." He pointed down the alleyway.

"Off with you now lad. Your work is done here." Jack boxed the boy's ears and attempted to kick him. The boy was too swift and ran off down the road.

Jack slipped into the carriage and pulled a box from under the floorboards. He opened it and felt the cool brass barrel of the pistol and thought of his father. It had been a gift on his eighteenth birthday—a Queen Anne flintlock pistol with a silver butt cap. The beauty of the polished brass barrel, contrasting dark wood, and silver along the underside, shone in the low light of the rainy afternoon. He kept it hidden in case of a robbery.

Seeing it again made him nostalgic for the days he and his father would hunt out on the glens and rivers. It had been awhile since he had held a weapon but with the strange behavior of his sister and the violence of Mathias of late, he thought it best to have some insurance. Mathias had overpowered him once and he did not like how that had made him feel.

A loud crack of thunder made him jump and he stepped out of the carriage to get a better look at the clouds. This would be a good time to make his move, with the noise of the storm to cover his entry.

"I will return promptly, please stay here," he said to the driver.

Jack made his way along the alleyway until he reached the back door of the cottage. It was locked. Jack pulled a letter opener from his pocket and slid it between the jamb and the door, hoping it was a simple latch he could lift. Success! It lifted and he slowly opened the door, stepping quietly into the small kitchen. He warmed his wet hands by the tiny fireplace. Jack listened intently to be sure he wasn't going to be surprised by anyone coming through the door to the next room. He heard voices and moved closer to make out what they were saying. It was Regina. Then he heard Mathias's voice too, as well as that of a woman he did not recognize.

He shifted position to stand behind a large coat rack near the door, intent on hearing every word of this exchange. Something jabbed him in the thigh. He removed the pistol from his pocket and ran his thumb over the curved engraving of the word London and the leaf pattern stamped into the gun's barrel.

The door opened and crashed into the coatrack, making Jack nearly drop the weapon. He glanced around the door that shielded him from her view to see an old woman pouring water into a large white bowl. As fast as she had entered the room she was gone. Jack looked at the ceiling and took a few deep breaths to calm down. Thank the good Lord he had not been found. Ear against the door, he strained to deduce what was going on. He was not versed in the arts of fortune-telling but knew there were a lot of charlatans. Why would Mathias bring Regina here of all places?

He listened intently, hoping to discover their purpose for being here. It was hard to make out the women's voices through the door. Mathias's voice was easy to understand. Jack's anger took over any semblance of logic. His cousin had taken it too far with this! In a flurry, Jack shoved the door open, found his target, and pulled the trigger. The weapon bit his hand as it kicked back nearly hitting his face. He had forgotten how much gumption the weapon had.

A deafening noise rang out in the small room. Mathias moved backward just as Jack pulled the trigger. The bullet pierced Mathias's coat sleeve and a spray of blood hit the floor and the wall behind him. Mathias yelled and managed to shove Regina out of harm's way.

Regina stumbled into the table with her arms outstretched to catch her fall, upsetting the candle on the table. The tablecloth caught fire and a puff of white mingled with the smoke from the fireplace.

"You cursed vile spawn of the devil!" Jack was furious that he had missed Mathias's head. His only hope now after failing to kill him was to take him by surprise.

It was Jack's good fortune that Mathias was distracted by the fire and did not prepare himself for the onslaught. He clubbed Mathias on the head with the pistol. Mathias fell to the floor, knocking over the water bowl and the burning tablecloth.

Regina screamed, "Mathias!" She scrambled to the floor to assist him.

The woman grabbed the pitcher from the cabinet behind her and poured it over the fire, putting it out.

Mathias did not move. Jack pulled Regina to her feet, "You wicked little vixen! How dare you run away with my cousin!" He grabbed her wrist and pulled her toward the door. She fought back pulling her hand free and made a dash for the kitchen. He grabbed her hair and stopped her. With his other arm, he caught her in a headlock and pulled her close, her heels dragging on the floor.

Regina clawed at his arm that encircled her neck, fighting to free herself, but Jack had a good grip. "This is the devil's work indeed, Sister, for now, I know beyond doubt that you are possessed. Even this fortune-teller says you have a black spot on your soul." He glanced back to ensure Mathias was not readying for an attack. The woman stared at him with hard black eyes. She made no move to stop him.

"I will see you back to hell where you belong!" Jack snarled at Regina, who responded by making another attempt to free herself. A quick tightening of his grip around her neck put an end to her struggles.

Jack dragged his sister out of the fortune-teller's residence and returned to the downpour. He tried to adjust his hat to protect his face and realized he still held the pistol. He shoved it in his coat pocket and fixed the brim of his hat to keep the rain out of his eyes.

Regina stopped struggling. Her hair was now plastered against her face, water streaming down her cheeks. Jack dragged her by her heels toward the carriage.

The driver stood under the building in an attempt to stay dry but opened the door to the carriage at Jack's approach. Jack roughly shoved Regina in, keeping hold of her hair in case she had any idea of exiting the opposite side.

Jack whispered into the driver's ear. The man looked at him in surprise. Jack nodded. He glanced at Regina and back at Jack. "Yes, sir." The driver adjusted his hat and climbed up onto the driver's bench.

The driver shook the reins, pushing the brake lever. The coach jerked and began the journey. Jack turned his attention to Regina who looked rather worse for wear. She was rubbing her throat.

"Where are you taking me?" That insolent look was back on her face.

"No more of your rude questions Regina. From now on it is *I* who will question *you*." He leaned forward resting his elbows on his knees, using every ounce of control to keep this a conversation and not another beating.

She narrowed her eyes at him, but before she could say a word Jack continued, "Regina Elizabeth Ingram, what in the name of all that is holy were you thinking, running off with Mathias? God's blood, you must have the very devil inside of you to come to a fortune-teller's home. Do you care nothing for what others will say about our family?"

Regina kept her eyes on the floor and continued to rub her neck. Perhaps she had recaptured her proper place as his quiet obedient little sister.

"It seems as though Catherine was correct about what evil has taken possession of your soul." Jack gritted his teeth. "You will obey me on this journey and make an end of your willful behavior." Since the accident, Regina had been so unpredictable. She had always been sufficiently afraid of him to obey his commands. Lately, he struggled to get her to do his bidding.

The coach slowed down at a crossroads. In a blur, Regina launched herself toward the carriage door and nearly threw herself out. Her foot caught on his boot, giving him a moment to grab her skirts and pull her backward. She landed hard on the coach floor. He heard the air rush out of her.

"Regina, you little hellcat!" He grabbed her arm and twisted her around so she was face down. He put his weight on her back and pinned her to the damp muddy floor.

"No!" she yelled. "Get off of me you sadistic bastard! I can't believe you shot Mathias. He is your cousin and did not deserve that!"

"Did he not?" He pushed his knee hard into her back. "I will teach you not to dare to speak to me in that manner!" He had no idea what sadistic meant, but he knew well enough what a bastard was.

She struggled to get up. "Ooooh!"

"I swear upon the good book you have changed, Regina. You are not the sweet obedient young lady you were but twenty-four hours ago." He shifted his weight to stand, jamming his knee deeper into her back. She let out another moan. Sitting back down on the seat he could see her face again. She wore a look of pain. At least the insolence was gone.

"Since the accident, you have not been yourself." He delivered a swift kick to her ribs to accentuate his frustration. Regina made an attempt to get up from the floor. "No Regina, I demand that you will stay on the floor. If you are going to act like a wild runaway dog I will treat you like one, by thunder!"

Hoping to see anguish or remorse, he leaned forward to see her face. The look of sheer hatred surprised him. Regina had changed into a wild, unruly child. He would get to the root of the problem.

"And is it not enough that you disobey me? You insult me further with each word from your poisonous mouth, your every action, dear sister, is designed to ruin me. You are disobedient, you tell lies, and you have made a foul jest of the fine marriage betrothal I worked so hard to procure. I will no longer try my patience with your ungodly disgusting behavior. You will pay for the damage you have done."

She struggled to move off the floor. He pressed her down with his feet. "You will remain under my feet in the mud until we arrive at our destination."

Chapter 24 - Torn Petticoats

Ronnie wanted to scream at Jack to stop being so horrible to her. Instead, she bit her tongue, not wanting to get kicked anymore. She settled to her fate and finally, the coach stopped. Jack grabbed Ronnie's elbow and jerked her to her feet. He brushed some of the mud off the front of her dress.

"Where are you taking me?" Ronnie said between chattering teeth. She wiped her face and tried to repair the hair that had come loose from the updo Margaret had done for her this morning. Jack dragged her off the coach and into a large building.

She broke free from Jack's grip and took a few steps away. A man was exiting the building in front of them. "Please, this man has kidnapped me! You have to help me!"

"Constable, I am delivering my sister into your custody," Jack shouted. "She is a danger to my household and to my unborn son."

The constable looked back and forth between them.

"No, don't listen to him!" Ronnie yelled desperately. "I just had an accident. I bumped my head and I can't remember everything. Can you see how he has mistreated me?" She held up the hem of her muddy skirts. "And, Constable, he is the one who has committed a crime! He shot someone just a half an hour ago."

"If you could have a seat over there, sir and madam, I will find someone to assist you," the constable said while holding the door open and pointing at a row of benches.

Jack grabbed her elbow and led her to the benches near the door. He leaned in close. "You will not tell such lies in here!" He squeezed her arm. He had the I-will-beat-you look. "And you will certainly not speak of Mathias."

"You shot Mathias! What will Catherine say to you? What if he is dead Jack? What if you killed Mathias?" Ronnie wiped away the tears that fell down her cheeks.

"Catherine will know nothing of this! She is with child and in a delicate state. I will not have my unborn son's life put at risk again with your tricks and your devilry!"

"Jack, I am not a witch. You *know* that!" she said. He tightened the grip on her arm.

"And what other explanation do you have for your lack of memory? How can you explain your odd speech, the words you use that are foreign to everyone? Your strange accent? Your erratic behavior? All of the evidence points toward the work of the devil. There is no doubt, dear sister, that you are possessed." He patted his breast pocket. "Even that dreadful fortune-teller agrees."

"I had an accident, Jack. It is the only explanation needed." Ronnie crossed her arms. Anger boiled around in her mind, mingling with the horror of Mathias being shot right next to her. The blood dripped down the walls of her mind as she fervently prayed for Mathias. There wasn't time to find out where he had been shot. Was he dead on the floor of Madam Zangari's parlor?

A gruff, older uniformed man walked toward them. Ronnie couldn't take her eyes off of the long bushy eyebrows.

Eyebrows said, "Good evening to you Mr. Ingram. I am Captain Green. If you would be so kind as to follow me to a private office."

Ronnie followed Captain Green with Jack walking closely behind. He led them down a dimly lit hallway into a larger room with dark wooden benches and a large heavy wooden table.

"Please have a seat." Captain Green motioned for them to sit.

They faced the Captain who stood with his back to the fireplace. "Mr. Ingram, what brings you to us on this damp dark evening?"

"I bring to you my sister who has become a danger to my household," Jack said.

Captain Green narrowed his small eyes, the large bushy eyebrows shading them enough to disguise their color.

"Please explain, Mr. Ingram," Captain Green said.

"I have the evidence for you." Jack reached into his breast pocket and pulled out several pieces of folded parchment.

Constable Green took them from Jack and glanced at her and quickly looked away. He turned and walked toward the small window and began reading the papers, twisting his eyebrows as he did so. He cleared his throat and darted his piggy eyes at her and then back to the parchment.

"What evidence is he presenting against me Captain Green?" Ronnie stood and took a step toward him.

"Enough of these outbursts, I tell you, Regina! You will remain quiet or I will be forced to teach you another lesson," Jack said with his teeth clenched.

KJ Waters

Captain Green held up his free hand and said, "Miss Ingram, remain seated if you please. I will return as soon as I can." He eyed her again and backed out of the room.

Jack gave her a fierce look, quelling any more questions. An overwhelming panic hit. She was not going to sit back and let Jack kill her only friend in this time and then trap her in jail for something as ridiculous as being a witch. This had gone way too far. Ronnie jerked the door open, and with no one in sight, she half-ran half-walked down the hallway. She made it as far as the lobby area where a constable stopped her.

"Excuse me miss, may I help you?" he asked.

Jack was right behind her and grabbed her arm, pulling her backward. "Regina, I have had enough of this!"

"Constable, I should not be here. This is a huge mistake," she yelled as she struggled with Jack.

Captain Green appeared, his small eyes wider now. "Miss Ingram, I requested that you stay seated in my inquiry room. Please come with me!" He took her arm and guided her back down the hall.

They passed the room they had been in and continued down the hallway with Jack following until they reached an open area with several desks. "Constable Peel, I need you to search Miss Ingram," Green said.

"Yes, sir! Miss Ingram, please come with me," the thin Constable Peel said. He put his hand on the small of her back and pushed her deeper into the stone-lined hallway of the jailhouse. He pointed to a small room and said, "Please Miss, would you be so kind as to go into this room. I need to search you."

Another tall man walked in, stooping down to get under the doorjamb. He shut the door and looked down at the floor.

"Place your hands on the wall, miss," Constable Peel said.

Ronnie's heart jumped into her throat. "Why is the door closed?"

"We need to search you in private before we place you in a cell." He said the words with irritation. "Please miss."

She put both hands on the wall, with her back toward the men, turning her head to keep an eye on the one talking.

He started at her boots, feeling around the top and then unlaced and removed both, handing them to the tall man.

"Please hold still while I search you. I don't want to hurt you but if you make this difficult for me I can search you while you are unconscious." He smiled, "No telling what may happen while you're out."

The tall man snickered and Ronnie shot him a hateful look. He abruptly stopped laughing and looked back at the floor. Constable Peel squatted down by her right leg, grabbed her ankle and worked his way up the length of her leg, stopping just before he reached her butt.

Ronnie pulled away. "Hey, stop that!"

He reached down to her left leg and pulled the petticoats up. "Look," he said to his friend. He bunched up her skirt and showed the other man her ankle and back of her knee.

She pulled her leg out of his grip and said, "Stop that!"

He grabbed the back of her neck and shoved her face against the wall. "I told you to hold still," he said close to her ear pinning her to the wall with one arm and pulled up her dress with his free hand.

Ronnie struggled but the man was too strong. She wanted to let out the panic that had built-up since Mathias had been shot in a long hard scream but logic won out and she yelled. "You know why I'm in here, don't you?"

The tall man took his gaze from her legs to her face. At least she had his attention. Constable Peel ignored her and slid his hand up her inner thigh.

Just before Constable Peel touched her delicate areas she yelled, "Witchcraft!" and managed to squirm away from the probing hands.

Huge eyes stared at her. The tall man made the same hand signal Father Blenheim had with his fingers and grabbed the handle of the door, ready to run out.

Constable Peel tried to pull his hand out from under her petticoats but the brass button on his sleeve caught on something in his panic to get away from her. He loosened his grip on her neck just enough for her to push away from the wall and look for his foot. She stomped as hard as she could but remembered too late that her shoes were in the corner. The fabric tore and she was pulled off balance as the man freed himself and took two steps away.

Ronnie spun around. "Ask Captain Green."

Both men stared at her openmouthed. Constable Peel looked at his hand and back at her.

"Do not touch me again or you will regret it!" she yelled.

The tall man ran out of the room and slammed the door behind him.

Constable Peel said, "I believe that you are telling a falsehood to scare us. Now that is not very nice, miss. I may have to punish you." He took a step closer, reaching out for her.

Ronnie put on her fiercest face. "Try it and I'll make your balls explode!" She pointed a finger at his crotch. "Do you want me to do that? Because I would really enjoy watching you suffer." She hoped she sounded tougher than the panicky girl inside.

He stopped, still not sure. The tall man opened the door sticking only his head in to say, "Green confirmed. There are papers to prove it."

She took a step toward both men and said in her best Hermione voice, "*Explosi-a-mus!*" And pointed at his groin.

Before she finished the curse both men were out of sight making a commotion in the hallway. Who would have thought that would come in handy? Ronnie smiled, but it faded quickly. There was nothing funny about this situation. The constables had left the door open and she took a few steps toward them. The noise in the hallway caught the attention of Captain Green and Jack, who were talking in the room nearby.

Captain Green opened the door, "What the blazes are you playing at Constable Peel? I have asked you to search—"

"—Get her away from me!" Peel interrupted. His shaking finger pointed at her as she entered the room.

"Your men need to learn some manners," Ronnie said and pointed at the constables. "You really shouldn't leave them alone with your female prisoners."

Constable Peel took a step away, both hands held protectively over his balls.

"I will take this under advisement, ma'am." He turned to the two men and said, "We will discuss this later. Back to your desks." The two men backed down the hallway, both making the sign of the devil.

Damn, she only meant to stop them from sexually assaulting her and now she had only succeeded in giving them more evidence. Jack's case against her was strengthened.

Chapter 25 - Bullet Holes and Booze

Mathias woke with a start, icy liquid dripping down his face. "Vat?" He wiped his face and sat up. "Vere in zee blazes am I?" he looked into the hard-lined face of Madam Zangari.

"Get up," she said. "You are far too large for me to be trying to move you."

A sharp pain in his upper arm distracted him from her hard stare. "Vat has happened?" His coat was torn and soaking wet with blood. His head pounded as he lay back down.

"Mr. Stohl, you should not have come here. You have brought bad luck to my house. I felt the badness when I touched your *friend.*" She stood up and left the room.

"Regina!" He cried out, as it came flooding back. "Vere is she?" He stood and steadied himself against the table, now devoid of the tablecloth or anything else that had been there. His head swirled and swam and he sat down hard in the chair. He put his head between his knees and tried to remember what Jack said to Regina. Ronnie? Did Madam Zangari say that was her name?

The door burst open and he jumped at the noise. Madam Zangari appeared with some cloths. "Take off your coat and shirt." She stared at him impatiently as he obliged her commands. Excruciating pain shot up his arm when he moved it.

"A man came in here and he set off a weapon. A flintlock pistol, I believe it was. Let me see your arm. The ball driven from the weapon has torn the flesh. He took your friend away, too."

Black spots fluttered around and he closed his eyes to make them stop. He took a deep breath and their jig promptly stopped. Removing the waistcoat was more of a challenge. Madam Zangari helped Mathias pull the garment off his right side and laid it on the table. He sat down on the chair, fingers fumbling as he unbuttoned the shirt and pulled it halfway off. Madam Zangari helped him and laid it on top of his coat. He looked at the damage made by Jack's bullet. Blood poured out of a small hole near his elbow, dripping onto the floor.

Madam Zangari handed him one of the cloths and said, "I do not want your blood all over my parlor floor, thank you very much."

He took the cloth and pressed it against the wound, blood soaking into the white material. He pushed hard, hoping it would reduce the blood spilling from his arm. She grabbed another cloth and wiped up the blood on the floor. "Let me see your head."

He held still while she poked the side of his head near his temple. "The skull is unbroken. It will cause you discomfort for a time but you should recover well. There is no blood. Show the arm again," she said.

He removed the towel and the bleeding had nearly stopped—just a small amount oozed out.

She prodded around. "Good. Good. I think there is no ball inside the flesh. Better for you. Not so good for me. It must have gone through your arm and no doubt smashed something in my parlor." She walked to the wall behind where he was shot. "Yes. It is here." She fingered a dent in the wall. "You will pay me fivepence for the damage and for cleaning up your wound."

He reached into his pocket and pulled out the money laying it on the table. At least the ball was not embedded in his arm.

"And, Mr. Stohl, when you can stand you must leave. I have more customers coming and I have to get the blood out of the floor. This kind of thing is not good for business."

"Madam I am truly sorry for bringing such mayhem to your doorstep." He grabbed his shirt, glad to not be feeling faint anymore. He had a long way to walk.

"Wait." She pulled a rag from the pile on the table and tore it into a long strip. She glanced at his arm and said, "You are too thick."

Mathias looked at his arm and laughed. "I suppose I am." His head was beginning to throb and he could feel his eye swelling.

She tore another strip, this time twice as long and wrapped it around the wound several times and tied a knot to hold it in place. Mathias bent his elbow several times, ignoring the pain, and tested the fabric. It was tight but not so much that it would prevent him from moving around.

"Do not take this off. It will help stop the blood from flowing." She grabbed his shirt and pulled it over his injured arm and held it for him. It was cold and sticky where the blood had soaked into it. He managed to put on the waistcoat without help.

"Thank you, Madam. I am most grateful for your assistance." He stood up and took a few tentative steps toward the door.

"Wait." She disappeared into the kitchen and returned handing him a small glass.

It smelled of spirits. He swallowed it in one gulp and enjoyed the burning sensation as it made its way down to his heart.

"Thank you, again." He handed the glass back to her. "Vat vas zat?" It was a spirit he had never tasted before.

"A home recipe for healing. Now go. I have many things to do."

He grabbed his coat and headed toward the door, difficultly pulling it on over his injured arm and struggling to pull it across his shoulders. She assisted him.

"About the girl," she said.

He turned around and looked down at her. "Yes. You mean Regina?"

"No. Ronnie. You will see her again another time. It will be better for you both but not without turmoil."

"Another time? Vat do you mean, Madam? Another day? Another veek?"

"Another life," she said, looking away.

"Another life?" he repeated, dumbfounded. "Madam, forgive me, but I do not understand vat you are saying."

"That is all I know."

"Do you know vere Jack took her?" Mathias asked, desperate for more information.

"I do not know. But the man said that he was determined that he would have her hung as a witch." Madam Zangari looked down at her hands. "Please Mr. Stohl. I would like you to go now. This was not an easy reading. That woman, she took me to a very dark place."

"It vas not an easy time for me either." He nodded toward his arm, making his head throb in the process. "But Madam I am very thankful for your help today. Blessings on your home and your place of vork." He reached for the door handle and walked into the rain.

Chapter 26 - Dark Thoughts

"Miss Ingram, please step in here." Captain Green motioned for Ronnie to return to the room where Jack waited. "I believe I have finished speaking with your brother." He turned to Jack and said, "Mr. Ingram, please let me know if you find any further evidence that would be helpful in this matter."

"Captain Green, please. I need to tell you that Jack has shot someone just before we came here. His cousin." Ronnie said.

"Captain, this is precisely what I have been speaking to you about." Jack interrupted, "My sister is not well, she is consistently telling stories, lies. And always those that harm me the most."

"Yes, yes, that is clear now. And the way she has terrified my men, I have never seen such nonsense from those constables. Thank you for bringing her to justice. We will pursue this will all haste."

Jack stood up and the men shook hands. "Much obliged to you, Captain Green." Jack bowed and reached back to the table for his hat. "Good evening, Sister."

Ronnie watched Jack walk away with mixed emotions. She had not enjoyed her time with him, but to be left alone here with these men was terrifying. Would the constables leave her alone? She hoped Constable Peel had spread the word and would keep them away from her tonight.

"Ma'am, please come with me." Captain Green opened the door and waited for her to follow.

They made their way along a dark damp corridor and down a few sets of steps. This part of the jail had stone walls and reminded her of the castles she visited with Steph in June. Too much adrenaline made her legs shaky. Captain Green opened a door at the end of the corridor and a putrid smell assaulted her senses. Male voices bounced off the walls. They made their way down the aisle between two rows of jail cells with two and three men each. Ronnie held her sleeve over her nose and mouth. A dirty-faced man reached through the bars and grabbed her skirt and pulled her backward.

"Help!" she yelled at the top of her lungs and lost her balance. She fell down hard on her butt with the panniers of her ridiculous dress around her ears. Peals of laughter echoed.

Captain Green reached down and helped her up. Low guttural sounds echoed around her, assaulting her from all sides.

A man's voice could be heard above the others, "By jingo, a virgin! Look boys, sweet fresh buttonhole! A nice tight madge!" More laughter.

Ronnie made herself as small as possible. Another man said, "I 'ave somfin' for your pretty mouth, lass." More men laughed and the noise level increased as the commotion escalated. "Come 'ere lady, I want to show you my Jolly Roger!"

Captain Green banged his club against the bars and yelled, "On your bunks!"

She jumped at the loud noise. Some of the prisoners returned to their bunks and the noise lessened slightly. Her heart nearly beat out of her chest and she shakily walked in front of Captain Green.

They turned a corner and went through another locked door, most of the noise from the raucous men now blocked. This area was cooler and the stench subsided a bit with two cells opposite of each other and a door just beyond. Ronnie took a deep breath in an attempt to calm down. A feeling of utter helplessness washed over her.

"You will stay here this night." He opened the barred gate with another key and pushed her in the cell. It was very small and had a rough wooden bench and a chamber pot. "There is a blanket and we will provide you with dinner and some water for washing later." He closed and locked the gate. "Good night, Miss Ingram." He turned on his heel.

She could see a few constables gathered in the next room, but didn't recognize any of them. In one way it was a relief there were police on the other side of the door since the opposite direction housed London's horny dregs of humanity. On the other hand, given her earlier adventure with the two constables, it wasn't clear who was more dangerous. Neither option was very comforting. Hopefully, everyone would leave her alone.

She looked out remembering her only other time behind bars as a tourist at Alcatraz. At the time it was fun to imagine what it was like to be locked up. Now, not so much. Ronnie leaned her head against the bars and enjoyed the cool metal against her throbbing forehead. Was this going to be the start of one of her massive headaches? It was hard to say since she was in Regina's body. Maybe it was just a hunger headache. Captain Green said they would bring her food. Probably horrid food, but it should make her feel better if it didn't make her sick.

Ronnie closed her eyes and took a deep breath. The image from Madam Zangari's parlor replayed and she gasped for air, feeling the panic from the vivid scene. It was still fresh in her mind, and she could feel the hatred of the crowd. Was that her fate? A terrible feeling welled up from the pit of her stomach. Madam Zangari's prediction had already come true for Mathias. He had risked everything to help her. He had to be okay. She tried to push out the image of him laying crumpled on the floor. In her mind she had him stand up, brush off, and smile at her.

"Please, please be okay, Mathias," she whispered. He was a good man and deserved better than to be shot by the likes of Jack. Goddamned Jack! He was responsible for Mathias's injury and maybe his death, and for her being in jail. Even if he had survived the assault, he would likely succumb to an infection. Antibiotics didn't even exist yet. How would they treat the fever and infection? Probably more idiotic bloodletting that would just sap his strength. If she had not shown up here in God-awful London, he would still be alive.

She eyed the bench. It was wet and smelled horrid. She went to sit on the floor but remembered the panniers and corset and spent the next twenty minutes trying to figure out how to remove them. Finally, the panniers were in the corner and the corset was looser and still on, and she sat on the dirt floor, legs bent with her head in her hands. Tears rolled down her face, but she didn't care. There was no use fighting them. She would rest her eyes and hope for the nightmare to end and for her to wake in her bed in Florida. Not that sleeping had fixed that yet. Ronnie tortured herself with dark thoughts as she fell asleep on the dirt floor of the prison cell, hoping for better things to head her way.

Chapter 27 - Cold Comforts

Mathias opened the door of Madam Zangari's cottage and was greeted by a downpour. He wished he hadn't left his hat back at the Ingram estate.

The smell of the rain was comforting and cool clean air filled his lungs. Pulling his coat around him, he knew what he had to do. He briskly walked the few miles to his sister's house, becoming hopelessly drenched. She would have a hot meal at the ready and could look after his wound. Would his brother-in-law Stephen be back from work yet? He looked at the sky. It must be nearly five, although it was difficult to tell with the rain.

His mind raced thinking of all he had to get done to help Regina—or Ronnie. How could she be called by another name? It made no sense to him, but somehow he felt it was right. She was different when he came into her room the night the doctor was calling upon her. The look she gave him, the smiles. There was a spark there that had not existed before. Prior to that day he only had glances from her, averting her eyes to avoid polite conversation. Today she looked at him with wonder, with excitement when he spoke, with laughter when he teased.

Standing at his sister's door he wiped the rain from his face and shook the water from his head, sending waves of pain through his skull where Jack had hit him with the pistol. He knocked on the door and waited while trying to clear his head from the blinding pain.

The door opened and Maria's smiling face greeted him. "*Brüder*! Vat brings you to my doorstep on such a dreadful evening? You are dripping *mit* rain."

He tried to smile back but the weight of what was ahead of him prevented it. "*Guten Abend*, Maria."

"Mathias, vat is amiss? Come in this moment and vee vill get you some tea." She stepped out of the way to let him pass. Her hair was covered by a kerchief, but wisps of brown curls escaped.

A small blur ran down from the stairs into the kitchen. "Uncle Mathias, come and catch me," his niece called out.

"Little Lumpkin, I vill tickle you if I catch you." It was their usual greeting. She would hide and he had to find her. When he did he would lift her into the air and tickle her ribs and she would squeal with delight. But his arms would do no lifting today.

"You look as though you have seen a ghost. Come *Brüder*." She removed his coat and he gasped in pain. "Mathias!"

"Sister, do not be alarmed. I have been shot *mit* a pistol, but I am vell."

"Shot? Lord preserve us, how be it zat you have been shot?" Maria didn't wait for an answer. "Stephen!" She yelled up the stairs. "Come here at once!"

"What is it, my darlin'?" Stephen's fiery red hair shone in the candlelight. "Mathias? Pray what brings you here, my lad?"

"Greetings, Stephen. I am—" Mathias started, happy to see Stephen was home.

"—He has been shot!" Maria interjected. "Come hither at once, Stephen, and vee shall examine the damage."

"What are you going on about woman?" Stephen said, but the smile left his face as he came down the stairs and saw Mathias's bloody shirt.

Maria led him to the bench near the door and pulled off his boots. "Come and lay down in the parlor near the fire. Mother, bring Mathias some tea," she called out toward the kitchen.

Mathias would allow his sister to baby him, but no one else. They were as close as siblings could get since she had mothered him his whole life.

Stephen took his good arm and helped him into the parlor. He did not really need the help but it was nice to be in the warm embrace of his family after such an emotionally and physically taxing day. "What kind of trouble have you got into lad?" Stephen spoke with a soft Irish lilt.

Mathias sat on the couch. His eyes were heavy and he was drained. He had to act tonight if his plan were to be successful, but he would have to choose his words carefully. "Cousin Jack shot me." He looked directly into Maria's eyes and registered her shock.

"That vile bastard," Stephen said, standing with fists clenched. "How did this come about?"

"Our cousin, Jack Ingram has done this to you? Vas it a hunting accident?" Maria asked twisting her apron.

"Alas no. Zere was no mistake to his actions. He shot me *mit* a flintlock pistol at Madam Zangari's cottage." Mathias noted the stark differences in their faces. Stephen's mouth was agape, whereas Maria's eyes were narrowed, and he could see the wheels turning, planning, and scheming.

That was another reason for coming to his sister's house. Maria was shrewd and didn't get caught up in the emotional aspect of any situation. Stephen, on the other hand, was a hot-headed Irishman who usually jumped to conclusions and passionately dealt with every situation without pausing to think, often making huge errors in judgment along the way, but forever loyal and willing to fight to the death for a friend.

Stephen's mother brought a tray into the room and set it down in front of him. "Mathias, how does this day find you?" She sat down opposite him and seemed oblivious to the situation at hand.

"Good evening, Mrs. McConnelly. Zis day finds me in a rather delicate state, I am afraid." Her eyesight was very poor, and she still did not notice the bloody garment he was wearing.

"Mathias is telling us how he vas shot today, Mother," Maria said.

"Maria!" Mrs. McConnelly said. "'Tis not a matter to be joked upon. 'Tis cruel to tease poor Mathias in such a way."

"Nevertheless, it is true, Mrs. McConnelly," Mathias said. "It is a very long story but I am hoping I may prevail upon Stephen for a new shirt and maybe a quick supper. I have an urgent matter to attend to, and I vill need Stephen's connections to help me."

Stephen smiled. "Ah, a scheme, Brother-in-Law. So you have a plan, then?"

Maria shook her head. "Mother, voud you be a dear and fetch a shirt from Stephen's drawer?"

Mrs. McConnelly nodded and left the room. Mathias could hear her thumping up the stairs to Maria and Stephen's room. Maria waited for her to get out of earshot.

"Mathias, you should not have eaten so much as a child, you have grown a fair bit more than my husband here. His shirt vill be a mite short in zee arms, I do fear."

"But a sight better zen no shirt at all," Mathias said, and continued to tell his sister and brother-in-law about his afternoon, leaving out Madam Zangari's predictions.

A small face peeked around the corner and disappeared. Mathias continued, "Stephen, might it be possible for you to help me gain access to your place of work?" This was crucial. He knew Stephen would go along with almost anything he suggested. It was Maria he was worried about.

"Mathias, I insist you tell me of zis plan of yours before I consent to my husband being put in harm's way. You have already met the business end of Cousin Jack's pistol. No need to make it a family affair," Maria pointed an accusing finger at him.

"Keep calm, Maria, have no fear. I ask for his advice, nothing more." Mathias took her hand. "And truth be told I have met both ends of Cousin Jack's pistol." He pointed to his temple and mimicked a hit on the head.

She whistled. "Zat is not pretty, little brother."

"No, that it is not. Neither is zis." He popped a pastry into his mouth whole, not bothering to bite it. He wiped the crumbs from his chest and stood up, unbuttoning the shirt. His arm was growing stiff and the dried blood itched his ribs. She helped him remove the shirt.

"Madam Zangari wrapped it for me," Mathias said.

"Madam Zangari looked after your injury?" Maria looked at him incredulously.

"Only after she charged me the princely sum of fivepence to clean up zee blood." He laughed and she stared at him, open mouthed. "I fear zee lady disliked zee idea of me spoiling her floor with my lifeblood. Red does not match her decorations, it seems."

"In zat case, we must look for another seer." She shook her head on her way to the kitchen.

Stephen pulled a chair up to the fireplace. "Here Brother. Sit ye down near the fire and get some warmth into your bones."

Mrs. McConnelly returned with a few shirts and set them on a chair near Mathias. "Oh goodness me!" she said when she saw him shirtless and bloody. "What in heaven's name have you done my dear?"

"Ma'am, I am vell and good." Mathias was used to her dotty behavior. She never was quite able to follow the conversation and always mixed up the facts. "I have met with an unfortunate mishap."

Mrs. McConnelly sat down in a dramatic motion. "Oh, my word!"

Maria returned from the kitchen with a large bowl of water and a bar of soap. Mathias patiently let his sister clean the blood from his arm and ribs. The warmth from the fire felt delicious on his back as it relaxed the shivering and subsequent tightening of his battered arm. However, his chest and stomach felt the chill of the room, since they were not on the side facing the fire.

Maria used some rags to bandage the arm. As she worked they discussed Mathias's plan. Mrs. McConnelly did Maria's bidding, bringing Mathias's boots and coat to dry near the fire, making some birch bark tea, and bringing supper to Mathias.

He ate stew and bread voraciously, as all the excitement of the day left him ravenous. He wondered what, if anything, Regina—or was it Ronnie—was having for a meal. "Are you nearly done, Sister? I need to attend to a few things."

"Patience, patience, I need only to fasten zee bandage and all is done." She pulled it tight and tied a neat knot. "Now let us see if my husband's shirt will fit over those vast shoulders."

He slid his injured arm into the shirt as Maria held it steady for him. Pain shot through the injured muscle when he flexed it. He sat down on the chair, catching his breath.

"Mathias, are you vell?" Maria asked kneeling down next to him. "Perhaps we should run and fetch zee surgeon?"

"Zis is of no matter, Sister, do not fret." He pointed to his arm. "It is a mite sore ven I move it, but it is of no consequence."

She disappeared and returned with another cup of birch tea, saying, "Zis vill help."

He sipped the bitter liquid and reached for his boots. They were still wet but had made some progress in drying out.

"Sister, might I ask you a small favor? I have been staying at the Ingram Estate, but I now find myself—"

"—Brother, bless my soul, as if you even need to ask. My home is yours for zis night and as many as you need to get back on your feet." Maria looked across at Stephen.

"Aye, Mathias, you must stay as long as you wish to. Indeed we will be right glad to have your company."

Mathias hoped to get Stephen alone to discuss a few details. His plan was a good one, but there were a few ways it could go terribly wrong. Stephen was scheduled to work in the morning at Newgate and this could be turned to Mathias's advantage. Maria would, of course, balk at his idea, knowing that Stephen could lose his job or worse.

A small form darted from behind a chair and crashed into Mathias's legs. He resisted the urge to pick the child up and give her a giant hug. "Sweet little Lumpkin." He knelt down and engulfed her in his arms and smelled her light brown curls. "I love you. And I will be staying here for a while."

"I love you too, Uncle Mathias. Will you breakfast with us then?" She looked at him with wide brown eyes.

He kissed her soft cheek and squeezed her tightly with his good arm. "I vill, little love." Mathias faced his sister taking a mug from her.

Maria smiled at him. "Here, finish your tea. Be sure to have more of zis brew before you take to your bed. It will conjure up restful sleep."

"*Danke*, Sister. I will be fine."

Chapter 28 – Raining Cats and Dogs

Fifteen minutes passed as Steph watched out the window to keep Mimi and Felicia up-to-date on the lack of sightings of Nick.

She looked at her watch. "Damn it, where is he?"

Mimi put her arm around Steph's shoulder, "He'll be fine, he's a very strong man."

"Um, Steph. I think Sugar needs to pee," Felicia said, holding the dog up and away from her as if he were going to explode any second.

"Okay, let's take her to the garage. Mimi, yell if you see Nick, all right?" Steph said.

Steph, Felicia, and Sugar quickly moved across the house to the garage. The image of a tree falling through the house haunted Steph's thoughts fresh from the pack-a-day lady on the radio. She sent a prayer to keep Nick out of danger, for the safety of the family in the burning house, and another wee prayer for poor Hamish.

"Oh Steph, look at your roof!" Felicia said when she saw the disaster in the garage. "I'm so sorry."

The dog was too terrified to pee so they waited patiently until she calmed down enough to relive herself in the corner of the garage.

"Steph, I'm sorry my dog is adding to the mess," Felicia said.

"Like it matters with all the water in here. It's going to be a big job to clean this up. What's a little dog pee thrown into the mix?" Steph said, too preoccupied with Nick's safety to give it much care. She just wanted the dog to hurry up so she could get back to the window.

"True." Felicia smiled at her and then scooped up Sugar. They made their way back across the house with Steph flicking the flashlight around as she walked. She saw an orange blur against the living room window. "Hamish!" She ran to the window to confirm it was her wayward cat.

"Felicia you go back to the closet, I'll be right there," Steph said, not wanting the dog to scare him away.

"Hamish!" Steph called out. Sure enough, the cat was on the window ledge. It was his usual way of telling her he wanted to come in.

Steph cranked the window open, but as she did it pushed Hamish off the ledge onto the ground. "Oh, Hamish, I'm sorry!" The wind blew rain into the living room. Usually, the cat would jump right inside. Where was he? She saw him pitifully drenched in the dirt below the eaves.

"You're hurt. Poor baby! Come on Hamish. Jump, kitty-boy." He looked up at her his golden eyes aglow from the flashlight. "C'mon boy you can do it." He didn't move. A loud whistling noise and a sound like a freight train accompanied a gust of wind, leaves, and water into her living room, soaking the table and chair nearby.

She cranked the window closed. "Damn it!" Now what? She could go out the front door and around to the side of the house to retrieve him, but what if he ran away and was lost again? "Crap! Felicia, come here. Leave the dog." She yelled out. Felicia must not have heard. Steph walked to the closet. "Felicia, I need your help, leave the dog." She glanced at Mimi. "Any glimpse of Nick?"

"No, not yet. I don't see any movement but the fire has nearly taken over the entire back of the house," Mimi said.

Felicia handed the dog to Mimi. "What do you need, Steph?"

"I've found Hamish but he can't get up to the window."

"Who is Hamish?" Felicia said.

"Oh, he's my cat. He got out when we were bringing in some potted plants."

They walked to the living room. Steph moved her painting from the wall and she shoved the table a few feet over so they would not get wet. She cranked the window open. "I'm going to hand you, Hamish. He won't let you hold him, but just make sure he stays inside. He'll probably run away."

"Okay," Felicia said.

Steph climbed out the window, lowering herself about four feet to the ground with the wind pushing her around. The rain soaked into her clothes in seconds. She reached down to grab Hamish by the scruff and lift him up to the windowsill, handing him to Felicia. The cat kicked and squirmed but Felicia got a hold of him and both disappeared into the house. Steph reached for the windowsill and tried to pull herself up. It was slippery and she couldn't quite get up. "Felicia!"

She appeared. "Help me!" Steph said. Felicia grabbed her hand but Steph's arms were wet and slippery. Luckily she was on the side of the house away from the major winds, the house blocking the worst of it.

"Hang on Steph ..." Felicia said and then disappeared out of sight.

156

Steph tried again but didn't have the strength to pull herself up through the window. "Crap!" She pushed the wet hair out of her face.

The bushes whipped around scratching her legs. "Felicia!" she yelled. "Open the front door for me!" Steph stepped out of the bushes hoping Felicia had heard her. Steph looked around wondering how the hell she ended up out in the storm twice! "Ah yes, the bloody cat."

Walking like a drunken person weaving back and forth with the wind buffeting her along, small branches and leaves pelted her arms and face. Without shoes on she made her way carefully, trying to avoid branches and sticks in the grass. Steph found the front of the house and banged on the door. Where was Felicia? She rang the doorbell.

A loud crack startled her and she moved instinctively away from the noise to press against the door. A huge palm tree crashed to the ground and landed a few feet away making the ground shake. It just missed her house but made a horrible noise as it completely demolished the neighbor's car. Fear choked her and she screamed before turning around and banging on the door. "Let me in!"

Chapter 29 - Ruby Slippers

Ronnie woke with a start to the clanking of metal. A man carried a small tray into her cell. "I have food for you, miss. Here is your water for drinking and washing." He set a pitcher down on a table outside the cell.

She rubbed her eyes and stood, feeling pain in the back of her head. The frightening dreams were fading but she was fully waking to a fresh nightmare in jail. "Thank you."

The man nodded his head and locked the cell door behind him. He opened the next door and continued into the men's area of the prison. Male voices and the waft of unwashed bodies floated into her cell. At least she wasn't in there with all those horrible beasts.

When she lifted the puce-colored napkin off the plate, Ronnie discovered a hard piece of bread and a bowl of colorless mush. Her stomach rumbled. It smelled like oatmeal and she looked around for somewhere to sit. *Why didn't I sleep on the bench?* she wondered. Ronnie remembered the foul liquid covering the bench, now dried and yellowish. A clean patch was visible near the end and she sat down, resting the plate on her lap. She cupped her hands on the bowl and the steam warmed her face.

Memories flooded her mind of hot chocolate on a snowy day, almost making her smile. Would she die here in London before she was even born? In her mind, Jeffrey smiled at her with his perfect face, light brown eyes, and caramel-colored hair. Was he freaking out that she was gone? What did he think happened to her? He would be really nervous about telling her mom and Steph she was gone. How could he possibly answer their questions?

The whole situation was baffling. How the hell did she even end up here? More importantly, how could she get back home? Madam Zangari had said the seeds of her destruction were planted. Destruction? Did it mean she was going to die? A flash of the terrible image from the bowl of water nearly made her throw up. She needed to eat something or she was going to turn into a super-hot mess. She stirred the lumpy mush and took another whiff. It smelled okay, but not exactly like oatmeal. Ronnie took a tiny test bite. Not bad, but not much flavor. She spooned some into her mouth and ate slowly as she thought.

An overwhelming urge to kiss the top of her niece's head hit her, forcing tears to her eyes. A smile nearly made it to her face at the memory of last Thanksgiving. They had played Monopoly and other games. Polly won every one despite her complete lack of interest by the end of the game. Her mom had made such a beautiful dinner with a huge turkey and her grandmother's special oyster stuffing. Her brother, Dave, slowed down enough to actually have a long conversation with her about his job and his upcoming promotion.

It had been a heavenly few days with all of them returning to the closeness that had evaporated since her father's death years ago. Now they would have to deal with her disappearance. Would her mom ever recover? When she spooned another bite into her mouth Ronnie found a lump of something hard and spat it into her hand. It was white and looked like a fingernail. She spat the rest of the bite into the bowl and set it on the bench.

"Gross!" Her stomach growled in protest. She picked up the bread and almost broke a tooth on it, but managed to soften it a bit by gnawing on it.

Her goal since she had shown up in London was to get away from Jack. Check. A lot of good that did her. Damn Jack. She thought of Mathias lying on the floor and cried. If he died all of his efforts to get her away from Jack would have been a complete waste. She picked up the napkin and wiped her eyes and nose.

"Fucking Jack!" She could hear her mom's disapproval at the cussing. "Sorry, Mom. Why did Jack have to shoot Mathias?"

How the hell was she going to get back home? Wouldn't it be nice to cross her arms and blink hard like Barbara Eden of *I Dream of Jeanie* and return home? It made as much sense as her being in 1752 and in jail for witchcraft. Ronnie set the bread down on the plate so she could stand and cross her arms. Not much to lose by trying. She had seen the show as a kid in reruns but couldn't remember if there was a catchphrase. She nodded her head dramatically and blinked her eyes.

Nothing. She clicked her heels together and said, "There's no place like home, there's no place like home." Nothing—not that she expected it to work. Out of ideas, Ronnie sat down on the bench and continued to gnaw on the bread.

Ronnie filled the cup with water and drank not caring that it tasted of metal and dirt. She grabbed the dingy piece of cloth that served as a towel, dipped it in the water, and washed her face. Ronnie rinsed the cloth and then used it to brush her teeth. It tasted horrible, but she didn't want to leave the fuzz on them.

The corset jabbed into her ribs and she remembered that there was no Margaret to make her wear the awful things. If she was going to be holed up in jail she should at least be comfortable. Ronnie loosened the laces and lowered the top of her dress so she could pull the wretched thing off and fling it on the bench.

A clanking noise startled her, making her almost scream. She adjusted the dress and covered the corset with the blanket. Two men walked into the room and came toward her cell.

The guard unlocked her cell door and stepped aside. "You have ten minutes, sir. Do you need me to stay nearby?"

Her heart leapt into her throat. It was Jack! Was he here to get her out?

"No, sir, I will be fine," Jack said to the guard. "Sister," he gave her an unfriendly look and locked the cell and walked out the door.

"What are you doing here?" she asked, her legs shaking as she walked toward him.

"I am here to talk to you." He looked around at the confines of the cell. "Did you enjoy your night?"

So it was morning. There was no way to tell in the windowless cell. "No, it's not the best of accommodations."

"Regina, you must listen. I need to ask you some very important questions." He looked very tired.

Her spirits rose. Maybe if she told him what he wanted he would drop the charges and let her free. "Go ahead."

"It is of vital import that I know what you told Lord Barton about the time-shift. As I understand it, he is under the impression that I am planning something—"

"—Time-shift?" Ronnie's heart sped up, nearly beating out of her chest.

He grabbed her by the shoulders and shook her. "You must tell me what you know, Regina! I know you're playing tricks, pretending you have no memory. It won't protect you." His face twisted in anger, making him look desperate.

"Stop it!" she yelled and pushed against his chest, trying to break his hold. "Look, I'll tell you what happened with Lord Barton," she continued. "Just get me out of here. But first, tell me, how is Mathias?"

160

"I do not know, neither do I care. I left the blaggard on the floor bleeding. If I had another pistol, I would have shot the disloyal scut in the head."

"What did Catherine say about you shooting her cousin, maybe even killing him?" Ronnie fought back tears.

"Catherine will not know of this. She is in a delicate state and it is of no matter. Tell me, Regina," Jack let go of her and took a step back, straightening his suit jacket, "what have you told Lord Barton?"

Ronnie took a deep breath. "Jack, he wanted me to do some awful things in exchange for signing the betrothal papers."

"No Regina. That is not what I am asking. What do you know about the deal with Mr. Prescott?" He seemed almost desperate. "What have you told Lord Barton about the time-shift?" His face was red and his lower lip trembled. Lord Barton must have been right about Jack planning something.

"Time-shift ... you have to tell me what that means Jack," she repeated. Maybe this could get her back to Florida!

"Regina, I have to know if you were privy to any of the conversation I had with Mr. Prescott about the New Style, and if you told Lord Barton of it," he yelled. "Enough with the charade and falsehoods, Regina. Silly child, you have no idea what you have done. Our family's fortune is at stake."

"Who is Mr. Prescott?" Ronnie wished she knew what to say.

"Do not play false with me, Regina. You are aware that Mr. Prescott has offered me a fortune for Lord Barton's ..." He stopped and looked at her. "Hell's teeth, child, I know you overheard my conversation with Mr. Prescott the morning before your accident, I saw you standing outside my office! The time-shift is coming and our plan is at risk. If he knows ... even without the betrothal."

"The time-shift? Please, Jack, you have to help me get back to the lab! Wait, is Mr. Prescott the one hosting the time-shift party? Lord Barton was inviting me to a party around the time-shift."

"Time-shift party? Gracious heavens, no! That is merely one of a hundred parties. Tell me what you know about the third of September. Verily, you cannot know how important this is to me. To our family." He emphasized this point by grabbing her shoulders and shaking her again. "Tell me right now or damn your eyes if I don't have you hung for witchcraft!"

"Jack, no! You have to get me out of here! I'm your sister!" She pulled away, afraid he was going to hurt her again.

"I insist that you tell me what you know, Regina, or by all that's holy I swear that my sister you will no longer be. For two days hence I will see you hang." He stomped his foot to accentuate his point.

"Jack, all I know is that I was in 2004 during Hurricane Charley in Jeffrey's lab and then I arrived in the road where you found me. Tell me how do I get back? Please!" She was crying now. He had to help her, there must be something he could do.

He shoved her hard onto the bench. "What in God's name are you talking about? Have you finally taken leave of your senses? Who is this man Charley you talk about? And what is this place you talk of called by the number 2,004?" He turned away from her and took a deep breath.

"Charley is a hurricane, Jack. I was in the future and got sent here from Florida. Can Mr. Prescott help me find a way back to 2004?" She stood up, taking a step toward him, hopeful for the first time since arriving here. "There's got to be a way, Jack!"

"I am so sorry Regina. Your words are madness, your senses are scrambled, indeed, I see now that the devil has possessed you finally and totally. The dark one is sending his vile words from your lips as though your stomach is heaving them forth—Florida? 2004? In the name of all that's holy, Regina you must know these words are the words of Beelzebub!" Jack held up his hands, walking backward.

The door outside the cell swung open and the guard stepped into the room, "Sir your time is up."

"No!" Ronnie grabbed Jack's arm. "It isn't nonsense. I need your help to get back home. Jack please!" Tears flow down her face. "Jack you have to help me!"

He broke her grip and stepped back with a look of horror. "Regina, let me leave. You are possessed. There is no more I can do to help you now." He backed up, tripping on the bench, spilling her cup of water.

"Jack, no! I'm not crazy. Please don't leave me here. *Please!*" Desperate now, she grabbed the back of his coat. "Don't leave me here!"

The guard pulled her away from Jack. "Miss, calm down, if you please." He restrained her as Jack walked out of the cell.

"Let go of me!" She struggled against the guard. "Jack you have to believe me!" The guard released her and quickly slipped out of the cell, locking the door behind him.

"Calm down Miss," he called through the cell door bars. "Do you need me to send in the chaplain or the surgeon?"

"No, I'm okay. I just need to talk to Jack." She grabbed the bars and reached out. "I need your help. Please!"

Jack came up to the bars, "If you cannot tell me what secrets you have shared with Lord Barton we have no more to say to each other. Catherine is with child. I cannot have you anywhere near her for she is persuaded that you have made a pact with the devil. Have you Regina? Have you?"

The guard opened the door to the police lobby area. Another man with a long black coat, white collar, and wide hat pulled low over his face waited patiently as the constable and Jack made their way into the hallway.

Jack nodded to the man and said, "Father, I warrant you will have much need of the good Lord's strength to deal with that unholy creature that is possessed by Satan." Another guard entered the room behind the priest.

Chapter 30 – Time-Shift

Ronnie wiped her eyes and made an attempt to compose herself. Why was a priest here? Her legs were shaky and she sat down on the bench, soaking her skirts with the water Jack spilled. She stood up abruptly and frantically wiped at the water stain on her butt. *Deep breath, let it out.* She closed her eyes and willed away the tears, hoping she could compose herself for whatever nonsense the priest would bring. She tried to get a better look at him, but his face was covered by a hat.

"Ma'am. Father Reynolds is here to see you." The guard unlocked the cell door, letting the priest in and relocking the door behind him.

Ronnie took a deep breath. "Thank you." She was not looking forward to talking to any more priests. So far they had proven to be less than fatherly.

"Ronnie!" The priest said. Shocked at hearing her real name she spun around.

He took off his hat and all Ronnie could see was a broad white-toothed smile. It took her a second to figure out why it seemed so familiar. "Oh my God, Mathias! Are you okay?" She stepped toward him and hugged him fiercely.

"Oh, zat is painful." He put his arms around her and clumsily hugged her back.

"I'm sorry." She stepped away from him. "How did you get in here? Are you okay? I thought you were dead!" She wiped away the tears of joy this time.

"Yes, Ronnie, vat is zis strange vord you keep using? Oh Kay. Never mind, vee do not have time. Indeed I have been shot, but I am still valking. Listen, Ronnie, I do not have long, for zee real priest vill arrive in a trice. Vat is your surname? I know it is not Ingram."

"My name is Ronnie Andrews. My real name is Veronica but only my mom calls me that. Where were you shot?" She stepped back and looked over his big frame.

"My arm, here." He pointed to the back of his upper arm. "The ball vent right through and did not lodge in the flesh, and the vound is freshly cleaned and wrapped." He put his other hand through his hair and looked out toward the door. "Madam Zangari told me zat vee vill be together again, in another time. I vill vant to know you zen." He looked at her intently. She could see the affection in his eyes and hear it in his voice.

Ronnie resisted the urge to hug him again and instead squeezed his hand. He squeezed back, smiling at her. "She said that? What does it mean?"

"I know not, Ronnie Andrews." It seemed as if he were trying out her real name, to see how it felt on his lips. A small sweet smile formed there.

"Can you get me out of here?" Ronnie asked, not sure how she felt about him knowing her real name.

"I have zus far used up a few favors already, to get in," he smiled. "But have no fear, Ronnie Andrews. I vill do all zat is in my power to set you free. Now, pay attention. I am hoping you vill be up to zee task I have prepared for you." He reached into his breast pocket and handed her a small knife.

She took the knife and felt its weight. "Wow, how did you get that in here?" Was she up for violence to get free?

He glanced toward the door again. He got close to her ear and whispered, "My brother-in-law vorks here."

"I can't believe you did this for me, Mathias. I really hope I don't get you in trouble. Or your brother-in-law." She bit her lower lip.

"As I said, vee have but little time before zee real priest comes here to examine you. Do not keep zis veapon about your person. Vee must bury it under zee bunk for now." He squatted down and used his good arm to start digging a shallow hole in the soil floor under the bunk. He held out his hand and she gave him the knife and he buried it, patting the dirt to cover it. "Take heed, Ronnie. It is buried directly under zee center of zee bench about a foot in."

"I'll remember. Mathias, there is something I need to ask you." Ronnie paused, struggling to come up with words that would make sense to him. "I know you've done so much for me already. But I really need the watch—I mean the bracelet—if there is any way to get it from Jack."

"Zee bracelet? Ronnie, vye on earth is zat of such importance? It is not a betrothal gift, is it?" he asked, letting go of her hands, his lips pressed together.

"Well, no, I, um …" That had taken her by surprise. Is that what he thought? It was sort of true. It was the most important gift Jeffrey had ever given her. But they were not engaged. "You see I had the watch on when I left and then I ended up here." There just was no way to explain this in a short time. "I think that I time-traveled here."

"So it has something to do with zee time-shift?"

"Yes! Mathias, what is that about? Jack and Lord Barton mentioned it but I do not think they were talking about the same thing."

"The time-shift is to be on zee second day of September by the King's decree. And I think Jack is up to something."

"I don't understand. How does the King know about this? And why September second?"

"Vye zee New Style, Ronnie, do you not know about it?" Mathias said. "Hold fast, forget this frippery, I do not have time to go into it, zee guard will be here soon."

"Mathias, you have to, it may be my way back. Please quickly tell me."

He looked harassed but relented. "England and zee colonies are shifting eleven days into the future. How in blazes can you be unavare? It has been zee talk of dinner parties across zee whole of England for almost a year."

"No, I don't know what you mean." She shook her head, trying to make sense of what he was saying. Was this another difference between her 1752 and this one?

"Zee Pope changed zee calendar in the year of our lord 1582 from zee Julian calendar to zee more precise Gregorian."

She looked at him blankly. "1582? What does that have to do with now?"

His hand combed through his hair and he turned away from her. "You are avare zat vee started our year on January first this year. Remember?"

"It always does. What does this have to do with the time-shift?" He was making no sense.

"Your education is sadly lacking, Ronnie, it is zee time-shift. See vere I come from in Prussia, vee have been using the Gregorian calendar since zee year of our Lord, sixteen hundred and two. Ven I come here, I have to adjust zee date in my head to match vat England's Julian date. Furthermore, England had always started zee year on March 25." He said. "Do you understand?"

"Not really."

"I vill say it another vay. England's calendar does not match zat of zee rest of the continent. Since 1582 zee time has shifted differently for England. Now after 170 years England is eleven days apart from France, Prussia, and all zee other countries in Europe. Zee King has finally tired of this nonsensical business and is undoing what Queen Elizabeth refused to do at zat time, in order to spite zee Catholic Pope, whom the Protestant Queen had religious differences *mit*. She voud not change to zee Gregorian calendar. And so England began it's time-shift in January, with zee new year of our Lord, 1752, starting on zee first of January instead of the twenty-fifth of March."

"I know we use the Gregorian calendar, but why have I never heard of the eleven day difference between the two?" This explained why she arrived on August second instead of the thirteenth—eleven days before her departure date. Was it a difference in this world rather than in her own? If it was, why did it make any difference in her world and 2004?

"I know not. In truth, it is all zee entire country has been talking of since zee King made zee decision last year. On Wednesday the second day of September vee vill shift forward eleven days. Vee vill awake on the morrow on zee fourteenth of September." He looked back at the door.

"So that's what Jack was talking about. He said something about Lord Barton, Mr. Prescott, and the time-shift. Who is Mr. Prescott?" she asked.

"Mr. Prescott is a shady acquaintance of Jack's *mit* whom he had met a few times. I do not know vat his business is, but he always arrived and took his leave at zee back door, shrouding his appearances in secrecy. Jack must think you informed Lord Barton of some particulars of Mr. Prescott's affairs. Did you?"

"I don't know if Regina did. I have no memory before I was hit by the carriage. That must be why Jack was grilling me again."

"Do you think Regina knew something?"

"I have no idea. He threatened to leave me in jail if I didn't tell him. He said I was faking having no memory so I could keep it secret. How do I get Jack to drop the witch charge and get me out of here?"

"Zat I know not, Ronnie. I vill have to make enquiries. Perhaps I may be able to convince him to drop zee charges leveled against you if I can locate some information concerning zee mysterious Mr.

Prescott." He gave her a small smile. "I've spoken to my brother-in-law about your situation."

"You have?"

"Yes. You are to be examined in a vater trial. I need to talk to you in haste about zis before the guard returns."

"Water trial?" Her stomach clenched. Oh, this did not sound good. She had vague memories of water trials from some of the historical fiction novels she read. From what she remembered the accused were either drowned or found a witch. There was no good ending to a water trial.

Mathias's big hand combed through his hair, making it stand on end. "Ronnie," his mouth turned down at the corners, his lower lip trembled. He cleared his throat, "Zey lower you into zee river to see if you can swim—to find out if you are a vitch. Fear not, I vill be on zee other side of zee river in a boat. There vill be time enough for me to rescue you, you cannot drown. For I confess zat I cannot lose you, Ronnie. I have only just found you."

"I will come to you," she said. "I can swim to the boat. I am very good in the water. But Mathias, what does a water trial have to do with being a witch?"

"The reasoning is zat vater vill repel a vitch because she has renounced her holy baptism as a result of zee pact she made with zee devil. Zerefore if you float you are a vitch. If you sink and drown, zen you are not."

"That is stupid! If I survive I'm a witch and if I die I'm not? How very convenient for them. You're a witch with a death sentence or dead either way!"

"Sadly, I do not make zee laws. Zey will bind you fast and have a rope around your middle to pull you out if you should sink. Zat is vye you have to take zee knife." He glanced at the door and then under the bench. He continued in a whisper, "Cut zee ropes and wait for me to row across. Zee guard will be here soon and zee real priest has arranged to come to you this afternoon. After zee priest examines you, you must grab zee knife, and hide it inside your stocking."

"But by swimming to you I'm showing them I'm a witch. If you don't get to me they will have more evidence."

"It is as you say. But zey will not expect a boat to come and act as your savior. Zey will expect you to float or sink, vile your limbs are bound to your sides. You have to cut zee ropes and make your way to me."

He wrapped his arms around her and hugged tightly. "Ronnie Andrews, I swear zat as Gott is my vitness I will see you again." He planted a kiss on the top of her head. "Until zat time, I beg you to be safe. Pray, take care. I will be zere for you in a small boat. You vill not drown."

"I definitely will not drown. Mathias, thank you so much for all you are doing. I know you are risking everything." Tears stung her eyes, and her throat tightened and made her voice higher. "I will swim to you. But don't get shot again trying to save me." Ronnie hugged him tightly, her face pressed against his chest, soaking in the warmth of his body, enjoying his arms around her. He touched her hair and bent down to kiss her cheek, cupping her face in his hands.

"Mathias, I can't thank you enough for helping me. You have been the only good thing to come out of all of this." She turned her head and kissed his hand.

"Ronnie, I vill move heaven and earth to help you." Mathias put his hands on her shoulders. "If you like, vee can vait and see if zee trial proves you are innocent. If you sink zey vill remove you from zee vater."

"But I float. Most women float—we are buoyant because we have a lung to body mass ratio that keeps us from sinking." She had learned that playing underwater hockey. "I'd rather take my chances at escaping. I think if they want me as a witch they'll find whatever they can to convict me. Who knows what other nonsense they'll come up with to put a nail in my coffin?"

"I am in full agreement. Vee must take charge of zee situation and flee as fast as vee can, using any advantage vee can create. I vill make all possible efforts to get zee boat to you but I vill have to take special care not to raise suspicion. I have planned our escape and according to my brother-in-law all should go vell, as long as you do not drown."

"There is no way I'll drown. I will make my way toward you but the water will be cold and I will not be able to stay in it for very long. Bring something for me to change into so I don't freeze to death on our way out of here."

"I vill attend to it. Have no fear."

"Mathias, is there any way you can get me the bracelet?" Ronnie asked. He stepped away from her. "I hate to ask any more of you but it may save me." She needed more time with him now to figure out what the hell was going on. What brought her here, to him, she felt it was about him, but she had no idea why. She had such strong feelings toward him. It was as if she had known him for longer than a mere two days.

He turned away and ran his hand through his hair again. "I do not understand vat zis bracelet has to do *mit* your escape? Please explain to me how it is of such importance to you?"

She reached for his hand and laced her fingers in his. "I don't know. I had the bracelet just before I came to this place, this time. It's connected I'm sure." How could she explain she was in another person's body and the watch was the only thing that existed from her other life? "Mathias, it is of the utmost importance." She bit her lip.

A clank startled them and they both stepped backward, putting space between them. A constable came into the room and said, "Father, your time is up."

Mathias grabbed his hat and took Ronnie's hand. "Bless you, child. I vill do all I can to try to fulfill your request," He mouthed "swim fast" and squeezed her hand.

"Thank you, Father." Ronnie squeezed his hand in return.

He ducked under the doorway to the cell and walked away. He glanced back, touching his lips and waving his fingers at her.

The two men walked out of the chamber and the door closed. She leaned her hot cheek against the cool metal bars. There were so many questions left unanswered. Did Mathias think she was crazy too? Would the guards find the knife? Would she be able to swim with all her clothes on? And most importantly, how the hell could she get back to her own time?

Chapter 31 - Chaplain of the Garrison

Ronnie slept off and on, hoping to be rested when she made her escape. She had moistened a strip of her petticoats with water and cleaned off the bench—not that the bench offered a bit of comfort, but it beat sitting upright on the dirty floor by a mile. Her mind ran through the new worries as she rested her body. Would Mathias be able to get the watch? Would the escape plan work? Even if it did, how would she get back to Florida? Her situation would no longer be dire, but it certainly wouldn't be rectified.

A loud noise behind her made her jump. It was the door to the chamber and a wafting of unwashed men came in with the guard, followed by the real priest this time. He was young, probably mid-twenties and his eyes were wide as if he had seen a ghost. The guard opened the cell, letting him in.

"Miss, the Chaplain of the Garrison is here to see you," the guard said. "Do you want me to stay in the chamber with you, sir?" He asked the priest.

"Yes, if you please, guard, right there by the door is perfectly acceptable," the priest said. The guard leaned against the wall, crossing his arms, leaving the gate to her cell open.

"Good day, Miss Ingram." The priest spoke to her as if she were a small child, enunciating everything slowly. "I am Father Fitzsimmons. I am here to examine you." His eyebrows danced above his eyes as he spoke.

"Hello, nice to meet you." She wanted to show him she was normal, and not a friggin' witch.

He nodded and smiled. "I have this drawing I must show you that I need to confirm." He pulled a small piece of parchment from his breast pocket, unfolded it and showed it to her.

It was the drawing the witch hunter had made. "Not that again?" Ronnie said. "Doesn't everyone have moles? I bet you have some too."

"Now miss, do not be alarmed. For I have not come here to cause you hurt, or to scare you. I merely wish to find out if this sketch is accurate. I do not need to see everything." His eyebrows arched high when he said everything making him look like a pervert.

She walked backward until the wall was at her back. "No thank you. I'm good. I've already been humiliated enough this week. The guard will undress for you. That'd be a whole lot more fun than me doing an encore performance."

He glanced back at the guard. "Save your jests miss. The guard here is not suspected of being a witch. You must know I have no choice but to do this. You can either let me do it or I'll have him hold you down while I examine you. I will let you choose."

"No, I'm good. How about I just tell you it's all accurate and we can move on?" The panic was returning full force. She had already been through this with Father Blenheim.

"And if the guard holds you down, your underclothes will be removed too." His eyebrows shot up for dramatic effect.

"Well, there's a deal." She looked at the guard.

"I would be 'appy to assist you, Father," the guard said, taking a few steps closer to her with a creepy smile on his face.

"No, no, please. I've already done this once. Why do I have to do it again? What does it even prove?"

"Miss, the court is preparing a very serious case against you. A court appointed man," he pointed his thumb at his chest, "is required to examine the evidence. In this case, you yourself are the evidence."

Ronnie took a deep breath. "I'll let you examine me in my shift." She pointed at the guard. "You are not part of this equation."

"Oh miss, ye've managed to ruin my whole day." The guard said and returned to his perch against the wall, not taking his eyes off of her.

"Can't he leave?" she said to Father Fitzsimmons. "This is humiliating enough."

"I fear not. I need a witness to attest that I have done as instructed by the court. He may be called to testify," the priest said.

"With compensation," the guard chimed. Uneven teeth showed in a broad grin.

"Yes, with compensation," Father Fitzsimmons agreed, giving the guard a sideways glance. He stepped closer to Ronnie with the paper in his hand.

"Don't worry you'll still get your show," she said to the guard.

"I'll do my utmost to try not to enjoy it over much, miss," the guard said with an ear-to-ear smile. "I'll pretend 'tis not me lucky day."

"Enough of this banter," snapped the priest. "Miss Ingram, I need you to remove your gown. You may leave your shift in place—I believe I can see what I need to with your underclothes protecting your modesty." He looked at the parchment.

"I do not think I can see what I need to with the shift on." The guard let his eyes fall to her chest.

"Please stop talking!" she said to the guard. "This is hard enough without your running commentary."

"Sir if you please, the prisoner is right to make you hold your tongue. You can watch, but you must remain quiet." The priest's young face made an attempt to look stern. It came off more comical than as a reprimand.

"Beggar me if I don't keep me gob shut but me eyes open." The guard wagged his eyebrows at her.

She shot him an angry look and his smile grew. Ronnie removed the gown and laid it carefully on the bench. The air was cold and goose bumps crawled across her skin. She crossed her arms, trying to cover the most offending display of the chill and regretted removing the stays.

"Miss, I must ask you to please turn toward the wall," Father Fitzsimmons said.

Ronnie turned her back to him. He pulled the shift down from her neck to expose her shoulder blade and back of her armpit.

"Hell's teeth, if it ain't the mark of Satan!" the guard cried out. She glanced backward to see him make the sign of the devil.

"Shut up!" Ronnie said.

Father Fitzsimmons continued his examination, moving the shift aside for various peeks at Regina's apparently mole-covered skin. Ronnie glanced at the guard. He had dramatically covered his mouth and was making his eyes bug out. She shook her head. At least someone was enjoying the moment.

"Please turn around," the priest said. "Pull your clothing down in front there." He nodded toward her chest.

"No. I won't." She glanced at the guard. He looked away. "You've seen enough."

"Miss one reason why I am here is that the examination by—" He paused and looked at the parchment, "—Father Blenheim was incomplete. We need to provide a complete statement to the court."

"I will not pull my shift down in front so you'll have to do without it." Ronnie eyed the guard in hopes Father Fitzsimons wouldn't insist and use the guard to hold her down.

"In that case, I will have to mark here that you refused to allow me to do my task," the priest said.

"I refused to show you only one place on my body. I cooperated with the rest—isn't that right, guard?" she asked.

He nodded while still dramatically covering his mouth.

"Think about this, miss. Is this really how you want me to report my findings?" he asked, eyebrows punctuating the question. "To tell the court that you refused to cooperate?"

"Yes. I will have to live with the consequences. Are you done?" Would he let her get away with it? She looked at the guard and he smiled behind his hand.

"Very well miss, yes the examination, such as it was, is done to the best of my ability. You may put your gown back on." He made a few marks on the paper and returned to his pocket.

She walked over to the bench and pulled the gown over her head. "Can you do the laces for me?" she asked the priest.

He walked out of the cell and pulled the door shut, ignoring her request. "Miss, I can now inform you that we have enough evidence for a water trial." He called the last words over his shoulder as he left the cell. The guard locked the door behind him.

"When?" Would she be able to escape? "Can you tell me how they do the water trial?" She asked, expecting more information from him, but relieved it was over.

He clapped his hat on his head and said, "Guard, can you let me out?"

After the guard relocked her cell door, the priest turned around and said through the bars, "The warden will inform you of the proceedings." The guard let him out of the chamber door and both men disappeared down the hall.

As soon as the door shut, Ronnie dug up the small knife Mathias had given her and hid it in her stocking. Her mouth was bone-dry. Would she be able to pull this off? What if they found the knife on her? She poured some water from the pitcher and sipped it. It had a strange metallic taste but she drank it anyway. It would be important to be hydrated. If only she had a full breakfast—she would need all of her strength to swim to Mathias in the cold water.

Ronnie debated taking off the petticoats to make her escape easier. Would they remove her shoes for the water trial? Maybe she should put the knife in the pockets around her waist instead of her stocking where a guard would be more likely to find it. She found the slit in her dress and felt for the pocket. The knife would fit nicely but the petticoats would have to stay on to cover the knife's bulge. Without the panniers, her dress dragged on the floor, but there wasn't anything she could do, there was no way she would put those damned things back on.

Ronnie lay down on the bench and tried to sleep, but her mind raced. How would Mathias know where to go? How would he not have been seen by the guards? Was there a strong current in the river? There were too many ways this plan could go wrong, but there didn't seem to be any other way.

A few hours later she heard the chamber door open and an older man in an official looking uniform and two other guards walked into the chamber. The younger of the guards, a man she had not seen before, opened the cell door and walked in, announcing, "Ma'am, please present your hands."

Ronnie held her hands out and the man tied them together at the wrist with a rough rope. He then tied a rope around her waist, leaving two long pieces dangling at her sides. She would have to cut her wrists loose first and then the rope around her waist to get free. It could be done but it would take some work.

The guard walked her out of the cell with the two other guards following behind. "We are going to conduct the water trial now miss. Please come this way."

Chapter 32 - Swimming, Swimming

Ronnie's heart beat madly. Doubt wormed its way in to diminish her already limited confidence. Would she be able to escape and get to Mathias without being caught? They made their way through the constables' area to a large metal door. Captain Green nodded to them, unlocked the door, and swung it open. A blast of cold air hit her face and forced her to take a deep breath. The icy air blew through her clothes. They made their way down a winding uneven path and a small crowd was gathered. Ronnie felt sick to her stomach.

"There she is!" yelled a man. The crowd murmured as she walked past.

"Witch!" yelled someone farther away. "Spawn of Satan!"

She could die right here and now if this didn't go well. It depended on how long they left her underwater. Could she get the knife out of her pocket? She was regretting putting it there—she should have listened to Mathias. What if she got the knife out but dropped it or failed to cut through the ropes? Surely she could get in a position to breathe. Her mom's face appeared and she could feel a soft caress of her cheek. "I'm sorry, Mom," she whispered.

They crested a hill and she could see the river below. The crowd followed them down to the riverbank toward a scaffold with a large rope blowing in the wind. All the bad outcomes danced before her, but she grabbed them by the scruff of the neck and shoved them in a bag, tying it closed. Using her mom's advice, she visualized the outcome she wanted, with the knife cutting the rope at her hands, then her waist, and a fast swim to Mathias and freedom!

The guards walked her up to the scaffold as Ronnie eyed the river. There didn't seem to be much of a current. She glanced back at the crowd with the vision from Madam Zangari's cottage turning around in her mind. As terrifying as this was, it did not have the horror and hatred of the scene in the water bowl. Madam Zangari's voice echoed in her mind—*the seeds of your destruction*. Ronnie swallowed hard, trying to create some moisture in her mouth. Her stomach protested and she nearly threw up the meager breakfast she had eaten.

The younger guard reached up and grabbed the rope from the scaffold. He clipped it to a simple metal circle attached to the rope around her waist. If she sliced the rope right next to the small metal ring it would release the entire belt of rope around her waist. She could get free in one simple cut if the knife was sharp enough.

The guard untied the rope at her wrists. Ronnie was tempted to jump in, but the rope was already tied to the scaffolding. Where was Mathias? She scanned the opposite bank but did not see anything resembling a small boat. There was a clump of trees just down the river. Could he be there? It would be nice to know which way to swim once she got free. A small bell tolled off in the distance and Ronnie followed the sound upriver to her right. There! A small white rowboat was hiding among the trees along the shore. It had to be him!

"Miss, please. I need you to hold out your hands," an older guard said, grabbing her right thumb and tying a small rope around it. He then took a second rope and tied it to her left thumb. The younger guard squatted down next to her feet, slipped off her shoes and pulled down her stockings.

She kicked her foot backward out of his reach. "What are you doing?"

"Miss, give me your foot. I need to remove your stockings," he said.

"Why?" Ronnie was glad she had chosen the pockets to hide the knife.

"Enough with the questions! You will allow my constables to prepare you for the trial." Ronnie lost her balance and stepped on the younger constable's hand.

"Owwww!" the younger constable cried out and stood up. "Miss, you will not assault me!"

Captain Green said, "Shut your mouth you prattling oaf and get on with your job."

The young guard gave her a don't-try-it look as he reached under her dress for the stockings, pulling each one off slowly.

"What are you doing?" she asked, her feet turning icy on the cold ground.

"Ma'am," the older constable said, "bend down toward your feet, if you please."

"What? Why do you want—" But before she could finish he shoved her so that she landed hard on her butt.

"That'll do nicely, miss." The younger guard quickly tied the left-hand rope to her right big toe and the right-hand rope to her left big toe. When he finished he pulled the rope tight to test it.

"Ouch, it is too tight!" she said. It was cutting off the circulation to her thumbs and toes. This would complicate things. Could she reach the knife in this position with opposing hands and feet tied?

"Miss," Captain Green said calmly. "We will lower you to the water to see if you will float or sink. We have attached the safety rope to your back there." He held the rope attached to the scaffold, showing it to her and then twisted it around to her back. "That's so that we can pull you to safety if you sink. Do you understand?" He signaled to a man out of her line of sight. She could feel the scaffold rope tightening, then lifting her off the ground.

"I understand!" she said, louder than she meant to, startled by the movement.

The crowd roared and she could hear voices cry out. "Drown her!" "Dunk the witch!" "Kill the spawn of the devil!"

The rope cut deep into her gut, not helping her nausea. She tried to lift her head to see across the water but she was leaning too far forward, her feet pulling her arms down. As she was lowered slowly toward the water Ronnie planned her first move—lift her left leg toward her right hand, and work her hand inside the pocket, if she could. She imagined exactly what she would do next, practicing in her mind each movement while taking deep breaths and expanding her lungs, getting ready for a long breath hold.

The crowd's noise level increased as she got closer to the water. The slight fishy smell of the river permeated her nose, making her think of her grandfather's lake. Ronnie wondered how deep the water was and hoped it wasn't too cold.

She hit the water hard, forcing air out of her lungs. The icy cold river encircled her and stole what remained of her air supply. Ronnie meant to take a large breath as she got close but they fooled her with the quick entry. Fumbling with numb fingers she reached for the knife but the rope held it short. Ronnie pulled as hard as she could and the rope came loose from her thumb. Her hand found the slit in the dress and rummaged around for the knife. Her lungs were protesting but she ignored the sensation. The last remaining warmth left her body and floated down the cold river.

She gripped the hilt to pull it from the pocket, then held the rope on her left wrist to saw through it. Her hands were free! Blindly she felt around her stomach for the ring and realized that now it was attached at her back. She sank deep into the river on entry, but now was heading back toward the surface.

Ronnie swam deeper into the water. Grabbing the rope around her stomach she sawed and pulled and sawed and finally, it broke loose, but in the process pulled the knife from her hands. The knife sunk quickly to the bottom and out of sight. Her freedom took her by surprise but she took advantage of it, swimming a few strokes to remain underwater as long as possible. Ronnie knew as soon as they saw her they would make an attempt to retrieve her. Lungs burning, she ignored the sensation. One thing playing underwater hockey had taught her was it was possible to hold her breath much longer than she had ever thought possible. She swallowed down the bit of air in her mouth and continued swimming with a wide deep breaststroke, pulling hard and recovering quickly, hoping they couldn't see her clothes under the water. The element of surprise would buy her some time.

She cut sharply to the left toward the copse of trees but had no idea how far she had gone. Finally, desperate to take a breath, she broke the surface to gulp for air. To her surprise, she heard a collective gasp from the crowd and guards yelling and screaming commands. She took a massive breath and a few smaller ones, packing the air in her lungs, another underwater hockey trick, and dove down, deep cutting sharply to the right again, making her way near the trees. It would be hard for someone to grab her from shore with the trees bunched so close together. The petticoats served their purpose but now were slowing her down, interfering with the breaststroke when they billowed out as she made the second part of her kick.

Ronnie surfaced and could not see the crowd with the trees blocking the view. Treading water she looked out across the river for Mathias. Where was he? A sharp whistle caught her attention to the right. A small boat was making its way toward her. She switched to freestyle for the better kick it offered, but the tight shoulders of the gown made it slower than she had hoped and would tire her out quickly. Sidestroke would offer her more freedom and the added benefit of keeping her head above water, where she could keep an eye out for Mathias. She paused to pull off the petticoats and managed to get two of them off.

Something caught her abruptly, jabbing her ribs and scraping along her spine. Ronnie turned around and saw a constable holding a long pole that was hooked around her. She grabbed the pole with both hands and kicked her legs with all her strength. The man on the other end of the pole was in waist-deep water. He lost his footing and fell face-first into the water. Ronnie threw the pole in front of her and watched as the current carried it downstream.

Another guard used a similar pole to pull the first man to safety. He made an attempt to reach Ronnie, but she was too far away. Ronnie ducked under the water, swimming briskly toward the small boat and away from anyone on shore.

The guards were gathered along shore yelling and waving their arms. She looked to her left and another boat was quickly gliding along the surface toward her. She was too low in the water to see either rower's face. Was that Mathias or was the other boat his? They were in opposite directions. She had to make the right choice.

Chapter 33 - Lost in the Stramash

"Felicia!" Steph yelled. "Let me in!" She banged on the door and tried ringing the doorbell but with the power out it didn't ring. "Hey, Felicia!" She yelled at the top of her lungs. "Where the hell did you go?"

The door flung open and Nick stood there looking nearly as shocked as she felt. He pulled her inside the house.

"What the crap are you doing out there, Steph? Have you no sense at all?" He glared at her.

"You smell like a campfire, Nick. The damn cat was on the windowsill and I knocked him off when I cranked the window open." She bent over to remove her muddy shoes.

"Sorry I was letting Nick in the back door." Felicia smiled behind Nick. "I saw him coming with the flashlight and wasn't sure if he would have someone with him."

"Did you?" Steph asked. "What did you find over there?"

"No, the house was completely empty. They must have left. Their car wasn't in the garage either." He wiped his face on his shirt.

"So what about the flashlight?" Steph asked while wiping the water from her face.

"Don't know, maybe it was a neighbor checking on them. Or maybe they were leaving." He took Steph's hand and led her to her room. Felicia followed.

"The fire is getting really close, Steph." He pointed out of her bedroom window. "You should grab a few things and we'll need to leave really soon."

"No! Damn! This is not supposed to be happening, Nick!" Steph made her way down the hallway to the guest room and pulled out her largest suitcase. "Oh my God, my house is going to burn down. Holy crap!" She rolled the suitcase to her room where she packed some clothes and photo albums. She rummaged through her drawers not sure what to take.

"Insurance papers, Steph. Are they already in your storm kit like I told you yesterday?" Nick asked.

"Yes, I've got those. But Nick, Hamish is lost here in the stramash." Steph was close to tears.

"I thought he was outside?" Nick said.

"Hamish, kitty, kitty," Steph called out making her way back to the guest room. He was not in his usual hiding place because the neighborhood had gathered in her closet. Where would he hide? "Kitty, kitty!"

"Steph just got him from the windowsill," Felicia said and scratched her head. "Nick, what does stramash mean?"

"Oh, it's one of Steph's Scottish words. It means mess, I think?" He rushed down the hall after Steph.

"Steph we have to get out of here—your fence is on fire. Your bedroom is twenty feet from the fence!" Nick grabbed her hand and spun her around. "Get your things. We have to go."

"My things? Hamish is the only thing I really want to save!" Tears ran down her face.

"I'll look for the cat, you get your important papers and we'll get out of here. Which neighbor are we going to?" Nick asked.

"Oh, two houses over. The Fitzpatrick's. Mimi knows them." Steph said and ran to the garage to find the kitty carrier. It was impossible to get him in there but he would never let her carry him in her arms.

She sloshed through the six inches of water on the floor and found the cat carrier on a shelf. "What else should I bring?" Nothing from the garage. "Oh, food for Hamish!" She reached for his bag of dry food on the second shelf and shoved it in the carrier.

Back in the house, she combed through the kitchen, gathering her address book, her laptop, attaché case, and a few photo albums to carry to the suitcase. She then grabbed three outfits and her favorite dress given to her by her mom on her last birthday. Her mind was spinning. This couldn't be happening. It just couldn't be!

"God, Steph, a dress. You have five minutes to save your most precious things and you pick a friggin' dress? You've lost your mind!" Nick said.

"Nick, my mum gave it to me!" Steph grabbed the framed picture of her family at her cousin's wedding in Edinburgh, and another picture of her parents and put them between her clothes. She found her makeup bag in the bathroom and shoved it in there too. "Should I take the car? I don't want it to be burned up too!"

"Yes!" Nick looked out the window. Mimi clutched the dog to her chest. Let's get in the car and get out of here before we can't get away."

"Where is Hamish?" Steph yelled at him. "HAMISH!"

"I don't know, Steph. Are you sure he's here?" he said.

"Yes, he ran to the back bedroom after I dropped him on the floor. He was scratching me. The bugger." Felicia rubbed the long lines of red on her arm.

Steph ran down the hallway. "Kitty, kitty. Damn it, Hamish, come here!" Her mind raced. What if she couldn't find him? "Hamish!"

Nick followed her into the room. "Steph we've gotta get out of here. Sparks are flying onto your roof and the house is going to be on fire any minute."

"Nick I can't leave Hamish! I can't!" Steph broke down again sobbing. "He is the only thing I want to save and I can't freaking find him!"

Chapter 34 - Swim Forest Swim

Swimming as hard as possible, Ronnie made progress toward the boat on the right. It had to be Mathias, he had whistled at her. Brass buttons sparkled in the sunlight off to her left. It must be the guards from the prison. Damn! They were going to reach her first!

She stopped swimming so she could kick hard and bring her hands wide, pushing down against the water, popping her head above the waterline. The man in the boat on the right wore a wide hat similar to the one Mathias had on when he visited her earlier. He was probably panicking, watching the other boat closing in. Hopefully, he wouldn't give himself away. *Keep cool Mathias—just appear as a friendly boater enjoying the day.*

She heard a low voice off in the distance. "Ronnie, swim to me!" It was Mathias. Damn, she would never make it. At least he could claim he was looking for someone else named Ronnie since the guards knew her as Regina. She glanced backward. The other boat was gaining quickly. The sun glinted off the eyes of the man at its helm.

"Witch, come to me!" he called. "You will not escape my grasp!" The rower stopped paddling and the boat slid toward her.

In a frantic effort, she sprinted as fast as she could away from the constables. She had to abandon the hope of reaching Mathias. There was no way they would escape. Even if she made it to him the guards would overtake Mathias's boat before she could get into it. It would take some time with Mathias's injured arm and then he would be in trouble as well.

Out of breath and muscles burning, she stopped and floated on her back. There was no point in using every ounce of energy. The shore was too far off and the men had nearly reached her. She glanced at Mathias saying a silent prayer for him, hoping he would be smart and start rowing in the other direction. He would only get himself caught helping her, a witch. Was that a hanging offense, too?

"Good afternoon. Enjoying this fine day?" Ronnie said as the boat approached alongside her in the water.

The man in the front of the boat reached out for her and she deftly swam under him, pushing on the front left bow, hoping to shake it enough to make him lose his balance. If he fell in he would probably drown. If all the historical novels she had read were correct not many people could swim in 1752. With both feet she pushed against the cold solid wood again, trying to flip the boat, but it was too heavy and she had nothing for leverage.

"God's teeth!" the man cursed as he fell heavily against the bow, narrowly escaping a dip in the river.

Ronnie grabbed the rope they used to tie it up. With her feet firmly against the boat, she pulled and made the boat rock violently.

"Rot your blood damned witch, you will stop this at once!" yelled the man at the back of the boat, reaching for her.

She grabbed his sleeve and pulled with all her might, feet still firmly planted against the bow of the boat, and was nearly successful in pulling him into the water, but the other man grabbed the back of his coat just in time and steadied him. "Hold me mate," he called out. "Reckon I've got the little hellcat!"

The man twisted to grab her upper arm and gripped her other wrist. He pulled her into the boat in one fluid motion and she landed on top of him.

"Agggghhhhh!" The man screamed inches away from her face, truly terrified. As quickly as he had pulled her into the boat, he flipped her over and landed on top slamming her hard against the beams of the boat, forcing the air out of her lungs. The other man scrambled to get out of the way and the boat rocked back and forth.

"Get off of me!" Ronnie yelled.

"Well caught, laddy! We should call you the witch snatcher!" the other guard said, laughing with relief.

"Stop your gawking you great lummox and get me a rope. Reckon this witch is still busting for a fight." In seconds the other guard had her tied in the bottom of the boat. Both men rowed with their faces turning pinker with each pull of the oars. Ronnie was entirely wiped out and shivered uncontrollably, the wind taking any warmth from her. She prayed Mathias had turned around and quit the pursuit. After fifteen minutes they arrived at a dock and several men crowded around the boat.

"Gentlemen, I present tae you the witch snatcher!" the guard called out with a Scottish accent. "You should hae seen him, lads. Lifted her clean out of the water, he did, and landed the little hellcat straight intae the boat."

"And then he screamed like a little girl," Ronnie added.

"That he did, that he did! 'Twas just like the screaming of a wee lassie!" The men roared with laughter. "Aye, gie her credit, the canny wee thing almost capsized our boat twice, nearly pulling both of us intae the water."

The men looked at her, some smiling, some making the sign of the devil. "Lads remove her from the boat if ye have the stomach for it," the Scottish man continued. Most of the men turned around and walked away. "Auch, so all yis want is a wee gander at the witch then, yer no gonna help us get her out?"

The constable who had screamed in her face reached down and grabbed her tied arms and pulled her to a standing position and then quickly lifted her over his shoulder. "I am the witch snatcher. It seems it's down to me to get this devil's baggage inside."

Ronnie's hands were stuck under her body and made for a very uncomfortable ride up the hill. The crowd was still gathered and she could hear voices yelling and cursing, "Burn her." "Hang the witch!"

A few people grabbed bits of her skirts and tore them off until a few guards walked on either side. Struggling was pointless. She looked out over the water and saw a small boat off in the distance but couldn't tell if Mathias was in it or not. Hopefully, he hadn't been suspected of trying to help.

The men brought her into the jail office. Someone brought a blanket to cover her up. Ronnie tried to stand but her legs were too weak and she crawled to a wooden chair, feeling like a cornered animal. She pulled the blanket around her and pushed wet hair out of her face.

"Well, well, Miss Ingram. It seems you have failed the trial by water. Do you understand what this means?" Captain Green was unable to look her in the eyes.

"No. Please tell me," she said, teeth chattering violently.

"The essence of the test is to discover if the water repels you. So that if indeed you are a witch, the renouncement of your baptism will occur as you will not sink in the water. If you are innocent of the charges made against you, you will sink." He spoke the words as if they made perfect sense.

"I sunk at first. Doesn't that count for anything?" she said.

He ignored her comment. "You not only prepared a spell to release the ropes, you floated across the river to attack the men in the boat. To my mind, madam, you are a very convincing witch."

"I didn't float, I swam. And I didn't cast a spell, I just pushed the boat. You think I conjured magical spells?" she said through chattering teeth.

"Miss Ingram, you have failed the water trial and have been proven a witch. There is no more to be said. You will be taken to court tomorrow where a judge will hear the evidence against you and your sentence will be announced," Captain Green said.

"What is the sentence for that bogus charge?" she asked.

"Hanging by the neck until you are dead." He looked triumphant but still would not meet her gaze.

"Hanging?" All the smartass comments fell away and this new reality set in. Her hand unconsciously went to her neck.

"You are hereby considered a prisoner of the King and henceforth will be allowed no visitors or comforts. May God have mercy upon your soul." He turned and called out, "Constable!"

A bright-faced man of about twenty turned and came toward them.

"Yes, Captain, sir?" the constable answered.

"Escort Miss Ingram to her cell. Block seven, number two."

"Yes, sir!" The young guard turned to Ronnie and said, "Ma'am." When he looked at her he shrunk back, visibly shaken at her appearance. He looked at the captain.

"This woman, who has been tainted by the devil himself has been swimming, if you please," the captain said with a smile that grew as the young man turned to face her. "And what's more, she has been proved to be a witch so treat her with care."

"Ma'am, please come with me." The constable motioned for her to walk in front of him. He was clearly afraid of her.

She tried to think of a way to take advantage of the young man but she was completely worn out and her mind felt like the bowl of mush she had for breakfast. It was difficult to walk a straight path. Thankfully, he did not take her past the other prisoners. That must have been a deliberate scare tactic when she had arrived. It had worked.

The guard opened the cell door and motioned for her to go in. He didn't say a word as he relocked the door and left. She wanted nothing more than to lay her head down and sleep.

Chapter 35 - The Devil is in the Details

A low creaking emanated from the solid oak chair as Jack leaned back. He was waiting for his lawyer to finish with another client. He steepled his fingers, tapping them together as he thought of the developments of the day. Regina had really rattled him this morning, what with all of her ramblings about the colonies and some strange numbers. It seemed as though Catherine had been correct about the devil. The idea of Regina's possession by evil spirits had begun as his excuse for removing Regina from polite society, but now she was a danger to his family.

The wild look in her eyes over the last few days seemed less like an act to convince him she had no memory of what took place at Lord Barton's estate than the expression of a woman who was afflicted by satanic possession. Regina had always been an obedient young lady, even as a child she had always done as she was told. Her insolence in the last two days outweighed all of her misdeeds to date.

Her removal would be difficult on Catherine, for they had been very close. Father Blenheim had provided plenty of evidence to convict her. The water trial though, that had been the final proof. It had been very dramatic. How she had got free was nothing short of a spectacle. To move across the water like that? It was ungodly. He rubbed his eyes. It was increasingly hard to get to sleep of late, what with all the worrying about Regina. He would lose his little sister if the trial went as planned. While that came with some benefits—not having to pay a dowry to any potential husband, and no more bad feelings between his family and that of Lord Barton, it would be sad to lose more of his kin. He had already lost his dear mother and father, and his older brother.

"Mr. Ingram?" Mr. Hallister's assistant called. "Mr. Hallister is ready to see you."

"Yes, thank you," Jack replied, standing and smoothing his waistcoat. He straightened his tie and thought of the day Regina was born. She was so small and pink and so delicate. It seemed inconceivable that he would be here with his attorney, plotting evidence to have her hanged. The memory of her rosy cheeks as a five-year-old girl and her sweet hugs would be all he would have left of her. Regina had always looked up to him as a father figure. Their own father had been busy with the business and had not been around much. Jack had taught her how to ride a horse and how to speak French.

"Mr. Ingram, your servant, sir," came the booming voice of Mr. Hallister, who shook his hand. He was a large man, with light brown hair, and the fact that his otherwise abundant flowing locks were thinning on top was his only physical flaw. The man was cut of sturdy fabric, with solid shoulders and thick legs.

Jack shook his hand. "Mr. Hallister, how does this day find you?"

"Very well, Mr. Ingram, very well, thank you kindly sir." He motioned to an empty chair near his desk. "Please take a seat."

Mr. Hallister set down a large folder on the desk. "Have you decided to pursue this somewhat troublesome matter, Mr. Ingram?"

Jack sighed, sitting down on the chair. "Yes. Sadly, it is clear to me now. It has to be done."

Regina's face on her last birthday, aglow with excitement about her special dinner and gifts, passed through his mind. What would Mother think about her actions of late? Would she be supportive of what he was about to embark upon? Father would be behind him, especially with the financial gains he would receive after the time-shift if the deal with Mr. Prescott worked out successfully.

Jack turned around to face Mr. Hallister. "Let us go through the papers."

"Mr. Ingram," the lawyer began, tugging at his lower lip, "I trust that you are aware that if they convict her the penalty will be hanging."

"Yes, I am aware. However I must not think of the details of this business, else I may not complete the task."

Mr. Hallister gave him a stern look. "The devil is in the details, Mr. Ingram, as you well know."

"Which is precisely why I need to proceed with this, my good fellow. Gracious, if you had only seen my sister this morning you would be in agreement with me, that she is possessed. Indeed she was ranting! Raving on about strange spells and places I have never heard of. The devil has her and I am certain now that she must be destroyed. I cannot have her near such a depraved ungodly creature in close proximity to my wife and my unborn son."

"Indeed I understand, sir, indeed I have the utmost sympathy for your plight. But are you quite convinced that matters have reached such a dire pass as this? Are you sure that the devil has quite taken possession of the poor child?" Mr. Hallister thumbed through a document.

"I fear there is no doubt, though it saddens me greatly to face it. It upsets me more than I can say. My sweet darling little sister spitting forth the vile utterances of evil and death." Jack covered his mouth to hide the tremble of his lips.

"Allow me to offer my sincere condolences for this dreadful affliction that has been suffered upon your family. Let us put together a strong case for you, so we can end this horrendous matter as soon as possible." Mr. Hallister pulled out a piece of vellum and placed it upon a blotter at the end of his desk.

Jack stood and turned toward the window, composing himself. There was no other choice about the matter. It had to be done.

"We will go to the magistrate now to discuss the evidence. I am quite sure he will agree that we should pursue it to trial," his lawyer said.

Jack steeled himself. He would have to retell the entire sorted tale to the magistrate. But in the end, it was the right thing to do.

Chapter 36 - Time to Steal

It had taken Mathias the last two hours to wrap his mind around the fact that Ronnie had not escaped the swimming as he had planned. Again, he had not managed to help her with his interference but had managed to make her situation significantly worse than if he had left her alone. Mathias worked his arm to get the stiffness out. Deep in his bones, he could feel the fever taking hold and sapping him of strength. But he could not fail—her life depended on it. He had no idea why the bracelet was so important to her but she needed it and that was enough for him. In his mind, he could see her soft hazel eyes looking up at him pleading for help.

Walking the final block he looked around for the telltale signs of Jack's presence. The two bay horses were not in the stable. Mathias walked through the courtyard in the back entrance, slipped in the kitchen door, and up the back steps. Several people were in the kitchen busily making the next meal. No one paid attention to his presence. At the top of the stairs, spots appeared before his eyes. The room spun. He knelt down, hoping not to blackout. Not now. Not here. Dark shadows shifted around the edges of his vision, like wolves coming in for the kill. He pressed his hands on his eyes, willing his head to clear.

Footsteps behind urged him to stand and move out of sight. He slipped into Regina's room and closed the door. He was hoping that it would be empty and it was. The room was cold without a fire and made him think of the last time he was with her here. It was painfully devoid of her lovely spirit.

The footsteps made their way past Regina's room and female voices drifted toward him. He pressed his ear to the door and listened. Footsteps continued past him and down the stairs. A cold clammy sweat broke out on his forehead. The birch bark tea must have worn off, for the ache was back. He listened intently—the hallway was quiet. Jack's room was at the end of the hall A loud creak sounded as he stepped on a lose board making his way down the hall.

"Margaret!" Catherine called out from her room.

Gott's gebiss. Mathias opened the nearest door and quietly closed it behind him. It was dank and musty, but thankfully empty.

"Margaret, is that you?" Catherine called out again.

Mathias's stomach lurched and a sweat broke out along his back. He slumped down in a small hard chair and took several deep breaths, trying to regain his composure. This fever was sapping his strength. Ronnie had asked for his assistance in collecting the bracelet. He felt it was his duty to return it to her possession. To what end he did not know, and if his scheming did not pan out, the hangman would likely get the bracelet even if she managed to keep it hidden before then. Equally as likely was that a constable would take it from her and neither of them would ever see it again. Stephen had said that if the swimming went against her that she would be hung in a day or two following.

The last words from Madam Zangari were that he and Ronnie would meet again, in another time and place. Deep in his soul, he felt that would be so. He did not know if that meant they would be together in a few weeks in the North Country, or something more ethereal, but he felt it was destined to be true.

Perhaps that was only the fever talking. He stood up, eager to complete the task and move on to the next more difficult one. He had not been in this room yet. Since taking up residence at the Ingram Estate a few months past, it had always been locked up. They must have been setting this room up for the nursery. A small box on the chest of drawers caught his eye. He walked over to it and slid the top off with the hope of finding Ronnie's watch inside. Only a slip of paper and a small needle and thread were there. Perhaps this room was too easy for servants to enter to leave valuable items in it, Jack would likely hide valuables in his own room.

Mathias listened closely for any noises in the hall, then he placed his hand on the doorknob. He would find the bracelet and then retrieve a few of his personal belongings in the room where he had lodged. A palette in front of his sister's hearth would have to do until he could see Ronnie to safety. Would someone try to stop him? If he were healthy he would have no trouble with anyone in the Ingram's employ, as he was taller and more powerfully built than anyone here. The only one equal to his strength was Simon, a lad in the stable, but he would be occupied out of doors with the horses.

The hallway was silent. He opened the door quietly and glanced around to find it empty. Mathias carefully stepped along the hallway, avoiding any loose boards this time. Would Mr. Ingram lock his bedchamber door? The question was answered as he tried the handle.

Mathias reached in his pocket for the skeleton key he had brought from his sister's house. It was his only hope of a quiet entry. If need be, he would break the door down, but that would have unwelcome consequences.

Mathias inserted the key and worked it around and after a few seconds, the lock turned. Murmuring a silent prayer, he quickly shut and locked the door behind him and searched the room. There was nothing in the chest of drawers. He went to the small elegant desk by the window. It was locked. He pulled out the skeleton key and attempted to fit it in the keyhole without success.

Stymied, Mathias continued searching the antechamber and then the bedchamber. There was no sign of Ronnie's bracelet. "Jack, vere have you hidden zis prized possession?" he whispered. A noise in the antechamber startled him and he froze. A key was working the lock.

Mathias looked around for somewhere to hide. Concealment was not an easy option for a man his size. He ran to the back room and stood next to the wardrobe. It was not visible from the other chamber and he hoped whoever it was would not venture this far. Footsteps clicked across the antechamber and back again. If the steps had been a hair faster they would have kept in time with his heartbeat. They came toward him—he had a matter of seconds before he was discovered. The important question was whose footsteps were they? A maid, or was it Jack?

Mathias's weakened state meant he would need to use the element of surprise to overpower Jack. He waited like a cat readying for the mouse. Mathias sprung on Jack and slammed him against the wall. Before Jack could cry out, Mathias grabbed his throat and squeezed hard enough to darken his complexion.

"Cousin, you vill listen to vat I have to say," Mathias whispered. "If zat rope is placed around Regina's neck I vill kill you *mit* zese hands." He clutched his throat further to make his point clear.

Jack stared back, eyes wide. He struggled to free himself but Mathias had a firm grip. "If you cry out I vill strike you. You do not doubt zat I can put you on zee floor again?" Jack nodded his head in agreement. "I had not intended to do so at Father Blenheim's, but if you force my hand, I promise my actions vill be *mit* increased fervor."

Mathias searched Jack's pockets and pulled out a rope. "Zis may be of some use." He released his grip and worked the rope around Jack's hands. A search in the other pockets found a small key.

"Stealing my property will land you in jail, Mathias," Jack croaked, his voice hoarse from the throttling.

"I vill not be taking your property, Cousin, and for zee record, attempted murder is a far bigger crime." He grabbed the back of Jack's head, pushing him onto the floor. Mathias landed on top of him and rammed a knee into his back. The air rushed out of Jack's lungs. Mathias tore a strip of cloth from the curtains around the bed and made a gag. There was no need to have the man ruin his chances of using the key.

He tore a longer strip and tied his cousin's feet. "Sorry for treating you so roughly, but all affection I felt for you, Cousin, vanished ven you shot me." Mathias stood up and brushed off his jacket and pants.

Jack mumbled something incoherent as Mathias worked the key into the locked desk, hands shaking, but managing to turn the lock. Rummaging through the desk, he found a sealed envelope with Lord Barton's name written on it. He stuffed it into his pocket and opened the right-side bottom drawer. In the back of a small box, he found a bracelet. Turning it over he examined the clasp to confirm it was the one Ronnie had been wearing the other night. He slipped it into his pocket and threw the key toward Jack. It hit him on the cheek and then skidded across the floor.

Jack briefly stopped fighting against his bonds and stared up at Mathias, hatred in his eyes. "Do not forget vat I have said. If you take Regina to court you vill not live another day."

He walked out of the chamber, using his sister's skeleton key to relock the door. It would be awhile before Jack was found. Enough time to get away and take care of his other task. He slipped silently down into the room where he had boarded for the last several months and gathered his meager belongings, throwing them into the bag he had brought them in from Prussia. He made his way down the stairs and out of the kitchen. Quickly, he walked out of the courtyard behind the Ingram estate and back out onto the street. Adrenaline coursed through his limbs.

194

Chapter 37 - My Kingdom for Your Shoes

A guard showed up a short time later and handed Ronnie a small tray with a bowl of brownish mush and another rock hard piece of bread. At least the mush was hot. Her clothes were still damp and any heat her body produced evaporated despite the blanket wrapped around her. She would take the wet clothes off if she wasn't worried about the guards finding her that way. At least the wet fabric would not be next to her skin.

"Any chance I could get some dry clothes? I'm really cold."

The guard darted his eyes toward her and away again. "Ma'am, you need to make a formal request."

"How do I do that?"

"The Captain of the Guard needs to receive a request." He wouldn't look at her and turned and opened the door.

"Wait. Can you formally ask him for me?" she yelled after him. The door closed midsentence.

She grabbed the bars and yelled. "How do I make a formal request?" Under her breath, she said, "You sack of shit!"

She scanned the cell for some paper. She could write a request. There was nothing but the food and a napkin. In the morning, she would ask for paper and something to write. The bench was hard on her sore rear end but the warmth of the bowl of mush soothed her cold hands. With her stomach rumbling, she decided it was going to be eaten regardless of any weird lumps. She savored each bite of the mystery mush, and thankfully found no anonymous stowaways, fingernails or otherwise.

The bread softened a bit when she left it in the mush. Ronnie devoured every bit of the meal, using the bread to wipe the bowl clean. At least her stomach was full. On Maslow's hierarchy of needs, a few in the bottom row were covered now: shelter, food, water, excretion, breathing. Keeping warm and sleep might be a problem. The bigger issue was the next row up—her safety. Would they hang her? Her hands went to her neck again.

An aching tiredness worked its way through her bones up to her chest. She set the bowl down with shaky hands. The hot meal had warmed her but not enough. She grabbed the blanket and laid down on the bench, physically and emotionally drained. Sadness poked at the edges of her mind. Would this be her last day alive? Would they hang her tomorrow? She could feel her mom's arms wrapping around her in a warm embrace. Too tired to cry she closed her eyes and fell into a restless sleep where she wondered what other differences there were in this time period other than the witches' law and the failed revolution. Frantic dreams pulled at her subconscious with harrowing escapes and death-defying feats of strength.

Waking with a start she sat up and looked around in the cold damp prison cell. It was nearly colorless in the low lamplight. Was it morning? Movement caught her eye in the corner of the room. A huge horrible rat sniffed around her empty bowl and then tipped it over. Startled at the noise, it scurried off under the bars and into the dark corners of the cell across from her.

Ronnie shuddered and pulled the blanket around her feet, tucking it protectively around her icy toes. Like that would help if the hideous creature wanted a bite of her flesh. At least the bench was up off the floor, but the rat could surely reach her if it wanted.

The weariness had subsided a bit. She must have managed a little sleep. Stretching, she sat up with her feet on the bench. *I wish they would give me my shoes back.* They had not bothered to return them after the swimming. They would at least have kept her toes from monsters' nibbles and added a layer of warmth between her flesh and the chilly air.

She sat cross-legged and took stock of the situation. The hope that had engulfed her yesterday was gone, snatched out of her chest the moment the men pulled her into the boat. Her family would be devastated. Jeffrey and Steph would be left trying to tackle unanswerable questions. How the hell had she gotten here? Something tickled her foot and she jerked it away sure it was the rat. It wasn't. Her foot was wet. She looked up expecting a leaky roof but she realized her eyes were responsible for the drip.

She wiped at her face. Damn tears. They were completely useless. "I'm sorry, Mom." Tears freely flowed as she thought of the police notifying her mother of her disappearance. How would she handle it? Would she spend her lifesavings hiring private detectives to find her? There would be no trace. But what explanation could Jeffrey give them? It was completely unexplainable.

Would he be accused of doing something to her? Steph and LT knew she had gone to his lab so there would likely be an investigation with him as the prime suspect. She pictured Jeffrey's handsome face with his mouth pulled down in sadness. What would he tell them? Would he lose his job for having her there during the storm? This had been his dream job—if her disappearance ruined his dreams, his life...

Steph would go ballistic accusing Jeffrey of all kinds of things. Of course, Steph would also blame herself for talking her into moving to Florida and not insisting that Ronnie go to her house instead of Jeffrey's lab. If she had only stayed in Virginia.

Her sweet niece, Molly, would be sad, but probably sheltered from the worst. Her brother, David, on the other hand, would be a mess. They were supposed to look after their mom together in her old age. Now it would all fall on him. They had not been as close since Dad's death a few years ago, despite her attempts to talk to him about it. They were just starting to get their relationship back.

Was there any possibility of getting back to Florida? Not from this jail cell. Would she have a chance to convince Jack to let her out? Was it even in his hands anymore? After the swimming "evidence" and the ploy she had used on the guards with her Hermione spell—and the moles. The stupid pointless moles. Would he be at the trial? He seemed truly terrified of her when she started talking about Florida and hurricanes.

She was supposed to start her new job on Monday. Her boss's smiling face popped into her mind and quickly changed to a concerned expression. What was his name? The tall dark and handsome Mike Walsh. It was a great job, too. Damn it, her life was just beginning, how on earth did she end up here?

The trial would be in a few hours. Surely they would feed her first and give her some clean dry clothes. Wouldn't they? She sat wondering how to prepare for the trial. Would Mathias show up to defend her? Would he try to get her free? It would be great to see him, but it was risky. Part of her wanted him to stay far away.

Chapter 38 - Lost in Space

Jeffrey stared at the screen. This was not happening! He rubbed his eyes and pushed away from the desk. Where was Ronnie? Why wouldn't the goddamned program pull her back? Every time he would connect to her it would bounce him out and disconnect. He imagined the call to his boss in the morning. "Well, you see I've begun human testing without your approval and I've lost the subject in 1752."

Yeah, that would go over well. It was supposed to be a one-time experiment as a gift to Ronnie. Now it had the upward potential to be a career and a girlfriend killer. All the years of planning and hard work and he had to risk everything. Why did he do this?

A message popped up on the screen. *Connection established.* "Please stay, please stay!" He punched in the return sequence. The wind speeds were dropping but it was still doable. "Ronnie hang on, I'm coming for you." He let out a sigh and typed like his life depended on it.

He hoped the coding had activated the backup plan. He had put the tracking pellets in her food as the backup if the watch failed or was removed. It worked on the cats but they had the collars on as well. He flipped through the notebook to his contingency plan. The storm was winding down and the window for rescuing Ronnie was slipping away. He needed sufficient power to bring her back.

With his heart beating fast and fingers trembling, he found the final sequence and keyed it into the program. He held his breath and hoped it would make the connection to Ronnie. It didn't bounce back with an error message so he flipped the page and entered the second part of the sequence. "Hell yeah!" It was working. She would be back in a matter of minutes and hopefully would be undamaged.

He watched the code scroll down the screen and silently begged it to continue. Ronnie's life depended on it and for that matter so did this project. Already on thin ice with his boss, he had been hired to use the weather's power to create useable, storable energy. Vastly improving the last scientist's design his results were stellar, but he was not storing as much as he really needed to call the project a success yet.

He had begged his boss to let him use the lab for a side project and he reluctantly had agreed as long as it didn't interfere with the safety of the lab and progress with his current storable energy project. If something happened to Ronnie that would destroy the trust and possibly end his contract with the lab.

The computer hummed along pulling massive amounts of power needed to return a human subject. With the cats, he could use standard power if it was configured correctly. That is why he had moved to Florida, the capacity had been reached with small mammals. There simply wasn't enough power to transport a human subject. This lab was using Central Florida's massive electrical storms for research in hopes of finding ways to capture the power of a storm. With Central Florida boasting the most lightning strikes in the world and almost daily thunderstorms in the summer it was a perfect place for this research.

The sad truth was that although he really did like Ronnie he never really saw himself with her in the long-term. The few months they had been apart had begun to unravel the spell she had had on him. Not that she wasn't amazing because she truly was. Just her grip on his soul was lessening and he liked it better that way. The separation these last few months drastically helped him stifle the emotions that would interfere with his research with her as the test subject. He was breaking the rules by sending her before he had all the kinks worked out—like a fail-proof method of staying in contact with the subject for example. Damn it!

What he really needed was solid proof that the subjects were, in fact, going back in time, not just disappearing into the vortex. Experiments with the cats recorded data with the special collar transmitters, but there was no way to confirm actual contact in the past. Ronnie could give him the confidence to put the project forward and apply for human testing.

He pushed his chair away from his desk and went to the carafe of coffee and filled his cup. He added one Splenda and looked around the room. The syringe was in his drawer—it would need to be ready when Ronnie returned. A sedative would be delivered so he could let her sleep off the after effects of travelling. The cats had always been highly agitated on their return. Ronnie would sleep soundly and then be fresh in the afternoon when he could stop by and confirm the time and location of the trip.

An alarm startled him out of his thoughts. He grabbed a stirrer and walked to the computer. The screen read, "Critical overload."

"Critical overload?" He set the coffee down next to the computer. Was it a power overload, or the computer system? He sat down and flipped through his notes. "What the hell!"

Chapter 39 - Rats!

A small noise drifted through the fog to reach her consciousness. It was her cat, Fluffy, purring. She could feel the warmth against her leg and the comforting vibration of her happy noises. Ronnie reached down to stroke her soft fur. Her hand touched something rough and felt a pinch on her finger. She sat up with a start. Fluffy never nipped her. A dark shape scurried off into the shadows.

"Eeeeeeewwwwwww!" she screamed. Her finger stung and she nearly put it in her mouth. Blood poured from her fingertip. She squeezed it, pushing more blood out. "Oh my God!" She had been bitten by the horrible hideous rat!

She looked around to see if it was still there and took three large steps to the pitcher of water. It was gone. What diseases would she get from that beast? Bubonic plague? Rabies? Blood dripped onto the floor and soaked into the dirt. She poured water into the cup and stuck her finger in. Man, she wished she had some soap or alcohol or anything to kill the germs. She took three large steps and she was back on the bench tucking her legs underneath her for protection.

She squeezed her finger again. "Oh my God, this is disgusting! Stupid freaking rat!" The water was a swirl of reddish pink. Now her cup would be full of funky rat germs.

***

In the busy prison kitchen, Davidson was preparing meal trays. Sweat rolled down his back and steam from the pot wafted around his face. He used his sleeve to wipe his brow. There was a loud crash followed by louder voices reprimanding someone. It was what he had been waiting for—a moment when everyone would be distracted. He wiped his hands on the front of his apron and slid one hand into the folded section he had created. It was still there. Taking a deep breath he looked to the left and then to the right. No one was watching. He palmed the small slip of paper, folded it a few times and slid it under the bowl. He filled the bowl with a double portion and set it on the tray, draping a cloth over it. Glancing around to be sure it was safe he dropped in a handful of cooked beans under the cloth.

The usual cacophony of noises continued as the workers returned to the task of preparing meals for the prisoners. He took the tray and walked a few steps to the canister of hard tack, grabbed one large piece, and set in on the tray. A prisoner, Jones, reached out to take the tray and he pulled it back protectively.

"Not ready. Take that one," he said, pointing with his chin. This tray was meant for ... what was his name? That Irish fellow. Well, it didn't matter. He knew what the bloke looked like. As long as no one mucked it up.

A voice behind him made him jump, nearly upsetting the tray. "Ready?"

He turned. A face with a ruddy complexion and flaming red hair greeted him. "Aye," he told him.

The redhead caught his eye. "Tis the one, right?"

"Tis the one," Davidson said and handed him the tray.

The redhead turned and walked out of the kitchen. Not realizing he had been holding his breath, he let it out. It was done. His hands shook and he glanced around, hoping no one had noticed.

"Look sharp Davidson, you're behind," his supervisor said, shaking his head. "Eighty-five trays and you're lingering in the middle of the kitchen?"

"Sorry, Gov." A small smile played at his lips. He busied himself with his real work now that the surreptitious task was completed, and he could now settle into the routine. Davidson lost himself in thought, calculating the ways he could spend the money he had just earned.

***

Ronnie felt the wicked rat germs race through her blood, working their way to her heart, her brain. Her stomach clenched. She felt like she was going to throw up. A burning sensation on the end of her left pointer finger was all that remained from the assault. It was just an overactive imagination. Surely someone couldn't feel germs attacking their body. Her heart skipped a beat. Oh no, it had made it to her heart.

A clanking of the door pulled her out of morbid imaginings. A man appeared at the barred grill with the now familiar black tray. He had a small bundle tucked under his arm.

"Miss, a change of clothes. And a nice plate of vittles." He had a lilt to his speech—he wasn't English. He paused to look around before he set the tray down on the table to free his hands to unlock the cell door. He set the tray inside the cell. He seemed to be nervous, not as comfortable with the procedure as she would have expected. He smiled at her. As he locked the door he whispered through the bars, "Under the bowl."

"What?" she asked.

"Miss Regina, under the bowl." He said it a bit louder this time before turning on his heel and opening the door.

"Wait, please sir!" she called out.

He stopped, looking nervously around.

"I've been bitten by a rat. Can you send a doctor?" she asked.

"A rat? Aye, I will pass along a word for ye, right enough. No guarantees they will give a care for ye though, miss," the guard said.

"Oh and sir, Can I get my shoes back? I'll need them for the trial."

He glanced at her feet and looked away. He mumbled something under his breath. "Sure, I will inform the captain."

"Thank you," she said. He lingered for a moment, looking at her with a strange expression. Why was he so different from the other guards? He gave a smile and a nod and he opened the door and walked out.

Wasting no time she lifted the cloth covering the bowl, to find it completely full with a serving of something oblong and brown on top. She picked it up and put it in her mouth. It was very salty but it had a good flavor—beans! Twice as much food as usual, and beans to boot. Now it made sense, the guard knew about the extra food and was looking her over to see why she was worth it.

"Under the bowl," he had said. Ronnie lifted the bowl and found a slip of the thick paper. Was this parchment like father Blenheim had used? She unfolded it and in small neat beautiful cursive writing it read:

> *Ronnie, I am so sorry I failed you. Please do not give up hope. I am working on a plan to assist in your release. If we are blessed with good luck at the trial you will be free and I will retrieve you. If we face difficulties with the trial I most humbly request that you prepare yourself at its completion. A man you do not recognize will call upon you and upon his lips a word you will be familiar with—Charley. If you would put your faith in him, I can assure you he is my man and will take care to reunite us. I will be there for you.*
>
> *With greatest affection,*
> *Mathias*

Tears flowed down her face and she held the paper to her lips. Mathias was behind the extra food and maybe the dry clothes. He was going to try to save her. How would he pull that off? It seemed completely impossible but if anyone could do it Mathias could. She remembered the night she met him everyone in the entire room was under his spell, except for Doctor Wiggams. He calmed Jack, he made her relax, and even Margaret seemed to be captivated by him.

She filled the spoon with the brown mush and beans and ate slowly, her other hand cupping the bowl for warmth. The bundle of clothes was in her line of sight. A few more bites and she would get dressed. Would anyone come in while she changed? God, she hoped not. She ate quietly and then stood and picked up the bundle.

The string that held the clothes came untied easily. It contained a long black dress, a corset, a linen shift, stockings with garters, and several petticoats. She wanted nothing more than to get out of these damp dirty clothes, even it meant she had to wear these ridiculous ones instead. What she wouldn't give for a pair of jeans, a hoodie, and her Nikes.

Ronnie rinsed the rat-germy cup with water from the pitcher and filled it up. It was the best she could do without soap. She grabbed the cloth that covered the mush. First, she peeled the filthy dress off and then lowered the shift to her waist before dipping the cloth in the cold water and washing off the stink of the river.

Ronnie was way beyond cold now but the dry clothes would help and she needed to look a bit more together for the trial. Listening closely for sounds of the door opening, she lowered the shift to the floor and washed the rest of her body quickly. Then put on the clean shift, corset, and petticoats. Damn horrible corset but if it added to the air of respectability she would need for the trial it would be worth it. When were they going to invent the bra? It was nearly impossible to pull the corset tight in the back but she managed to tie them awkwardly, then reached for the black dress.

She held the dress up in front of her—it would be very warm and with the shift next to her skin hopefully wouldn't be itchy. It was ugly as sin, but it didn't matter, it was dry and clean. She put on the dingy stockings and still had no shoes, but at least her feet were covered. The dress was a lot smaller than the one she had just taken off, and there were no stupid panniers. Eyeballing the bowl of steaming mush she returned to the bench and finished it. Her full stomach pushed against the corset and she lay down on the bench to stretch out.

Her mind shifted to the trial. She had no idea what to expect. If she only had a notebook to organize her thoughts. In grad school, she over prepared for every oral report to help calm her nerves and allow her to concentrate on the presentation and not have to worry about the material. It would be a lot easier to do this in PowerPoint. Even a legal pad would vastly improve her likelihood of remembering what she wanted to say with the courtroom of staring strangers.

Was she supposed to present her defense or would they pepper her with questions? For that matter what was her defense? Could moles be argued as a method for proving or disproving witchliness? Her argument would be weird, especially coming from a twenty-first century woman. Would that convince them further that she was a witch?

How could she explain her ability to get free from the ropes and swim across the water? Ronnie couldn't mention the knife because the guards would be suspicious about someone helping her. The thought of Mathias's smile warmed her. Was he okay? He must have been crushed with sadness when the guards pulled her from the water. What was his new plan if she got convicted? God, she would have to focus, her mind was racing all over the place.

Over the next hour, she worked out her defense and tried to practice it a few times. Nerves would be a problem for sure. Ronnie was not a fan of public speaking, and in this time and place, in an appeal to save her life the stakes were as high as they could get. Most likely she would freeze up and not be able to defend herself.

Chapter 40 - Smoked Out

"Steph, you have to leave Hamish. Open a window so he can get out." Nick pulled her toward the kitchen. Mimi was rolling Steph's suitcase toward the garage.

"I need my purse and keys." She ran to the front door to grab them and then looked around hoping there wasn't anything she wished she had taken. "My jewelry box!"

"Steph!" Nick said.

She ran into her room and snatched the small cherry wood box that held her family heirlooms.

"Steph! Come on!" Nick yelled.

Smoke permeated the room now. "Hamish, Hamish!" Steph cranked open the window near the front door, the one furthest from the fire, and glanced around the room. Nick was heading her way.

"I've got the hurricane kit already in the car. Mimi and Felicia are waiting! Let's get out of here!" Nick said.

Steph followed him to the garage. Tears rolled down her face and she sniffed. She pressed the automatic garage door opener. The door didn't budge—the power was out. She saw the branch sticking through the ceiling and wondered how much that was going to cost. Like that mattered since the whole damn house was going to burn down.

"I'm on it Steph!" Nick splashed to the Jeep and shined the flashlight near the rafters. He found the red handle that hung down and pulled it to release the automatic door latch. "Oooh, man." He bent over and clutched his shoulder.

"Are you okay? Nick, I could have gotten that," she said. He was a mess. "Here I'll get the door." Steph went to the metal garage door and pulled it up.

"Steph, let me get that," Nick said, standing now, his pants soaked from the water on the floor.

"You're hurt. I can get it. I'm not a helpless wee lass." She wiped the spider webs from the inside of the garage door off her hands.

"Um, Steph. There's a tree down across the driveway! We're not going to be able to drive in this." Nick waded through the water toward her.

Steph looked behind her at the huge palm tree across the driveway. "Oh no! I forgot about that tree." It had fallen right in front of her while she was ringing the doorbell. "Now what?"

Everyone got out of the car and splashed in the water.

"I guess we can make a run for it," Nick said.

Steph lifted her rolling suitcase out of the trunk and shoved some of the contents of the hurricane kit inside the outer pockets. Felicia and Mimi took a few bottles of waters and put them in their pockets and purses.

Sugar whined and Mimi patted her head. "It's gonna be all right, honey."

Steph wished that were the truth. At least the damn dog couldn't understand false hope.

Nick stuffed a few waters and some snacks in his cargo short pockets. They all stood looking out at the storm. It was much calmer than it had been. Nick took a few steps closer to the open garage door. "The wind—it's hardly blowing."

Steph looked up from messing with the bag. "Is the storm over?"

Nick climbed in the car and Steph threw him the keys. He clicked it to give power to the radio without turning the engine over.

Mimi opened the car door near her and sat down. Felicia came close to Mimi and listened.

"There is a tornado warning for the following counties." They listed every county in Central Florida again. "This is Terry James of WKJB Orlando with your first alert forecast. The eye of the storm is over Altamonte Springs. It is one of the smallest eyes I've ever seen. It may only be five or ten minutes of relief from the winds. But don't be fooled, we still have the back half of the storm to contend with."

Nick switched off the car and tossed the keys to Steph. "This is our chance to get to a safer location. Grab your stuff ladies let's go for an evening stroll." He gripped one of Steph's bags and put it over his good shoulder. Mimi and Felicia hesitated under cover of the garage.

"Come on the eye of the storm is here, we have a chance to get to a safer place," Nick said.

They looked at each other and stepped out into the rain. Steph followed behind rolling her big suitcase. "Nick, my car too?"

"I know Steph. There is nothing we can do about it. I can't move that tree!" Nick stepped toward the tree. He shined the flashlight around and then back toward her. "If I could I would, but we're running out of time. We have to get somewhere safe before the storm cranks up again."

Steph stepped out into the rain and closed the garage door, surprised at how heavy it was. She rolled the suitcase over leaves and small branches. Nick helped Mimi over the tree and then took the dog from Felicia so she could climb over the obstacle. Steph picked up the suitcase and flung it over the tree, and then climbed over it. The rain was still coming down hard but was not blowing in her face like it had earlier.

They walked up the street away from the fire and everything Steph owned. "Hamish! Here kitty, kitty!" Steph looked back at her house where a stream of orange smoke billowed over the roof. It must have caught on fire. Would wee Hamish make it out? She couldn't bear the thought of something bad happening to her precious kitty.

"Which house are we going to?" Nick asked. Another tree was down on the neighbor's house and they walked around the huge root ball. It was slow going with the suitcase rolling over all the sticks and branches on the ground.

"The one with the tree on it," Steph said. "The neighborhood is not going to be the same after this storm!"

"No, we should pick another one and fast." He looked up at the treetops swaying more violently.

They walked past the next house and didn't see any lights on inside. On the left side of the street, though, there was a flickering light within. A bit further away from the fire too.

"How about here?" Nick said.

Mimi answered, "Yes, my friend Ona lives here."

The rain was torrential now with the wind picking up. "Thank God, we need to get inside!" Nick said over the noise.

Steph wiped away her tears and tried to calm down. Her house, her cat, her car—everything would be gone! She looked back hoping to see Hamish following them on the road. He wasn't.

Mimi knocked on the door and they waited. Mimi knocked again. "Ona? It's Mimi. There's been a fire. Please let us in!"

The door opened and a tiny elderly woman stood there in her robe and slippers. "Oh my, you have a crowd with you. I'm in my nightclothes." She pulled her robe to cover up, looking up at Nick.

"Hi, Ona. I am so sorry to surprise you like this but a fire is burning close to our houses," Mimi said as they all walked into Ona's house. It smelled musty and old, like a library.

"Hi, I'm Nick, Steph's friend. It's very nice to meet you." He held out a wet hand and she shook it politely.

"Ona, this is my neighbor Steph, and you know my granddaughter Felicia?" Mimi said.

"Yes, yes, very nice to meet you." Ona smiled at Steph and Felicia.

"Hi Ona, we met at bingo a few weeks ago," Felicia said.

"Yes, yes. I remember. Nice to see you again," Ona said.

They all stood dripping wet and not sure what do to.

"A fire you say? What has happened? Whose house is burning?" Ona asked.

"Just behind Steph's house and next to mine. We had to leave with nothing but Sugar and our purses," Mimi said while pushing her wet silver hair out of her face.

"Oh, I am sorry about that! You can borrow some of my clothes if you need to," Ona said. It was a nice thought but she was about a foot shorter than Mimi and Felicia.

"I grabbed a few things for you two if you'd like to change into something dry," Steph said.

"Thank you, dear. Would you mind terribly if we stayed here until morning? We've had to leave Steph's house because the fire is about to …" She stopped and looked at Steph.

Steph numbly looked back. It was hard to believe everything she owned was about to be burned to bits. In all her fears about the storm she never thought to worry about a fire. Nick saw her expression and hugged her. That was it. Steph lost her composure and began sobbing, hiding her face in Nick's chest.

Chapter 41 - Bars and Scars

Mathias reached into the breast pocket of his coat and pulled out Ronnie's bracelet. It was a brilliant design and beautifully made. No wonder she wanted it, but how it could get her back to, how did she say it? To her *own time*? It was quite baffling.

He reached into his other pocket and pulled out the money Stephen had lent him. Was there enough to get a hackney coach? Struggling with Jack had taken a lot out of him, it would help to avoid the walk through the dingy streets. He would need his energy to help Ronnie out of London. It would be a difficult few days if they made it that far. For that matter, it would be a difficult few days if she didn't make it out of jail. He sent a prayer up with a fervent wish that all of this would work out so he could save Ronnie.

He flagged a hackney coach for hire and spoke to the driver about his destination. Mathias climbed inside and sat heavily on the polished leather seat, remembering a similar coach and Ronnie sitting opposite. There was no way he would be in this situation if it had not been for Jack. The evil bastard.

He had to play it perfectly, fever or not, for there would only be one shot at this. He formed his words for the next part of his plan. A short ride and he was in the place where Stephen had instructed. Alighting from the coach he handed the driver a single coin, "Many thanks to you, sir." It had been years since he hired a hackney coach and in this span of a few days, it was becoming a habit. He stopped for a minute, trying to clear the spots from his vision. His legs felt shaky but he could not rest them. Time was of the essence. If this failed, Ronnie would likely hang.

Mathias looked up to recheck the address and was surprised to find it was a small inn. He opened the door and walked in to have a glance around. It was nearly full and seemed to be all men in expensive clothes, and from their conversation and accents, apparently well above his social status. He straightened his coat and smoothed down his hair, hoping he didn't look too out of place. He realized he had no idea how to find the man. All he had been given was the address, and he assumed it was going to be a private home or an office. This could be a wasted trip, for how would the man know who he was? Damn.

A movement caught his eye. In the back corner, someone held his hand up. Mathias made his way across, squeezing between tables, trying to steady his nerves. Was this the person? He wasn't even looking at him, what if he had gestured to someone else?

"Get me a pint and the special." The man's voice was low and raspy.

"I am not your server," Mathias replied. Surely the man did not think he worked here?

"If you wish to discuss something with me we will break bread together." It was a command. The man barely glanced at him as he spoke. "Jump to it lad, do you think I want to sit here all day? Believe me, I have other fish to fry."

Mathias stared at him incredulously. The cheeky arrogant bastard. Anger boiled within him as he turned to do the man's bidding. Was he to buy the man's dinner as well? Nodding, he made his way back to the bar. He calculated whether he had enough money for dinner and for the services he hoped the man could provide.

The bartender took his order and he pointed to the table where he would be. "Just one dinner, sir?" he asked.

"Yes, only one. Vait, I will take two pints of ale as vell." Mathias could take supper with Maria.

He returned to the table with two pints and sat down. The man looked at him squarely and he finally got a good look at his face. A huge scar sliced through his left eye and down the cheek adding greatly to his already menacing look. "Dinner vill be here shortly," Mathias said, eying him over his tankard of ale.

"So what brings you here this night?" the man asked, lifting his pint and looking him up and down. He took a sip and placed the metal mug in front of him.

"I need your help," Mathias said, glancing around to see if anyone was close enough to hear.

"Aye, I 'ave no doubt." The man took a sip of his ale.

Mathias chose his words carefully. "First tell me your name. I vant to know vat to call you."

The man paused, giving Mathias a hard look. A shudder ran up his spine. He knew it was the fever, nothing more, yet he paused, checking his gut to be sure that explanation for his reaction rang true. Something about this man was distinctly strange and disturbing. He felt he should leave but then he remembered why he was here, cursing Jack for putting him in this position.

"They do call me Ned."

Should he delve into the unknown with Ned? He was running out of time and options to help Ronnie. *It was only money*. Maybe more than money if things went awry, but if all went according to plan it would mean Ronnie would live and they could escape the hellish position they were in. It was worth so much more than the gold.

A serving wench placed a plate with a chop and potatoes in front of Ned and left without a word.

"Ned, a friend of mine needs a jailbreak." He decided it was time to get the heart of the matter.

"Jailbreak indeed?" Ned sat forward a bit, more interested now. "From where pray? Newgate?"

"Yes, Newgate. The trial is on the morrow and the gibbet the day after," Mathias said, trying to keep the emotion out of his voice.

"The gallows, eh?" He looked sideways at Mathias, the shadow from the scar separated his face into three sections, making him look other-worldly. "Tell me, sir, how certain are you of the court's verdict?"

Ned scared the hell out of him, and that said a lot. Not many people scared Mathias, who was a head taller than most men, and a fair bit broader as well. He ran his fingers through is hair. "I have no knowledge, but it is a possibility." Against his bold nature, Mathias found himself looking down, losing his nerve. He normally locked eyes with an opponent, as a way of asserting his dominance, but it seemed impossible with this man. Maybe it was the fever sucking away his mental reserves, along with his physical strength. Maybe it was the man's slithery soul and evil countenance. He usually found that most sticky situations could be manipulated to his advantage with either charm or force. He felt that neither would suffice here.

Ned nodded to someone across the room. After a hand gesture, two men in long coats made their way to the table and sat down on either side of Mathias, boxing him in.

"*Gott*, you have friends," Mathias said eyeing each man.

"Jailbreak will not be an option." Ned ignored his remark and took another bite of his meal and chewed his scar bunching and separating grotesquely. "What say you to a commotion and kidnapping as they leave the courtroom?"

Mathias looked away and took several swallows of his ale to give himself time to think and to calm his nerves. Confident and in control was how he had wanted to be, but it was the total opposite of how he felt. He looked directly at the scar, hoping to draw strength from the weakness of Ned's flesh. He stole a glance at the man to his left and then to his right. Their expressions remained neutral, their greasy hair and unshaven faces looking like mangy dogs from the alleyway.

"Zis type of skullduggery is your calling, or at least zat is vat I have been told." Mathias forced his eyes to not blink—to not shy away from the man's gaze.

"Why should I take this on? What reward is in it for me?" Ned narrowed his eyes, crossed his arms, and leaned back in the chair. The man on his right mimicked him, crossing his arms as well.

"Payment of course." Don't show weakness, his brother-in-law Stephen had told him. He flexed his arms and felt the injured muscle cramp make him wince. Damn it. Sweat dripped down his back. He wanted this to be over, to be arranged. There was so much left to do. Please just say yes, he thought, forcing the idea out toward the scar.

"Leave us for a moment," Ned said, waving his hand in dismissal.

"Pardon me?" Mathias had not expected that. "Leave you? Vat is the meaning of—"

"Leave us, we will talk together and decide if your friend can be grabbed from the arms of the gibbet," Ned told him firmly. "Now go!"

Mathias leaned forward for the first time and claimed dominance in the conversation. "I vill tell you a few things first, so you can best decide. Firstly my friend is a woman. Secondly, she is on trial for false accusations of vitchcraft. I need her returned to me unharmed, untouched."

Ned leaned forward, putting his face a mere foot from Mathias's. He could smell the whiskey on his breath. As their eyes locked, he felt the man's spirit worm its way into his mind, raising doubt, creating fear. Mathias resisted but was overcome with the power this man possessed. "A woman!" his two henchmen laughed. "Now I will not tell you again. Leave us!"

Mathias stood suddenly as if controlled by him, making the chair fall to the floor. It clanged as it hit the boards, causing several of the inn's patrons to look their way. The man on his left stood up and grabbed Mathias's injured arm, squeezing it and moving Mathias backward.

213

"Arrrrrrgh!" Mathias jerked his arm away, clutching it and glaring at the man. "Zere's no need for zat. I vill step away and leave you." Mathias was at least a foot taller than the other man and took a step toward him with his fists clenched.

The man flinched, stepping backward and nearly tripping over his own chair. Mathias started to turn away but looked back at the scar-faced Ned, leaning on the table to make his point. Ven I return I hope to have an answer. Zere are other matters I must address."

Mathias glanced at both men. The one on the left took another step back holding his hands up as if in defeat, clearly afraid of him. Ned smiled at him the scar puckering and bending unnaturally. Mathias turned and walked to the bar, ordering another pint of ale. Maybe the drink would calm the shaking that started deep in his gut.

If there was any hope of saving Ronnie, Ned had to say yes. But he could not let him know how badly he needed his help. He glanced back toward the table where the men talked heatedly. Mathias gulped the ale and ran his fingers through is hair. He finished the pint and walked through the back door breathing in the damp musky air. He walked a few yards to the alley and took a piss, trying to clear his mind. He had to be steady, solid, and confident. He thought of Ronnie and her sweet lips, her smile. Her sad eyes. A noose around her neck. His belly clenched. He had to save her.

Urine, smoke, sewage, and damp earth mingled in his nostrils. He had no back-up plan. If Ned refused to help him … Well, he couldn't allow himself to think of that. Taking a deep breath, he pulled on his hair at the crown. How in *Gott's* name had he got into this situation? A week ago his life was beginning here in England with everything going so well. Now all was at stake, his very life, and a woman he loved was nearly at the gallows, while he mixed with cutthroats and rascals to risk planning a prison break. It was exactly the scenario Madam Zangari had foretold.

Mathias said a few prayers, hoping he was capable of the effort that would be needed. The words of Madam Zangari floated around in his mind like the smoke in her parlor: *Too late to save yourself.* So perhaps it didn't matter. He should have no fear if the worst that could happen was death. The reward was equally substantial—having Ronnie as a friend, alive, maybe as a wife and lover if things went well. A dramatic situation required a dramatic solution. Isn't that what his father had said before his death?

He patted his breast pocket, satisfied the payment was there and returned to Ned and his henchmen. Ned was eating his meal carefully, cutting the meat slowly as if he enjoyed tearing the flesh with the blade. The two men stood up as he approached the table.

Mathias squared his shoulders and stood up to his full height, glaring down at them. A weight had been lifted off of his conscience. He was no longer undecided. It had to be done. Confidence coursed through his body, renewing his strength. Even Ned's cold hard stare didn't shake him this time. Ned flicked his hand and the men left the table. Mathias sat down without being asked. This was his transaction. Ned could either do his bidding or he would do it himself and keep the money for their escape.

Mathias sat back in the chair, crossed his arms, and looked down at Ned. "Vat is your decision?" He kept his voice calm.

Ned paused and narrowed his eyes at him. "God's truth, I am not sure it can be done."

"Vye do you not think it can be done, surely you have helped people escape before?" Mathias asked, certain it was a ploy to maximize the price. "I am thinking it can be done at less cost to me if I use another method."

Ned shot him a dark look. "Do you have a price in mind?"

"Perhaps you should tell me your plan, zen I will measure it against mine," Mathias said.

The scar puckered and Mathias was given a brief glimpse of gray crooked teeth. "As I reckon it, the prisoners are brought through a courtyard between Newgate and the courts of the Old Bailey. I could fix it so there is a group of my men waiting for them. The lady should stand out from the male prisoners like a rose in a dunghill. But you had best describe the wench in case she be not the only woman in the gang."

"She is small, dark, with ivory skin. About seven stones in weight—"

"—I'll not be bringing scales to weigh her. A general description is all we need, lest there are mistakes."

"I have provided her *mit* a black dress, simply made. Use zee name Charley as zat is our agreed code word." Stephen had confirmed she got the note, explaining his plan. She would be ready. "Are zee guards armed?"

"With clubs, but my men are better equipped," Ned said. The gray teeth displayed in more of a snarl than a smile.

"Zee prisoners, are they chained to each other?"

"The menfolk are most times." Ned inserted a long strip of meat into his mouth. "But the women most usually are not," he said with his mouth full.

"Vat if she is chained? After all, she vill be a convict, Mathias said. This was all so complicated.

"If necessary we could hack off her foot. Better the lady be lame than her pretty neck stretched tight from master gibbet." A disturbing smile played around Ned's lips.

"You cannot mean vat you say!" Mathias was aghast. A horrible image of a mutilated foot passed in his mind's eye.

"Settle down, all I seek to know is the limits of your interest in her freedom. If she is held fast by the ankle, how else are we to ensure her escape?" Ned asked. The large thick necked henchmen nodded and the other started to talk. Ned hushed him by placing a dirty hand over his mouth. "Smithy, do not speak, you are far too foolhardy to add anything of value."

The man pulled away from Ned and shot him an angry look. "Sir, that is false."

Mathias interrupted the two, "She vill have all limbs intact. *Gott's* blood, if she does not survive her escape, vat point is any of this?" Mathias could feel his face grow hot.

"Very well, sir. If our first attempt fails there will be one more chance when they bring her to the gallows. The poor condemned souls are brought on a cart and we could try our luck as they unload. But there is a much bigger crowd to get through, and hardly room to swing a mouse by its tail. There are often pike men accompanying the prisoners to Tyburn."

"Zen by all zat is holy let us hope she vill not be shackled ven they bring her back to Newgate. Is zere not a way to unchain her from zee other prisoners?" Mathias asked.

"We could try, but time would be against us. The guards would be on us in a trice and my men would be at risk. If any of my lads are harmed, it will cost you extra," Ned said as he boxed Smithy's ear. Smithy stood up and moved out of reach leaning against the wall behind them.

"How will I find you after you've taken her?" Mathias asked. Would these men take his money and not perform the agreed upon task? There was that risk.

"We will arrange a meeting place."

"I will pay you the remainder of our agreed sum when you deliver her unharmed," Mathias said.

They worked out the final details. Mathias stood up and held his hand out to Ned. "I vill see you on zee morrow. I vill pay you zee first half after zee verdict is read out in court. Zee other half vill be yours ven I have her safely in my arms."

Ned stood for the first time that evening and held out his hand. He was taller than Mathias had expected. Long, skinny legs unfolded, bringing Ned to the level of Mathias's chin. They shook hands and Mathias turned away, wiping his hand on his pants. He felt a glimmer of hope for the first time since Jack had shot him.

Chapter 42 - Clown Shoes and Courtly Affairs

A guard walked in carrying a pair of black boots. "Miss, please put these on, you are wanted in court momentarily." He unlocked the cell door and handed Ronnie the boots.

She sat on the bench and looked them over. They were much worn, mud encrusted, and the left one had a small hole in the sole. Other than that they were a perfect pair of boots if her feet were three sizes larger. She got a whiff of Gorgonzola. They smelled, too. Nice.

"These aren't my shoes, constable," she told him.

"Well they are yours now," he said, crossing his arms over his chest. "I have my orders. Get 'em on your feet and let's get a move on, miss."

She slid them on her feet and looped the laces over the eyelets—they reminded her of ice skates she had used as a kid. They were better than nothing but she felt like Bozo the Clown. The foremost three inches of the shoe flopped around uselessly as she walked.

The constable snorted and held the gate open for her. "A most elegant addition to your wardrobe, madam."

Ronnie bit her lip and walked ahead of the guard, legs feeling weak and shaky with each step. They walked to the constables' quarters and on to the side of the building where a few other prisoners were gathered. One grimy man looked her up and down and smiled, showing brown spotted teeth. His evil breath wafted in her direction and she turned her head to get some fresh air.

"Sit!" the guard said. Ronnie sat in a chair and eyed the other prisoners. Fifteen minutes later a dozen or more men waited nervously, with many more arriving since Ronnie.

An older guard appeared and addressed the group. "Right then. Let us make our way to the courtroom. I expect you to accompany me without any trouble."

They walked as a group out of the building led by two constables in the front and two in the back. The men were cuffed at the ankles and Ronnie was thankful she was free. The men coordinated their movements to progress forward clumsily due to the chains dragging on the ground.

A stiff breeze greeted them and Ronnie hunched her shoulders to try to stay warm. Butterflies fought to get out of her stomach but thankfully did not. The note replayed in her mind and she couldn't help but look around for Mathias's man.

They made their way under a covered walkway, passing through a small courtyard, and entered an adjacent brick building. One of the men fell to the floor and began writhing. It was the one they called Brown Spots. The two men shackled to him fell to their knees. The guards stopped and kicked the fallen man until he curled into a ball.

"Stand up, you useless toss bucket!" the taller guard barked. He grabbed his arm and hauled him to his feet.

Brown Spots held his stomach. The second guard pulled out his club and beat Brown Spots about the head and neck until he passed out.

Ronnie didn't want any part and stood back. One guard supported Brown Spots. Blood trickled down the man's neck onto his shirt as the guard carried him into the courtroom.

They proceeded down a long formal corridor, turned the corner, and walked into a crowded lobby. The stench of hundreds of unwashed bodies hit her hard. She covered her nose and mouth with her sleeve. The crowd parted as they made their way toward a set of large wooden doors and entered a huge courtroom that was filling quickly with spectators. Would Jack be in the courtroom? Would Mathias?

Her worries gathered like flies on a soda can, buzzing around her annoyingly. Would she remember anything she had prepared? The guards ushered them to a long table in the center of the room. Ronnie looked around at the other prisoners. A few prayed quietly. Brown Spots weaved back and forth in his seat.

"I dunno what the worst is," the man next to her said, his foul breath hovering around him like a green cloud, "the trial or the Gaol Fever."

"Gaol Fever?" she asked.

"Aye, miss. Do you not remember this two years past when sixty men and women died from sittin' in this very courtroom? A plague of Gaol Fever took them down as if the devil were reaching for their throats for witnessing the goings on."

"No, I don't remember that." Ronnie covered her mouth and nose again in self-defense. Gaol Fever was what they used to call typhus? She couldn't remember.

"The Lord Mayor and a judge or two met their maker." He looked at her with big bloodshot eyes.

"That's horrible." There were more than a hundred people in the courtroom now and more were filing in. It was certainly a playground for germs, especially amongst the mass of filthy unwashed bodies. At this point in history, Ronnie thought, germ theory was a zygote.

"And would you believe it?" He waved a thick finger around, stabbing the air to accentuate his points. "Each and every man and woman has paid to get in to this trial. Well, with the exception, of course, for the judges and jury. They get a free pass. Just imagine it, young miss. Just imagine paying to die!"

"And us too," Ronnie said, "we have a free pass, but they can keep mine."

He smiled. "Mine as well."

"Why did they charge all these people to get in here?" Ronnie looked around at the masses of people. It would bring in a lot of money.

"Thins the crowds if you get my meaning, miss. Shame it could be money that buys them a ticket to their grave." He crossed his arms over his ample stomach. "Wait and see, young miss, wait and see. They will try and staunch the worst of this hellish air with some smell goods."

"Smell goods?" Ronnie felt like a parrot repeating everything he said. "What do you mean?"

"Shhhh young miss! They're startin'."

A man walked to the front of the room in a black suit. "Hear ye, Hear ye, the Honorable Judge Faust presiding upon the City of London. Ye will all rise and remove your hats." Ronnie decided he must be the court shouter.

The sound of people shuffling and murmuring echoed around. Another man sauntered to the center of the room. He wore a black robe with a long gray wig that came down below his shoulders. He stood behind a chair and waited.

"Honorable Judges Reardon, Arden, and Hudson presiding alongside Judge Faust," announced the shouter.

Three other judges of various sizes and shapes entered the room from a door along the back wall. They joined Judge Faust at the table, two to the left of him and one to the right. In unison, they sat down at the table.

"You may be seated," the shouter said. An extended shuffling echoed around the room as the vast audience took their seats.

Two men came from either side of the room, each with a lantern on a long chain. No, it wasn't a lantern, it was an incense holder, like the ones priests used in old movies. They walked awkwardly, swinging the containers of incense, with smoke billowing out, making their way to the judges' table, to the jury, and around the audience.

A man came out with a small basket of flowers that reminded her of a Friday night in Georgetown, where the vendors sold roses for the drunk men to impress the equally drunk ladies. Surely they weren't going to sell flowers during the trial? The man made his way to the judges, who each took a bundle of flowers from the basket. Then he made his way to the jury. Each man took a bundle until the basket was empty.

"What are they for?" Ronnie asked the man sitting next to her.

"Why they are nosegays, young miss. As I said, smell goods. 'Tis said that they keep the Gaol Fever at bay."

"No, actually they don't. They only make the smell less offensive," she said, but really it was a pointless statement. He would believe what he had been told all his life.

"The court will hear the case against William Petrey," announced the shouter.

The constable standing near her poked Brown Spots, who was bloodied and battered and seemed to be sleeping. The guard helped him to his feet and shuffled him over to an area in the front of the room between the judge and the jury where a small banister marked it off. The guard placed his hands on the handrail.

Brown Spots, or rather William Petrey, was not in good shape. The beating had left him in a stupor. He weaved back and forth a bit. The bailiff swore him in and then Judge Faust said, "William Petrey, how do you plead to the charges of theft on July twenty-seventh of the year of our Lord, seventeen hundred and fifty-two?"

William Petrey looked at the jury, the judges' table, and back to the bench, showing a brownish grin. "Good day to you kind sirs."

"How do you plead Mr. Petrey? Guilty or not guilty?" asked Judge Faust.

William Petrey weaved and leaned heavily against the banister. "If you please, sir, I plead nothing because I done nothing," he said slurring his words like a first-class drunk.

"So you plead not guilty?" Judge Faust said, not bothering to hide his irritation.

"No. I refuse to plead in this house of lies!" William slurred and waved a hand around, nearly falling backward with the motion.

The crowd gasped and a few men in the back clapped.

"There is no plea, Mr. Petrey? Is that what you are saying?" Judge Reardon asked, marking on a piece of vellum as he spoke.

"Yes, I am saying that," Petrey mumbled something to himself and nearly fell over backward, but caught himself at the last second.

"It will be noted that Mr. William Petrey has refused to plea. A punishment of *peine forte et dure* will be carried out in Newgate Prison directly after the trial," Judge Faust said and then banged a gavel.

The crowd began murmuring and a man from the balcony whistled loudly.

"Alas, alas, a *piene forte et dure*. That I declare is something to behold. Never in my days have I seen the likes of that," the man next to her murmured.

"What does it mean?" Ronnie asked.

"If there is no plea then the man will die in a most horrible manner." He wiped away a tear.

"But he's injured. The guards beat him and he's not thinking clearly!"

"Aye, tis true enough, I grant you. But there is no one to give a care for him. Will you stand and support him? A common thief? A low cutpurse?" She shook her head. "Aye, tis as it goes in this sad world. You will not and no one else will either."

"What will his punishment be then?" Ronnie asked.

"He will be taken to his cell, stripped, and splayed on the dirt floor. Heavy stones will be placed upon his belly until he dies. A meal the first day, water thereafter."

"They will just leave him like that?" she asked, imagining Brown Spots in agony on the dirt floor of the cell.

"Aye, leave him like that they will sure enough young miss. William is a dead man walking. He's not so very big come to think of it. I warrant that three large stones will do for him. How many would you guess?"

"Are you kidding me? That's horrible," Ronnie said.

Two guards came and escorted William Petrey out of the courtroom. He weaved and swayed along until one of them grabbed his elbow to help support him. The crowd became louder with shocked exclamations.

"That's it? His fate was death just for not making a plea?" Ronnie asked.

"That's about the size of it. Listen carefully, miss, you have to say not guilty. You have to say those words because if you say guilty they will give you the roughest ride they can. Say not guilty, then they have to give you a punishment handed down from the jury. But no plea is certain death. Certain death. Unless of course, you plead your belly." He had to raise his voice over all the noise.

"Plead your belly?" Ronnie asked.

"Yes." He put his hands on his substantial paunch. "Say you are with child."

Ronnie tried to gather her thoughts. She felt like she was going to be sick. All of her earlier preparations were hiding in a dark corner of her mind. She chased them around but, like a scared dog, they wouldn't let her catch them. Ronnie scanned the crowd and to her surprise, Jack was there in the front of the courtroom. "Oh God." Her heart raced and she hoped that they would not call her name until she could grab the rascally arguments she had prepared by the scruff of the neck.

Chapter 43 - Crazy-Eyed Witch

"Miss Regina Ingram, how do you plead to the charges of witchcraft, threatening behavior, and perverting justice?" Judge Reardon said.

Ronnie forgot to breathe. She tried to stand up but her body would not respond. Her one and only friend in the court stood up, pulled her out of her seat, and shoved her toward the box. As if floating across the room, she reached out for one last attempt at capturing her trial preparations. They scampered to the far reaches of her mind when the courtroom erupted with a few people yelling, "Burn! Burn the witch!"

Completely intimidated by the crowd, she stood in the box and looked around. A bright light shined in her eyes and she looked up to see a large mirror-type contraption directing light from the small window above her head. "Yes. I am present," she managed to call out at last.

There were a few snickers behind her. Her face flushed. That is what she had said every day in eighth grade social studies class. A bailiff held a Bible up and Ronnie placed her right hand on it.

He said, "Do you solemnly swear to tell the whole truth, and nothing but the truth?"

"I do," Ronnie said.

"Miss Ingram how do you plead?" asked Judge Faust.

She looked at the judges' table and said with all the confidence she could muster: "Not guilty," and added, "Your Honor," for good measure.

"Prosecution, it is your case," Judge Faust said. "Mr. Hallister. Good to see you again."

A thickly built man stood up. "Good morning Your Honors. I have met with Mr. Ingram and the magistrate on this case to be sure it had merit. I can assure you that we will prove without a doubt that Miss Regina Ingram is, in fact, a witch."

Jack sat smugly and shot her a piercing look, making her knees turn to jelly.

"Mr. Jack Ingram, the accused's brother, is afraid for the safety of his wife and unborn son." He motioned to his left and Jack nodded. "It is believed that on The Year of Our Lord 1752 on the second of August, Miss Ingram was struck by a carriage and at that moment the devil found a pathway into this good Christian woman's body. For, according to Mr. Ingram, ever since that moment his dear sister has not been present, despite her claims otherwise."

He looked around the room with utter confidence. "In fact, not to put too fine a point on it, she has been unruly, difficult, and has on numerous occasions physically assaulted Mr. Ingram."

"That is not true!" Ronnie shouted out. "He assaulted me!"

"Silence!" Judge Faust said, his long wig shaking as he pounded his gavel. "Miss Ingram, I will give you time to speak when the counsel has presented their cases, and not before."

Ronnie crossed her arms and fumed. How could he say she had assaulted Jack? That was ludicrous.

Hallister resumed his speech, "You can see how it has been, Your Honors, she is doing it now, very unwomanly behavior do you not agree?"

One judge nodded, and several members of the audience yelled out. "Witch!"

"Because of this dramatic behavior change, my client, Mr. Ingram, procured his own clerical expert to examine Miss Ingram. I would like to present the results of this examination and call to the stand Father Blenheim as our first witness."

He handed over a piece of thick yellowed paper to an official-looking man who carried it to the jury, who were in a box next to where Ronnie was sitting. Some blushed deeply, and others glanced at it and quickly passed the paper as if it were on fire.

Father Blenheim, wearing the same clothes he had worn on the day she met him, waddled up to the stand and mopped his forehead with a handkerchief. "If it pleases the court," the priest began, "I will explain the evidence that has been presented. What you are looking at now is a sketch from my own hand. Mr. Ingram arrived at my estate a few days past and asked me to examine this woman." He pointed at Ronnie with a shaky finger. "As a group, we began by reciting the Lord's Prayer. I hesitate to have to tell you now that as we recited the holy words, Miss Ingram kept looking at me with her large insane eyes. Her eyes were twitching. They were monstrous, her gaze was filled with evil."

There was a loud murmur from the crowd.

"I did not! I don't have insane eyes!" Ronnie said. She wanted to add, "You fat bastard," but thought better of it. "And they certainly don't twitch."

He looked over at her and dramatically took a step backward as if the sight of her was so disturbing.

Ronnie blushed deeply. This man was the one with the crazy eyes, but it seemed to be working. The men of the jury were looking at her, but not directly. The demeanor of a few of them changed and one man shifted his legs away.

"This woman was not able to say the Lord's Prayer," announced Father Blenheim, his face as stern as stone.

"That is not true!" Ronnie interrupted. "I was very nervous and misspoke once, maybe twice. And my family says it a bit differently." She immediately regretted it.

"Mr. Ingram said the prayer without error. Is he not your brother?" challenged the priest. "So what is this family you speak of, Miss Ingram? The devil's brood?"

The crowd exploded with whoops and hollers. Ronnie put on her best hateful look but Father Blenheim had his eyes on the jury. If what Mathias said was true, this man was trained in convincing a jury that someone was a witch.

"I had my horns at the ready." Father Blenheim held up his pointer and pinky fingers so they stuck out like a bull's horns. "I asked if I could make my examination. She refused. But after Mr. Ingram threatened her with bodily harm she acquiesced." He wiped his brow as if it had been a harrowing experience for him, not a dirty old man's glimpse of a young girl's bared flesh.

"My lords, and ladies and gentlemen, you can see from my sketch on the vellum that Miss Ingram has devil's marks on her. There are at least ten and some of these are in very exceptional parts of her body."

One man of the jury held up the paper and Father Blenheim walked over and grabbed it. "You members of the jury have seen my sketch. Is it not extraordinary the number and locations of these devil's marks?"

Several of the jury members nodded their heads. The bailiff took the paper and walked it over to the judges.

"They are not devil's marks," Ronnie said calmly. "They are moles. The judge over there has a mole on his face." She pointed to Judge Reardon. "Are you accusing him of being a witch as well?"

A few people in the balconies clapped but more people booed. Some spectators behind the jury started chanting: "Witch! Witch!" Ronne felt like she was in Wonderland where nothing made sense.

226

"I am an expert in these matters," Father Blenheim replied. "And they are witches' marks, young lady! And if I may say so I have had more than enough insolence from you—"

"—Moles, Your Honor," Ronnie interrupted him. "They're simply moles. I think the term witches' marks is inflammatory. It leads the jury. I am willing to bet each one of your jurors has a mark on them. Everyone has moles. It proves nothing."

"I grant you that the mark itself does not provide conclusive proof. But if Your Honors would allow me to prick them." He held up a metal tool that looked like something a dentist would use. "I will, without doubt, be able to prove to you that this young woman is a witch. If the regular flesh bleeds but the moles do not, that is proof that they are the marks of the devil."

"Your Honor, you're not going to allow this man to use his prick on me!" Ronnie realized too late what she had said. Gales of laughter rang through the halls and it took five minutes for the judges to regain control of the room. The bailiffs were busy removing the rowdier the spectators.

"Why yes, Your Honor," the priest said, a light of excitement in his eyes. "I would very much like to do the demonstration here and now, before the jury, if I may. It is not something that is easy to describe, and you will agree that a demonstration, in front of witnesses cannot lie."

"Father Blenheim, pray tell us what this demonstration involves?" The youngest judge asked.

"I will use this pricking device to probe Miss Ingram's flesh. The normal flesh will bleed and the devil's marks will be impervious to the assault as these accursed monstrosities will not release blood. Toughened flesh from the devil's suckling," Father Blenheim added dramatically.

The courtroom quieted down. Ronnie stared at him in disbelief. "You are not going to strip me in front of this courtroom?" Her face felt even hotter and she was sure she was blushing deeply.

"To preserve the young lady's modesty I would be prepared to use the mark on her forearm for this demonstration." He glanced at the vellum and back to the judge. "You can, therefore, remain clothed." He didn't look at her as he spoke but was looking at the judge, awaiting approval.

The judges whispered in conference and Judge Faust quickly came back with a decision. "We will allow this demonstration, however, you must stand together near the jury for their eyes to witness."

"You are allowing this?" she said in disbelief.

Father Blenheim walked to the front of the jury box. A bailiff came toward her, opening the small gate in the banister and guided her to the stand, a bit closer to the jury. She glared up at Father Blenheim and could see the sweat beading on his forehead and smell his stench. He would not meet her stare.

He reached out for her hand, and Ronnie took a step backward. "Tell me what you are going to do first."

An impatient look crossed his face, quickly covered by the oily smile. He mopped his brow and said for everyone to hear, nearly shouting. "I will simply push up your sleeve and lightly prick your skin and then do the same thing again, on the mark."

She looked at the jury and a few met her gaze, but most of the men looked away nervously.

"Miss Ingram, please let Father Blenheim continue his examination. We are all waiting," Judge Faust said.

Ronnie took a deep breath and let it out. Shoving her sleeve up, she held out her arm.

"Miss Ingram, this will be more comfortable for you if you look away during the process. I have found that such surgery can be more disturbing if you watch." He smiled a fake, slightly twitching smile.

She grit her teeth and stared at his face, wishing she had telekinesis powers to poke him in the eye or give him explosive diarrhea—anything to make him stop.

"First I will prick her normal flesh. Miss Ingram, please look away," he said more sternly this time.

"I will not. I want to see what you are doing." She scowled at him, clenching her jaw, readying for the pain in her arm.

"As you wish." He moved the instrument to her arm and glanced at the jury. The light from the mirror reflected off the metal of the instrument. Ronnie had given up worrying about the germs since the rat incident and the bloodied tools used by Doctor Wiggams. This seemed like the least horrible of the events that had been thrust upon her so far.

"I will merely touch you with this and you will feel a pinch. Like a bloodletting," Father Blenheim said.

He took her hand and steadied her arm. His fat dirty fingers shook as he approached her with the metal instrument. There was a small poke, a sharp pain, and a few drops of blood welled up on her arm.

"Behold! The normal flesh bleeds." He held her arm up for the courtroom to see. She jerked her arm away, not liking a spectacle being made.

"Now Miss Ingram, please allow me to use this instrument on your mark." She noticed his word choice, purposefully avoiding the word prick.

He held her arm again, looking at the blood pooling, readying to drip down her arm. He dabbed at it with his handkerchief, the same one he had dabbed his forehead. She closed her eyes, trying to push this horrid fact out of her brain. She had caused enough of a scene and wanted to show the jury she was reasonable and calm.

He took her hand again, twisting her wrist a bit to have the mole facing the jury. "Now the mark, please watch carefully." He glanced at the jury, making sure they were watching. The courtroom quieted down with everyone focused on her arm. The end of the instrument looked a bit fatter this time, but before she could say a word he poked her with it harder than he had on the other jab.

"See! No blood!" He held her arm up dramatically. "The devil's mark does not bleed!" There was a collective gasp from the courtroom and the judges banged their gavels.

Chapter 44 - Trickery

"Bailiff, please bring Miss Ingram to the bench so we may see the results ourselves," Judge Faust said.

"Your Honors, I would like you to examine the instrument Father Blenheim used. It is merely a trick. One end is sharp and the other end is blunt!" She was spitting mad that the priest would use such trickery on the jury and that everyone was so damn gullible they believed it.

"It is no such thing!" Father Blenheim said.

Ronnie made a grab for the instrument but Father Blenheim shoved it in his pocket. "The woman is clearly a lunatic. You all saw the effect it had on her flesh. She is grabbing at any explanation to suit her defense."

"Father Blenheim, please accompany Miss Ingram to the bench so that we may examine your instrument," Judge Faust said.

Father Blenheim shot her a hateful look and Ronnie was sure she had him. The bailiff walked both of them across the main part of the courtroom to the judges' table.

"Miss Ingram, please present your arm," The younger judge said. As he spoke Ronnie could see he was missing a few teeth, and there was a coldness in his eyes.

Ronnie held her arm out for them to see. Father Blenheim came close and poked her arm with his pudgy finger. "Observe, please your honors. Here is the normal flesh. You can see the smear of lifeblood that I wiped away with my kerchief." He held the item out with a small dot of blood on it. The two other judges stood up and moved closer to see.

"Father Blenheim, please present us with the instrument you used," Judge Faust said.

Father Blenheim reached in his jacket pocket and fumbled around for a bit too long and handed him the pricking instrument.

"It appears to have a handle on one end and a very sharp point," Judge Faust said handing the instrument to the younger judge. They held the instrument each in turn and put a finger on the sharp end lightly checking its sharpness.

Father Blenheim looked at her triumphantly. Ronnie smiled and said, "Your Honors, I saw the instrument he used on the mole. It was not this one. Could you have the priest empty his pockets to see if there is another blunt instrument in his pocket?"

The younger judge looked away annoyed. "Miss Ingram, you have stalled this process enough. Can we please just get on with the trial?"

Judge Faust looked at Father Blenheim and then at Ronnie, and there was a long pause. "Father Blenheim, please allow the bailiff to empty your pockets."

The younger judge crossed his arms and sat down hard on the chair. Father Blenheim visibly blanched but acquiesced to the search. The bailiff removed two other instruments and a few coins from the priest's pocket and set them on the table in front of the judges.

Excitement welled in Ronnie's chest and a smile broke out on her face. Father Blenheim shot her another hateful look and made the sign of the devil holding it high for the jury and the audience to see. Murmurs and shouts from the crowd drowned out anything the judges were saying. They picked up the instruments and handed them back and forth. Ronnie could see a double-ended instrument with a different handle than the one he had shown the judges.

Ronnie pointed at it and said, "That's the one he used, he merely flipped it over to use the blunt end on the mole. He is a charlatan!" Ronnie then yelled as loud as she could, "Father Blenheim is a fake!"

Judge Reardon reached out and grabbed Ronnie's arm. "Hush woman! We will never quiet the crowd down! Bailiff, please return the subjects to their original positions." The judges tried to regain order.

The bailiff guided Ronnie and the priest back across the courtroom. Father Blenheim clenched his jaw, again making the sign of the devil for all to see. Shouts of "Charlatan!" and "Witch!" echoed through the courtroom as they made their way back to their original places.

Finally, the courtroom calmed down and Judge Faust said, "Father Blenheim, is there anything else you would like to present to the court?"

"No, that is all." Father Blenheim wiped at his brow again and glanced at Ronnie.

Ronnie smiled at him. "Fake!"

Judge Faust then said, "All right Miss Ingram. You may question the witness."

"Oh, I can?" She felt stupid as she said it, but gathered her thoughts and glanced at the jury. They whispered to each other. Hopefully, they were confused about who to believe.

"First I want the jury to be clear on what happened over near the judges' table. Father Blenheim, would you like to tell them about the double-ended instrument?" Ronnie said.

His face turned red again and he shook his head.

"Okay, then I will tell them." She turned to face the jury. "Father Blenheim had three instruments in his pocket. One with a sharp end, one with a blunt end, and a third double-ended instrument. When he pricked my skin and it bled when he used the sharp one. When we weren't looking he turned the instrument around and used the blunt end to prick my mole, and it didn't bleed. Is that correct, Father?" Ronnie said, looking at Father Blenheim.

"I did no such thing," the priest snapped indignantly, but his lower lip quivered and his jowls shook. She was breaking him down.

"He's lying, but you know that, right?" Ronnie said to the jury. One man nodded in response, another crossed his arms and looked away.

She knew what she had to do to finish him off. "Father Blenheim, are you a real priest?"

"I beg your pardon!"

"Were you not hired by my brother to prove that I'm a witch? You are a paid consultant and not a man of God."

"Do you see how she talks to men?" The priest was practically foaming at the mouth as he yelled at the jury. "She is insolent and disrespectful."

"She has the cheek of the devil!" yelled out a spectator, to a chorus of titters.

Father Blenheim took a deep breath, trying to muster his dignity. "This is not the Miss Ingram everyone knew before the accident, who was a sweet and innocent young lady. It is as if the devil has taken this person and replaced her with this foul creature."

Someone called out the word creature and it made Ronnie think of Gollum. That certainly did not describe her.

"Please answer Miss Ingram's questions, Father," the younger judge said.

Father Blenheim flustered and puffed. "This is quite preposterous! I am a man of God. How dare you imply I am not? You should be held across my knee for saying that."

232

"I bet you would like that Father, wouldn't you? To put me over your knee and spank me. I saw how you were looking at me when you made that sketch. If you really think I'm a witch why did you take so long drawing my legs?"

Several guffaws could be heard and a smile crossed a few lips in the jury.

"Do you see her insolence?" Father Blenheim called out, but with considerably less conviction than earlier.

"You didn't answer my question." Ronnie was gaining confidence now. "Tell me, where is your church, Father? Are you a man of the cloth or a paid consultant to convict innocent men and women of witchcraft? You should be the one rotting in hell. Not me! How many necks have been wrung from your false testimony? How much blood is on your hands, Father?"

"How dare you? How dare you?" He blustered angrily and his face turned beet red. "What right do you, a creature of Satan, to accuse me of—"

"—Answer Miss Ingram's questions, Father Blenheim," Judge Reardon interjected. "It is a simple enough question when all is said and done! Are you affiliated with a church?"

Father Blenheim looked at the judge, stuttering and subdued. "I, I, I am a priest. I am addressed as Father."

"So you have fathered how many children?" Ronnie asked. "Does that makes you a man of the cloth?"

Father Blenheim looked at her with hatred. "You are a defiant, rude, insubordinate young lady!"

"Now you're saying I'm a young lady. Are you taking back the horrible lies about me being a witch?"

"Forgive me, Father Blenheim," Judge Faust asked, "but I am curious. Pray tell me, where is your church? Are you part of a clergy that we need know of?"

Father Blenheim wrung his hands. "I have no church. I was ..." He began to weep as he spoke. "I was dismissed from my parish."

"Is this so? Why, did you rape some farmer's daughter?" Ronnie asked.

The crowd collectively gasped. Maybe Ronnie had gone too far. It did seem like she was discrediting Father Blenheim though and that had to be a good thing.

"I ... They ... All seemed to agree it was better that I move on to another location. Or so said the church elders."

"Why was this?" Judge Faust asked.

"I am not the one on trial here, Your Honor," the priest protested, sweat pouring down his loose jowls.

"Nevertheless I do believe that since you are sitting in judgment on Miss Ingram's life, she has a right to ask for your credentials. Tell me, why did you leave the church? Did they strip you of your post?"

"Aye, that they did Your Honor. It was a lie, every part of it. I swear I didn't do it, they set up a vile plot to discredit my name. The lad was not supposed to be there. He was not supposed to be in my bed ..." He looked up in horror, realizing what he had just confessed.

"You are dismissed Mr. Blenheim," Judge Faust said. "Mr. Hallister do you have any other witnesses for the prosecution?"

Mr. Blenheim turned a fair bit redder and said, "What? I ... Please, Your Honor, wait. I have more testimony."

A bailiff took his arm and led him out of the courtroom.

"Miss Ingram, do you have any further questions for this witness?" Judge Faust asked.

Ronnie made the mistake of looking at Jack. His arms were crossed and he frowned at her. Panic rose, derailing her train of thought.

"No, Your Honor," Ronnie said.

"Mr. Hallister, do you have any other witnesses you would like to call to the stand?" Judge Faust asked.

Mr. Hallister stood and said, "I do. I present the Captain of the Guard at Newgate Prison, Captain Green."

The man who had first spoken to Jack at the jail stood up and walked to the stand. They swore him in. He observed Ronnie with his piggy eyes under those caterpillar eyebrows and quickly looked away.

"Captain Green, what is your evidence to present?" Judge Faust asked.

"Your Honors, with the evidence that Mr. Ingram presented upon bringing Miss Ingram to our facility, we determined that a swimming—that is a water trial—was necessary," Captain Green began.

A woman cried out, "I was there! Wholly unnatural!" A few women chanted, "Burn the witch, burn the witch!"

"Order! Order!" Judge Faust banged his gavel. "I will have order in this court!"

234

The noise died down. A few courtly looking officials made their way to where the ladies were chanting and removed one woman.

"What evidence was presented to you to convince you to do the swimming, Captain Green?" Judge Faust said.

"The diagram that the priest, or um, as it turns out de-frocked priest, passed around to the jury." Captain Green shot a dark piggy squint her way. She peered into his eyes. He looked away.

"Captain Green," the younger judge said, "please tell us of the swimming."

"We carried out the swimming yesterday afternoon. I can tell you in all my years working at Newgate Prison, I have never, ever, seen anything close to what happened in the river." He barely glimpsed at Ronnie. The room fell silent and all that could be heard were a few coughs and shuffling of feet.

"First, if I may, I would like to explain the purpose of this procedure to the jury." Captain Green turned toward the row of curious faces. "A witch is rejected by water, whereas a woman of Christian and upright character will sink. We prepare the swimmer by tying a rope around the midsection so we can remove the good woman from the water if she should sink. If she is a witch the water will reject her and the rope is to keep her from escaping. This person—Miss Ingram—very nearly escaped. Were it not for a few of our fine constables she would have fled."

The noise rose and the crowd was so loud the judge's gavel could not even be heard.

"Silence!" Judge Faust roared. "It is within my jurisdiction to clear the court and proceed without all of you!" He stood this time and glared at the spectators. Ronnie's palms were soaking wet and her legs began to shake. Her defense so far had gone pretty well, but this was where it got dicey. Superstitious beliefs were so ingrained in people's minds it would be nearly impossible for them to believe her version of events.

"Very well Captain. Please tell us what happened in the river," Judge Faust said.

Captain Green proceeded with his explanation. "We tied the ropes to her toes and thumbs, crisscross." He held out his hands and mimicked what he was describing. "Rope around her midsection, standard procedure you see." He described in detail how the rope lowered her into the water. "Then she disappeared. I'll warrant that she cast a spell to release the ropes and in an instant, she had made herself fly about twenty feet away from where we put her in the water."

"You cannot say that I cast a spell!" Ronnie said, "That is conjecture." She thought that was the right word.

The crowd erupted in murmurs and shouts. All of the judges stood up and called on their bailiffs to remove the louder members of the audience. Ronnie wished there was somewhere to sit down, she was sick with nerves. Gavels banged and finally, the crowd settled down enough to carry on. The jury stole glances at her and she tried to make eye contact. They would not look at her. She was losing them.

"Captain Green, pray continue if you please," Judge Faust told him calmly. "But you must stick to facts and do not embellish your account with your thoughts on what might or might not have taken place. Simply the facts."

"Yes Your Honor. Somehow Miss Ingram broke free of the ropes on her hands and feet, as well as the rope around her waist." He glanced at the judges' table and a few of them nodded. "Then," he paused and rubbed his eyes dramatically, "then my men took a hook on a pole and chased the wench along the shore. They were instructed to save her life. We mortally feared that the current would take her away. The most baffling thing was that it appeared as if the river's current was running against her—it should have been dragging her in the opposite direction from the one she moved along. It was if she somehow transported herself to a different location."

"Transported? Really Captain Green?" Ronnie said.

"Well tell us what did you do Miss Ingram?" Judge Faust asked her. "How did you manage to get free from the ropes and move upstream?"

"I ... Well ..." Ronnie had prepared this section. She rummaged around in the recesses of her mind. Just as she was losing hope of any rational explanation it came to her. "The ropes came loose. The river water was very cold and I believe the ropes stretched or my hands and feet shrank." She tried to swallow but her mouth was too dry. "The volume of my skirts helped me float and I propelled myself with my hands and feet. I read about it in a journal. Swimming is something the Indians in the colonies perform in the water. I merely used my hands and feet to move away from some sharp rocks on the riverbed. I was as surprised as everyone else was."

Ronnie studied the jury to see if they bought it. A few looked up at her. Two men in the back row were shaking their heads.

"Your Honor," Captain Green commented, "If I may say so, I have never in my life seen anyone, and most especially a woman, perform such a feat. The practice of swimming, using the breaststroke, is something a few men—particularly sailors—have learned to do, as you may know. But a woman swimming in full petticoats? Whoever heard of such a thing! And this talk of savages in the colonies swimming? Dear me, how does she know of such things? Frankly, I do not believe her account. I was there, sir. It was very, very disturbing to see her disappear under the water, and then reappear twenty feet away."

"Tell 'em about the boat!" a spectator yelled.

"Yes, yes," Captain Green said, waving his hand at the spectator, "the boat. I had placed a few of my men along the other side of the river. When they saw she had broken free they set about on their rowboat to apprehend her. She was making her way across the river moving in the water. It was quite astonishing, and I confess I have no explanation as to how this was possible."

"I was swimming Captain," Ronnie said. "You have never seen anyone swim?"

"Swimming, miss. Whoever heard of a woman swimming! The idea is preposterous. But then, yes, I suppose perhaps *swimming* is a good term for what you were doing. We were swimming you to see if you were a witch. And in my professional opinion we proved our case," Captain Green said.

Applause broke out and several people yelled out, "She is a witch! Burn her!"

Ronnie looked at the judges. Judge Arden looked stunned. Judge Faust was conferring with Judge Reardon. No one attempted to quiet the crowd.

Finally, the noise subsided on its own when Captain Green began again. "The two men on the boat rowed near Miss Ingram. She leapt from the water and nearly capsized the boat."

"I did no such thing Captain Green! I merely yanked on the arm of the man who tried to pull me out of the river!"

"That is not how he tells it, Miss Ingram," Captain Green said. "He says you nearly drowned him. She cast a spell on the boat as it was rocking uncontrollably in the water!"

237

"No!" Ronnie said. But before she could carry on, Judge Faust stood up again.

"Please, Miss Ingram, I insist you must let Captain Green continue!" he eyed Ronnie angrily. "You will have a chance to cross-examine him when he is finished. Please carry on Captain."

"Yes, yes, the boat. As I recollect, the boat was rocking and it nearly capsized again when she grabbed the other man who was onboard. He managed to pull her on deck and bind her fast."

"And thank the Good Lord that he did, praise be to God!" yelled a man from the balcony. "The witch will hang!"

"SHUT UP!" Ronnie responded. "Your Honor, the spectators should not have a place in this trial. They are tainting the jury! I should have a retrial in front of the jury and judges alone!"

Judge Arden stood and glared at Ronnie. "How dare you question the proceedings of this court! Bless me if you're not a mere woman at that!"

"I present a good argument judge. The jury is being swayed by the commoners who yell out during my trial. You can see it on their faces." She pointed to the jury. "They are being influenced by the rude spectators who can't keep their mouths shut!" A mistrial would buy her some time and maybe Mathias's back-up plan would work if he had one. It was a long shot but she had to take it. "This is my life, Your Honor. I deserve a fair trial!"

The judges gathered close together at their table and whispered. A few boos could be heard from the crowd. It started quietly but as the judges conferred a low chant of "Witch! Witch! Witch!" was growing in intensity as more spectators joined. Finally, the judges banged their gavels.

Judge Faust yelled, "Silence! Silence! Order in the court!"

Finally, the courtroom quieted and he continued "Verily, it is most unusual to have a request such as this, Miss Ingram. We have discussed the matter and have made a decision. The amount of time required to file every last person out of this courtroom would be prohibitive for us to complete the docket for the day. The spectators will remain in place but any troublesome or unruly ones will be removed from this courtroom."

Damn! It would have been a more fair trial if it was held in private, Ronnie thought. It has been going so well with her discrediting Father Blenheim. Captain Green's testimony seemed to be shocking enough to change the judge's demeanor. How could she undo the damage to her case?

Chapter 45 - Home Fires

"Stephie," Nick held her close and wrapped his arms around her. "It's going to be all right. The storm is half over we should be fine. It's just your house, right?"

"And Hamish," Steph said. It was the cat she was most worried about. The house would be a devastating loss, but to lose her kitty would be too much. He had been with her through her divorce and her mom's illness. He was like her child."

"Steph, he'll get out I'm sure if it. He's a smart cat. You left the window open, right?" Nick asked.

"Yeah. I did." She wiped at the tears, but they wouldn't stop.

"He'll get out and hide somewhere else. I know it." He held her tight and stroked her hair. Steph took a deep breath and tried to let out all the stress and worry.

"Now you can get that new washer you've always wanted." He squeezed her tighter.

She pulled away and looked up at him. "My new ... oh yeah." Her washer had been acting up lately, spewing water on the floor every so often. "True, could get a new one of those." Small consolation for all the losses, but he was trying to cheer her up.

He lifted her chin up and wiped away her tears. "I'll go shopping with you. It'll be fun."

"You hate shopping," she said.

Nick planted a kiss on her forehead. "For you Steph, anything!"

The other women busied themselves figuring out beds and sleeping arrangements. Ona got over her initial shock of visitors at her door and seemed genuinely pleased to have them there to ride out the storm. Nick set up a cot in Ona's closet so she was sleeping in a safe place. Steph and Nick set up a palate of sorts in the hallway, closing the two bedroom doors to make it a safe zone. Mimi, Felicia, and Sugar were set up in the master bathroom.

Nick pulled out the clock radio from her bag and turned it on. Hurricane Charley was tearing through the area with the slightly weaker back half battering them now. The wind direction changed 180 degrees and all the weakened trees and structures from the first half of the storm were being put to the test. Everything that had been protected behind buildings was now in the full force of the wind.

Steph tried to sleep but the thought of her house burning down was too horrific. She went through all the things she should have saved—the special things that couldn't be replaced. Nick lay on the floor and shifted positions often. He needed a doctor and stronger pain meds.

He smiled at her and winked. "It'll be okay, Steph. I promise."

"When do you think we'll be able to get you to the hospital?" she asked.

"It'll wait until morning. I don't think we can make it in the dark. There will be so many trees down blocking roads. Not sure it would be very smart to attempt it. Besides, it's not like I'm dying or anything." He shifted position again only to finally sit up so he could lean against the wall and cradle his arm. His mangled finger was still wrapped in the dishtowel. "Do you think we can get back to my house at some point tonight? I can't stand the thought of not knowing."

"It sounds like Charley is heading out. Once it stops we could walk down the street if you want."

Steph turned the radio down and listened to the storm. It did seem quieter now. She stood up and opened the guest room door and looked out the window. The rain came down in torrents and rivulets blurred the window. She tried to look down the road to her house but it was the wrong angle and too far away. The orange glow from the fire still came from that general direction but it was too hard to tell if it was her house burning. Steph leaned her head against the window. It was warm and smooth.

Nick came up behind her. "It'll stop soon and we'll go back to the house, okay? We can see what's happened and at least you'll know." He put his good hand on her neck and rubbed away the tension. She leaned back against him. He put his arm around her and kissed the top of her head. "We'll both be fine Steph, you will see."

Chapter 46 - Revenge

Jack stole a glance at his little sister. She was not the shy immature girl of last week. He was utterly stupefied at the way she handled herself. Mr. Hallister assured him that this trial would be quick and painless, but had been nearly two hours with all of the evidence and her constant interruptions. She stood tall and confident. Not the awkward girl without worldly experience he had expected.

He shook his head and glanced at the jury. They were a tough looking bunch and he hoped they were as disturbed by Regina's strange explanations as he was. At least they had seen the aggressive unwomanly behavior he had witnessed of late. She gave him a steely gaze and he returned it.

"When will we be finished with this court case?" he asked Mr. Hallister.

"It is nearly over, providing she stops the endless questions."

"Please continue, Captain Green," Judge Faust said.

"Well, my officers carried her to shore in the boat and then brought her to the jail. The wench looked a fair sight too!" Captain Green wiped his forehead with a large kerchief.

"I was soaking wet. How was I supposed to look?" Regina said.

"Your Honor, I submit to you, sir, that there is little more of import to tell. Except to say that the water trial was heartily convincing. In my twenty years as a public guardian of the peace, I have seen a good few swimmings and this was by far the most convincing one I have ever borne witness."

"Is there anything else you wish to add?" asked Judge Faust.

Captain Green wiped his brow again. "No, Your Honors."

"Miss Ingram, your witness," Judge Faust said.

Jack prayed Regina be done with her incessant questioning. Did she not know how foolish she sounded? His thoughts turned to Catherine and the baby—it was getting close to her time and he would meet his new son soon. A shame the lad would never know his aunt.

"Captain Green, I would like an explanation about what a swimming is supposed to prove. Aren't there some people who naturally float, maybe your heavier customers, and others who sink? Is that a reflection of their being a witch?" Regina said.

Where did she get these odd notions?

"Miss Ingram, I have already told the court that a witch is an unholy person, a woman, who has retracted her baptism. If such people are thus rejected by the water this is the good Lord's way of proving this retraction of the divine power," Captain Green said.

"Here, here!" yelled Jack. Mr. Hallister shook his head and grabbed his arm.

"So you are saying that if you float the water is rejecting you?" Regina asked.

"Yes, for that is the purpose of the swimming," Captain Green said.

"What about the Indians in the American colonies who swim and have taught their colonial friends to swim too? Are they witches as well, since they are moving about on the top of the water?" Regina asked.

"Indians! Good God, what is she going on about?" Jack said. He tapped his fingers alongside his thigh. He willed her to stop talking but to no avail.

"Miss I confess I have not seen any Indians moving about on top of the water, as you describe, nor am I ever likely to. But I'll warrant that these Indians have not been baptized as good Christians, and so the water would naturally reject them."

"But what about their colonial friends? English folk like you and me, learning to swim? As you mentioned before, sailors learn to swim as part of their profession. It's like learning to ride a bicycle or sew. It has nothing to do with witchcraft. Swimming is a skill like any other learned behavior."

Mr. Hallister shook his head. "Why does the judge not stop this ridiculous line of questioning?"

"Miss Ingram, are you calling into question the vast experience gathered in hundreds of years of witch hunting? I think the jury will see the folly of such an outlandish idea. Goodness me, to cast out one of the most tried and tested principle methods for ascertaining if a person is possessed by the devil, simply because a few unchristian savages in the colonies delight in splashing around in the water?" He laughed and looked around, waiting for others to join in his mirth.

Regina's cheeks were pinker now but she continued. "I am as you say, 'calling it into question.' You know we discover new things every day. In fact, just recently a man in the colonies discovered electricity. This new force is going to change the world, light up our rooms and streets." She looked around. "Look, we discovered the colonies

243

because Columbus thought the world was flat. Swimming could be the flat Earth of the eighteenth century."

"Miss Ingram, I am decidedly unclear as to what point you are trying to make," Green responded. "You furnish more and more evidence to the court that your mind is indeed weakened and corrupted by the devil! You are on trial for your life, yet you speak about the explorer Columbus and some insane gibberish about candles being powered by an unseen force. Savages in the colonies who can walk on water, perhaps making a mockery of our Lord Jesus Christ, as only one possessed by the forces of Satan would dare to do. What is next, pray tell us, miss? Monkeys who can talk? Fish that can walk?"

When the crowd quieted down, Judge Faust asked, "Miss Ingram do you have any further questions for Captain Green?"

"No, Your Honor," she said, feeling utterly defeated.

Jack clapped his hand. "Good God she is finished!"

"There is one more witness," Mr. Hallister called out from the lawyers' bench.

"Very well Mr. Hallister call your witness if you please, then we will allow Miss Ingram to do the same," Judge Faust said.

"My witnesses?" Regina said. "How was I supposed to find witnesses, I've been in jail for goodness' sake!"

Two men Jack had not seen before approached the stand and were sworn in. "Your Honor," the priest began, "I am Father Fitzsimmons the Chaplain of the Garrison at Newgate Prison. I examined Miss Ingram yesterday to see if the claims set out in Mr. Ingram's vellum were correct and worthy of the effort of arranging a water trial—a swimming."

"Yes, Father," the youngest judge said. "Please tell us in your professional opinion what you found in the examination of the accused."

"Mr. Hallister, I would like to take the stand. My testimony is stronger than this fool's," Jack whispered.

"Are you certain Mr. Ingram? This may draw more attention than you are willing to accept. Think of your business. If you remain quiet they will not attach the witch to you and your family ever so much. Besides this case is a strong one, your testimony will not make a difference at this juncture."

The priest continued, "I have brought this constable who was my witness while I examined Miss Ingram." He pointed to the man next to him.

The guard nodded, a grin splitting his face. "And what uncommon sport it was, seeing the lady in her shift! And now I have the great good fortune of being paid to testify to that rare privilege." He smiled stupidly at the crowd, some of whom laughed while others clapped.

"Very well, I believe I have more to gain by keeping quiet." Jack listened to the Father provide his testimony. What other troubles had Regina caused at the jail?

"I visited Miss Ingram in her cell yesterday. She was most unfriendly and unwelcoming. She refused to allow me to do my complete examination," the priest said. "Thus I had scant choice but to make as thorough an examination as I could in those trying circumstances. She was in no way agreeable, nor did she respect the cloth. However, I was able to confirm the existence of several witches' marks."

"I didn't cooperate because he wanted me to strip in front of this pervert—Would you?" Regina asked a woman in the audience.

"No, I surely would not!" said the woman.

"Miss Ingram, we have covered this ground already," Judge Faustus told her wearily. "I demand that you hold your tongue. You may present your defense when the good Father has finished."

"I did confirm most of the witches' marks," the priest continued. Miss Ingram was frightfully rude to me." He held his head high but his hands were nervously twisting his long black shirt. "I can tell you that she disported herself no better than a common doxy on the street. All ladylike manners were absent during my exam. She deeply insulted my character."

There were about twenty minutes more of the prison chaplain shifting about, blushing, and stammering. Jack could not tell whether Fitzsimmons's testimony had helped her case or not, but he had grown bored with the whole business. Surely they would convict her. All of this talking was a waste of time. There was enough evidence of her guilt. He watched the jury, some were nearly asleep. One man had a scowl on his face whenever Regina spoke.

Mr. Hallister stood up, "No Your Honor. We rest our case."

Judge Faust turned his attention to Ronnie. "Miss Ingram," he said. "You may call your witnesses."

Regina's ivory face turned a few shades pinker and she said, "I apologize Your Honor. But I have not prepared any witnesses."

"Praise be to God!" Jack said.

Mr. Hallister smiled and squeezed Jack's arm. "I do believe that we are within a gnat's whisker of finishing, Mr. Ingram."

There was more talking from different officials, and finally, the jury was instructed on the charges. The chairs were arranged by the outside jury members to face each other and within a few minutes, they were in a heated discussion deciding Regina's fate. Jack observed her sitting quietly on the bench with the other prisoners, all of whom looked as if they belonged there. Regina looked like a fish out of water. It had been easier to despise her when she was acting in such an unwomanly manner, but now, watching her fight back tears, he was reminded of the times when she was a little girl and had cried over some upset. Jack pushed aside his emotions. She was in league with the devil and he could not afford to be fooled by her outward appearance. Regina Elizabeth Ingram was gone. His dear sweet innocent sister had left him forever, but a few days ago.

"How does the next segment of the trial proceed?" Jack asked his lawyer.

"The jury will discuss the case and come to a conclusion. It should not take very long. These witch trials are usually decided with all Godspeed. And thankfully, ours is a mighty solid case."

Jack leaned in toward Mr. Hallister so he could hear him better. The crowd had grown louder, inpatient for a verdict. "About Mathias, my wife's cousin, I wish to press charges against him for the many assaults he has visited on my person." He rubbed his wrists and tried to push the humiliation aside. It was not enough to blacklist him with everyone he knew in London, he wanted also to be sure he did not have the opportunity to complete the threat on his life for bringing Regina to trial. "How do I go about setting the wheels in motion?"

"Mr. Ingram, forgive my saying, but I believe you need to take special care over this matter," Hallister said. "Remember, you assaulted him with a deadly weapon. He would be within his rights to press charges against you for attempted murder. That is a grave charge indeed, sir. In my professional opinion, you should abandon this idea. And, mark you, Mr. Stohl is your wife's cousin. Think of what dragging him through the courts might do to her, on top of the tragedy of losing her sister-in-law."

Jack pressed his lips together and frowned. He knew Mr. Hallister was right, but nevertheless had the overwhelming urge to ruin Mathias's life, after all, his cousin had betrayed him so thoroughly. He scanned the crowd again, this time turning to look at the faces behind him. Mathias had to be here somewhere, watching and praying for a not guilty verdict. A third of the way up he found a familiar face. The dark-haired man turned away. Was it Mathias, or was his mind playing tricks on him? There were not too many men of such a large stature in London.

Still not sure if it was Mathias, he waited. Jack watched the jury for a few more minutes, forcing himself to not turn around. In a quick movement, he twisted his head around to look at the mystery man's face, catching him off guard. It was him—the mangy cur! He flicked his wrist at the attention of the hired man. "Fifteen rows up, directly behind us. Black suit. Count to eight along. Do you see him? Very tall."

The hired man nodded.

"Don't lose him," Jack said. "Take care. I am going ahead with the plans we made this morning."

"Trust me, sir," the hired man answered. "I will attend to the matter."

Jack smiled and thought of his coming revenge on Mathias. His blood still boiled thinking of the ways Mathias had humiliated him. Twice in as many days Mathias had got the better of him. His maid Margaret had to get the cook to help untie him after Mathias had left him bound. The servants had talked about nothing else than the handsome rogue Mathias. The women were sighing and men making him out as a fine hero, for goodness' sake! How could he have misjudged the lad so much? After all of his kindness allowing him to live in his own home, to be repaid by such confounded treachery.

A loud banging noise quietened down the courtroom. The head judge stood up and addressed the jury. "Have you a verdict for us, members of the jury?"

Chapter 47 - Verdict Vertigo

The bailiff motioned Ronnie to return to the stand. Her stomach did a flip and she pressed against it hoping it would calm down. A tear snuck down her cheek and she wiped at it. The judge nodded at the man with an unkempt lamb-chop beard, who stood before the courtroom.

Lamb Chop looked down at his feet. "Your Honor, the jury has found Miss Ingram not guilty of the charges of threatening behavior."

Not guilty! Ronnie wiped her sweaty hands on her dress and bit her lip. Maybe they would not convict her on anything. She crossed her fingers, hiding them under part of her skirt. Please God, help me here!

"And the charge of Perverting the Course of Justice?" Judge Faust asked.

"To the charge of Perverting the Course of Justice, we, the jury, find the defendant, Miss Regina Ingram, not guilty." The man's hands were shaking and he stole a glance at her and quickly averted his gaze.

Ronnie closed her eyes and sent up a prayer. *Please, please, please say not guilty for the last one.*

"And to the charges of Witchcraft?"

The paper shook and Lamb Chop's lips trembled. He cleared his throat and said, "G-G-G—" He cleared his throat again. "Guilty as charged."

Ronnie's knees buckled and she fell to the ground. The bailiff lifted her to her feet. Another bailiff came to her left and held her elbow.

"No, I'm not guilty. I'm not!" She yelled, but the courtroom was too loud, she couldn't even hear her own voice. "No! No!" Her face felt wet and her vision blurred. The bailiffs supported her and stayed near as the spectators yelled while some of them threw things at her.

"Witch!" called out a man with a caved-in mouth and only one big tooth. "Hang her!" He came close and tried to grab her but the bailiff pushed him back. The bailiff on Ronnie's right led her by the elbow to sit down near the other prisoners. The judge banged his gavel and a slew of constables removed the rowdier spectators. A solid twenty minutes of outbursts and chaos ensued until finally the courtroom settled down. Ronnie tried to calm her shaking hands but it was impossible. She was definitely going to be sick. It was only a matter of when and where. Glancing around, she looked for a reasonable place and came up wanting.

"Mr. Vernon Baggins. How do you plead to the charges of Petty Theft and …" Judge Faust introduced the next case on the list.

Ronnie sat through the next four trials, none taking more than ten minutes. Most of the defendants had no clue what to say or do. She looked down the bench and found two defendants remaining. The hall was getting darker and the day was fading away. She looked at her hands and wondered where her real ones were. What had happened to her body? And where was Regina? Was she with Jeffrey in Florida? Man, she would have had a strange few days. At least Jeffrey would not hit her and send her to her death by hanging. She imagined Jeffrey's face, his dark blue eyes looking back at her. His soft kiss and the feeling of his fit body pressed against hers, his arms around her waist.

"Miss! Miss, if you please we are standing for the sentencing." The constable was motioning her to come along with the other prisoners. The group to her left had already filed down, forming a line.

They stood before the judges in a long scrappy line. Judge Faust spoke to the group, "After a lengthy and arduous day of trials it is within my duty as Judge to sentence you according to the verdicts as determined by our jurors. Miss Ingram," he looked down at his papers and then whispered to Judge Reardon before he turned his attention back to her. "Please step forward."

Ronnie's shuffled forward, her legs were shaking and an overwhelming lightheadedness washed over her. This was surreal to be standing before an eighteenth-century courtroom awaiting her fate. She tried to read the judges' expressions but they returned her gaze blank-faced.

"Miss Regina Ingram, you have been convicted by a jury of your peers on the charges of witchcraft. For this great offense to the crown, I hereby sentence you to death by hanging."

The crowd roared and Ronnie swayed, nearly fainting, but leaned over with her hands on her knees taking deep breaths. "No, no!" Her head spun.

The man next to her helped her back up. "Aye, miss, I am greatly sorry for your poor outcome." He held on to her elbow as the judge addressed him. Ronnie searched the audience for Jack but the judges were in the way. The remaining sentences were read as they all stood before the judges. Ronnie wanted nothing more than to sit down, to make her legs stop shaking, and to get away from this crowd. Finally, the last man was handed a light sentence of branding a 'T' for theft on his thumb. He seemed very relieved that was his only punishment. It sounded horrible but not nearly as horrific as her sentence.

A constable motioned for the group to make their way out of the center of the courtroom back to the benches they had sat on before. While the prisoners were seated he shackled the men's feet together and tied a rope around their hands. They left her unbound, as they had when she was brought into the court.

She glanced around remembering Mathias's note. She had nearly forgotten. Was he sending someone to help? Or was that only if she was not convicted? She shook her head, trying to clear her mind. At this point, she had nothing to lose. If Mathias was willing to risk everything for her, even if she died in the escape, it was still better than a damn rope around the neck.

"Come on miss, hurry along if you will, we are all waiting for you." The constable sounded impatient.

The line moved and she followed the men out. A terrible odor trailed behind them. She covered her mouth and nose with her sleeve, the black fabric smelling of smoke. They made their way out of the courtroom and into the hallway. A huge crowd of hundreds of people clogged the door into the halls of the courthouse.

A constable pushed the crowd backward but not quite in time, a man grabbed Ronnie's sleeve and pulled her toward him. "Ya scabby godless witch, be it true? Are they gonna burnt you on the morrow?"

Ronnie jerked her arm away. "Get off of me!" He put his face right up to hers, grabbing her shoulders to pull her closer. In a quick motion, she brought both arms up and around his arms, striking hard. "Stop it!"

He stepped back in surprise and rubbed his forearms. The man's expression changed rapidly from anger to fear. He turned and pushed his way through the crowd to get away.

Other people were shouting and shaking their fists at the prisoners. The constables had their clubs out and were hitting anyone who got close as they made their way down the hallway and out to the courtyard. Cold air hit her face and she hunched over, trying to stay warm. The noise died down and it was a relief to breathe fresh air. Her heart was beating out of her chest and she tried to calm down. On the left, she saw a group of five or six men but no one else was in the courtyard area.

"Charley," a deep voice called out from her right.

Her heart leapt to her throat. "Charley! Yes, I'm here and ready!" she said.

The man was about ten feet away with wavy dark hair and a greasy beard. He raised his hand and made a fist. A commotion to her left caught her attention. The group of men were walking toward the constables and spreading out.

The officer in front said, "What are you ruffians doing back here? The court has adjourned for the day." The other constable took a few steps toward them.

"Tis but a quick matter we wish to discuss with you, gentlemen," the tall thin man said. There was something odd about his face but the prisoners were in her way, so she couldn't quite make out what it was.

"Listen, miss, I'm Charley. Stick tight to my side and I will get you free," the man with a deep voice said.

Ronnie turned her head. "Okay." Her stomach lurched and she could feel the panic rise. Charley grabbed her hand and they ran away from the prisoners. Ronnie was dragged along with her large shoes flopping against the cobblestones. She glanced back to find the two constables in a scuffle with the group of men. The prisoners were kneeling on the ground.

"Make haste lass." They ran to the end of the courtyard and were blocked by a fence.

"Miss, crawl through." Charley pointed to a small hole in the fence, "Through this gap over yonder, another man is waiting for you." He smiled and showed a large chip out of his front tooth.

"Thank you so much!" she said.

She crawled through the fence and heard a constable say, "Halt!" The hem of her skirt was caught on a lose nail on the fence, but she pulled until it came free. Noises of a struggle were audible on the inside of the fence.

A small man in a dark-brown suit reached for her hand. "Ma'am this way." He stood up and walked briskly across the street, shoved her into a carriage, slamming the door behind her. The carriage took off immediately and Ronnie could see a number of constables running out of the front of Newgate Prison. Her carriage was heading the opposite direction.

Would she see Mathias soon? The carriage careened around a corner, speeding up now. She glanced behind them and saw a man on horseback galloping in pursuit. It was a police constable she could see the shiny buttons and a flashback of the swimming ran through her mind.

Chapter 48 - Blood and Guts

Mathias tried to ease his nerves. There were so many ways this could go wrong. The worst thing had already happened—Ronnie had been convicted. Damn Jack could just have let them run off together and his problem would have been solved. Now Mathias had to throw everything away, his life, his family, his future. If Ronnie lived through this they could start a new life but where? How? Even if he moved away they would still be adrift and she would be wanted by the Crown.

He fought his way through the crowd, taking the back route, trying to avoid Jack. The bastard had nearly seen him earlier. Ned was waiting just outside of the rear door to accept the first portion of the promised fee.

"God's Blood, what has kept you?" Ned's scar bunched as he grimaced.

"I have zis for you, please take care *mit* my friend. Remember zee name is Charley. She vill be expecting you to use it." Mathias handed him the package of bank notes.

"Aye, we have been over this. I will attend to the matter and find you at our rendezvous location," Ned said and scurried out the door and around the building.

Mathias turned around and made his way back toward the front of the building. He would start the journey on foot toward the rendezvous spot so he would not miss the meeting. Ned was as likely to keep Ronnie as he was to return her so he felt compelled to get there early and be prepared to take Ronnie away as soon as she arrived.

The crowd was thick and it was slow to work his way through to the other side of the court. A man in a long black coat stopped in front of him and Mathias was pushed by the crowd into the back of him. A sharp pain in his side made Mathias scream out, "*Gott's gebiss!*"

He turned around to find a mustached man, "A gift from Mr. Ingram."

Mathias's knees buckled and the crowd made their way around him. One man tripped on his legs, landing next to him. The crowd behind them pushed and more people were forced to either step on Mathias or step over him. A woman in boots stepped on his hand, crushing his fingers. It seemed an eternity until she picked up her foot and freed his hand. He tried to stand but the crowd continued to push forward, knocking him over. Mathias landed hard on a smaller man, knocking the air of him when the man's shoulder jammed into his stomach. He crawled out of the flow of the crowd and leaned against a wall, trying to catch his breath. A trickle of warmth flowed down his back and he reached around to feel it. Looking at his hand he realized it was covered in blood.

His shirt was soaked through with blood. In a light-headed daze, he leaned over, trying not to faint. "Stabbed! I have been stabbed," Mathias said in a panic. "How will I get to Ronnie?" He moved into a hallway that was not quite as crowded and lifted his jacket, twisting around to try and see the wound. He pulled his shirttail out from his pants and lifted it. It dripped blood onto the floor and a woman behind him screamed.

"He is hurt!" she yelled out. A few constables heard her scream and made their way toward him.

Mathias began walking. He did not need anyone asking questions and detaining him. He worked his way to the front of the building. His height made it hard for him to get lost in the crowd and the constables made their way toward him in pursuit.

"Sir, sir. Please, we will help you," they called out. He made it to the front of the building and moved quickly to an alleyway. He stood panting, leaning his head against the bricks. "Nein, nein, nein," he cursed. There was no way he was going to make it to Ronnie. The meeting place was a mile away. Energy sapping away, he touched the wound again, trying to gauge how much damage the knife had done. The gash felt as if it was only an inch or so wide but blood poured out and ran down into his boots, his foot squished in the warm puddle in his boot.

He made his way to the end of the alleyway, crossed the street and went into the next alleyway, hoping it was far enough away from the constables. He sat down hard on the dirty wet ground, legs feeling weak. "I curse Jack to hell and back," he said under his breath as his eyes closed. He was so tired. He remembered something that Madam Zangari had said to press against the bleeding to make it stop. Taking his handkerchief out of his breast pocket he folded it, setting it against the wound and leaned against the wall, pushing with all his weight. The man had sliced him between his hip bone and his ribs. *Gott* if the blade had penetrated deeply there would be no stopping the bleeding until he was dead. He pulled out the wad of bank notes and stuffed it down his crotch in case he passed out. Hopefully, that was one place where brigands would not look.

"*Gott* and hell's damnation!" He was not meant to be here wounded and bleeding in an alley. He was supposed to be rescuing Ronnie and taking her away from London.

Chapter 49 - Escape to Rape

Ronnie gasped as the mounted policeman drew closer. The driver of the coach whipped the horses and he had to swerve to avoid other vehicles and horsemen on the road. The effort slowed them down. Ronnie held on tight trying not to slide across the seat and finally crouched on the floor wedged between the two facing seats. It helped a bit but she was still buffeted around the cabin.

A man on horseback rode up and grabbed the reins of the constable's horse, making the animal careen sideways and dismounting the rider. They make a sharp turn at a crossroad and Ronnie scanned the road behind them and saw no sign of any pursuit. Thank God. It was horrible to think that she might be taken directly back to jail. The coachman must have noticed he was no longer being pursued and slowed down to a normal pace for several blocks. Finally, she poked her head out of the window and said, "Where are you taking me?"

"Don't you worry miss," he assured her. "I will have you at your destination in God's speed. I apologize for the delay, I believe I was a bit turned around getting free of that constable."

Ronnie sat back against the seat, heart racing, imagining Mathias's broad shoulders and long arms around her. It was mind blowing to think he was still alive and had planned all of this to get her free. What a miracle. It was so nice to be out of the courtroom and especially out of the prison. She filled her lungs with fresh air and let it out enjoying the view of Londoners going about their business. Still, it was shocking to see the costumes of the eighteenth century. They were a hard-looking people. Of course, the ladies wore no makeup and the men were shaggy haired. She caught a glimpse of her reflection in the glass of the window and immediately set out to repair her hairdo. She smoothed her black dress and tried to wipe off some of the mud on the hem from climbing through the fence. There wasn't anything she could do about the tear in the fabric.

Trying not to think too far ahead she imagined Mathias smiling and lifting her off the coach. The first thing she wanted to do was kiss him. He had given up so much for her. A mixture of emotions assaulted Ronnie. There was nothing more she wanted than to get back home to Florida, but how could she after Mathias had done so much for her?

Of course, there was the monumental problem that she had no clue how she got here and equally had no clue how to get back. They certainly couldn't go to Madam Zangari's house again to ask for her help. That bridge was burned with napalm.

Maybe Mathias would have some idea about what they should do now. After all, she had been through she felt like she could trust him to listen to her story and maybe have something to add to the craziness of it to help her figure out the next steps.

The coach stopped in front of a wooden building with several men standing out front, pulling Ronnie from her thoughts. She scanned the faces staring at her but none of them were Mathias. The coachman opened her door and offered a grimy hand to help her down. She took it, not trusting her giant shoes and stepped down into the muddy road.

"Miss, if you please, follow me," said a stocky man, who led her up to a shabby porch. He held the door open for her and motioned for her to go inside. Several men followed them into the building. "Miss, down that hallway and to your left, if you will."

She glanced back at the two men behind her and caught the stocky one mimicking grabbing her butt. Ronnie turned around to face him and gave him a hard look. "What are you doing?" she asked with her hands on her hips, wanting to call him a jackass or something, but thought better of it after looking at his face. The man looked very stupid and yet capable of doing her some real damage, his meaty forearms showing through his rolled-up shirt sleeves.

The offending man smiled, "Miss, I most humbly beg your pardon," then broke into a snaggletooth grin. The two men laughed and shoved Ronnie forward. "Don't tarry now. We need to get into the back room." The two continued laughing.

She wanted to see them laughing when Mathias got hold of them. Hopefully, he was there waiting. The man in front opened the door and they all went inside. A large fire crackled in the hearth and warmed the cold damp air. The room held sparse furnishings all faded and shabby. A far cry from Jack's lush appointments. Her heart raced, Mathias might be here. She scanned the faces and again was disappointed.

"Ma'am, sit yourself down if you please," the stocky man said. He kicked a man sitting sideways in the only upholstered chair in the room who stood up, taking off his hat and bowed.

Everyone in the room watched her sit and she looked around confused. "Where is Mathias?"

"It's like this Ma'am," the stocky man said, giving a sideways glance to the man he had kicked out of the chair. "Truth be, no one's seen hide nor hair of him. He was supposed to meet us here as soon as the trial was done."

"Does he know where to go?" She looked around the room and the men were staring at her like they had never seen a woman before. Leaning forward, she fixed her skirt to cover her ankles. One man openly gazed at her chest and she moved her hand to cover it up.

"Stop staring at me, would you?" she said. "You're making me very uncomfortable." The men laughed and some averted their gazes.

"Wench is a real spitfire ain't she, George?" one man said to his stocky friend, elbowing him in the ribs.

George nodded stupidly and said, "That's about the size of it. Juicy little hellcat, she be, I reckon. Just the way I likes my women. Fighting hard, drumming her little fists against me as I splice her!"

Laughter filled the room and Ronnie crossed her arms and legs, saying a prayer for Mathias to show up. She turned away from George and his friend to find another man sitting near her.

He licked his lips and stared at her intently. "Hello kitten, do not let those men make you nervous. I'm the one you really need to worry about." He broke into a wide grin.

"Aw, do not be telling her stories Michael, 'cause we all do know your dangle's been jiggered these past years, leastways, that's what all the maids hereabouts tell me." Everyone but Ronnie and Michael laughed.

"Tis a dastardly lie, miss." Michael leaned in closer to her, talking conspiratorially, "My jigger stick be a right fine specimen and works just fine and dandy."

Ronnie stood up and stomped her foot as she spoke. "Mathias paid you good money to get me here safe. You will not treat me with such disrespect!"

The men laughed again and she heard the words spitfire and wildcat.

A tall man walked into the room and was followed by two greasy smaller men. "Miss Ingram. Mathias did ask me to return you unharmed, so don't nobody lay a hand on her. And any more filthy remarks I been hearing just now, I'll crack your dirty skulls against the wall." He looked around the room at each man and several hung their heads.

"Because if anyone is going to ride the little wench, I reckon as how it's going to be me." A deep scar ran down his face, almost splitting it in two as he smiled. Ronnie shuddered.

"How 'bout if you at least let us watch, Ned?" George said. A few guffaws filtered around the room. "And after you're done with the wench, surely you would give leave to give her a second helping?"

"We will give the lad a bit longer to make his way to us. If he does not see fit to put in an appearance in the next hour or so, we can take turns to make merry with her." He smiled and chucked under the chin. "But 'tis me as gets the first crack."

Ronnie nearly vomited at the thought and looked around the room to count the men—all eight looked back at her, some smiling, others making rude gestures. Why would Mathias let these men near her, much less trust them enough to not murder him when he arrived? Aware of all eyes on her she turned away and took a few deep breaths, rubbing her temples. A headache was edging in. If Mathias was supposed to be here she couldn't run away, it might be her only chance to find him. If he didn't show up there was no getting away from this group. They looked bloodthirsty. Where was he? Ronnie felt a chill run up her spine. She wasn't so sure if the hanging were the better of these two options, although yesterday she wouldn't have guessed in a million years she would have any options at all.

"Hell and damnation, where the devil is he?" Ned, the man with the scar eased himself into a chair next to her and steepled his fingers. "Do you know that he still owes me money?"

"Something must have happened to him. He would not leave me in this situation,"

"Tell me, pretty lady, where should we seek him out?"

"Where was he supposed to be before he came here?" The last time she had heard from him was with the note in jail.

"I saw him m'self at the courthouse but then right quickly afterward I left. He was late with the first payment, he nearly made me miss the capture. Michael? Get my coach. The lady and I will be making a quick trip."

"You're taking me to the courthouse? What if someone sees me?" Ronnie felt her heartbeat quicken. She did not want to go back to jail.

"I would be pleased either way. If the law spies you, I can pocket the reward for your return to Newgate. But if the angels are with us I might find our friend Mathias and screw the rest of my dues out of him. It is all the same to me, luv, I will make-do with whoever pays me most handsomely. Smithy, you come along for the ride." The beefy dumb man walked over to them. "Step outside and check on the coach. The matter of my payment is right heavy on my mind, and I fancy it must be settled one way or another," Ned said.

"Yes, sir." Smithy walked toward the back of the house and out the rear door.

The man was a snake. Mathias's hard-earned money was going to this loser and his band of unwashed rapists? He must have been desperate.

After a few minutes, Smithy walked back into the room. "Ned, the coach is ready and waiting." He turned to Ronnie and held out his hand. "Miss?" She refused his help and stood up, making her way down the hallway to the back door. The two men followed.

"What's the hurry miss, don't you like my men?" Ned said. He and Smithy laughed.

She ignored the comment and opened the backdoor. A terrible thought hit her. What if Mathias showed up while she was gone? Ned would return her to prison if he couldn't find Mathias, or worse, leave her to be entertained by his men.

A beautiful black horse stood rigged to a small coach. Ronnie walked up to it and, without waiting, climbed inside, sitting as far over into a corner as she could. It would be a tight squeeze with the two large men in there with her. At least she didn't have the stupid panniers on anymore.

"You are eager to find your man, are you not, miss?" Smithy said. "Perhaps you 'ave not yet had your field plowed by a proper fella? Some of us know right well how to please a lady, I will warrant you need to be shown what's what." He reached out to touch her sleeve.

She smacked his hand away. "Stop that!"

"Hold your filthy tongue, Smithy, and do not harass the lady, or you will feel the edge of my blade against your neck," Ned said as the coach started to move.

Ronnie kept her eyes on the two men, not liking the aggressiveness of Smithy. They rode in silence for several blocks toward the courthouse and Ronnie sat lower in her seat hoping there weren't constables out searching for her. Ronnie looked down each cross street and alleyway hoping to catch a glimpse of Mathias. Finally, down a dark damp alleyway, she saw something.

"Stop, there was a man back there!" she yelled to the driver. A large shape sat on the ground. "Back up!"

"Back up? What do you mean, miss, how can a carriage go backward?" The coach driver stopped and she opened the door and climbed down the steps. Smithy was right behind her. "Mathias! Mathias." She ran toward the still form and reaching him knelt down and turned his face toward her.

Chapter 50 - Stealing His Breath

"Mathias! Oh my God!" she cried out. His skin was clammy and took on a horrible grayish-blue hue. She felt for a pulse and, not finding one, laid him flat on the ground and put her face to his mouth, hoping to feel his warm breath on her cheek. Nothing. "No! Mathias!"

The two men stood watching her dumbfounded. "That's our man, right?" Ned said. "What in the devil's name is she doing?"

"Damned if I know, Boss," Smithy said.

"Yes, it's Mathias. I think he's dead," Ronnie quickly went through the steps of CPR. Tilting his head back and lifting his chin, she blew air into his mouth. His lungs filled and stale air came out when she released his mouth.

"What is the meaning of this cruelty, miss?" Smithy said taking a step toward her. "By heavens, you are stealing his breath. You must desist!"

"No, I'm helping him." She began the chest compressions, not quite sure how hard to push since she had only done it on a CPR dummy in lifeguard training. It was so much harder on a real person. "Mathias!" She stopped and shook him. No response.

After several puffs of air into his lungs, she continued chest compressions again. She turned back to the men. "Can you run for a doctor?"

"Stop, you creature from hell! By God, you're stealing his breath!" Ned called out, aghast. "Do you see this Smithy? She is pushing the very air of life from his body. Make her stop. It is an abomination to God!"

"No! Stop a witch stealing the breath from a dying man? Then I wager she will steal mine!" Smithy's voice was getting higher and he grabbed the other man's arm as they both backed away from her.

She ignored them, counting compressions, desperate for Mathias to come back to life. She could not lose him. He had given up everything for her. He couldn't lose his life as well! Tears flowed down her face but Ronnie did not stop.

Suddenly Mathias coughed and let out an unearthly moan. "Ahhhhhh." He made an attempt to sit up.

Ronnie sat back on her heels. "Oh thank God, Mathias!"

The two men stood staring, mouths agape. "Miss, did you just bring that man back from the dead?"

Her face grew hot, realizing what they must be thinking. "No, he was just nearly dead. I managed to get enough air to his brain for him to wake." How the hell could CPR be explained to someone of this time period?

"By thunder, she is a witch Smithy," Ned said. "We've seen her sorcery with our own eyes. Mathias said so himself. She was convicted of witchcraft and now the maid's cast some pretty spells indeed!" They took a few more steps backward. "Now the pieces of the puzzle are in place. He had to spirit her out of jail because he had need of her ungodly magic."

"No, that's ridiculous, I simply pumped his heart and gave him some air." She loosened the cravat at Mathias' throat—his color was returning.

"Uuugghh," Mathias winced, still trying to sit up. Ronnie pushed him back down. "Where the hell am I?"

Ronnie stood and helped Mathias to a sitting position. "Don't stand up yet. Just get your bearings and we'll get you in the coach in a few minutes," Ronnie said looking around for the two men. Smithy had disappeared but Ned still stood nearby.

"Aye young sir, how about the money? Let's take care of that little bit of business right now, if you have the mind," Ned said, his voice shaking.

Mathias's face twisted in pain and he reached into his coat.

Ronnie helped him sit against the wall. "Mathias, do you have the money to pay Ned?"

"The money?" He combed through his dark hair and shook his head. "I'm ..." He stopped and looked into her face. "Ronnie? Is that you?"

"Yes." She was surprised he remembered her real name but did not know where he was. "Where did you put the money, Mathias?"

He reached into the front of his pants and pulled out some wadded up bank notes. Ronnie took the money, stood up, and walked the few steps toward Ned who retreated with his hands up. "Stay back miss. I do not want to be the object of your sorcery. Just leave the bank notes on the ground there and step back."

"Don't get carried away." She glanced back at Mathias smiling. "I'm not a witch."

Ned reached down and picked up the money, counted it and turned around and walked briskly back to the coach.

"Wait!" Ronnie yelled as she ran toward the coach. "Wait for us!" Ned climbed in and shut the door, looking at her intently.

Ronnie ran toward them, "Wait for us!" And stopped short when they were out of sight. She walked breathlessly back to Mathias. "They left us! Now what the hell do we do?" She knelt down next to him. "How are you feeling?"

"I feel like death warmed over." He touched his back as he spoke and then winced. His voice sounded different, must have been made deeper with tiredness.

"Are you in pain?" She pulled up his jacket and then the shirt in the place where he was touching his back. A blood-soaked handkerchief was wadded up pressed into his flesh. She peeled it away to reveal a cut about an inch-and-a-half long still oozing blood, but not too copiously. "Oh my God, how did this happen?"

He shook his head and smiled at her. "You have no idea how happy I am to see you."

"Mathias, how did this happen?"

"What?"

"This injury?" she asked.

He shook his head.

"The bleeding is slowing down but there is a pretty big puddle under you. I wonder how long you were unconscious." Ronnie moved around to crouch in front of him touching his face in an overwhelming wave of affection. "Thank you for getting me out of that hellhole." She kissed his cheek and he put his arm around her back holding her close. "That was quite a feat, Mathias!"

"All that matters now is that you are free. We can get away." He smiled weakly.

"Yes, thanks to you. You have done so much for me Mathias. I hope you won't regret it!"

"No." He smiled his eyes reflecting the gesture. "The only thing I regret is that I did not kill him when I had the chance."

"Who? You mean Jack?" She pressed the cloth against his back again and looked around for something to tie it in place. He was not making much sense. She lifted the hem of her dress and tore at the white shift to pull off a long strip and wrapped it gently around his waist and tied it in front.

"Jack? No, I'm talking about ..." He looked away in thought and licked his lips. "Yes, Jack. None of this would have happened if he had ... If I had," He leaned his head against the wall. "And I would not have been stabbed in the back."

"Jack is responsible for this?" Ronnie said through clenched teeth. "He has caused so much pain and suffering to us both." She took a deep breath and let it out. "God I hate that bastard." Angry thoughts rolled around in her mind but they had to be pushed aside to focus on the task at hand. Mathias was in bad shape. "We have to clean you up and stop you from going into shock." The ground was damp and his pants were soaked with blood and water from the alley. "Can you stay put for a few minutes? We need a carriage. Crap, do you have any money left? I might have to hire a car, I mean, um, a carriage."

"No, we are staying together," Mathias said it in such a way that she couldn't argue.

She shot him a dark look. "Why?"

"Because we cannot be separated." He looked at her and the corner of his mouth turned up. "Women are not usually alone and standing around hiring carriages in this area. I need to go with you. That will be less suspicious."

"Oh, I see. So how do I get you down to the end of the alleyway then? You're a lot bigger than I am and not so steady on your feet yet."

"Just let me catch my breath. So sleepy. I can hardly keep my eyes opened."

"Mathias, listen to me. You have to fight the urge to sleep. You've lost a lot of blood. I really need to get you out of here but you *can't fall asleep.*" His eyes blinked drowsily. She shook him by the shoulders. "Stay awake Mathias!"

"I will do my best," he said, words mashing together.

"You have to do better than that." She wasn't sure if he would die if he fell asleep but there was no way she would be able to move him if he weren't helping. He had to weigh nearly 200 pounds, as tall and broad as he was.

"Do you think you can stand up?" she asked, doubtful.

"I can if you will kiss me," he said, a small smile playing on his lips.

"Ha! That will help? Okay." Ronnie leaned over and pressed her lips against his. A wave of excitement bubbled in her chest and he wrapped his arms around her. He kissed her, parting her lips with the tip of his tongue, his mouth firm but soft on hers. He pulled away and smiled. She smiled but looked away, embarrassed at the intensity of her feelings.

"Now we have to get you standing," Ronnie stood. He had dark circles under his eyes and his skin was the color of ash. "Mathias, you've got to stay with me. I cannot lose you now."

"Ronnie, stop talking like that. You are not going to lose me. We are at the very beginning of us. We can get through this, I just need a little support from you and everything will be fine." His mouth smiled but this time it didn't make it to his eyes.

She bent over to help him up. He put his arm around her and leaned heavily to get off the ground. As he stood his legs gave out but she caught him, using every ounce of strength she had. "Oh my God! Why are you so damn heavy?"

He stood now, legs still unsteady. Ronnie gave him a minute to get his balance. She could feel the muscles beneath the shirt and couldn't help but imagine what he would look like shirtless.

"Are you all right, Mathias? You're not going to faint are you?" He was at least a foot taller. If he went down, she would be in trouble.

"Ronnie, are you looking forward to your job?" he said and then looked away. "Um, forget I said that."

"My job? What are you talking about?" The only job she could think of was the one she would start in Florida on Monday but he would not know about that. "Mathias, what job?"

"I misspoke. Please let us focus on getting down this alley." He leaned on her for support and took a tentative step.

"So what is our plan here? We are walking down this alley and then what? Do you have a wagon waiting somewhere for us?"

"Yes."

"Do you have money and supplies?"

"Again, yes Ronnie. I have made arrangements for us."

She laughed. "I know. I'm sure they are great arrangements. We haven't talked about it yet so I'm just asking."

"You have been in jail. How could I, never even thought I'd get this far?" He leaned down and kissed the top of her head. "I must rest. Can you hold me up against the wall here?"

They walked arm in arm to the brick wall and he leaned against it. He pulled her in close and she thought of Jeffrey with a twinge of guilt pulling at her heart. He circled his arms around her waist. She hugged him and felt the long lean muscles on his back. He rested his chin on top of her head. They stayed like that for a few minutes.

"Okay, let's get you somewhere safer. I'm worried about you," she said.

"What the devil is this?" A loud male voice interrupted them. "What have we here? If it ain't the two love birds."

Smithy stood ten feet away smiling at them. Ronnie pulled away from Mathias and took a step toward Smithy. "What are you doing here? You got your money, now run along."

"Dear me no, miss, I cannot do that as an honest upright citizen. In conscience, I am indeed driven to do the right thing for God and England. I fear I must make things right with the law." Smithy rolled up his sleeves.

"Well there's an interesting concept," Ronnie said, looking around for a weapon.

"I have paid you, now piss off you leach." Mathias pushed away from the wall.

"Tis nothing personal my friend, I assure you." Smithy took a few steps toward them. "I am merely looking out for my own interests—I am sure you can relate to that." He closed the gap between them and stood a few feet away. "The constables will be delighted to know that while I was out on an evening stroll it was but my good fortune to come upon a pretty lady who has a price on her head, and a goodly fellow with gold in his pockets. It is a dreadful shame that he is stricken, and can no longer defend her. Something of a rare opportunity for a catch-hand chancer like me."

"I said piss off, you piece of shit." Mathias squared his shoulders.

Smithy cupped his ear with a hand. "Eh? Is my hearing awry miss? Will you allow him to address me in such terms when we have shared so much?" Smithy made a grab for Ronnie's arm. "For shame, miss."

Mathias leapt forward taking Smithy by surprise. The men wrestled, but Mathias shot low and grabbed Smithy's legs, knocking him to the ground. Ronnie grabbed a rock she spotted and returned to the two men scrambling for control.

"Run away now, I cannot hold him for long!" Mathias yelled as Smithy nearly succeeded in pushing off Mathias.

"No! Mathias, I will not let him hurt you!"

"Ronnie, run away where he can't find you!" Mathias bellowed.

Smithy shoved Mathias and stood up. He pulled out a knife. "I will sink this sharp steel into your belly, then I will strike deep into the belly of the witch and carve out her sins." He waved the knife around.

Mathias rushed him again, this time grabbing Smithy's knife hand. The two men wrestled for control of the weapon.

Smithy tripped over Mathias's foot and they both landed hard on the ground, a grunt of air exploding with a whoosh from someone's lungs. Ronnie couldn't tell for sure, but Mathias was on top again.

"Run, Ronnie, this is your chance to be free!" Mathias bellowed.

"Smithy, you son of a fucking bitch!" Ronnie screamed holding the rock over her head. Both men looked at her momentarily surprised.

Ronnie smashed the rock down with all of her strength on Smithy's face. It skidded off his hard head and bounced away.

"Witch! No!" Smithy said, fighting hard to get his hands free from Mathias's grip.

Mathias took advantage of Smithy's distraction and punched him square in the jaw, nearly falling forward in the process.

Ronnie grabbed the rock again aiming at Smithy's head for another attempt. This man was hard to knock out! Mathias held Smithy's arms down against the cobblestones and Ronnie brought the rock down with all her strength. She aimed for his nose this time. It hit its intended target with great effect. Blood splattered across Mathias's face. Ronnie struck again and again, afraid Smithy would get up and kill them both.

After several blows, Mathias yelled, "Stop, stop. He is no longer a danger." He stood up slowly and took the bloody rock from her hands and threw it away. It skidded across the cobblestones.

Smithy was finally quiet, his nose was destroyed and blood poured down his cheeks.

"We need to be on our way." Mathias grabbed her hand and they made their way to the end of the alley and stopped to rest.

Something did not seem right with Mathias. In fact, she couldn't help but notice that as he spoke during the exchange with Smithy his German accent was weaker, maybe even non-existent. Had he been faking it this whole time? The comment about her new job was weird too. An eerie feeling echoed around in her mind. They needed to get somewhere safe where she could examine this further.

Chapter 51 - Blood on Her Hands

Ronnie put her arm around Mathias's waist. Walking like two drunks they made their way down the alley to the connecting street. They turned left and away from the courthouse. Ronnie guided them to a bench outside a shop and eased Mathias's big frame down. They both sat quietly for a minute out of breath.

"Oh my God, did I just do that?" she said.

"Yes, I believe you have taken care of Smithy," Mathias said. "But for how long he stays down God only knows."

"How are you feeling? Can you make it further?"

Blood and beads of sweat covered his forehead despite the falling temps with evening coming on. "I cannot walk another step," he said. "Why did you not listen to me and run away? You could have been killed." He reached out and pushed her hair behind her ear.

"But Mathias, you are hurt and in no condition to fight! Then, when he had his way with me, he would probably have turned me into the prison for a reward."

"You should have left him to me. I would have broken him." There was no fight in his words. He was exhausted.

"It doesn't matter. We have to get away from here." Ronnie looked around. Would there be police on the streets looking for her? "Where is your wagon—is it very far?" He didn't answer and she looked more closely at him. "Mathias!"

He was not responding. "Mathias!" She touched his face and he looked up at her.

"Yes?" His eyes were glazed and then he seemed to refocus. "Ronnie. I am sorry."

She stood up. "Don't fall asleep. I'm getting a coach. Where are we going to go? What should I tell the driver?"

He leaned forward and dry heaved a few times. An older couple walked by and gave them a funny look. The man said, "Sir, excuse me, but do you need some assistance?"

Mathias smiled. "Oh, just feeling a bit sick. Would you help my, er—" he looked at Ronnie, "wife get a carriage? We are trying to make our way home and I fell ill."

269

The woman shrank back in horror. "They are both covered in blood!" She pulled her husband away down the street, talking to him heatedly.

Ronnie wiped her hands on the black dress, hoping to remove some of Smithy and Mathias's blood, but it was dried and not coming off. She took her sleeve and tried to wipe Smithy's blood off of Mathias's face. "Mathias, we can't be out like this. We need to get off the street. Where can we go?"

He looked at her sleepily. A commotion down the road caught her attention. It was the older couple and they were talking to a constable. "Oh no, Mathias, that's all we need." She pointed down the street.

"Ronnie you have to run away. LISTEN TO ME NOW!" Mathias said.

"Mathias, I can't leave you."

He pushed her away. "You have no choice! Leave me now, Ronnie. I cannot see you back in jail. I cannot watch you hang."

The constable was walking briskly toward them. "Where will I find you?" she asked, holding his hand.

"There is no time, Ronnie, I will find you. Get away from here!"

She kissed him on the lips, her hand on his cheek, forcing herself to remember how this felt, how he smelled, how he tasted. "Do not let them bleed you, Mathias. You've bled enough today!"

Ronnie looked around, not sure where to go. She ran inside the closest shop and asked the clerk, "Where is the back door?" The shopkeeper looked at her in shock. Without waiting Ronnie rushed to the back of the store and found a door leading to the alleyway. Looking left and right she saw a few constables from the jail walking briskly her way. Turning on her heel she ran back through the store and out the front door, the shopkeeper yelling after her.

Mathias was still on the bench with a few men talking to him. The tallest of the men noticed her and she ran as fast as she could away from them, shoes flopping oddly on the cobblestones, dodging people walking toward her. Loud male voices yelled after her but she couldn't make out what they were saying. Ronnie ran across the street and nearly got hit by a man on horseback. The horse reared and slowed the men chasing her, allowing her to step unseen into another small shop. Quickly closing the door behind her she made her way to the back of the shop looking for a back door. A woman followed.

"Stop thief!" the woman shouted. "How dare you try to steal from me!"

"No, no you don't understand," Ronnie said. When the lady saw the blood on Ronnie's hands she stepped back.

Ronnie ran to the back of the store and opened the door, running into the alleyway, and smack into two constables.

"Well, well, well, just look what the cat dragged in." One of the men said while grabbing her arm.

"Miles, that's just stupid. She wasn't going *in* anywhere. She was on her way out." The other constable said, eyeing her.

The door opened and the shopkeeper came out, wringing her hands. "That girl is a thief!"

"I am not. I was just running to the alley," Ronnie said.

"Ah but what are you running away from?" Miles said. "That's what I've got to ask myself."

"Now why would you ask yourself, Miles?" Miles's colleague shook his head in exasperation. "Why don't you ask the maid herself, you simpleton."

"I … well," Ronnie stuttered, "My friend is sick and I was going to find a doctor."

"In the alley? You're looking for a doctor in the alley? Brilliant, that's just brilliant, miss," Cranky said.

"Well I can tell you that oftentimes old Dr. Mercer stumbles along here in his cups," Miles said while weaving his hand back and forth, "Blind drunk and throwing up against the wall, but he ain't in no fit state to do any doctoring!"

The cranky man ignored Miles and looked at her. "What's this on your hands?"

"It's blood. My friend is hurt. He needs help."

"You look a bit familiar like. Where have I seen you, miss?" Miles looked her up and down.

Ronnie recognized him from the courthouse. "I don't know. Maybe you're my neighbor or something,"

"Do you think that maybe, just maybe this could be the girl we are looking for, Miles?" Cranky put his hand on her neck and gripped tightly.

She shrugged her shoulders and tried to pull away, but he held tight.

"She fits the description," Miles said, pulling out a small piece of parchment. "She is the right height and wearing a black dress."

"Are you ever going to get around to questioning her? God's teeth man you are thick as a cathedral stone. Miss, please identify yourself." The cranky constable shot another angry glance at Miles.

"I'm Ronnie Andrews, sir," she said.

"Miss Andrews, can you tell me why your hands are covered in blood?" Cranky asked.

"My friend was stabbed and I was helping him." She was trying again to wipe off the dried blood.

"Stabbed you say?" Cranky looked at Miles. "We have had a report of a man bleeding just after the trial at the courthouse. Miles, really, surely you remember? She needs to be processed at Newgate. We will question her there."

"No, oh please don't take me to jail. I've done nothing wrong, constables. I just need to help my friend." Tears flowed down her face and Ronnie wiped at them until she realized she was smearing blood everywhere. Using her sleeve she wiped again, hoping her face wasn't covered in blood. Was it Mathias's or Smithy's blood?

"Stuart, why can we not ask her a few things here. The maid is in distress, what is the harm in treating her with a bit of Christian charity?" Miles said.

"You are a fool indeed, Miles. Our task is to find a woman matching her description, and pound her to a pudding once we have found her. It is our duty to return her to Newgate and allow the captain to question her. No more delays, Miles. You have tried my patience enough today." Cranky grabbed her upper arm and dragged her along, walking just ahead of Miles.

"Please, my friend is near here and he is sick. You need to help him first," she couldn't let Mathias die in the street.

Stuart walked briskly ahead with a strong grip on her arm. Miles trailed behind.

"Come on Stuart," Miles said almost whining, "what's the harm in talking to her friend?"

Maybe she could use the green Miles to her advantage. "I tell you, he will likely die if we don't do something!" Ronnie said.

"We can send for help once we get you settled. We are but a few blocks to Newgate, miss. What did you say your name was?" Stuart asked as cranky as ever.

"Andrews. Miss Andrews," Ronnie said.

"Aye, I do not recall the name, but I do recognize you from the trial." Miles smiled down at her. "Very pleased to make your acquaintance, miss."

"Miles, really!" Stuart pressed his fingers into his eyes. "You have not been introduced to the maid at a dinner party. She is a wanted felon. Are you going to ask for her autograph?"

"But I tell you she was a rare one at the trial, Stuart. She made that fat pig of a priest look like he was a buggering boys!" He laughed and Stuart shot him a dark look.

"Well, she did!" Miles said. "Right clever questions she asked, I reckon. Tied 'em up in knots she did."

"Miles, you need to learn to keep your trap shut. This is not helping matters." Stuart led her down the street. "Lord give me strength," he mumbled under his breath.

They walked in silence and Ronnie was glad for the opportunity to think. How could she get someone to help Mathias and not connect him to her escape? They were close to the jail. Ronnie's heart leapt when she remembered Jack bringing her there the first time. Would Constable Peel be on duty? What about the other man she had scared so badly with her Hermione impression?

"Please constables, can't we go back and help my friend?" Ronnie tried to pull away from Stuart, who merely tightened his grip.

"He might be dying. For pity's sake, can't we do something for him? It is our duty as constables and Christians—" Miles continued.

"—Yes Miles!" Stuart stopped abruptly. "If it'll stop your infernal whining maybe we can bloody do something for him." He turned toward Ronnie. "Miss tell me where is your friend, assuming that he even exists?" He looked at Miles as he said the word exists.

"He is down the main street here, just past that alleyway," she said, pointing beside the shop where she had left Mathias.

"Miles, here is your opportunity to do your Christian duty. Get the man and take him to the doctor if you can find him. By Jiminy, Miles, if you're not one of the most annoying baskets in all of London I will eat my ruddy hat! Why in heaven's name did I have to be stuck with you?"

Miles looked down the street and back at Ronnie. "Miss, can you give me a description of your friend?"

"He is tall." She held up her hand to indicate his approximate height. "Dark cropped hair and very broad in build. He is wearing a black coat and pants."

"Fear not, Stuart, I will report back to you when I return," Miles said.

Stuart ignored Miles and with a huff continued down the road and through the door into the outer courtyard of Newgate Prison, pushing Ronnie in ahead of him. A half an hour later Ronnie was back in the jail cell she had been in but this time she was not alone. The cell reeked of booze and urine, and a woman slept on the bench. It was not the bunkmate she had in mind for the night.

Chapter 52 - Back at the Ranch

Nick and Steph returned to the hallway where they listened to the radio. Steph studied his handsome face. He laid flat on the floor with his arm on a pillow across his chest with his eyes closed, his face wearing an expression of pain and exhaustion. She imagined kissing his full lips. Her weakness was high cheekbones, and Nick's were perfect for framing his big eyes. He had a thick neck and broad shoulders but looked somehow younger in that vulnerable position.

He had handled everything so well, despite being hurt and everything possible going wrong. He was a very well put together man, physically and otherwise—strong but sensitive. Steph had always been attracted to the strong and silent men. Of course, that is why she had to leave Scotland because of her ex-husband. He was a violent man in the Royal Navy but hadn't shown his true colors until their marriage was a few months old. That is when the beatings began.

The first time she had wrecked his car in an ice storm while he was away for five months on tour. But gradually it didn't take much for him to hit her over the smallest thing. Her sister, Cynthia, came to her house one night, grabbed her things while Sully was out drinking with his mates. Sully must have had an absolute fit when he came home that night but Steph was hidden away at her sister's cottage and left in the morning on a flight to Virginia Beach, supposedly on a holiday with her sister but Steph ended up staying. Cynthia had a close friend in the tourism business who gave Steph a job until she got her green card. Ten years had passed and her new life in the States, while a bit lonely, was calm and without drama. The hot South was not the climate she would have chosen, being from Scotland the heat and humidity in the summer was enough to make her crawl out of her skin, but it was home now and she coped well enough.

Nick sat up abruptly and startled her. He cried out in pain, "Ooooh, damn." He cradled his arm.

Steph went to him. "Are you okay? What happened?"

"I must have dozed off and tried to roll over. Oh man, it fucking hurts." His face twisted in pain.

Steph pulled out her phone and looked at the time. It was 11:20. "Let's peek outside and see if we can go for a short walk. That'll distract you."

275

They made their way to the window in the guest room. It was hard to see much from the condensation and the debris stuck to the window. She took his hand and walked over to the front door. They stepped outside and a wall of hot wet air hit them. But it was not raining and the wind was light.

"The storm is over! Nick! You up for a short walk?" Steph's heart leapt into her throat. This would be the moment of truth. Her life would be turned upside down if her house was gone.

"Yes, let's do it," he squeezed her hand and smiled at her. "It will be okay, Steph, you'll see."

Steph decided to not even think about what could be, just to be optimistic and take what God presented and make the best of it. They found their shoes and flashlights and quietly slipped out of Ona's house and made their way down the street. Steph's mind was racing, hoping to find the house intact and the cat asleep in a dark corner. Nick walked stiffly down the road but soon walked with a more normal gait.

Everything seemed too quiet. The neighborhood was usually abuzz—air conditioners running, frogs croaking, teenagers cruising down the street blaring their stereos. It was silent. Not a single noise natural or otherwise ruined the quiet night. The darkness of the streets added to the hushed silence. No flickering TVs or porch lights aglow. The only noise was the crunching of leaves under their feet.

"Nick. Where is the glow? I don't see it anymore!"

"It's there, but farther away," he smiled.

The glow seemed to be several streets over but it was hard to tell. She grabbed his good arm and squeezed. "Maybe it missed my house? Do you think?"

"I don't know. Could be, Steph," he said excitedly. They quickened their pace and shined their flashlights ahead hoping to see signs of her house intact. The neighbor's yellow siding was unsinged and their plants seemed to be in order.

"That's a good sign, right?" he said. She nearly ran the twenty-five yards to the next house. Near the end of the road was her house. It was not on fire, or at least not the front. She tried to not be too excited, it was too early to know but so far it looked good. "Hamish!" She yelled hoping to see him climb from the front bushes.

They made their way to the corner of her lot. "Nick, it's still standing!" He jogged a few steps and they walked to the front door together. She pulled the keys out of her pocket and unlocked the door.

The house was smoky but not terribly so. She automatically flicked on the lights with no results. "Nick! Nick!"

He squeezed her hand. "I can't believe it!"

Steph ran to her bedroom. Everything was in place. Nick came in behind her. "All okay?"

"Yes! It bloody is!" She jumped up and down. "I was sure there would be some damage. The fire was so close when we left."

"Man you got so lucky, Steph. The eye of the storm came just as we were leaving. It must have pushed the fire back."

"How, Nick, it doesn't seem possible?"

"Well, remember the winds shifted to blow from the opposite direction. Apparently, just in time to save your house. How lucky is that?"

"Lucky as hell. Let's make sure the kitchen is okay." She walked out of the master bedroom and into the kitchen, Nick followed while shining his flashlight in every corner. "I can't believe it!"

"Steph, you are the luckiest woman in the world! I can't believe it either," Nick's face broke into a wide grin showing the crinkled skin near his eyes. Before the night was over she would kiss that spot. He opened the back door and walked out onto the patio. "Steph let's see where the fire line is."

She followed him outside. Her fence was a bit singed and no longer white PVC but more of a grayish slightly melted mess.

"Oh man, that is about as close as you can get!" He looked over the fence and shone the flashlight on the neighbor's house. "They weren't so lucky."

"Tell me what you see," Steph was too short to see over the fence.

"The house is still smoking, but I don't see any flames. Hard to tell though." He stood on tiptoes to see over the fence.

"We shouldn't be out here very long." He looked up at the tall trees. "They may still have a few presents to drop on us."

"What presents?" Steph asked.

"Branches. You can't see the ones that may be damaged by the storm. They could drop at any minute."

"Oh, I see." Steph walked back into her house. Everything seemed to be working out all right. The house was fine. Her fence, another matter, but really was small potatoes.

"Help me find that damn cat, okay?" she said to Nick as they walked into the kitchen.

Chapter 53 - Doom and Gloom

Ronnie woke to the sound of retching. A horrible smell of vomit and alcohol swarmed around her like bees. Her cellmate was throwing up her dinner that appeared to have been mainly booze.

She plugged her ears and buried her nose in her sleeve. The smell was nearly enough to make her get sick herself. Finally, it stopped and she managed to steal a look at the woman who lay dramatically on the bench, her arm covering her eyes. A puddle of vomit was soaking into the dirt floor.

It seemed like an eternity had passed since Mathias first visited her here. Even longer ago was the romantic dinner with Jeffrey and news reports of Hurricane Charley. How the hell would she get back to 2004 now? Despite the escape, she was still no closer to finding a way home, and with the imminent hanging there seemed little hope of her getting away to make another attempt at something.

The woman moaned and rolled over again, dry heaving with no success. Ronnie's stomach lurched. She was beyond hungry. They had not fed her last night as a punishment for escaping. The smell was doing a good job of tamping down her appetite but she was feeling very weak. The last time she ate was before the trial, a day ago at breakfast. Was today the day of the hanging or were there other proceedings?

Last night before falling asleep she had nearly cried her eyes out thinking of Mathias in such bad shape. Was he alive? Without antibiotics, he would likely be ravaged by infection with his multiple injuries. He might be lying in the streets unconscious again, or worse, dead from Jack's stabbing. Maybe he was in jail down the hallway with those horrible men. It was overwhelming. She tried to stop the tears but they had a mind of their own. There were too many things to be crying about.

This was likely her last day alive. She would never get to see her family again. Her mom and brother would not even know what had happened. Steph and Jeffrey would be baffled at her disappearance only to be left with questions and accusations. Steph would tear Jeffrey apart, she already hated him and would not stop until he was destroyed over this. Would someone find Fluffy before she starved to death? How long would it take for them to give up hope on her return? It was too sad to keep thinking about.

She shifted her thoughts to saving herself. How could Mathias, or anyone else, get her free again? Even if she escaped how would she get home? There was no explanation for her being here to start with. What had caused her travel in time to this place, this time? Ronnie rested her forehead on her arms as she leaned against the stone wall and tried to calm her fears. Her stomach growled.

"Water," the woman said in a gravelly voice. "Please miss, would you be so kind as to fetch me some water."

"Oh, sure." Ronnie stood up, feeling dizzy, and leaned on the wall to steady herself. She took a few steps toward the pitcher and glass and poured some water into the pewter mug and carried it to her. "Here you are."

"Thank you." The woman took the cup from her with shaky hands and spilled most of it down her ample chest. "I am terribly sorry for the mess I've made. I will clean it up as soon as I am able."

"Oh no, don't worry. It's okay," Ronnie said. How could she clean it up anyway?

The familiar clanging of the door made both women turn their heads. "Miss Ingram," a man's voice said.

"Yes," her heart beat fast.

"Please bring your hands to the bars," the constable said.

She walked to the cell gate and held out her hands.

"Turn around," he said and then tied her wrists.

"Oh, my dear. What have you done?" the woman said.

"She's a witch," the man whispered.

The woman's eyes grew big and she made the horns with her fingers like Father Blenheim.

"She will be hung today. I am delivering her to the gallows now."

The woman covered her mouth, "Blimey. That I spent the night with her. Has she cast a spell on me whilst I slept?" She touched her face and hair frantically.

"Yes, I do believe she has turned you into a fat ugly whore," he said. "Unless you looked like that when you came in last night."

"Bullocks," the woman said. "I swear Samuel, you always say that to me."

Ronnie's heart leapt to her throat. "You're taking me now?"

"That I am. Do not get any witchy ideas, Miss Ingram." He held up his devil horns with his index and pinky fingers.

"Will I get any breakfast? I'm very weak from not eating much yesterday."

"You had time enough for a meal when you were running around free yesterday," he said pushing her forward with a short stick. The rough rope cut into her wrists. "I do not think it a wise investment to put food in you when you will be dead in a matter of hours." He unlocked the door and pushed her through, locking it behind him.

"Dead!" Ronnie said. "The hanging is today?" Her airway seemed to close off a bit. "What time do they take me out there?" Her knees wobbled with every step.

"We are gathering the convicts as we speak and will load you on a wagon within the hour," he said. "Enough with questions, miss, you need to be silent."

Each step she took brought her closer to death. She saw her mom's smiling face, felt her warm hug. The constable walked her to a crowd of other convicts and they waited for more to show up. Her stomach clenched and began to cramp. Ronnie sat down on the floor and leaned against the stone wall and pulled her legs up to her chest. She closed her eyes and took a few deep breaths. The sensation began to fade and she wondered how long she would have before the noose was around her neck.

"Why are ye here?" A man asked from a few feet away. She opened her eyes and looked into crystal-clear blue eyes.

"I'm convicted," Ronnie said.

"I know that, or yee'd no be here." He had a Scottish accent making her think of Steph. She fought back tears and bit her lip.

"Yer no the witch ever'ones been talking of, are ye?" his red hair caught the light from the rush on the wall above his head.

Ronnie sighed. "Yes. But I am not a witch." She felt like she had to say it but there was no fight in her words.

"Ach I know, lass. None of us here are guilty. I've no killed my brather, he's no stolen from his master," he waved his arm around pointing at each innocent as he spoke, "and she's no whored around on her husband and stolen from her neighbor. We are all sweet angels, we are."

It wasn't worth arguing. As far as these people were concerned she was a witch. If only her magic could get her back to Florida. Resting her head on her knees she tried to shut everything out. Her stomach would not settle down. Deep breath, let it out.

An authoritative voice bellowed above the din of the convict's chatter. "Quiet! Quiet! Please form a single queue for me starting here." He pointed to his feet. The mangy group sorted themselves and Ronnie was midway in the pack.

"I fully expect you to sit in the cart without any trouble. I have guards on every side and you will be chained in place. There is no escaping. If you try we will be happy to beat you until you cannot move. In fact, we enjoy it, so please, give us a reason to use our sticks." The other guards nearby nodded.

The Scottish man was near Ronnie and said, "God bless ye, miss. I hope ye die a fast and nearly painless death."

"You too," It was a strange thing to say, but there wasn't much that would suffice under these circumstances.

"Ye have loved ones to attend the hanging?" he asked causally like they were discussing ordinary things.

"No one." Ronnie bit her lip and wiped away a few stray tears. She couldn't get the thought of Mathias dead somewhere out of her mind. Maybe Jack would be at the hanging just to confirm the job was done. Jeffrey, her mom, her brother, all of them were not here, would never know what happened. To them, she would be gone without a trace.

"Do ye think it hurts overmuch? The hanging I mean," he asked.

"I don't know. It's horrible to think about." She wished the man would be silent.

"I 'ave got me wife. She is coming to pull me to my death," Ronnie was surprised to see him smiling.

"Pull you?" Ronnie asked.

"Auch aye. She will stand nearby and when I am hanging by the neck she will grab hold and help me go fast." He looked down at her.

"Why would she do that?" Ronnie asked.

"Lass, if I die faster on the account of her extra weight it will no be so bad."

"Oh, how awful. She said she would do that for you?" Ronnie asked.

"Aye, she loves me ya ken, she will do it for me. She has promised to get a good position so she may jump up and help me go to my maker," he said almost cheerfully.

"How horrible for her." Ronnie imagined a woman with a baby in her arms trying to help her husband die. Women who were widowed were not taken care of in this time period, especially if her husband was hung for a crime. Her life would likely be miserable.

"She is a strong woman," he scratched his hairline.

A thickly built constable knelt before the Scot and put a chain around both ankles and locked it into place. He then tied a rope around each bicep and the remaining length around his waist leaving his hands free, but not able to move his arms much. The man came to her next and put chains on her ankles. He tied her arms the same way he had for the Scot. After all the convicts were chained and tied they began putting them in groups of three or four. Ronnie was pulled aside with two other women, both heavyset and miserable. One mumbled prayers and sobbed intermittently giving her the outward appearance of a mental patient.

The other woman stared at Ronnie, looking away quickly. Ronnie was in no mood for friendly talk. "Just stop staring at me, okay?"

"Do you not know who I am?" she said her eyes growing preternaturally wide as she spoke.

"No, I don't?" Ronnie said. "Should I?"

"I was yer maid, Elsbeth, Miss Ingram. When you were a lil girl."

"Oh, I don't remember you. But why would I, I'm not Regina anyway," Ronnie said tired of the lie. It didn't matter anymore she was about to die for it.

"You are not Regina? Why are you saying that?" Elsbeth's big blue eyes stared at her in disbelief.

"Look, I'm not Regina. I don't want to chat much now. Just let me sit here and gather my thoughts."

The woman looked away, turning her body slightly. Another hour or so passed and thankfully the woman left Ronnie alone. Finally, the guards called their group. Ronnie and the two women walked outside and were helped into a wagon by a few grimy men, not from Newgate, by their appearance. Twenty or so men were mounted on horseback and even more were standing with large pikes in their hands. Three long boxes filled the cart and Ronnie looked around for somewhere to sit.

"You in the middle," he pointed at her, "that is your seat." He pointed at the middle box.

She sat down on it and the other two women sat on either side of her. It was a horse drawn wagon open to the air. "What's this?" she said to her former maid, touching the box she was sitting on.

"Miss that is your coffin."

Ronnie looked down at it and cringed. So very practical. When they were done they could just plop her inside for burial. The sobbing one began to wail. A crowd had gathered and people were yelling horrible things at them. Father Fitzsimmons, the prison minister, climbed onto the wagon bench next to the driver and the wagon took off. He glanced back at her and made the sign of the devil.

"Nice touch," Ronnie said wishing he had chosen another wagon. Captain Green had probably asked him to keep an eye on her. The wagon jerked forward and Ronnie slid off the coffin but caught herself before falling onto the filthy wagon bed. The crowd was gathered along the street yelling and cursing at them. Something hit Ronnie on the side of the head and dropped in her lap. Her head rang from the impact. It was a dried piece of cow crap. She flicked it off into the floor. "Oh my God, that is so disgusting!"

The women on either side of her ducked down to avoid the rocks, clumps of dirt, and other gross things raining down on them. Finally, they were away from the crowds in town and were in the wide expanse of the country, leaving only an occasional traveler heading in the opposite direction. The huge army of mounted men rode between the carts and the pike men walked on either side, making crude comments about the women.

An hour passed and Ronnie sat in silence numb to her surroundings. The woman crying next to her was calmer now with only the occasional sniffle. As the procession of prisoners made the journey the wagons spread out along the dirt road. Ronnie counted at least five prisoner wagons behind her and two ahead. In the front of the line, three wagons carried constables from the jail and other dignitaries.

They entered a small village and a few minutes along the road a crowd had gathered but thankfully the only thing they were throwing were insults. The wagons meandered through winding dirt roads and stopped in front of a church. A man stood on a wagon and addressed the prisoners. "Do not give me leave to let my men upon you with their fists. You will stay seated and be silent or they will have permission to enforce this request."

After fifteen minutes, all of the wagons had made their way to the churchyard. A loud bell tolled for several minutes adding to the eerie feeling. Ronnie observed the faces of the prisoners. All of them would be dead today. She searched for the Scotsman and found him with head bent in prayer, hands pressed together.

"Your attention please!" Father Fitzsimmons stood on a podium near the front of the churchyard. A large crowd had gathered, filling the spaces between the wagons, more filling in the churchyard every second.

"Those of you who are condemned to die, repent with woeful tears, ask mercy of the Lord for your soul's salvation." He waved one arm dramatically, his long black sleeve flapping in the breeze.

A prisoner called out "Praise the Lord" and another "Forgive me of my sins, Father." More similar calls came from the convicted.

Ronnie silently sent up a different prayer, "God if you are there, please save me from this fate. Return me to Florida, to my family, to Jeffrey."

The priest continued, "All fine people, pray heavily unto God for these poor sinners are now going to their death, for whom the great bell tolls."

The priest walked back to the cart and quietly climbed back in the wagon. The procession slowly began moving again and they made their way through the beautiful stone buildings lining the road. In other circumstances, it would have been a pretty drive with no modern trappings to mar the view.

Ronnie was numb, her hunger well beyond comfortable. She let the rhythm of the cart lull her into a sleepy and sad place. To her surprise, the wagon stopped.

"What are we doing now?" Ronnie asked Elsbeth.

"Miss Ingram, we break the fast."

Chapter 54 - The Last Supper

Ronnie turned around to see a stone building with a small wooden plaque above the door that read Bowl Inn. The priest and the driver stepped down off the cart and walked to the back to help the women out of the wagon and into the inn. The rich, hearty aroma of cooked vegetables and meat hit her hard. She was beyond hungry now and it smelled amazing. With shaky legs, she followed Elsbeth to a small table in the back, away from the soldiers and horsemen that crowded around the bar and the tables near the door.

A small dark-haired man approached the table and set a pint of golden liquid in front of each woman. Elsbeth and the crying woman took the pewter mug and lifted it to their lips. Ronnie was tempted but it looked like alcohol. Hungry and still queasy she thought better of drinking anything before she ate. Ronnie glanced around the room with a glimmer of hope that Mathias would appear to steal her away. Not likely with all the guards, but it was a nice fantasy.

"How much longer?" Ronnie asked the driver.

He laughed. "Miss, you never have gone to a hanging, then?"

"No, I have not."

"Well, it is our most famous form of entertainment in London."

"I thought we would be outside of Newgate. Where are we going?"

"Miss, we hang folk at Tyburn. Always have," he told her. "Ah, here is our food now."

A small man set down a plate full of steaming fried potatoes, carrots, onions, and a small sausage. Ronnie looked around for a fork but found nothing. They must not allow prisoners to have utensils.

Elsbeth and the other woman were using their hands to eat—the crier shoveling food in as fast as she could. Ronnie looked down at her dirty hands. At least she had cleaned Mathias's blood off before she had gone to sleep. She shuddered at the thought of what she had been in contact with on the ride here but it wasn't like there was a risk of getting sick, she would not live long enough to grow germs. Her hunger overtook logic and she managed to eat every last bit on her plate. It did a lot to settle her stomach.

Once she was full, Ronnie took a sip of the drink. Sweet cool bubbles danced on her tongue and for a second she forgot the horror of the day. She drank the rest of it feeling the effects of the alcohol, hoping it would give her a little liquid courage.

They finished the meal in silence and returned to their perch on the coffins. The drink had made Ronnie sleepy, but it was impossible to fall asleep sitting up. Another few hours passed and the long slow journey gave Ronnie time to imagine the hanging over and over. Her mind found endless ways to say good-bye to everyone important in her life.

She imagined hugging Steph and thanking her for her friendship. Steph hugged her in return and said, "Dinna fash yerself. You will be just fine." Something she had heard Steph say a million times.

Saying good-bye to her mother was not so easy. She imagined looking into her mother's face. Her father joined in and they all hugged each other, something they had not done since she was a kid. There was no way to hold back the flood of tears that had been building up all day. Maybe she would see her father today. Would he be waiting for her beyond the pearly gates?

Ronnie went through her family and made it to Jeffrey. She imagined holding his face in her hands and telling him she was sorry for doing this to him. What would it do to his position at the lab? She was not supposed to be there. In her mind he was sad and a bit angry at her for screwing everything up.

The thought of Mathias dead in the alleyway tormented her. Where was he now? Would he survive the latest assault from Jack's wrath? If she had not come back to this time, this place he would be undamaged, carrying on with a happy life. Not dying somewhere.

Her thoughts drifted to her new job. What would her new boss, Mike Walsh, think when she didn't show up for work on Monday? Would Steph or Jeffrey know how to contact him? She had felt such a strong connection to him during the interviews. He seemed like a really good guy.

She continued along this path until there were no more tears to cry, surrendering herself to her fate. As if on cue, the rhythmic jostling of the wagon stopped. The wagons in front of them were all stopped waiting for something out of sight up a small hill.

The priest stood and stretched. "I will go ahead and see what is afoot," he said and then jumped off the wagon and walked up and over the hill.

Ronnie looked at the women next to her. The crier seemed all cried out. Elsbeth returned her gaze.

"Will you have family at the hanging?" Ronnie asked.

"No. My husband is also in jail and without his income, I was unable to feed my children. I stole a few pieces of silverware from the dining room at the Hampden's." Elsbeth wiped away a tear. "Now my children are with their auntie. A burden on my sister. I am afraid for her and my wee ones."

"I cannot take it anymore," the crying woman said. "I want it to just be done."

Ronnie nodded in agreement. "The waiting is horrible."

Father Fitzsimmons returned, "Just over the ridge are the scaffolds."

The wagon lurched forward and she could hear the rocks pop and crunch under the wheels. As they climbed the small hill her panic escalated. She tried to focus on the sun peeking out from behind the clouds, shining on the crowd below. Hundreds of people gathered around a structure in the shape of a triangle. The crowd was moving aside for the first wagon in the procession. Her stomach clenched and her lunch nearly made an appearance, but she managed to keep it down.

The structure was a scaffold with three thick posts in the ground and crossbeams forming a triangle above. As Ronnie's wagon crept down the hill the first wagon in their procession was pulled under the scaffold, and the three prisoners were asked to stand.

A man in a three-cornered hat took the rope that was wrapped around the first prisoner's body and put the loop over his head and around his neck. He then threw the rope up to a man who was perched on top of the crossbeam of the scaffold. He deftly snatched the rope to pull it over the beam, tying it securely. He then reached for the second prisoner's rope.

"They hang us right in the wagon?" Ronnie asked. She had envisioned a platform they would stand on.

"Yes. In this very place," Elsbeth said, stomping her boot on the floorboards.

Ronnie looked down, wondering how many others had died in this spot. She closed her eyes. This was it—the moment she would end. Their wagon had stopped on the hillside to wait their turn. A second wagon was directed to another space under the scaffold. The process continued until eleven men were in position. Father Fitzsimmons was now up on a platform near the scaffold making a speech. Ronnie was too far away to hear his voice but he flailed his arms around getting a rise out of the crowd.

Elsbeth began to pray fervently, muttering under her breath. The crying woman started up again, becoming louder as each minute passed. A few of the pike-wielding men stayed near the remaining wagons but most were near the hanging, controlling the crowd and keeping an eye on the convicted.

Whoops and hollers escaped from the onlookers. Some of the convicts were crying, several were praying. One was making a speech and the crowd booed him when he was done. About half of the men to be hanged had a strange white hat pulled down over their ears.

"Why do some of the men have hats on?" Ronnie asked once Elsbeth was finished praying.

"Oh," she glanced back toward the hanging. "They have money to buy a nightcap. It is so they can cover their face while they are dying." Elsbeth wrung her hands and her lower lip quivered.

"Do you have a nightcap?" Ronnie asked.

"I have not. There is no money for such things. Have you arranged a cap?" Elsbeth asked.

"Only if my brother bought me one. I have no money myself," Ronnie told her.

"Mr. Ingram would surely buy you a cap if you have money. He will claim your body, won't he?" she asked.

"No. He thinks I'm a witch," Ronnie said gloomily. There would be no one here for her.

"A witch? Surely not. Mr. Ingram, had you convicted? But you were so close as children. Why would he do that to you?" Elsbeth asked.

"I don't know." Well, she had a few ideas, but it was not worth sharing them. "You could say we're not so close anymore."

Their wagon jolted forward, creeping toward the scaffold and Ronnie felt light-headed. She grabbed Elsbeth's hand, trying not to watch the men hang, but it was like a car wreck. She couldn't look away. A few men had their caps pulled over their faces.

The Scotsman was crying and yelling out something. A woman with long blonde hair jumped up on the wagon but the soldier pushed her down. It must have been the Scotsman's wife. Ronnie began to sob hard now. That was true love! He was a lucky man to have such a brave wife during such a horrible moment.

Their wagon moved slowly down the hill. Ronnie strained to see the scaffold through the crowd. Elsbeth squeezed her hand. Tears were rolling down her face.

"God Bless you," Elsbeth said.

Ronnie said, "God Bless you, Elsbeth."

A loud call came from the man in the three-cornered hat and the horses strained against the weight of the wagon, inching it forward. The men walked the length of the coffins until they dropped off and began dangling—only falling a few inches. Every one of them was still alive, legs kicking in the air, hands straining to reach their throats, but unable to because of the rope around their arms and bodies. The faces of those without caps contorted and turned bright red. One man's eyes began to bulge gruesomely.

The crowd roared with pleasure. A few people ran to grab the legs of their loved ones. Ronnie looked for the Scotsman and could see the top of his blonde wife's head, holding on to his legs, guessing her feet were off the ground.

There was a loud gasp from the crowd and Ronnie moved to the side to see around the driver's head. One of the ropes was untied and a man fell to the ground. No, a soldier had cut him loose, she could see the sun shining off of his blade just before he sheathed it. The man was hauled up by two soldiers and carried off.

"Where are they taking him?" Ronnie asked.

"I do not know," Elsbeth said, a look of utter despair on her face.

Two soldiers made their way to the front of Ronnie's wagon, at the ready to push it under the scaffold. One of the soldiers, a dirty-faced man with dark hair answered her, "He is to be drawn and quartered." He showed her a gruesome smile with a few teeth missing.

"Why? They just hung him?" Ronnie said, stomach turning at the thought of them tearing the man apart.

"They are just carrying out the sentence. We make sure they've not quite met their maker, so they can enjoy the second death twice as much." He laughed and the soldier on the other side smiled.

"That's right miss, we carry out the letter of the law with pleasure," the second man said.

The hanged man was unconscious. The larger of the two guards slapped his face and made an attempt to revive him, the rope still tight around his neck. The smaller man loosened the rope, exposing a red and bloodied neck underneath.

Ronnie turned away, covering her mouth. Her heart ached for the man that would no doubt die an agonizing death. The ligatures on his neck were cut deep into his muscles. Nearly panting now, she was in a full panic. There had to be a way home! This could not be her fate to end here alone, with one knowing what happened to her.

Chapter 55 - Hide and Seek

"Hamish!" Steph called. "Here Hamey wamey!" She grabbed his treats out of the cupboard and then shook the can. That usually got his attention.

She half ran, half walked to the back of the house where Felicia said he went. Nick was calling out for Hamish in the master bedroom. If he were hurt he may not come out. For that matter, the wee idget had been a spaz all day with the storm approaching. He may be sound asleep or cowering still terrified or worse.

"Hamish!" He was pinned by a branch earlier. She could feel her cheeks get hot and her stomach did a flip. Oh no. "Hamish!" A terrible feeling took over.

The back bedroom was a few feet away. Steph paused and said a silent prayer. "I'll go to church. I will. I promise. Just make wee kitty boy okay."

The room didn't smell right. Her mouth tightened. No. No, it couldn't be. "Nick," Steph yelled, "come here now!" She needed his strength if what she feared was in this room.

"Nick, please come here." She pinched her nostrils shut. It smelled like a litter box, but a bit stronger.

"Haay-mish," Steph said more quietly. "It's okay. Come on out boy. The storm is over." Panic welled in her chest. She shook the treat can hoping he would crawl out.

Nick walked into the room. "Oh God, what is that smell." He held his nose. The way he looked at her said it all. He thought Hamish was gone too. "Steph, have you found him yet?"

"No." She knelt on the floor. It was okay right now with it unknown. Better than a definite answer at this point. She shook the can again. "Hamish."

Nick looked in the closet, under the chair, behind the door, and lastly under the bed. Just at the frontcorner he found the reason for the smell. "I guess he didn't make it to the litter box."

"Stephie, I can't get down on the floor to look under." He nodded to his shoulder and handed her the flashlight.

"No, I will just sit here and wait for him to come out."

"Steph, c'mon. You need to do this," Nick clutched his injured hand. "Here kitty," he said. "Shine it under there Steph."

Tears ran down her face. "Hamish come here boy." Maybe he was just really hurt.

Steph lay flat on the floor and shined the flashlight under the bed. "Oh my God, Nick. I see him. Hamish! Hamish!" she sobbed.

"He's there! Steph! Grab him!"

She stretched and tried to reach the cat deep under the bed. "Got him!" She pulled Hamish out. He was limp and didn't respond at all to being dragged along the terrazzo floor, making her heart sink. He was gone.

"Nick, Nick, he's dead. He's gone!" She sobbed, picking Hamish up and cradling him like a baby. His fur was wet but he looked like he was just sleeping. She buried her face in his fur and breathed deeply. "Oh, Hamish. Oh, baby. I'm so sorry I left you. You needed me didn't you?" She sobbed and hugged her cat who was no longer breathing, his life slipped away during the storm.

Nick sat next to her putting his good arm on her shoulder. "He was a great kitty, wasn't he?"

"He was the best cat in the world!" she said.

Nick held her tight, kissing the top of her head as she cried hugging her cat. They sat like that for what seemed like forever and finally Steph took a deep breath.

"Steph, I'm so sorry. The branch must have hurt him pretty badly," Nick said.

"He couldn't jump up from the ground into the windowsill. I knew he was hurt. I just didn't know how badly. What do you suppose happened to him?" She wiped away the tears.

"I don't know. It could be internal bleeding or spinal cord injury. It's hard to say. Could have hit his head too."

"I don't see any blood on him, except where the branch hit his back," Steph said. "Poor wee chap. If he had only stayed in the house. He was so afraid of the storm."

"Yeah, he had every reason to be afraid of the storm. Do you suppose he knew he was going to die tonight?" Nick said.

"I don't know. I guess. Maybe he's just a dumb cat who freaks out with storms." Steph was numb. It was not real, holding her cat in her arms for the last time. She looked at his limp body, he had always been so full of life. "So now what?" Steph said. "What do I do with him? The vet won't be opened for a while."

"Did you want to cremate him? If so there is no way to really keep him from … rotting. Unless you want to put him in a cooler with some of your ice? Who knows when they'll open after the storm?"

"Ugghh. What a horrible thought. I can't bear to think of him in the corner in a cooler." Her stomach lurched. She started to cry again. "Why did he have to go out in the storm? Stupid cat!" She shook him and his front paws and head dangled gruesomely. "I wish I'd been there for you Hamey-wamey. I could have held you while you passed." She cried some more.

Nick stood up and sat on the bed cradling his arm. "Look, he'll be fine for a bit. Let's wrap him in a blanket and get something to eat. I'm starving."

"Nick, how can you eat at a time like this? That's so gross." She looked down at her dead cat and her stomach lurched again. He handed her a red throw blanket from the guest bed. "Wrap him in here."

"No, not that, that was my grandmother's." She got up and handed the cat to Nick and went to her room to get a towel.

They wrapped Hamish up and brought him to the guest bathtub. Steph gently set him in the tub pausing to say a prayer as she did. She washed her hands, now grossed-out that she had held her dead cat for so long. How could Nick be hungry at a time like this? On her way to the kitchen she passed the window she had left open for the cat and sobbed. Poor wee Hamish.

All of the excitement Steph felt in finding her house intact was gone. Whoosh, out the window she had left open for him. Heading to the kitchen she found Nick looking in her cupboards for food.

"I guess the ice cream isn't gonna make it." She pulled out rum raisin and grabbed two spoons. "Here."

She sat down at her small kitchen table and dug into the mushy creamy pain-killers. They sat in silence eating until Steph scraped the bottom of the container.

"Now what? Do we go back to Ona's house and get our stuff or just wait till morning?" he asked.

"Oh, Ona's?' Steph didn't want to do anything but sleep. Her stomach was full but it didn't push out the bad thoughts rolling around in her head as she had hoped. "I don' think I can move anything but my go-to-sleep muscle. It's been a horrid day."

"Yeah, it really has." He threw the empty ice cream container in the trash.

Steph walked toward her bedroom. "Nick, I need to take a shower." She then added for good measure, "Alone."

"Okay. You sure?" he said smiling. "Sorry. You need a minute, don't you? Okay where do you want me, I'm rather soggy."

"It doesn't matter. Just try to get comfortable." She shut her bedroom door, peeled off her wet clothes, took a flashlight into the bathroom and set it up to shine into the shower. Would there be hot water? She was already numb, it wouldn't make a difference. A flash of Nick's naked body in the shower hit her as if his essence lingered from their earlier encounter. God, what a chicken. Nick was a great guy, she should have just jumped his bones. What if Hamish hadn't yelped would she have gone through with it?

The water was still hot—a small miracle. She stepped into the shower and let it wash away her sorrow. Tears mixed with the steamy goodness and she got lost in the memories of Hamish. He had been such an adorable kitten, and had been her therapy after leaving her husband, and had brought comfort to her in bed every night since, except for her trips home to Glasgow.

Finally, the water began to cool and she quickly washed and got out. She felt better having let out all that emotion. Nick was comforting but she really didn't need him to see her blubbering. She dressed and towel dried her hair and got dressed.

Nick was sitting in the dark living room. "Hi, what are you doing?"

"Hey there. I'm eating again. Sorry. Just hungry. I guess I never ate dinner, Steph."

"No, it's okay. Eat whatever you want. Do you want to take a shower or change your clothes?" she asked. "I think we should try to get some sleep if we can."

"I'm nearly dry now." He stood up slowly.

"Nick, are you okay?" He looked like he was in a lot of pain. "Let me get you some pain-killers."

"Got anything stronger, Steph? It would be nice to get some sleep."

"Glenfiddich. That's about it."

"Whisky will do nicely." He reached into the bag of chips. "You sure I'm worthy of your precious Glendfiddich?"

"Of course you're worth it Nick. I'll make you a peanut butter sandwich, too. Goes great with it." She wanted to laugh, but her heart was heavy. He followed her into the kitchen and watched her make the sandwich. She took ice from the freezer and put it in her best two glasses, and poured two fingers in each one.

"To Hamish. The best cat in the world." Steph held up her glass.

"To Hamish." They clinked and downed it.

She filled his glass again. "Bottoms up, Florida boy."

Chapter 56 - The Surgeons

Ronnie felt short of breath and had to pant to catch up. There was no room for prayers or thoughts of any kind, sheer panic dominated. Death by hanging. This was not on her list of ways to die. Her morbid imaginings had led her to car accidents, a long hard fight with cancer at an old age, or a shark attack while enjoying a dip in the ocean. But never in her worst nightmares did she imagine being hung.

The rest of the men dangled by their necks. One man made horrible choking noises and tried with all his might to move his hands to his throat. All the while blood poured from his forearms where the rope had cut him. Another looked as if he were laughing, his chest and shoulders shaking, his face covered by the white hat. The man closest to her hung quietly, his blinking eyes the only thing moving until his entire body began to shake. A dark stain appeared on the front of his pants and it continued to grow.

The blonde woman still held tightly to her husband's legs and she readjusted her grip a few times. Her face looked sad but she was not crying. The Scot's face had turned blue, his eyes unblinking. He must have passed quickly.

A young man pushed through the crowd. He pulled out a small knife to slice a vein at the wrist of one of the hanged men. He held up a pewter goblet and filled it with blood. Ronnie watched in disbelief as put the cup to his lips and swallowed. He passed the cup to another man in the crowd. Hands reached and it was quickly drained. The cup was passed back up to convict's body again and refilled. The man took another sip and passed it the other way to more of the crowd.

Elsbeth looked at Ronnie in horror, both women covering their mouths. Ronnie tried not to get sick but this was too much. She leaned over the wagon and emptied the contents of her stomach.

Elsbeth pointed to two men who were cutting some of the hanged down, "The surgeons!"

"The surgeons what are they doing here?" Ronnie asked.

Elsbeth looked away and shook her head. "Early summer they started allowing the surgeons to take the bodies away."

Ronnie watched as the men cut a body down and the crowd began clawing and clutching at it. Within seconds the body was stripped of its clothes. Another man cut the rope off and began selling pieces.

People swarmed around the body and walked away with clips of hair and bits of flesh. It reminded Ronnie of the zombie apocalypse. Fear choked her. Was this going to happen to her? They cut down another body. The man was still alive. His legs kicked but no one seemed to notice. Loud screams could be heard over the noises of the crowd.

A man leaned over a body and pushed others away until he held up a bloody severed hand. "Look! I've got the lucky hand!" he yelled to the crowd and shoved it in a small bag, hiding it quickly inside of his coat.

Two other bodies were cut down right in front of Ronnie's wagon. This time the hangman stood over them wielding a sword. "These fresh ones are mine! Do not make any attempt to take them!"

A woman came forward from the crowd and grabbed the hand of one of the dead men. "This is my husband," she wailed and another man came forward and helped her pull the body away. The surgeon pulled the man's legs.

"Noooooo!" The woman yelled and picked up the dead man under his armpits. "He's my husband! He is mine!"

Elsbeth leaned over to Ronnie to explain, "That is the surgeon. He is gathering bodies to cut apart in his private rooms. He is akin to the devil!"

"How can he take her husband's body? It's her property isn't it?" Ronnie asked.

"She can only keep the body if she can overpower him. He can take any of the bodies that he chooses. He has a very big knife."

Ronnie turned away. It was too much! They were like animals tearing apart the newly dead. "Why does that man have a hand, and others take the hair? It's so horrible!"

"It's thought to be lucky to have the hangman's rope or hair from a newly dead man. A hand especially is considered very lucky indeed." Elsbeth's lips quivered.

"Will they do that to us?" Ronnie asked.

"Yes, they will. Parts of a hanged woman's body are rare prizes indeed."

Ronnie looked around for the Scotsman and his wife but they were not in sight. Did the wife get his body or did the surgeon grab it away? The second round of hangings was set up and carried out with the same gruesome effect. This time a small child near Ronnie wailed throughout the proceedings, "Papa! Papa!" drowning out all of the other ghastly noises. Who would bring a kid to this horrible scene? The child's mother sobbed adding to heartbreak.

The third round was worse since Ronnie's wagon was directly in front of the ropes. She could smell the fear of the men as they lined up. The acrid smell of excrement hung in the air, adding to the odors from the crowd. The chaos was even more frenzied afterward, with the crowd behaving like wild animals, grabbing and tearing at the newly dead. The surgeons claimed a few bodies and the hangman wielding his big knife claimed a few of the wealthier looking citizens.

Once the remaining convicts were cut down and placed in their coffins the horses were whipped and the dead were pulled away. The pikemen pushed Ronnie's wagon under the scaffolding. Another cart was pushed to the second section of the scaffold, as these were the only two wagons left. People from the crowd pushed in to fill the space where a third wagon would have been. The faces in the crowd were dirty and tired but their expressions were eager for more bloodshed and death.

Ronnie squeezed her eyes shut. Terror nearly made her blackout. This was not happening. It couldn't be it was too horrific. Would Jack be here to watch her hang? Ronnie was startled by someone grabbing her ankle. She looked down to find a soldier there as the hangman asked her to stand. He unwound the rope from her body as he had done with the other prisoners and waited for his man to climb the ladder to the top of the scaffold to place the rope.

This was it—the last minutes of her life. Great sobs wracked her body. All the things she had not yet done. She wanted kids, she wanted a successful life full of love and a wonderful husband to share that with. Why did she move to Florida? She could be sitting on the couch with her mom, reminiscing of the life they had before Dad died.

Maybe she would see her father. What would she say to him? She imagined hugging him with all of her might. What if he was not there? What if he was in heaven and she went to hell or the other way around? All of the visions of heaven and hell came together, now swirling with the words that started the witch hunt—The Lord's Prayer. Tears flowed down her face, aware of the irony of it all. It was, after all, the first bit of evidence they had gathered on her.

Our Father, who art in Heaven, hallowed be thy name. Thy kingdom come, thy will be done ...

Was this God's will, to put her in the noose? She didn't believe in a punishing God, a spiteful God. There was a bigger purpose to what was happening to her, but what? Why was she here? What did it mean? She willed herself home but nothing happened. Scanning the crowd, she saw a familiar face but it took her a second to focus on him. The hangman brought the noose over her head and blocked her view. He pulled the noose tight around her neck. Her hands went to her throat but the rope around her upper arms prevented it.

Ronnie's pulse pounded at the back of her skull from the injury she got on her arrival to this strange place. She squeezed her eyes shut and tried to block out this horrible moment. Then she remembered the familiar face in the crowd. Her eyes scanned the faces again hoping for someone she knew. Even Jack's sour expression would be welcome at this point.

The hangman blocked her view again as he prepared Elsbeth for the hanging. Ronnie's heart broke, watching the tears fall down Elsbeth's face. She would never see her children again. It was too painful to watch the agony of her new friend. Her eyes locked on a man she knew. He waved and called out, "Ronnie!"

"Mathias," she yelled back. "You're alive." Her knees were weak with the sight of him. He had come to this despicable place for her.

He shoved his way through the crowd, pushing closer. "Ronnie, I am here for you!" He called to the hangman, "I will pay for her body now. Please do not let the surgeon take her." He held out his hand with several coins and the hangman nodded to Mathias.

The hangman waved his knife around and forced a few bystanders back, making room for Mathias stand next to the cart. Tears flowed freely down her face and her vision blurred. She was terrified but Mathias was here for her, to take care of her. Overwhelming affection overtook her fear and she got lost in his eyes. He mouthed, "I love you."

She mouthed it back and tears flowed down her face. "Thank you for everything you have done for me." She tried to yell over the crowd so he could hear over the increasing noise. He did not take his eyes off of her.

"Look at me. Don't look anywhere else. I will smooth your journey to heaven!" he yelled, his eyes shone with tears and she began bawling in earnest.

He reached out and touched her leg. "I will help you. I will care for you in death. I will bury you." He continued telling her what he would do to help her and she tuned out everything else, focusing on his face, his words, and his touch. The sounds of the crowd, the hangman, and the prayers of the priest were fading away. All she saw was Mathias's face. It was a miracle he was alive and was here for her.

Father Fitzsimmons spoke in her ear, "Miss, have you any last words?"

She shook her head. "No, I don't."

"May God have mercy upon your soul," he said and turned to Elsbeth. She could hear Elsbeth's voice but tuned it out. Ronnie's attention was all for Mathias. She did not want to miss a second of the time she had left with him. His lips were moving again and she strained to hear him over the noises of the people around her. The noose cut into her neck. Reaching to loosen the noose her hands were stopped by the rope again. What was he saying to her? She refocused and watched his mouth move so she would not miss a single word.

"I will see you soon," he said.

What did that mean?

"The seer, Madam Zangari, told me so. We will be together again," he said, squeezing her ankle.

She heard the command from the hangman. The wagon moved and she tried to look down at her feet but the noose didn't allow it. Walking backward she began to panic. This was it. She was going to die. "NO!" Ronnie screamed. "NO!"

Mathias held something up toward her hand. It was shiny. The wagon pulled away and Ronnie fell, her feet paddling in the air. A loud gruesome popping noise followed by excruciating pain in her neck overtook all thought. Her jaw snapped shut and the rope pulled just below her ear. For a few seconds, all she could see was white and her mind was overcome with pain—searing horrible pain.

Something gripped her legs and a hand reached up, pressing a hard object into her palm. It was warm and smooth. The pain cleared and she looked down now, her head tilted at an odd angle, her neck stretched. Mathias was holding her hand, clasping something in it.

Chapter 57 - Connection

Overwhelming pressure in Ronnie's head made her face feel huge. Her lungs exploded. Her air was cut off.

All of Mathias's weight was pulling her down. "The watch, Ronnie. I have the watch for you." His words floated around in her mind, but she was unable to process them. Her neck stretched more and she could hear his voice. "Watch!"

Oh my God! He brought the watch! Blackness hit her like a light switch turning off. Her hearing was still working and the crowd yelled louder.

Mathias sobbed, "Ronnie! Please take the watch!" Was Mathias shaking her or was she convulsing? "Ronnie!" Why did he call it a watch? He had always said bracelet.

She was gasping and choking, trying to loosen the noose, but to no avail. Her lungs were going to explode! Pain blinded her, deafened her. It was so intense it was hard to tell what hurt. She fought to stay conscious. It was her last few minutes alive and she wanted desperately to be connected to Mathias, to be aware of his hand in hers, to hear his words, hear his voice. To not be alone.

The watch! She forced her hand to grip the watch and squeeze Mathias's hand. All of her attention was on that connection to him. The pain subsided. Noises were muffled as if she was underwater and a comforting warmth surrounded her. Mathias squeezed her hand crushing the watch in her palm. An electrifying energy shot through her hand, up her arm to her heart and it felt like it would burst. A flash of white and darkness covered her eyes. A faint smell of almonds and wet Earth hit her.

Her hand was crushed by his. "Ronnie, I love you. I will see you soon."

Involuntarily she gasped for air and to her surprise, her lungs filled. She touched a smooth white surface. The air smelled of bleach and the horrid stench of death was gone for a split second. Then it returned and she heard sobbing and yelling and felt the pressure lessen on her neck.

"Ronnie, please forgive me." He sobbed and she could feel him kissing her face. "I will not fail you now. I will not fail you when we meet again."

A flash of the white room again and she gasped for air and her lungs filled. She pushed up and saw a toilet and white tiles. She was desperate to feel the connection to Mathias but it was severed. Everything went black.

A horrible wrenching sensation pulled at her soul—tearing, ripping, detaching. Her body fell for what seemed like an eternity and a sensation of moving a million miles an hour downward disoriented and terrified her. Smells changed, air pressure changed. She reached and tried to reconnect with Mathias. Her heart broke knowing she would never see him again. Light sped past her, the wind blew against her face, and she felt cold wet air against her skin. Everything spun and twisted making her feel drunk and out of control.

Then it stopped.

Ronnie gasped and gulped greedily filling her lungs and then expelling it as quickly as possible. Her hands touched something cool and hard. Stones? Was she on the ground? The acrid smell of smoke assaulted her nostrils. Oh, my God, they're going to burn me. "No! Please no!" Ronnie screamed, shocked at the strength of her voice.

Someone helped her up. She took a breath and expected excruciating pain. Instead, her vision cleared and Ronnie was surrounded by white tiles, a white sink, and a toilet.

"Ronnie, are you okay?" A male voice said, but it wasn't deep enough to be Mathias's. Her hands went to her throat and her arms were no longer tied.

"Where am I?" She was standing up now and she looked down waiting for the noose to restrict her movement. Instead, she could see bare tan feet and naked legs. The man turned her around and she looked into his face expecting the tired stubbled face of Mathias.

"Ronnie, where is the watch?" It was Jeffrey. He sounded angry.

She stared in disbelief. "What are you doing here?" She asked not even sure if she could trust her vision. Like E.T. she reached out touched his face. Her knees buckled and he pulled her in tight hugging her close, kissing the top of her head, keeping her from falling to the floor.

"Ronnie, are you okay" Jeffrey repeated.

It was merely a death vision, one experienced as a body fades away into the light. She had seen a movie in eighth grade from the perspective of a man about to be hung. The entire movie was his death vision about the rope breaking, him swimming away downstream and escaping. In the second it took him to fall on the rope, the death vision played out in a long stream of hopeful thoughts with his life being saved. That's all this was. It was a very wonderful vision of her back in Florida in Jeffrey's arms. It made sense as it was where she had been so desperate to return.

He grabbed her hand and looked at her wrist. "The watch! Where is the watch, Ronnie?" The room was filling with smoke and she started to cough. She reached for her sleeve to cover her mouth and realized she was wearing Jeffrey's shirt, just as she had when she left. The black dress was gone. Her eyes watered and the smoke was making her choke.

Jeffrey shook her. "Ronnie, focus. Where did you put the watch?"

"Mathias has it. He held it in my hand ..." This was her death vision, he needed to be hugging her. Happy to see her again. Why was he asking about the watch?

A sharp pain pierced through the vision. She reached for her leg hoping the surgeon wasn't cutting it off. Ronnie crumpled to the ground. Everything faded to black.

Chapter 58 - Time Lapse

A strange but familiar noise woke Ronnie and pulled her from a deathlike sleep. Crisp white sheets were under her cheek and the sun shone through the blinds. Had she survived the hanging? Was Mathias nearby? Excitement rose in her chest and she slid her legs over the side of the bed. Immediately she reached for her throat expecting to feel pain. Her neck had been broken, the muscles were stretched. She had a terrifying thought—what if the surgeon had cut off her legs? She reached down. They were intact. She looked at her pink toenails and brown skin. It did not fit. Then it hit her, this was her Florida apartment and those were *her* pink toes! "I'm home! Oh my God I'm back home!"

"Ronnie, please pick up the phone." It was Jeffrey's voice! "I hope you slept well but I've not been able to come over yet. There was a fire at the lab last night." Ronnie reached for the phone, but it wasn't there next to her bed. She had set it up in the kitchen a few days ago when she unpacked. Ronnie ran to the kitchen and picked up the receiver and heard the dial tone. There were seven new messages on her answering machine.

"Noooowww!" Someone said from the other room. Her heart beat madly and she listened waiting for it again. It was her cat meowing louder stretching the call out to last a few seconds. It was her panic cry. "Fluffy!" Relieved Ronnie dashed across the living room, into to the guest room and opened the bathroom door. The cat launched herself at Ronnie purring loudly, rubbing against her leg. Ronnie picked up her kitty and buried her face in the white silky fur.

"Precious baby-cat, I missed you so much!"

Ronnie took a few steps to the closer of the two twin beds and lay down on her side petting her cat. Fluffy lay next to her offering her stomach for scratching purring like crazy. The clock on the bedside table read 4:00 p.m. How the hell did she get here? She had on the shorts and shirt she wore to Jeffrey's lab. She pulled at the collar and peeked down her shirt to see her lacy silk bra. No horrible stays. No hideous filthy clothes.

"How did I get home Fluffy?" Ronnie said.

A loud pounding on the door scared her out of bed. Fluffy jumped down and followed her to the living room.

"Who is it?" Ronnie looked through the peephole.

"Oh thank God. Ronnie, you're there!" Steph's head loomed huge with the distortion of the peephole glass.

Ronnie opened the door. Her friend hugged her ferociously. A man with light hair stood behind Steph and waved awkwardly. His left arm was in a bright white cast.

"You're okay! I was so worried about you," Steph said.

Ronnie hugged her back. "Steph, it's so good to see you."

Steph pulled away. "I heard on the radio that Jeffery's lab caught fire during the storm. I was terrified that something happened to you."

"A fire? Are you sure Steph?" Ronnie had a vague memory of smoke but couldn't place it. "Jeffrey just left a message about a fire. Strange I don't remember it. Come in Steph." She stood aside and let her friend into the apartment. "Hi, I'm Ronnie." She held her hand out to the guy that followed Steph inside.

"Oh hi, I'm Nick. Good to meet you." He awkwardly shook her right hand with his left.

"Ronnie this is my friend Nick. Nick this is Ronnie." Steph said.

"Hi, Nice, really nice to meet you," Ronne said. "I'm so glad to see you, Steph. Here sit down." She motioned for them to sit on the couch. Fluffy was underfoot making attempts to greet Steph by rubbing on her leg.

"Why haven't you answered your phone? I've been calling for hours." Steph looked at Nick. He nodded in agreement.

"I just woke up, Steph."

"Sweetie, it's almost suppertime. Are you okay?"

"What! I slept all day?" Ronnie around for a clock but remembered the one in the bedroom said it was 4:00 o'clock. "I think so. I'm still groggy. Why did you come over here? Is everything okay with you?" Ronnie nodded toward Nick's arm. "And have a seat, please."

"I've had the worst day, Ronnie. You will never believe what we've been through." Steph sat down on her red velvet couch. Nick stood nearby and Steph patted the couch. "Honey, sit next to me." Nick obeyed and looked uncomfortable.

"Steph, I think I've got you beat for worst day ever. Not in a million years will you guess what happened to me the past several days." Ronnie sat on an over-stuffed armchair across from her friends.

"Past several days? What are you talking about, I just saw you last night." Steph looked at Nick and back at Ronnie.

"Last night? Steph, come on that's crazy. I've not seen you for days," Ronnie said.

"Ronnie, seriously? We sat right here just yesterday before Jeffrey called." Steph reached out to take her hand. "What's going on with you? What did Jeffrey do to you?"

"No that can't be! Steph, what day is it? I saw you just before the hurricane hit." Ronnie's mind was spinning. "Poor Fluffy has been all alone here since!"

"Today is the fourteenth. Hurricane Charley hit last night!" Steph's eyebrows bunched together.

"She's right. It's Saturday," Nick said. He shifted in his seat, looking like he was in pain.

"Saturday. No, no, no. Steph, I've been gone for days."

"Hey, I know we just met but what did you smoke last night, Ronnie." Nick laughed but stopped when he saw the look on Steph's face.

"What did Jeffrey do to you, sweetie. You did go to Jeffrey's, didn't you?"

"Yes, I did. And then I ..." Ronnie put her head in her hands. What was happening? Tears fell down her face and she tried to compose herself. She stood up and walked to the Kleenex on the breakfast bar behind her.

Steph stood up and followed. "Ronnie. What happened at the lab?" Steph put her hand on her back.

Ronnie turned around and hugged her friend while looking toward Nick. He returned her stare with his mouth opened in shock. He finally looked away obviously uncomfortable with the odd turn of the conversation.

"Ronnie, I think you better tell us what happened after you left me here last night." Steph grabbed the Kleenex box and walked her back to the couch.

"The beginning, Steph?" Ronnie said. "You're gonna have to sit down for this." Ronnie took a deep breath and tried to piece it together. It was Saturday the fourteenth. She hadn't even been gone a full day. It made no sense at all. She wiped away the tears and started at the beginning.

The End

Want More?

To continue the adventure, get the first two chapters of Shattering Time, the next book in the series, on my website. Sign up for my newsletter on my website (www.kjwaters.com) and get the first five chapters delivered to your email NOW! Visit my website www.kjwaters.com and be the first to hear about special deals and events.

Acknowledgements

I have so many friends and family members to thank for helping me over the past nine years as I have worked on the Stealing Time series. I apologize in advance to anyone I forgot to add to this list. I'm sure tomorrow I'll cringe at the omission.

First and foremost, I need to thank my family for putting up with our messy house, dirty laundry, and my distractedness over the last two years when I dove deep into the completion of Stealing Time. I can't guarantee it will get any better going forward because I'm addicted to being an author. I have so much more of this story to tell, so I hope you will forgive me for putting so much into this, but know I'm forever grateful for the freedom to pursue my dream of writing.

The one person who has helped me the most with the story development is my son who has been there for all of the big and small twists and turns. He has a very logical mind and has been a huge help in sorting through the myriad of possibilities with the time travel science and repercussions.

I need to thank my diligent and expert editing by Jeri Walker (jeriwb.com) and Geoffrey West (GeoffreyDavidWest.com.) Jeri was my 'everything' editor and Geoffrey was my English historical editor who helped this blonde American with all the odd subtle and not so subtle British eighteenth-century issues.

A huge thank you to Jody Smyers for the excellent work on the cover artwork (jodysmyersphotography.com.) This was our first joint effort on a book cover that blossomed into our business, Blondie's Custom Book Covers (www.blondiebooks.com). Jody was also one of my first beta readers and had a lot of great suggestions on increasing the tension and excitement of the story.

Other people to thank are my mother and late step-father for being my first true fans and were so encouraging throughout the process, my step-mother for all of edits and suggestions before it went to my editors, and my father was my clock and watch specialist along with the proper terminology for priests and such in England.

I have had so many friends I've met on social media that have been extraordinarily helpful and very kind. There is no way I can list them all but a special shout out to Suzanne Kelman, Christie Poole, Frank Watson, Marc Mimouni, Kirkus MacGowan, Wendy Potocki, Ron Chapman, Shawn Wickersheim, Katia Antoine-Rochet, and Michael Blair.

Stay in Touch
The best way to keep up to date on my new releases and projects is to follow me on my Amazon Author page (and signup for my newsletter.) Look me up on Amazon and follow me.

You can also find me on these social media sites:
Blogger: www.kjwatersauthor.blogspot.com
Twitter: @kamajowa
Facebook: KJ Waters Author
Pinterest: kamajowa
Instagram: @kamajowa

I am also CEO of Blondie's Custom Book Covers providing book cover service for authors and publishers.
Website: www.blondiebooks.com
Twitter: @BlondiesBookCov
Facebook: Blondies Custom Book Covers

In October 2015, I started a podcast called Blondie and the Brit with Suzanne Kelman. It is an author podcast with interviews, social media tips and more. Check it out here. www.blondieandbrit.com and on podbean at www.blondieandbrit/podbean.com and iTunes.

I also help authors manage their book marketing and social media. If you're interested in my consulting services, please contact me at kjwatersauthor@gmail.com.

Printed in Great Britain
by Amazon